The Bridge:

The Book of Necessity

A historical fantasy by

Jodie Forrest

Wishes Three!
Jodie Forrest

Published by Seven Paws Press

POB 2345; Chapel Hill NC 27515 USA
919.929.4287; fax 919.929.7092; alyra@intrex.net
http://www.intrex.net/alyra7paws

Printed in the United States of America.

First Edition
First printing, Nov. 1998

ISBN 0-9649-113-2-9
Library of Congress Catalog Card Number 98-090438

For information and orders of additional copies, contact Seven Paws Press at the above address.

Cover art by Michael Weaver, tel. 770-924-8426, mweaver@mindspring.com;
http://www.mindspring.com/~mweaver

For my husband Steven, of course.

TABLE OF CONTENTS

ACKNOWLEDGMENTS

Another separate book would be needed to thank all who deserve it, including, since Time has long arms, everyone who encouraged an introverted child's love of reading or made no attempt to limit her vocabulary...

My gratitude to the following people and organizations whose kindness or expertise were invaluable to me as I wrote this third volume of the *Rhymer* trilogy:

Gary Ace, Joyce Allen, Antero Alli, the Baton Rouge Jung Society, Cyril Beveridge, Frederica Bishop, Poppy Z. Brite, Thomas Brown, Caffe Driade, Keith Cleversley, Lisa Creed, Mike and Carol Czeczot, Chris DeBarr, Ben Dyer, Cholena Erickson, Peter Estep, James R. Evans, Dick and Bunny Forrest, David Friedman, Jean-Michel Garcia, Kristen Gooch, Jeff Green, Dave and Donna Gulick, Kathryn and Scott Hammond, Diana Hawes, Sam Heaton, Mary Kay Hocking, Becky Jackson, Bill and Sharon Janis, Catherine Jones, Steve Jordan, Gloria Karpinski, Dan Kee, Kittisaro, Sinikka Laine, Steve Lautermilch, Alphee and Carol Lavoie, Rob Lehmann, Catherine Losano, R.A. MacAvoy, Doug Margel, Carolyn and Richard Max, Dominic and Judy Miller, Daphna Moore, John G. Moore, Luna Mountainsea, the Nalbandian family, Mary Beth Peterzell, Rick and Cathy Petty, Michael Rank, Sara Romweber, Sharon Rossman, Savannah Scarborough, Ken Schonwalter, Diana Simmons, Maria K. Sims, Sid Smith, Sting, Trudie Styler, Meg Switzgable, Yota Switzgable, Thanissara, Triangle Yoga, Michael Weaver, James Weinberg, Robin Williamson, Henry DaVega Wolfe, Rosales Wynne-Roberts, Tom Young and my extended family.

Affectionate thanks to the other members, past and present, of the band Dragonship: Christen Campbell, Michael Chandler, Steven Forrest, Mike Roig, Linda Smith, Roger Windsor and Scotty Young; to Theresa Arico and the Valkyries Dance Troupe; and to Robert Griffin for his musical inspiration, encouragement and patience.

I am deeply grateful to my fellow teller of Norse tales, Dag Rossman of Ormsgard, for generously permitting me to use his poetic interpretation of the Ørlög—as far as we know, it's the only extant interpretation. It was first published in his article, "Ancient Nordic Spirituality: A Quest for Wisdom and Balance," *Scandinavian Press,* Blaine, WA: Oct.-Dec. 1996. Dag's audio work, including the Norse legends as Tomas might have told them, is distributed by Skandisk, Inc., 1-800-468-2424.

To my husband, Steven Forrest, who wrote the music and lyrics to Dragonship's Tomas-inspired rock operas, and without whom I might not be writing at all: there is simply no way that I could ever thank you enough, Steven, but I'll keep trying.

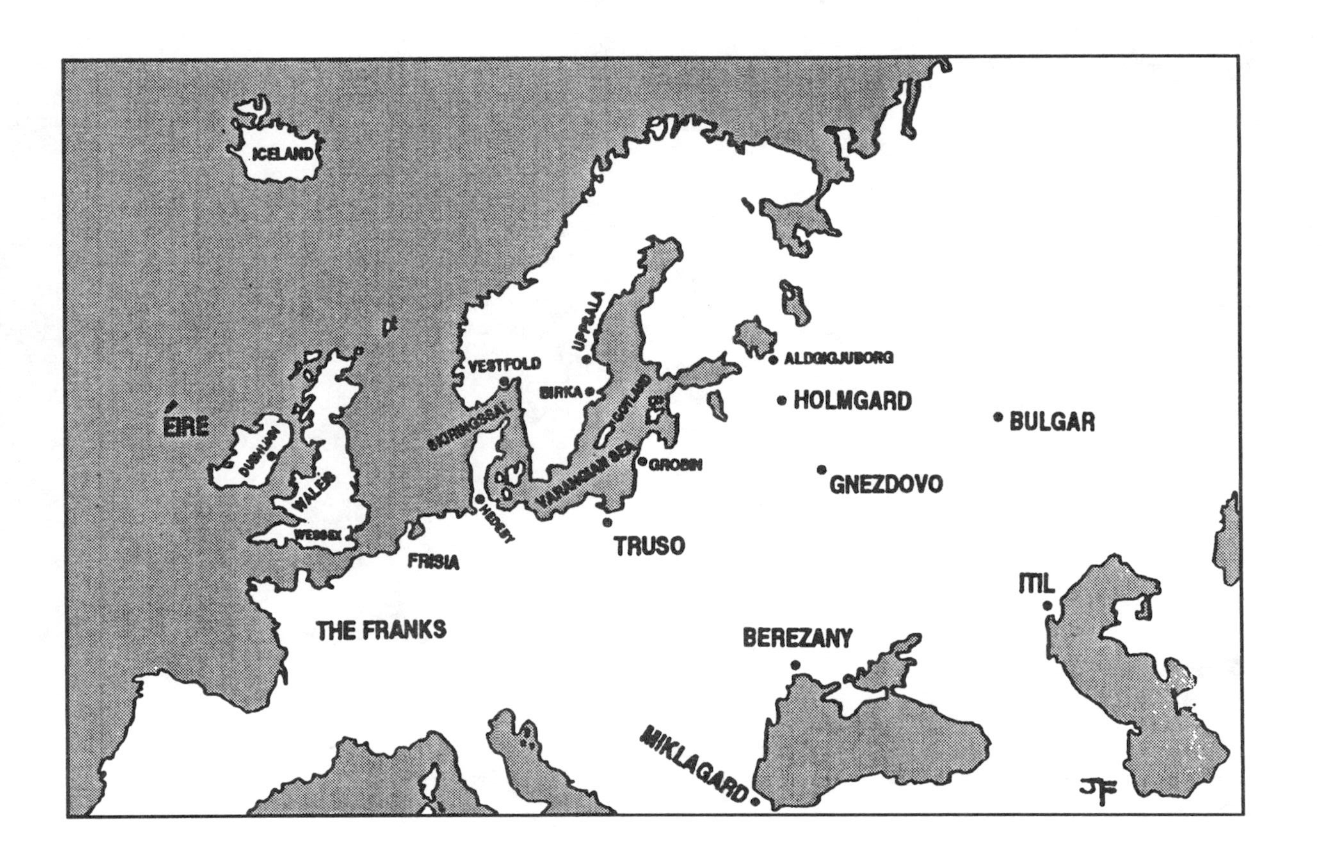
ICELAND
ÉIRE
WALES
WESSEX
FRISIA
THE FRANKS
VESTFOLD
SKIRINGSSAL
HEDEBY
UPPSALA
BIRKA
GOTLAND
VARANGIAN SEA
GROBIN
TRUSO
ALDGIGJUBORG
HOLMGARD
GNEZDOVO
BULGAR
ITIL
BEREZANY
MIKLAGARD
JF

IONIAN SONG

Though we have broken their statues,
though we have driven them out of their temples,
the gods did not die because of this at all.
O Ionian land, it is you they still love,
it is you their souls still remember.
When the August morning dawns upon you,
a vigor from their life moves through your air;
and at times a figure of ethereal youth,
indistinct, in rapid stride,
crosses over your hills.

C.P. Cavafy
translated by Rae Dalven

THE EIGHT POINTS OF THE PAGAN YEAR

The first or second of the relevant month are the dates usually given for Imbolc, Beltane, Lammas and Samhain. However, these festivals were probably meant to bisect the timespan between a solstice and an equinox. If we place Imbolc, Beltane, Lammas and Samhain symmetrically, at a date precisely between their immediately neighboring solstices and equinoxes, as I feel that our ancestors must have done, then Imbolc, Beltane, Lammas and Samhain fall on the sixth of the relevant month, not the first.

For more information about the meaning of these ancient seasonal festivals, an excellent reference is Stanley J.A. Modrzyk's *Turning of the Wheel*, York Beach, ME: Weiser, 1993.

"In the midst of darkness, light..."

Winter Solstice or Yule

Approximately December 21, when the Sun reaches zero degrees Capricorn.

The shortest day of the year. Signals the start of the light's return to the earth, and the beginning of the fading of the dark.

Imbolc or Candlemas

Approximately February 6, when the Sun reaches fifteen degrees Aquarius.

The midpoint between the first lengthening of the light at Yule and the Spring Equinox, when day and night will be equal. The days continue to lengthen; the light is clearly gaining in strength.

Spring Equinox

Approximately March 21, when the Sun reaches zero degrees Aries.

Day and night are equal and in balance. From now until the Fall Equinox, day lasts longer than night. Marks the beginning of the ascendancy of the light over the dark.

Beltane or May Eve

Approximately May 6, when the Sun reaches fifteen degrees Taurus.

The midpoint between the Spring Equinox, when day and night were in balance, and the Summer Solstice, which will be the longest day of the year. Light continues to hold its power over the dark. Traditionally a fertility festival with fertility rituals, although dates for the actual planting of crops undoubtedly varied from one locale to another.

Summer Solstice

Approximately June 21, when the Sun reaches zero degrees Cancer.

The longest day of the year, when light is at its peak, after which the days will start to shorten. The moment of the supremacy of the light—and also the beginning of the dark's return.

Lammas
Approximately August 6, when the Sun reaches fifteen degrees Leo.
The midpoint between the Summer Solstice, which was the longest day of the year, and the Fall Equinox when night and day will again be in balance. Traditionally marks the beginning of the harvest—reaping the gifts of the light—although actual harvest dates undoubtedly varied according to crop and locale.

Fall Equinox
Approximately September 21, when the Sun reaches zero degrees Libra.
Night and day are in balance again, after which the nights will start to lengthen and the dark will become stronger than the light. In some locales, the end of the harvest.

Samhain, or All Saints' Day, or All Hallows' Eve, or Halloween
Approximately November 6, when the Sun reaches fifteen degrees Scorpio.
The midpoint between the Fall Equinox, when day and night were in balance and the nights began lengthening, and the Winter Solstice, which will be the shortest day and longest night of the year. The dark continues to extend its power over the light. Samhain was traditionally associated with death, as growth and activity were slowed or stopped.

Yet, as the Ørlög says, "in the midst of death, life"—the cycle begins again at the Winter Solstice.

THE NORSE RUNES

The Runes were the letters with which the Norse wrote until approximately 1000 A.D., and they can be seen carved on ancient Runestones throughout Scandinavia to this day. They also had oracular, mythological or psychological import. The chief Norse god, Odin, was voluntarily wounded with a spear and hung for nine nights on the worlds' axle-tree, Yggdrasil, to obtain knowledge of the Runes' meanings and their use in magic—a kind of Norse shamanic initiation.

Many historians, mythologists, occultists and modern pagans have published work about the Runes. One good place to start reading about them is Freyja Aswynn's *Leaves of Yggdrasil*, Llewellyn: St Paul, 1994. What follows are my own interpretations—those of a novelist, not a scholar.

FEHU: Possessions, Manifestation. You are invited to define the meaning of prosperity for yourself. Materially, this is a fortunate Rune, if you don't abandon yourself to other people's definitions of success. What resources, inner and outer, do you need in order to thrive in your personal journey? Seize them at all cost, and discard the rest. This is the Rune of Right Nourishment.

URUZ: Strength, Endurance. Pressures arise which tear away everything except your essential nature, revealing levels of instinctive strength and self-knowledge untapped in less stressful times. Psychic bedrock is struck; you must respond decisively from your core, or be wounded. This is the rune of Endurance.

THURISAZ: Force, Giant, Thorn. In the circumstances you now face, enormous destructive power, neither good nor evil, is available to you. Although dangerous, it can defend that which is dear to your heart. You can choose whether to release its devastating force—and incur your choice's responsibility. This is the Rune of Blind Force.

ANSUZ: Signals, Omens. A message is coming to you through omens and natural signs, perhaps through some human channel or oracle. If you're fettered by your unconscious wishes and fears, they may distort that message. This is the Rune of Omens.

RAIDHO: Wagon, Journey. A Rune of rhythm and order, Raidho counsels strategy and persistence. A demanding journey, literal or metaphorical, lies before you. You must proceed step by step, aware that natural laws govern all motion and that no shortcut, however tempting, will do anything but lengthen the journey. This is the Rune of Right Action.

KENAZ: Torch, Insight. Resourcefulness and practical inventiveness are essential if you are to devise a strategy to improve your present circumstances. There is no magic cure; creative thought, clear analysis, and pragmatic application of skill are necessary now. This is the Rune of Ingenuity.

GEBO: Partnership, Gift. Any partnership must be bound together through a mutual exchange of gifts. Perhaps the exchange is material, but it may be mystical, mental or sexual. Perhaps it is a gift of trust. This is the Rune of the Ritual of Commitment.

WUNJO: Joy, Fulfillment. Knowledge and willpower now blossom into wisdom and illumination. You have matured spiritually, and unity is growing between your soul's inspiration and your daily life. Peace arises within you and is reflected in your relationship with the human family. This is the Rune of Harmonious Merging.

HAGALAZ: Hail, Disruption. Shock, too, is part of the great Pattern. Overwhelming events arise now, around you or within your unconscious, and demand radical responses. You must adjust your plans, perhaps change your course. Be wary of stubbornness; you cannot fight the Divine hand. Return to your spiritual center, let the dust settle, then refocus your will in the light of the new reality. This is the Rune of Disruption.

NAUTHIZ: Need, Self-Preservation. Resistance within you may create your experience of resistance in the world. Where have you limited yourself? To what have you given so much power that it can cause you such pain? Claim the wisdom of patience and attend to what's needed now, or your hurt may have no meaning. This is the Rune of the Forging of Character.

ISA: Ice. Progress is temporarily frozen. Take comfort in patience, stillness and caution. The blockage is not inside you but around you. Don't relax your concentration; remain alert enough to detect the early signs of thaw. This is the Rune of Waiting.

JERA: Harvest, Reaping. You are in a cycle of events whose seasons must all be respected: sowing, cultivation and harvest. Well-planned right action, constancy and patience yield the best results and the most gentle evolution. This is the Rune of Fruition.

EIHWAZ: Defense, Striving. Although you are facing a trial, you are protected. The skill you most need lies in trusting that protection. Unforeseeable power and wisdom await you if you avoid panic or precipitous overreactions. Be strong, and judiciously bold, and no harm should come to you. This is the Rune of Testing.

PERTHRO: Fate, Secrets. Although your circumstances may seem random, a group patterning beyond your comprehension is active in your life. You cannot grasp the flow of events because they involve the Nornir—the three Fates of past, present and future—and because other lots than yours are being cast. This is the Rune of the Web of Fate.

ALGIZ: Watchfulness, Protection. Alertness, not defensiveness, is the best shelter. Be wary; watch for omens, which are plentiful now. Be fluid; avoid predictability and routine. Like the elk, watch ceaselessly for rustles in the sedge grass. Danger seldom arrives unheralded. This is the Rune of Watchfulness.

SOWILU: Sunlight, Life Force. Primal vitality is the issue now. The spark within you must be fanned and renewed. What feeds your spirit and your Self? What give you joy and energy? Turn to those sources now, and restore your elemental enthusiasm for living. This is the Rune of Wholeness.

TIWAZ: Warrior, Justice. Conflict arises now, but the first battle you must face is within. Your primary enemy is your failure to face squarely your own trepidations, attachments and personal history. Only with that inner battle won can you see clearly what constitutes right action and justice in the outer battle. There, do not fear your own ferocity. This is the Rune of theWarrior.

BERKANA: Growth, Goddess. In each person, the adolescent must die to make way for the adult. Drawing this Rune indicates that a rite of passage is at hand. Something within you must be sacrificed to allow the birth or creation of the new. Mysteriously, mourning and joy now coincide. This is the Rune of Transition.

EHWAZ: Movement, Partnership. As the leaping horseman must trust his mount, you too must share your Fate with another person or force, leaping across the abyss in a spirit of trusting self-abandonment. You and another power or entity face a common dilemma, resolvable only through the fusion of your alien natures and skills. This is the Rune of Effective Cooperation.

MANNAZ: Individuation, Humanity. Use intelligence, memory and reflection to integrate your inner self with its outer expression. Inauthenticity or falseness in your social position may interfere with your journey and that of others. The question, "What should I do?" is always rooted in the deeper question, "Who am I?" This is the Rune of Individuation.

LAGUZ: Water, Lake, The Sea. The watery mysteries of death and rebirth surround you now. Something is dying, being ferried across dark primal waters. Release it. Something is quickening deep in the psychic womb of your soul, awaiting baptism. Flow now, surrendering old, spent patterns of living, all the while trusting the new birth even though it is still beyond comprehension. This is the Rune of Radical Release.

INGWAZ: Fertility, Beginnings. You have reached the end of one cycle and the beginning of another. Complete what is past to make room for what is to come, then prepare a safe cocoon for your own gestation. This is the Rune of Rebirth.

OTHALA: Retreat, Roots. Charging headlong into impossibility is foolish. Circumstances now arise in which strategic withdrawal and timely assessment of your inner resources are the right actions. Rely now on your "fastnesses": friends, family, power places, familiar spiritual practice. This is the Rune of Regrouping.

DAGAZ: Daylight, Dawn. Night shifts into day; for a moment, opposites are reconciled, the paradox of spirit and flesh transcended. One liminal instant arises in which, if radical faith and intense willpower are fused, a leap can be taken which will forever alter the Pattern of your life. Be alert: recognize this moment and seize it. This is the Rune of Breakthrough.

SYNOPSIS OF *The Rhymer and the Ravens: The Book of Fate*

The first novel of a historical fantasy trilogy loosely inspired by the thirteenth-century manuscript of Thomas the Rhymer, the book is set in late ninth-century Europe, during a paradigmatic conflict among waning indigenous Celtic religions, the Viking invaders' brand of paganism, and the new religion, Christianity. The Vikings' more violent faith and Christianity's exorcisms both constrain the Elves and drive their world further from ours.

When Tomas, a young Nordic-Celtic bard, deserts his half-brother's Viking raid on Wales, he's seduced and inveigled to Elfland by the Welsh Elf Queen, Moira. Under pain of death, she assigns him a quest that takes him on a journey across medieval Europe all the way to the Norse gods' realm, Asgard, to steal the chief god Odin's ravens, Thought and Memory. Gambling that the Norse world-view will predominate, Moira wants Odin's ravens as hostages to bargain for Elfland's retaining as much power and vigor as possible. After giving Tomas two harps, a flute, a sprig of Celtic mistletoe and a perfect inability to lie—"true speech and prophecy"—Moira abandons him in Wessex, where the Christian king, Alfred the Great, and his men are hiding from Danish invaders.

Despite the facts that the touch of iron now sickens Tomas just as it would an Elf, and that Tomas has mysteriously lost seven years in Elfland, the Saxons barter with him. For spying on the Danes, Alfred gives Tomas a seal of safe-conduct and a horse to take him to the Welsh coast where he can continue his journey to Uppsala. The Saxons don't know that the horse is actually a pooka, a shape-shifting Elf—but Tomas does, since they've already met. Aubrey the pooka is Moira's loyal servant, sent to make sure Tomas continues his quest.

He books passage on a trading vessel which founders in the Irish Sea. A dolphin carries him into Dublin harbor, where he has a romantic interlude with Caraid, an Irish Seer whom the Elf King, Rhys, had taken to Elfland under much the same conditions as Moira brought Tomas. The Norse King of Dublin wants to meet the man whom a dolphin had brought in from the sea, and summons Tomas to court. There he encounters his half brother Olaf, whose Viking raid he'd deserted seven years ago, and kills Olaf in self-defense. From Dublin, Tomas sails to Birka, a Norse island trading port. In Birka he meets a wise woman, Mother Aud, who urges him to make full use of his Elfin gifts. He goes to the Norse gods' temple at Uppsala, then to Asgard, where he meets the demigod Loki the Trickster. They trade: Moira's mistletoe for the iron key to the ravens' hall.

Loki uses the mistletoe to have the god Baldur slain, which signals the beginning of Ragnarök, the collapse of the Norse pantheon. The numinous ravens Thought and Memory, their own masters now, elect to leave the falling Asgard with Tomas, after revealing that he has some Elf blood. With their help, Tomas realizes that he's begun the transformation from a hapless wandering Fool to a Magician. He has an audience with Moira, who says that since Elfland's Fate was linked to Asgard, it's suffered a similar collapse. She doesn't tell him she's with child by him. Tomas and the ravens leave for Birka to consult Mother Aud about his newfound powers, while Moira reflects that their paths will cross again.

SYNOPSIS OF *The Elves' Prophecy: The Book of Being*

The novel begins in the lucrative Norse trading port of Birka, where Tomas meets Aud's friend Brubakken, a half-Saami Mage. Aud, a Seer, and Brubakken advise Tomas about magic. He has an animal ally in the ravens, and passes a first test: an encounter with a water Elemental magically bound to Brubakken.

Tomas goes to Dublin to see the Irish Seer, Caraid, who'd once been taken to Elfland by the Welsh Elf King, Rhys. He asks Caraid to go to the court of the Saxon King, Alfred, who'd promised Tomas lands in Wessex should he return. Caraid insists that Tomas is still enmeshed with Moira. When his true speech won't let him deny it, she sends him away. In Wessex, he accepts an unprecedented offer of unbound allegiance from a powerful air Elemental, Nissyen. Tomas's Saxon friend, the bard Linley, becomes reeve of Limecliff, the estate granted Tomas by King Alfred, who still needs Tomas's auguries about the Danish invaders.

In the decaying Elfland, Moira's life is at risk; if an Elf woman carries a child by a mortal father, she assumes that child's mortality and sickens. Rhys doesn't want Moira's mortal child on the throne, nor Tomas as regent, and imprisons her. The Irish Elf rulers, Finvara and Isolde, plot to seize the child and the regency. Moira escapes Elfland with the help of the Parcae, a race of matrilinear, winged Elves. Their ancient prophecy says the children of a mortal Mage and an Elf Queen may save Elfland from fading, and keep the other worlds green. Pregnant, ill, with her innate Elfin magic virtually gone, Moira goes to the mortal realm to beg Tomas's aid.

Loki the Trickster travels there too, in search of a world where he could be *the* power, not just one among many. If Moira's child survives, the Elves will retain too much power in the mortal world for Loki to have total sovereignty. He masquerades as an angel and recruits an ignorant Christian Mage, Daniel, who has designs on Tomas's estate. Meanwhile, Isolde plots with Rhys to doublecross Finvara, after which she'll betray Rhys.

After Tomas takes Moira under his protection at Limecliff, the Parcae attack Daniel, who accuses Tomas of sorcery. He and Moira leave for Birka, seeking Aud and Brubakken's aid. When Moira gives birth to twins, Isolde kidnaps them. As Aud and the Parcae heal the dying Moira, Tomas pursues Isolde to Elfland, followed by Nissyen and by Moira's servant Aubrey. Tomas, Isolde, Nissyen, Aubrey and Loki have a confrontation in Elfland. Tomas saves the twins from Isolde and Loki, and so Elfland survives and stays linked to our world, Midgard. According to the Elves' prophecy, not only Elfland but Midgard will remain green and thriving because of the link between the two worlds.

PROLOGUE: THE NAME-FASTENING

Birka, Horning (Winter's Month), 879 A.D., Christian reckoning

From the start all the omens, both Elfin and mortal, boded ill.

Aubrey the pooka came late for the name-fastening. So did Jared, captain of Moira's guard, and Aidan, who showed promise as a Seer among the Elves. So did Tallah of the winged Parcae.

Moira's face was calm as the minutes lengthened into hours, but she cast not a few glances at the door of Brubakken's two-roomed steading, while the afternoon shadows pointed long narrow violet fingers across Birka. When the latecomers arrived, the ceremony would be held in the Mage Brubakken's stone-lined cowbyre, whose connecting door was propped open for the event.

Holding the twins Owein and Fraine, Aud the Seer waited behind Moira's straight-backed wooden chair, and Brubakken stayed near Tomas, who had a silent raven perched on each shoulder. Before Tomas was a table that held a soapstone bowl of water and two folded pieces of soft and finely woven cloth. A few paces behind Aud and Brubakken hovered Nissyen, Lord of the Air, its greenish-blue eyes glittering in the low light from the torches thrust into holders along the walls. Beside the Elemental stood Gillian, the water-Elf from Lake Malar which surrounded Birch Island.

They'd begin the rite as either Elves or mortals would, by hallowing Brubakken's steading. Tomas had no idea when the pooka and the others would arrive, nor any notion what kept them. Judging from Moira's half-resigned, half-preoccupied expression, she'd no idea either, and would prefer her own thoughts to any words. As would Tomas. He let his mind drift while they waited.

Yesterday he'd asked Moira, "To what gods do the Elves hallow their steadings?"

She gave the twins' cradle the gentlest of nudges with one slippered foot. "The twins are mortal and so are you. It should rather be hallowed to yours."

"What gods are those?"

The Elf looked at him, tilted her head.

"Have I any? Do any remain?"

"Yes. Of that much you can be certain."

"Which ones, then? Where are they? Aren't the Norse gods fallen with Asgard?"

Moira made him no answer, though she was watching him, her eyes grey pools of light, reflective and opaque.

"No three years' winter began before Asgard fell," said Tomas. "No

battles with the giants or Fenrir Wolf or the Midgard serpent, as I was taught would happen. Loki was already unbound when I arrived in Asgard; he'd no need to sail there in a ship made of corpses' nail parings. And he left without fighting Heimdall the Watcher who guards the rainbow bridge. I crossed it into Asgard and back, and had never a glimpse of Heimdall."

The Elf kept silent.

"I no longer know what to believe." He suppressed a frustrated gesture. "Nor in whose name we should hallow this or any steading, nor whose protection to ask for the twins. Asgard may have fallen, but the gods appear to have escaped the rest of the wyrd that I was told would come upon them."

"As you've escaped yours, Tomas, or one of them. As I've eluded mine. Or so it appears." She had cast a pensive glance at Aud's spindle. "The Nornir weave our Fates as they will, and beyond any reckoning of mine."

A scrabbling came at about the midpoint of Brubakken's door. As far as Tomas knew, an Elf could have simply arrived within the house itself. Maybe the visitor was observing mortal etiquette by knocking. Whoever sought admittance wasn't very tall. Gillian shot Tomas an inquiring look.

It is Tallah, said Nissyen down its mind-link to Tomas, who nodded at Gillian to admit the caller.

Tallah wavered into the cowbyre, breathing in ragged gasps. Except for the pouch slung across her chest, she was naked. Her whiteless green eyes were sunken with what he took for fatigue, and she held her wings close to her body, as if warding off blows. Brubakken slipped into the other room and came back with a mug of water.

She drank half the liquid at one swallow and pressed his hand by way of thanks. As always, her stench was overpowering at close quarters, yet Brubakken's round flat-planed face, half Saami and half Swede, appeared utterly unperturbed. Perhaps the smell bothered Tomas more than anyone else.

Tallah went to Moira and said something in a low apologetic voice. The one Elf who'd even tried to learn the Parcae's archaic language was Moira, and she'd acquired only a few basic phrases. She asked Tallah a halting question that produced a torrentially indignant reply. Tallah fished her stone knife from her pouch and used the tip of the blade to draw on Brubakken's dirt floor, talking all the while. Nissyen leaned forward to listen, its eyes gleaming.

Moira said neutrally, "Exorcisms. More than ever before and more potent, Tallah says. Or it is we who are weaker. They obstruct our routes between Elfland and Midgard, especially to the Christian lands. For some time it's been easier to travel to the north of Midgard, but Tallah could scarcely win through just now."

Gillian whispered something to Brubakken, then fetched a blanket which she draped round Tallah's shoulders.

"There are more Christians in the North these days," said Brubakken. "They've been on Birka the past fifty years. Longer, but that's when they sent us a Bishop. Ansgar, his name was."

"Ah," said Moira. "Even to Birka."

Tallah chittered a diffident question. No sooner had she received a smile and a murmur from Moira than she sank down on the floor. Her wings drooped; she wrapped herself in the blanket.

Moira put a long elegant hand on the little Elf's head. "She was separated from the others on the way. She says they're coming as soon as ever they can." The fleeting look she gave Tomas told him she'd no idea when that might be, so when Tallah stretched out and closed her eyes, he let his thoughts ramble again.

"You're right," he had told Moira. "We were each like to die. I at my brother's hands, and you giving birth to mortal children."

"Our children." A smile. "Yet we escaped those Fates."

"I'm glad of it," he said softly. "Still, lately I wonder if eluding one wyrd only brings another and darker one in its stead."

"Meaning?"

"Frigg is wise. She knew her son Baldur's Fate but traveled the whole of Midgard and Asgard both to try to prevent it. If the gods hadn't thought Baldur was made safe by her efforts, they'd never have cast weapons at him. And if Loki hadn't been roused enough by their sport to go prying till he learned that the mistletoe had given Frigg no oath to spare Baldur, no weapon would have felled him."

Moira was contemplating the hearthfire. "I cannot say what Fate we may have called upon ourselves by averting another one." She transferred her gaze to the twins. "Nor upon Owein and Fraine. Yet I know the gods still exist, Tomas. They are immortal. Loki escaped Asgard; others may have. They might dwindle like the Elves, as their worship fades with ours." A grave look. "Ask the protection of whomever you please for the name-fastening. Still, we should not ask lightly."

She came to where he sat tuning his harp, kissed the top of his head and began combing his hair. He put down the harp, enjoying the sweep of the polished tines. From the corner of his eye he caught an occasional glimpse of his hair, long and thick, pale as winter wheat and all flyaway tangles in the Birch Island damp. The scent of crushed roses hovered about Moira, as it always had. What was new was a richer, yeastier fragrance. Milk. Dampness. Clean baby skin.

He reached up to encircle her shoulders with his arms. "I've considered invoking whatever Powers and beings are well disposed towards ourselves and the twins."

"That would be a potent summons," she said, and the comb paused in his hair. "We've no idea who might heed it."

A hoarse voice said from beyond the door, "It's Jared, my lady. And Aidan."

Aidan was leaning a little on Jared when the two Elves came in, with Aidan stumbling slightly. Snowflakes drifted from their cloaks into melting powder on the floor. Aidan's blue eyes were ringed with dark smudges, while Jared's dark gypsy's face was grey and tight. His gait was that of an aged mortal man, all of his powerfully fluid energy gone for the moment.

"Exorcisms?" asked Moira quietly.

Aidan shuddered. His eyes were closed; he appeared dazed.

Jared said, "Everywhere. Like living fire."

"For a time I thought we were lost," muttered Aidan. "Thought we'd stay lost, I mean. You can't find your way for love nor gold now. All guesswork, it is. He opened his eyes and spotted the winged Elf huddled at Moira's feet. "Tallah!" He sounded relieved. "She brought us partway before the bars got thick as pea soup and we lost track of her."

The Parca gave him a feeble smile, got laboriously to her feet, shook out her blanket and offered it to him. Tomas wrinkled his nose; by now the fabric stank almost as much as Tallah herself.

"Ah, no thank you, my dear," said Aidan, spreading his hands apart with his palms turned up. "Most kind of you, though."

Jared turned his head aside to conceal a grin. Tallah didn't seem offended. With a philosophical shrug, she dropped down at Moira's feet again.

"Still, here we are and at your service," Jared told Moira. He glanced from her to Tomas and said, "I don't know when Aubrey will arrive." His expression was that of someone bracing himself for a long wait. "When or how."

Tomas had twisted round until he could see Moira's face, then asked, "Wouldn't such a summons be rather like how you first called me?"

He'd kept his voice neutral; still, she stiffened at the question. "Yes," she said quietly. "Yes, I suppose it would." Her tone wasn't defensive.

Tomas studied the set of her shoulders and the tension about her mouth. When he drew her into his lap, she twined her arms about his neck. The shade of crumbling slate, her eyes were somber, shadowed with fatigue and her recent ill health. Her eyes softened beneath his gaze, but their haunted expression remained.

They were both silent for a little space before he asked, "Can you tell me what you most fear?" For the twins, he was about to add. For the name-fastening.

Moira had taken his face in her warm narrow hands and said, "The day I lose you."

The pooka didn't knock.

Without warning he appeared in the middle of the cowbyre, his eyes tight-closed, rocking on his cloven feet and flinging his arms out to either side to keep his balance. Tallah scrambled out of range of the fall that looked imminent. He was as naked as she was. His tufted ears were laid back; his chest labored. Jared moved forward as if to steady him, but got a warning glance from Moira. "You've found us, Aubrey," she said.

The pooka's back was to her and Tomas. Taking small shuffling steps, he turned completely around before he opened his eyes. They were bloodshot. He wiped the sweat from his forehead, tossed his matted grey hair from his face. "I'm late. Your pardon, there were—"

"Exorcisms. The others told us," Moira said gently. "Save your breath. We'll not begin till you've rested."

He waved aside the mug that Gillian offered him and drained the water pitcher dry instead. "We may be cut off from the rest of Elfland now. From the Norse, the Franks, even the Sidhe and the other Celtic tribes." He smiled wistfully at Gillian. "And from the water family...I've never lost touch with them before, Norse, Celt or other." The lake Elf gave his elbow a sympathetic squeeze. "I've a message from the Parcae who accompany Tallah. Her scouting party."

His glance at Tallah was ambivalent. Faced with an insurmountable language barrier, both he and Tomas had formed a temporary mind link with the winged Elves. The link wasn't anything like the telepathic and kinesthetic fusion that Tomas and Moira could share when they chose, nor did it resemble Tomas's carefully constructed mental link with Nissyen, a door that either of them could open and shut. It was more like Tomas's unexpected natural affinity with ordinary birds of prey, with their instincts and reflexes, their primitive minds and body-centered awareness. But the Parcae were intelligent, intelligent and conscious in a way that mingled jarringly with any awareness of their highly physical selves. At least it had jarred Tomas, who had no desire to repeat the experience.

From the queasy look on the pooka's face, he hadn't relished his link with Tallah either. "The Parcae are holding the paths near the palace as open as they can, but they don't know how long that might be," he said. "They say it would be well if you were to leave Birka as soon as possible."

Before long, all of the tardy Elves had eaten and rested and declared themselves ready for the name-fastening. Brubakken had already produced his astrolabe and calculated another time to begin the ceremony. When the chosen moment finally arrived, Aud handed Tomas and Moira each a twin. Fraine opened her milky grey eyes and blinked up at her father. Except for the opening and closing of her small fists with their moist pearled skin and miniature fingernails, she was quiet in his arms, but he thought that her skin seemed pinker than usual. Was that the faintest of shimmers in the air about her head?

Then the whole cowbyre began to glow. In a trice Aubrey was wreathed in iridescent crimson that lightened to pink near his heart. The shade of new spring leaves pulsed around Aud, turning to pale yellow about her head and shoulders. All those present wore a multicolored halo. Still more color stained the air, which was cold yet smelled rather as it did before a rainstorm, heavy and damp and clean, and vibrant with some all but tangible energy. The ravens shifted their grip on Tomas's shoulders. He wasn't surprised at the charge in the atmosphere: magic was afoot.

"Moira and I hallow this steading to the Aesir, to Frey and Freya of the Vanir," he began. Fertility deities, the Vanir might help keep all nine worlds green and linked. And Frey and Freya were twins, too.

"And to the gods of the Welsh," he added, for through him the twins were partly of that blood. "And to whatever benevolent Powers might turn their attention our way. Therefore we cannot sanctify only one object for this hallowing. Not the hammer of Thor alone, nor the distaff of Frigg, nor the sword of Tyr. Nor do these ravens represent Odin and his spear."

One of the ravens stretched a wing, then the talons of one foot. The air tingled and throbbed so much that Tomas wondered what hues were swirling about his own head now. "So we draw and sanctify Runes to whatever Powers may heed us."

With a long pointed stick, Aubrey carved a bind-Rune of Tomas and Moira's design into the earthen floor. Composed of the intertwined forms of several Runes, it would be large enough to surround all those present. First Aubrey drew Othala, Rune of Inheritance, Blood-Ties and the Hearth. Next he added Algiz, Rune of Protection and Sanctification—and for the East Franks, according to Brubakken, the Rune of the Twins.

To Tomas's eyes, the incised lines glimmered and sparked like marshlight on the floor. The pooka was drawing Gebo now, Rune of Partnership and Commitment. Gebo ruled the giving and receiving of gifts, and the tenuous balance between giver and recipient. Then Aubrey carved Ansuz, Rune of Omens, Rune of Words. It was the first Rune that Moira had suggested since, for the Elves, a name was akin to an omen. Last came one of Tomas's choosing: Perthro, Rune of Fate, the Nornir's Rune he'd seen in the sky when Moira first called him. The bind-Rune's Perthro was so bright that it was difficult to look at directly.

When the pooka finished his task, Tomas beckoned to Tallah, who came forward with his Rune bag. Her eyes appeared to have caught some of the glimmer in the air. After fishing in the bag with one hairy hand, she held a Rune aloft.

"This Rune stands for Owein and Fraine," said Moira. "Dagaz.

Daybreak. Rune of opposites and that which links them. Rune of paradox." She glanced down at Owein. "Above all it is a Rune of change," she said quietly. "Night becomes day, and autumn begins at midsummer. Good and evil may walk hand in hand. Dagaz rules the rainbow bridge to Asgard and all other links between the worlds."

Tallah cast the Rune into the bowl of water and drew again.

"The second Rune belongs to Urd, the Norn who rules Fate and the past," said Tomas. "It is Berkana, Rune of the Goddess, sacred to Freya and Frigg. It lies at the roots of this birth and rules every thread woven into it. Rune of growth, birth and creation. Rune of Transitions." It was also the Birch-Rune, though what that might portend beyond its rulership of Birka, he couldn't say.

"The Norn Verdandi rules Being and the present, and the third Rune is hers," said Moira. "It signifies any Powers who stand with or against the twins."

When Tallah held up the Rune, there was a collective intake of breath. "Thurisaz," said Moira. "Thorn-Rune; Giant-Rune." It represented both Loki, the child of two frost-giants, and the giants' greatest foe, Thor of the Aesir. "Thurisaz carries tremendous force, which is neutral until bent to either protection or attack." But such attacks, from a simple sleep-thorn or war-fetter all the way to murder, could easily backfire. Holding the Rune edgewise, as if it were hot to the touch, Tallah slipped it into the bowl.

"The last Rune belongs to Skuld, Norn of the future," said Tomas. "She rules Necessity: that which derives from Fate and the past when they collide with one's acts in the present. This Rune rules whoever may shed light on the twins' future." The light and motion in the air had gone to whirling cold blue icicles, yet Tomas could see through the haze they created. He felt no surprise when Tallah drew Perthro for the last Rune. "The web of Fate," he said, ignoring a sudden weight like a mail-shirt on his chest: depression or fatigue, or a presentiment. "Rune of the Nornir and their loom, and of Frigg who spins what the Nornir weave." He met Moira's troubled eyes, and thought of Frigg's hopeless attempt to save Baldur. "We cannot grasp the fateful flow of events, because other lots than ours are being cast," he said quietly, as Tallah dropped Perthro in the bowl. "Let this steading so be hallowed."

Aud stepped up to the table. When she halted, it was as if a door through which she would gaze but not venture had opened before her. Her amber-centered blue eyes were distant as she studied the water with its four Runes, and she stood as fixedly as the past. In the air about her masklike face hovered a vast and terrible stillness, an emptiness, an intent. Aidan stared at her with parted lips from which all the color had drained.

Tomas forced himself to look away, lest he follow Aud into trance. With an effort, he said, "We are assembled to welcome the twins into their clans, both mortal and Elfin. We honor these children, give them their names and seek guidance and protection for them." He looked at Moira. "What wyrd might go with the Welsh names you've chosen?"

"'Owein' means 'nobly born' and 'young warrior.'" Moira was gazing at the drowsy infant in her lap. "Once I heard the tale of an Owein who served a Countess of the Fountain, but so long ago that the whole of that story eludes me. Perhaps the Fountain was akin to your Norse Wells."

Which one? The Nornir guarded a Well with whose water they bathed the roots of Yggdrasil, the nine worlds' axle-tree. From that tree Odin had hung for nine nights and given one of His eyes besides, to obtain the knowledge of the Runes—and the wisdom that came with a drink from the Well of Mimir, the Well of Memory. There was a third Well at the Norse gods' temple at Uppsala, where Tomas had narrowly escaped becoming a sacrifice. The air in the cowbyre was so thick and ominous now that he might have been breathing water. Perhaps they were all the same Well...

"And Fraine?" he asked.

"'Fraine' means 'stranger.' I know no stories in which that name appears."

Did no stories mean no wyrd, for good or ill?

"Let this girl be named Fraine. Let her brother be named Owein. For their blessings we call upon the twins Frey and Freya of the Vanir," said Tomas. "We call upon any of the Vanir who are disposed to aid these infants. And upon the Aesir, Thor and Frigg above all. We invoke the Disir, the spirits of these children's Norse ancestors, and the spirits of their Welsh kin." A flashing image came: his enslaved mother's tired face and sorrowful grey eyes. "We call upon the Nornir whose Rune we have drawn tonight, and upon whatever personal Norn these children have."

When Tallah held the bowl aloft, Aud blinked. Looking as if she had lost something whose passing would cause her no grief, the Seer let out her breath and retreated to her original place.

Moira said, "May the blessings of those Powers be in this water."

The bowl was passed about until everyone had taken a small swallow. When Tallah brought the bowl to Tomas, he dipped a finger in the water and sketched Dagaz upon Fraine's forehead. Moira did the same for Owein. As a libation to the Powers they'd invoked, Tallah poured half the remaining liquid on the floor, then carried the bowl outside to pour the rest of the offering onto the frozen earth of Birch Island. The tree-dwelling Parcae did not care for mortal houses, nor put much trust, Tomas suspected, in rituals conducted withindoors.

A tall figure, completely swathed in voluminous grey robes that showed none of its face or body, followed Tallah back into the cowbyre.

With its appearance, all the shimmering colors of magic abruptly vanished, and the air grew hot and clammy and immobile. Tallah spun about to look behind her. When she saw the veiled form at her heels, the soapstone bowl slipped from her hands and thudded to the floor. Tomas tried to rise, to demand the creature's name and errand, but found himself pinned to his chair as if by a giant's unseen fist.

"I saw Her in the water just now," said Aud as she put a trembling hand on Moira's shoulder. "She comes in peace."

With inexorable slowness the entity moved towards Tomas, Moira and the sleeping twins. It made no sound at all. Either it had no feet or it floated a few inches above the floor. Sometimes Nissyen moved that way.

The guard-sylphs! said Tomas down his mind-link to the sylph. *Why did they give no warning?*

Because they are subject to this Being. As are the gods themselves.

It was a Norn, then. It must be Skuld, who ruled the future and whose face was veiled to mortals. Skuld had come to the twins' name-fastening.

The room was stifling. Tomas's face was damp, his chest constricted. Tallah dropped to her bony knees, but Tomas felt bound to his seat. Gillian clutched at Aidan and Jared, who both put an arm about her, though Tomas could not have said who was steadying whom. Staggering slightly, Aubrey came to grip the back of Moira's chair.

Moira had gone the color of whalebone bleached by the Sun. When she reached for Tomas's hand, her palm was slick with perspiration, and she clamped down so hard on his fingers that he stifled a grimace. Brubakken edged a step closer to Aud. Only Nissyen appeared relatively unperturbed, though its eyes had grown round and still and glassy-bright with attention. The air was growing so hot that Tomas could scarcely breathe, and the twins must be sweltering in their blanket. In a moment one of them would begin to fuss, and the spell would be broken: the veiled Norn would dissolve into nothingness. Nissyen would announce that it had fooled them all this time. Moira would let go of Tomas's hand before he lost the use of it.

The Norn came to a halt, so close that Tomas could have touched Her grey garment. A stillness emanated from it, a deafening silence, an oppressive heat. Tomas could see the shape of Her nose beneath the veil. Sweat trickled down his neck; the back of his shirt clung to his ribs. His stomach heaved. Would Skuld lift Her veil? He didn't want to see Her face.

Moira was gazing up at the Norn. The Elf's eyes were black pits with a narrow rim of grey, and a muscle at her temple twitched like a living thing beneath her skin. She moistened her colorless lips. "I did what I must," she whispered, so low that Tomas suspected that only Skuld and he could hear. "No one can do more than what You and Your sisters have allotted."

The Norn's robes lifted at either side of Her body, until the shapes of two extended fingers showed. Moira's face turned from white to almost green as she pulled Owein closer. The Norn was pointing at the twins.

Tomas should say something. He should argue. Not my children. Find someone else. He sucked the cowbyre's molten air into his lungs. *Nissyen,* he thought at the sylph, *lend me strength. Thought and Memory, aid me. You have seen Skuld before; you've seen all nine worlds from end to end.*

The birds made no answer, yet he felt a current of reassurance flowing from them. Skuld was still pointing. The byre was taut with silence but for a light pattering upon the roof: the beginning of an ice storm. The skies above Birka had cast their own Rune: Hagalaz, Hail-Rune, Rune of Disruption.

As hard as he could, Tomas bit his lip. The pain, coupled with the flat taste of his own blood, seemed to break the immobility that had enshrouded him. Like a plucked harpstring, for an instant he rocked against the back of his chair. Then he pulled his hand from Moira's grip. Still holding Fraine, with the ravens perched on his shoulders, he rose and faced the Norn.

Skuld kept pointing at Fraine with one hand; Her other hand was aimed at Owein in Moira's lap. Beneath Her veil Her head turned. She was looking at Tomas. Studying him. Something like heat, with motion as well as temperature, pulsed from Her in waves. His skin grew tight over his cheekbones and his eyes felt parched. Nausea stirred at the root of his stomach. He locked his knees; he stood his ground. She came in peace, Aud had said. When he stole a glance at Moira, she was staring at him as if he were a dangerous and volatile stranger.

"Why have you come, Lady Skuld?" His voice was a husky whisper. He heard Nissyen's gasp of exhilarated interest; of a sudden Thought nibbled at his hair. Upon the floor the Rune Ansuz gleamed a blinding gold, but the rest of the cowbyre went dim, all its colors muted to the grey of Skuld's robes. Power beat at Tomas's face, his neck, his arms that cradled Fraine against his torso.

Then a question formed in his brain, as distinctly as if it were carved in tiny letters on the pulsating air between the Norn's veiled face and his own. Very softly, as Moira drew an incredulous breath, he asked, "What word do you bring?"

Skuld chanted:

"In the midst of darkness, light;
In the midst of death, life;
In the midst of chaos, order.

In the midst of order, chaos;
In the midst of life, death;
In the midst of light, darkness.

Thus has it ever been,
Thus is it now, and
Thus shall it always be."

The Norn's voice was deep, sonorous, the sound a mountain might make as it shifted on its roots. The sound of an Age turning. Her chant filled Brubakken's small crowded cowbyre, flowed out into the hailstorm and deafened the tapping of the hail-Rune upon the roof. Her words rolled about in Tomas's skull and boomed against his eardrums, excruciatingly loud and then louder still. Tomas pulled the blanket over Fraine's ears; what might that sound do to an infant's delicate hearing?

Nissyen stood alone, its sylph's assumed and illusory body transparent and quivering and its wild green eyes trained on the Norn. Except for Nissyen, Moira and Tomas, everyone had cried out in pain or surprise or both. The others stood with their hands covering their ears and their white-rimmed eyes glazed with awe. Tallah had gone from her kneeling position to full prostration before Skuld, her face against the dirt floor, her palms flattened on either side of her head and her shivering wings folded above the back of her neck.

The Norn's echoing words beat against the walls, the rafters, the ceiling. Moira was bent protectively over Owein. Skuld's speech expanded, hammering against the earthen floor and its bind-Rune and rocking Tomas back on his heels before Her.

The room had grown hotter. He was panting; sweat glued his trousers to his thighs. Skuld's face was still turned towards him. He swallowed, twice. "What do your words mean?" he whispered.

To his lasting astonishment it was one of the ravens, Memory, who answered. Never before had he heard either raven speak aloud. With him they communicated in mind-speech, which had been halting at first, comprised mainly of images, yet grown in power and fluency since he'd twice assumed raven-shape. Still, their conversations had always been conducted within his own mind.

"It is the Ørlög," said Memory in a rasping bird's croak that wasn't remotely human, and sidled closer to Tomas. Warm feathers pressed against his temple. Through the fabric of his jerkin, he felt the clasp of its talons on his collarbone. Those sensations, and Fraine's weight in his arms, were all that anchored him in that hot grey whirling room.

The *Ørlög.* The Nornir chanted it daily as they applied their Well's water to Yggdrasil's rotting trunk. The Ørlög, the collective destiny of the nine worlds and of their inhabitants, their all-encompassing wyrd. The web of Fate, its myriad spinners and that which they spun. The Ørlög, the power of Fate, its force driven by the weight of the past and, therefore, its self-created limits in the present.

The Norn was nodding slowly in Memory's direction.

Don't speak again, Tomas thought desperately. Stop pointing at my children. Begone. Take the ravens with you. Take my magic. I cannot endure it.

Skuld jabbed a finger at each twin. "*Remember,*" She said softly, though even Her lowest voice filled the room beyond bearing and ground an echoing pathway through the air. Then, wholly and instantaneously, She vanished.

CHAPTER ONE: BEFORE THE JOURNEY

Two hours after the name-fastening, Tomas, Moira, Aud, Brubakken and Aubrey all met in Aud's steading. The twins were asleep in their double wooden cradle, with the pooka sprawled beside them on a pile of furs. In his own lanky form rather than horse-shape, Aubrey lay on his back with his arms folded beneath his lantern-jawed grey head and scowled at the ceiling. From time to time he peered into the cradle as if he expected Skuld to have spirited the infants away. A more unlikely child-minder could hardly be imagined, but Aud was glad of his presence, for it meant that Moira and Tomas would be less distracted.

She found it hard to look away from the twins herself. At first she'd thought she was imagining their rapid growth, but now she was sure of it. They filled the cradle that had dwarfed them only a few days ago, and at this rate they'd soon be too big for it. Likely that was part of why Aubrey kept eyeing them. Halfbreeds could reach physical maturity with preposterous speed, but she'd never known any to grow this fast. She only hoped their minds and hearts would keep pace with their bodies.

Aud offered the pooka a tankard of ale, which he refused with an amused little shake of his head, so she poured her other guests a round and took a seat beside Brubakken. While he arranged two copies each of the twins' horoscopes on the table and made a last calculation, Aud studied Moira. The Elf shared a bench with Tomas and was leaning against him, her head on his shoulder, her eyes closed, her lashes ragged crescents of black that cast wavering shadows on her cheekbones in the lamplight. Her color was more sallow than it should have been, nor had she gained as much flesh in the almost nine days since the birth as Aud would have preferred. The Elf's face was a hollow mask of exhaustion. It was thanks to the Parcae's nursing that she'd survived. If only so many shocks would stop coming so thick and fast for her. She needed at least a Moon of nothing but rest and ease, while three or four Moons would be better, but she insisted that she and Tomas must be off to Elfland immediately. She wasn't fit for the journey, nor for whatever waited at the other end of it.

Neither was Tomas, though he was in better fettle. He sat quietly, an arm about Moira's waist, his face bemused. When he caught Aud watching him, he flashed her a grave smile. Brubakken said that Tomas was learning as rapidly as he could, Runic charms, defenses, sendings and more—but one could hasten instruction in the Ars Magica only so far and no further. One needed time to practice, gain confidence and learn from mistakes as well as victories. And Tomas had precious little time for errors.

That he had allies was a comfort. Of the ravens' allegiance and those of the Welsh Elves Aud was certain, though less so about Nissyen. The air Elemental felt no loyalty, scruples or emotions; it would remain in Tomas's service as long as it found him interesting. Moreover, unlike the Elves, it was perfectly capable of lying about its plans. No Elf could tell an outright lie. Nor, since his encounter with Moira, could Tomas. Something about that trait he shared with the Elves made Aud determined that she would never give him anything more or less than the truth.

"Are you ready to hear what I saw in the water?" she asked calmly.

Tomas nodded; Moira opened her eyes.

"I saw Dagaz, and some images within it. A young man and woman whom I'm sure were Owein and Fraine, he in one section of Dagaz, she in the other. With their arms outstretched and a current of energy flowing between them. They were building something."

Moira sat bolt upright. Two spots of color flared high on her face, and her eyes were narrowed. "A *bridge*," she said. "Dagaz rules the bridge between Asgard and Midgard. They were building one between Elfland and Midgard."

"Yes," said Aud slowly. "That's precisely what they were doing." She looked at Tomas. "I think you may have been involved with it too. I didn't see you, but I sensed you nearby."

"The prophecy said they would link the worlds," said Moira, her face pensive now. "Literally, perhaps."

After an instant's debate, the Seer said in a neutral tone, "As literal as the Sight may be. Then I saw Loki in both sections of Dagaz. He was hunting for the twins. He means them no good, nor you either."

"Did he see you?" asked Tomas.

"No, I wasn't the one he sought. And I was well-protected, thanks to all the Elementals that you and Brubakken posted." The Norn had got past them, but Elementals were as subject to the Nornir as was every other creature in the nine worlds. "Then Skuld appeared in both halves of the Rune. She held a scale. A market scale for weighing out silver." The Norn hadn't brought one, but Aud's Sight often added something to her visions. "I saw nothing more."

"Might you know why She came?" asked Moira.

"No. I'd no idea that She would. I only knew she meant us no harm. And no good either." Aud hesitated. "I'm not certain that Skuld could intend either good or harm. Can the future have an intent? I don't believe it's fixed." She hunted for words. "Yet it grows out of the past and the present, and they must give it some rough shape. Skuld may be more bound by the Ørlög, in her own way, than we are."

Aud's listeners didn't appear to find that thought any more comforting than she did. Aubrey mumbled something; Moira gazed at her lap. After a searching look at Aud, Tomas put his head in his hands.

Brubakken met Aud's eyes calmly. No one knew the truth of these matters. Moira might comprehend more than either Aud or Brubakken did; the Elf had certainly had more time to learn. Yet it was Tomas who'd risen to his feet and asked the Norn her intent, while the rest of them sat stunned and gaping.

"Perhaps She's not more bound by it. Perhaps She's just more aware of it," said Tomas, and reached for the water jug.

Brubakken considered him. "Do the ravens know why She spoke the Ørlög here?"

"No, they only knew what it was. They'd heard it before." Tomas looked a bit awed. They all did. The ravens had heard the Ørlög chanted when they'd flown through the nine worlds for Odin. There was a protracted silence before Tomas said, "All they could tell me was what we already know, that it has something to do with the twins."

Small help that. The Ørlög had something to do with all of them, whether they knew it yet or not. Perhaps the ravens would have another view to lay before Tomas. Presumably they were outside in the night at that moment. Aud had decided that they weren't made of flesh and blood, at least not like her own. She'd seen them dozing but, as greedy as ravens were, she'd never seen these two take any food or drink, and they didn't appear to feel the cold. Not only that, they could materialize in her home at any moment without the benefit of an open door.

"The twins will need shields," muttered Tomas. "If Loki's looking for them."

"They'll need a Mage's training," said Moira. "They'll be apt for it."

Brubakken rested a hand on one of their horoscopes. "So they will. Aud asked me to say a few words about their nativities."

Her face brightening, Moira said, "I'll listen gladly. I have no skill in that art." She smiled a little. "We have no Sun or Moon in Elfland, nor any planets. Not even a single star."

"It's as well I don't practice there," said Brubakken with an answering smile. "And the craft isn't always conducted the same way here. I learned mine in the East, in the city of Miklagard. I won't speak for long; the hour's too late. You may ask me for more whenever you wish." He pointed at the charts. "They were born at the full Moon. Which means that the tides of their feelings will run high, and their links with women are important for good or ill. The Sun tenants the fourth house, so their ties to their roots are deeply felt. Yet the Sun's in Aquarius: they'll need to follow their own counsel, not merely the path of their ancestors." His glance at Moira was gentle. "Likely they won't feel well-suited to either half of their kindred, nor will they be biddable or easy to read. You hardly required my services to tell you that, I expect."

She gave him a half smile.

"Their Moon is in the last degree of Leo and tenants the tenth house. To be happy they'll need recognition or some share of authority. And affection as well." He paused. "Affection is best earned by deserving it. If one must rule, then, that means ruling well." He turned to Tomas. "With that Moon and a well-tenanted fifth house, they'll find their way as easily into the heart as you do, and have something of your artistry besides. Some gift that needs to bear fruit, though what I could not say."

Tomas nodded.

"Scorpio was rising in the east at their birth, so they'll walk all their roads with the Scorpion's face showing, regardless of what's beneath it. That's the mask of the sorcerer. I'd start their training in magic as soon as may be." Brubakken looked at Aud. Over the years she'd absorbed enough of his star lore to have some sense of what would follow. Besides, they'd discussed how best to word it.

"Scorpio rules death," Brubakken told Moira. "The rising sign rules birth. It's how we enter the world, as well as how we make our way through it. You nearly died at your lying-in. Death attended it."

The Elf's brow was furrowed, her eyes fixed on Brubakken. No strain in her face, only concentration.

"Death will walk at their sides throughout their lives," he said quietly. "As it does for all mortals, yet Owein and Fraine will hear more of its footsteps. They must make their peace with it."

"And if they do not?" asked Moira.

Aud glanced at Tomas who, his expression somber, was watching Moira.

"Then their death will haunt them," said Brubakken. "They'll tempt it, or deny it, or flee from it."

"If they make peace with it, how will they act?"

The Swede's smile was kind. "That I could not say. That we all do in a different manner."

Tomas was nodding. The Elf took his hand. "So I've been told," she said softly, then pointed at the horoscopes. "Do they differ?"

"Hardly any. They were born only moments apart." Brubakken rolled up the charts, tied them with a strip of leather and presented them to her. "Take these with you. I've drawn copies."

Aud, Brubakken and Aubrey had left, and the twins been fed and fallen asleep again. Tomas and Moira lay on the pile of furs by the cradle. Fatigue seemed to have settled in Tomas's bones like the damp, but he wasn't drowsy. The hearthfire tossed and turned and mumbled to itself in its stony bed, and too many shadows danced upon the walls.

Moira was wakeful as well. After a while he asked, "Are you sure you're fit to travel?"

"No. But we must. I don't know what's afoot in the palace. The sooner we learn, the better."

He was glad that Jared and Aubrey, formidable and well-respected figures in Moira's former court, would go with them. And Aidan; they'd need of a Seer who was skilled at that craft. And the Parcae, for he and Moira were stepping into their prophecy together. "How do you feel about

Gillian's staying behind?"

"Content. She's of more use to us here. I'm glad to have an ally among the Norse Elves, and one close by Aud and Brubakken." A small chuckle. "Though I'd like to see her kin's faces when she announces she's our ambassador and claims Lake Malar for the twins."

"Are the lake-Elves liable to attack her?"

"No. Only to argue." Another giggle. "Most water-Elves are nearly as contentious as the Sidhe. Five or ten of them may have come near to claiming Lake Malar already."

"Then they may not pay Gillian any heed."

Moira raised herself up on an elbow to look at him. "They will. They know the prophecy, and who the twins are. They'll take her most seriously indeed. Some will pledge loyalty and some won't." She was eyeing him quizzically. "Have you ever been to Lake Malar?" In the lake itself, he could tell that she meant. To visit the Elves there.

"No. Though I've been invited. Will that be the way of it at your palace? With pretenders to the throne already bickering?"

She was silent for so long that he thought she might have fallen asleep before she said, "I've no idea, Tomas. I can't even bend my own Sight there, and it's little more use asking Aidan. All the threads are too tangled to see through."

CHAPTER TWO: ROSE, LINLEY AND MATILDA

Midgard, Wessex, spring 885 A.D., Christian reckoning

Rose stamped her feet on the trodden earth of Limecliff's courtyard and blew on her finger-ends. Before dawn, it was, and not fully light. King Alfred's niece Matilda, holding a torch, smiled wanly and huddled into her cloak. The gesture made the torch wobble. Rose coughed as a wisp of smoke reached her eyes, pulled her hood further over her face, and shoved a tendril of her sleek brown hair beneath her kerchief.

"Pardon," said Matilda.

Blinking tears away, Rose saw the girl bite her lip as she moved the flaming brand aside. "No harm done," said Rose, determined to be cheerful despite the cold and Linley's imminent departure, neither of which was Matilda's doing. Alfred was off to the defense of Rochester town, which was besieged by the Danes. Linley bore arms with Alfred's thegnhood one month out of three, and while he'd not been eager to leave Limecliff, that he should go to Rochester had not even been in question.

Not by Alfred. Rose had questions a-plenty about warfare in general and this skirmish in particular, though none she could put to Alfred or the Danes. Not and expect a more than cursory hearing, let alone a reply.

She pulled her hood away from her face just long enough to smile at Matilda. Alfred's dead brother's by-blow, the girl was pretty, slight and soft-spoken, with the maple-brown hair and unusually dark blue eyes that ran in Alfred's family. Lapiz eyes, large and watchful in Matilda's case, dominating a reticent face. She was pale, in sharp contrast to her uncle's healthy color.

A royal bastard's life was seldom easy, less so for a girl. Neither Rose nor Linley was surprised at Matilda's silence during their visits to the various royal estates that hosted Alfred's court. What had intrigued Rose was the girl's wary attentiveness to her surroundings and the way that, whenever asked a direct question, she took a moment to ponder her reply. Like a half-wild barn cat with an instinct to seek safety, she eluded the coarser or more lecherous members of Alfred's court and gravitated towards gentler folk. She sat near Rose and Linley at meals, though she said never a word until Rose struck up a conversation.

The girl wasn't a shining intellect but neither was she feeble-minded, and what she'd most wanted to talk about was Limecliff's mews and its birds. Even then it had taken her nearly an hour to approach the topic. Moreover, it had taken Linley, charmer though he was, nearly another half hour to win a smile from her. A genuine, unguarded smile, warm as Spanish oranges and, Rose suspected, twice as rare.

Her mother, Theodosia, saw Matilda squander that breathtaking and infectious smile on a simple countryman, Linley, who hadn't any noble blood and wasn't even a landholder. Theodosia probably supposed that Matilda found him comely enough to commit an indiscretion. Linley had thick soft dark hair, shining and sufficiently unruly that it put most women in mind of smoothing it back from his forehead. He wasn't tall but he was well-formed, and his round, olive-brown face had a lot of good strong bone about the jaw and temples. He had fine clear brown eyes whose gaze was warm and amiable. All in all, his was a most pleasing face, ready to listen and quick to smile, albeit easily mistaken for guileless.

For a casual acquaintance to notice Linley's discretion and sensitivity would take unusual perception, and Theodosia had little of it. She would see only that any dalliance with Linley would be profitless for her daughter. He and his equally low-born wife were not wealthy; they merely managed the estate of some Norseman of peculiar repute who'd been gone for six years or more. Though it was fine land; the King himself often went hawking there. Such an estate was wasted on a pagan—though it was whispered he'd remained in good odor with the King if not with the Bishop—who couldn't even be bothered to oversee his own holdings. Theodosia saw Matilda's smile, and called her away from Linley and Rose.

"She's not been ill-used, at least physically," Linley had allowed when they were alone. "But bullied to a fare-thee-well, if I'm any judge."

He was the best judge of people that Rose had ever met. "And starved for a kind word," she said indignantly, and he agreed. They'd both taken to the girl.

Which was why, after a few circumspect words with Alfred, at the next court supper they'd proposed that Theodosia to send her daughter to them. Rose claimed that Limecliff needed another pair of hands, and Linley offered to bear Matilda's keep himself.

With a wild glance about the hall and its well-heeled prospective suitors, a couple of whom were suppressing scowls, Theodosia opened her mouth.

Alfred, who never interrupted anyone, spoke before the woman even drew breath. "An excellent notion," he said, smiling. "It could only benefit Matilda to learn the management of an estate. I'm delighted she'll have good instruction." And to Theodosia: "Wouldn't you agree that knowledge can only add to a dowry, my lady?"

Smiling, as if with a mouthful of green persimmons, she nodded.

The King said to Rose, "For your kindness to my niece, I thank you," and to Linley, "And you for your generosity, but I should like the pleasure of paying her keep myself."

A few hours later, Matilda found Rose in the kitchen where she was reviewing Alfred's stores of medicinal herbs. Without a word, her eyes damp and shining, the girl had hugged Rose for so long that Rose's own eyes grew wet.

During the three months that Matilda had been housed at Limecliff, she'd gained confidence, some much needed-flesh, a steadily increasing trust in her hosts and even a hint of more color, although nothing approaching Rose's warm complexion. Though Matilda was a hard and willing worker, she showed no real interest in Rose's herbs or midwifery, nor in needlework, the kitchen or the stables, where they now stood waiting for Linley to finish saddling up and bid them farewell. Matilda had spent days on end riding the fields with Linley, learning how crops were harvested and stored and how livestock was tended. The rest of her time she passed in the mews with the falcons and sparrowhawks. Linley took her hunting a few times, then said she was perfectly capable of flying the birds alone.

"I've never seen such patience. She hasn't Tomas's touch with them, but if she wanted a falconer's job, I'd give it her in a heartbeat," he told Rose.

Ah, Tomas. Linley's eyes were wistful whenever he spoke of his absent friend. Rose missed Tomas too. Six years was a long time away, unless he'd gone to Elfland again. Gone with Moira and their child, if she'd survived its birth. Linley said that Tomas had spent seven mortal years there once before, yet it was hard not to fret over him and Moira. The hermit Daniel could spread fewer rumors about them if they'd put in an appearance and belie his tales of demons with their own flesh and blood and quiet presence. Even Matilda had asked some cautious questions about Tomas. About his skill with birds, and the way he had Alfred's ear. About the strange dark-haired woman who, bearing Tomas's child, had come to Limecliff during an eclipse, and with whom he'd departed not long afterwards. And finally, daringly, about those small naked women with wings who'd once or twice been seen on the estate.

Life with Tomas and his Elf Queen had left an imprint upon Rose: she'd not lied to the girl, but neither had she told her the whole truth.

If Tomas and Moira returned, Daniel would likely make as great a hue and cry to Alfred and the Bishop as he'd done directly after Tomas and Moira left, though he'd not got Limecliff signed over to him or anything near it thereby. He'd be less likely to get it now, when Alfred wouldn't be inclined to pay more than lip service to any ill words about Tomas. For Wessex was going back to war with the Danes, just when and as Tomas had foreseen that they would.

During the past six years, whenever Linley had attended a court function, Alfred met him with a face full of anticipation and uncertainty, and each time Linley had been obliged to shake his head, yet still convey his faith that Tomas would return. And faith he had. Rose wasn't sure if she did, nor if Linley's convictions came from his limited second Sight or his heart. Alfred needed Tomas's Sight, but Linley missed his friendship.

"There he is," said Matilda. Linley was leading his roan mare from the stable. The girl's glance at Rose was hesitant. "I'll just say a word and leave you two alone then, shall I?"

Rose squeezed Matilda's arm. "No, my poppet, though you're kind to offer. We said that sort of good-bye last night. He'll expect to see us both now."

"So I do," said Linley, knotting the mare's reins to the pommel. "Though I'll not be gone long enough for either of you to miss me. Alfred should make short work of this; never fret. Don't sell my harp while I'm gone, Rose, and 'Tilda, don't let your birds nest in my lute." He was taking it with him; still, no one contradicted him. He enveloped both women in a hug and reached up to kiss Rose, who was taller than he. "Simon's stopping for me at the ford, so I'll be off now. If any couriers are traveling your way, I'll send word, but don't trouble yourselves if none comes. Agreed?"

Rose said something cheerful as he kissed her again and vaulted into the saddle. Dashing a hand across her eyes, Matilda proffered a smile.

Linley leaned down from the roan, beckoned to Rose and breathed in her ear, "Say a word to the old gods, will you? And goddesses."

"To all the Powers there are," she murmured back, and kissed him one last time.

CHAPTER THREE: CARAID AND LOKI

Dubhlinn, spring 885 A.D., Christian reckoning

Brendan O'Quinlan stood in his doorway gazing at Ennis, who was halfway across the common grazing lands with Brendan's son Scully. From time to time their two heads, one dark-haired with strands of grey, the other dun-colored and curly, bent together over a single chunk of wood. Chips flew whenever they conferred. While the two of them took a turn at minding the sheep, Ennis, a master carpenter and fine wood-worker, was teaching Scully how to whittle.

"A good man, your Ennis," said Brendan. "I'm not nearly so patient myself."

Caraid glanced up from carding wool. "A very good man."

"With age comes patience, they say. And he already has chick and child of his own. Nearly grown now."

Brendan's back was to her, but she knew he was working himself up to a question. "We may have a child yet ourselves. Ennis would like that."

"And would you?"

"I've not ruled it out." Her voice sounded sharp. "I would, yes," she amended.

After a moment Brendan left his doorway and came to stand looking down at her. "It would be good for him, I think," he said, then added mildly, without a trace of his usual heartiness, "And better for you, after the hard road you've had of it. Losing Tomas and all."

He meant well. Brendan always meant well, simply and utterly and with no artfulness whatever, and he always told her exactly what he was thinking. He'd been that way since childhood, long before she'd spent eleven mortal years in Elfland and came back to find her adored younger brother, her favorite, suddenly older than she was—and the only person to accept her story and herself entirely and without question. You'd no more justification for losing your temper with Brendan than for losing it with a simpleton, though he wasn't dim-witted. He'd never say to Ennis what he'd just said to her.

Although Ennis knew, along with all Dubhlinn, that Caraid was a Seer and that she'd traveled to Elfland and back, about Tomas he knew very little and she'd just as soon keep it that way. Fortune had smiled upon the skill in Ennis's hands; he earned a more than comfortable living. She liked all three of his children and they liked her: no feigned affection there. He was generous, honest, even-tempered, trustworthy, whole-heartedly devoted to his family and now to her, the first woman in whom he'd shown any real interest since his wife died three years ago. She'd never met anyone with such a capacity for single-minded allegiance.

But Ennis had no love for the Norse and, though Caraid's powers fascinated him and he accepted them, he had nary a drop of the Sight. His world was bounded by weights and measures, the grains of wood, the temper and balance of a saw, the orderly foundations of houses and barns. He had the physique and vigor of a man who'd done physical labor all his life and done it wisely, knowing his limits.

Still, he was older than she was and by no small margin: nearly nineteen years. She had a feeling he might be troubled by too many tales of the soft-spoken Norse harper she'd met in Elfland, and who had not only come back a Mage but who had also—which would matter more to Ennis—disarmed and killed a berserker at King Ivar's court, and done so with no more weapons than his empty hands. She'd no idea what Ennis might have heard in the town, but she herself had told him only that she'd had a Norse lover named Tomas who'd left her.

"A child might be good for me, too," Caraid agreed. Against her thigh she could feel the jet comb that Tomas had bought her, a light weight in the case she'd sewn from the creamy lapiz silk that he'd also given her.

A faint line deepening between his eyebrows, Brendan studied her face. Then he sat on the bench beside her and pulled her into his arms. "I'd not have mentioned his name if I'd known you were still grieving, lamb."

She'd gone for a walk to get away. She didn't want to weep in front of Brendan or discuss Tomas with him. She didn't care to speak of Tomas at all. If she stayed and let Brendan hold her, even if neither of them said a word, the tears would come, and when Ennis returned he'd ask what troubled her.

So she'd fabricated a need for some herbs that the Welsh traders brought to Dubhlinn, and said that she fancied a stroll to the harbor, and promised she'd be careful when Brendan lectured her about slavers. There were always slavers, and she was always careful. Besides, they preferred easy pickings: small coastal villages whose men were off fighting for some chieftain or other, and where dozens of younger lasses could be captured. Slavers wouldn't exert themselves to take one lone woman from the busiest port in all Éire, and she likely to have friends and family there in the harbor to come to her aid.

With an empty basket slung across her back by a strap, Caraid slowly made her way down the path to the docks. Mud and springtime had arrived together, along with even more rain than usual. A fine thing it was to see the return of the full palette of greens all about her, and hear the riotous birds in the hedgerows. Even the moss on the north side of the half-buried boulders looked fresh and new. Overhead a corncrake sailed by on the soft afternoon air, and once a hare bounded across the field to Caraid's left. She climbed onto a crumbling stone wall and walked atop it for a while with her arms extended to either side, not that she needed any help keeping her balance. The gesture was one from her childhood and always made her smile. It made old man Doherty smile, too, as he labored up the steep hill from the harbor, and they waved at one another.

What had Tomas's childhood been like? The son of a Norse earl and a Welsh bondwoman, he'd told her he was. What if his father had been among the Norse invaders who'd settled here, and Tomas had grown up in Dubhlinn and they'd met here? In that event, would she have spared Ennis a second glance?

But Tomas had been born in Vestfold and sailed to Waleis with his half-brother's crew, where he'd fallen afoul of the Elves. She should put him out of her mind once and for all. A miracle had happened and she'd been granted some sort of reprieve, an opportunity for a peaceful life close to Brendan and his family, and secure with Ennis who asked for little more than a chance to make her happy.

Ennis had no Sight at all; he was head-blind. But that she could live with and easily. Sometimes it was a relief to be the only one who knew something she'd no business to know. Ennis's smile was never a map that pointed to some unexpected and strange new country within him. He was an open book, one that held no surprises. His silences were those of a kindly and tranquil nature, not the strained defenses of someone whose wyrd was to speak the truth or nothing at all. There was no uncanny grey light in Ennis's eyes; he didn't move like a cat stalking the darkness, and no magic, thick and turbulent as a migrating swarm of bees, hung in the air about his head.

Tomas was lost to her; Moira had taken him. Caraid hadn't seen him for six years, neither in the flesh nor by her Sight.

After their last meeting, her Sight had told her she was lucky to be alive, for all that she'd done no more than speak to him and not tried very hard to stop him from kissing her. That conversation should have been the death of her; it was a pure miracle that she was still breathing. She knew that, though she'd never consciously bent her Sight in Tomas's direction since the harrowing moment when she'd summoned all her resolve and sent him from her garden. She knew it because she still dreamt about him and Moira, all too often and with a hallucinatory lucidity that meant her Sight was working unbidden while she slept. And because in those dreams, though Tomas's body and clothing looked just the same as when she'd last seen him, and though everyone else seemed to find him perfectly normal, to Caraid's eyes he had only a hollow-socketed and yellowing skull where he should have had a face.

Somerset, Cheddar caves, spring 885 A.D., Christian reckoning.

In his own shape, ginger-haired, slight and narrow of shoulder, Loki lay atop a jagged shelf of rock overlooking a sheer and giddying drop to Cheddar gorge and scowled at the water below. The salamander Plirok was late. Still pretending allegiance to the hermit Daniel, the fire

Elemental was now wholly Loki's creature, assigned to spy on Daniel and subtly influence him via its reports and suggestions. It was a cumbersome way to keep track of Daniel, but Loki's assumption of the role of the Christian arch-demon, Lucifer, had made such roundabout measures necessary. The hermit had been afraid of Loki while thinking him only a fiery seraph. Now he was terrified and could no longer be worked with directly.

Eeling farther out on the ledge, Loki tossed a stone into the gorge. He harbored no fear of the drop. If he overbalanced and slipped, which wasn't likely, he could simply grow wings before he'd fallen thirty ells. He threw another, larger stone, and listened till he heard a series of thuds from the rocky shelves below.

Before he announced his new role as Lucifer and parted ways with Daniel, Loki had tried to reason with him. The fellow was informative, if nothing else. Loki had learned a number of useful facts about the worshippers of the white Christ and the sort of behavior they'd expect from Lucifer. All manner of tidbits that would help keep Loki the primary Power in his new world, Midgard. The stories were wrong, all those skalds' ravings that had him bound under a mountain and enduring torture by venom before Ragnarök began and he was freed. Such a pleasure to be unbound and gaining strength in Midgard. The stories were wrong; the Aesir were wrong, and he was the master here.

Or he soon would be. What in blazes was keeping Plirok? The one thorn in Loki's side was the Parcae's prophecy. Clearly, the major threat to his undisputed sway over Midgard was the Elves, specifically Moira, Tomas and their children. The stronger that Faerie's link to Midgard remained, then the more magic would remain there—particularly magic that had to do with the earth of Midgard itself—and the less central Loki's influence would be. And that he would not abide. After coping with Asgard and its pack of gods, not to mention Vanaheim and the Vanir, he was more than deserving of his role as the main Power here. Yet although Loki knew every blasted word of the prophecy, at first he'd no idea what the twins would *do* to keep the worlds linked and green. Plirok wasn't his only spy: he'd sent a pack of salamanders to trace Tomas's every step since he first shipped out of Vestfold.

They had told him of the air Elemental who'd volunteered to assist Tomas. A Lord of the Air was one thing, and small rank and file sylphs quite another, particularly those whom Nissyen deemed not powerful enough to join the Elementals under its command. Thwarted sylphs would pry and sneak about any activity from which they'd been banned. Moreover, to prove how much they knew, they would natter away for hours to anyone who would listen. Even salamanders...

From that handful of rejected sylphs, Loki's agents learned something of what the half-Saami Mage, Brubakken, had said of the twins' nativities.

A most enlightening report: Loki had conceived not a few notions about turning the twins' character traits against them. He also knew that Skuld had attended the name-fastening, but so far he'd seen no way that event could be twisted round to his advantage. And he'd discovered that Moira thought the twins might build some sort of bridge between Elfland and Midgard, perhaps rather like Asgard's Bifrost had once been. Finally he had learned of Caraid, the Irish Seer whom the lord Rhys had brought to Elfland, and learned that Moira might not know about Tomas's dalliance with Caraid in Dubhlinn. That last particular set of facts could lend themselves to many a use...

Loki heaved another rock, this one about the size of his doubled fists, into the gorge. After falling perhaps fifty ells, it stopped in midair, cleanly, then held still for an instant. Slowly, a wisp of smoke began to curl about the stone. Smoke and then flames, though they didn't consume the rock. They danced about it as it started an ascent.

"*There* you are, Plirok," said Loki, sitting upright when the stone and its fiery halo paused before him. He was more irritated than relieved. "What kept you?"

Mouth first, a face was materializing in the flames, an ugly face with narrow wide-set eyes and a crumpled snout like a parody of a pig's muzzle. Plirok must have been practicing; it looked more like Daniel's description of a demon all the time. "Your business, my lord," it said as soon as its lips were fully formed.

Its breath smelled rotten, like spoiled eggs. Like sulphur. Loki grinned. "You've brought tidings. But first, how fares your charge?"

"Prepared to petition for Limecliff should Linley not return from battle." It grinned. "I have convinced the good hermit to wait long enough not to be offensive."

"You've done well by him. And Alfred?"

"Gone to defend Rochester. There's a Viking fleet bound that way. With live slaves in the cargo." Plirok's wink was more of a sneer. "And a few dead ones."

Precisely what he wanted to hear. Loki stood up and stretched, luxuriously, savoring the moment. "I'm off to Dubhlinn. Fetch your brothers Paimon and Oriens and meet me at the harbor. And stay clear of peat fires! This is to be done as quietly as possible."

Caraid didn't need any herbs and besides, she preferred to grow them herself. Still, since the good-natured Welsh traders with whom she and Brendan had grown friendly were in port, she asked what plants they carried.

"Only what we'd need ourselves," Morgan said cheerfully. "Ginger and mint for the sea sickness, though we'd no call for it this time. I've never seen the Irish Sea so calm." He glanced over Caraid's shoulder down the plankway, then reached for her elbow. "Though the same can't be said for the docks. Stand back, love; I don't like the look of this lot."

Joining him, she kept her eyes prudently downcast. Half a dozen Norsemen came striding along, their thighs big as treetrunks and their beards braided with glittering thread. They all wore those billowy kneepants that the slavers brought back from the Saracen lands, and soft-soled leather boots that looked new.

Turned out in their best they might be, yet it was easily seen that these were fighting men. Armbands glittered between their wrists and their elbows, where the jewelery could dull a blow and not impede the full use of their biceps. Their short cloaks were pinned at the shoulders so their arms could swing freely. Small wonder that Morgan had drawn her aside. She felt the men's eyes on her as they passed, though their pace didn't slow.

"Slavers. Pack of trolls," muttered Morgan when the Norse were out of earshot. "All the water clear up the North Way's crawling with dragonships, off to Mercia or East Anglia or thereabouts."

"Why?"

"Likely because the Danes are besieging Rochester, and marching through Wessex if they can. Which means both an army to supply, and that same army selling a fresh lot of slaves."

Caraid said nothing. Tomas had gone to Wessex. Was he still there?

"But they're not raiding Dubhlinn these days," Morgan said cheerfully. "Not while one of their own has the rule of it. So give us a smile, Caraid, won't you? Come see the fine cloth my wife's sent your sister-in-law." He tipped her a wink. "It could be she's sent something for you."

It was nearly dark when Caraid left the harbor, fortified with Morgan's ale and the bread and cheese his shipmates had pressed upon her. She made her way quickly through Dubhlinn's warren of narrow streets until she reached the common grazing fields, then started across them at a more leisurely pace.

In no time her shoes were soaked with dew. The sky was getting blacker by the second, but plenty of times she'd found her way home when she'd had more ale and less light than this. From the common fields on, she'd likely meet no one but sheep and cows, and not many of them at this hour. By the pale illumination from a waning Moon low in the sky, she spotted the silhouettes of a few great boulders. Ancient, they were. Who had tossed them there and never come back for them? The great goddess Dana and Her people, the Tuatha de Danaan? The Gentry. The Sidhe—the Elves.

Strange how Dana still seemed so near, how She'd always seemed closer than the blood that beat just beneath Caraid's skin, while the Sidhe had turned alien in her eyes. They'd taken her to Elfland, and there the Welsh

Elves and their King had treated her worse than ever the Sidhe had.

Mostly she kept any thought of Rhys at bay. But sometimes a fragment of memory flooded in, sharp and unwelcome as a splinter working its way towards her spine. Before she'd learned that the Elves meant to compel her Sight, all of Rhys's actions had seemed to have only one end: to give her pleasure. The only memories she'd allowed herself were a dim mass of sobbing breaths, whether hers or his she'd no idea, and of hazy red vistas receding behind her closed eyes before she'd slept like the dead. If she let herself recall how much more had happened, she'd sink clean down into this soggy grass and weep. Not from shame, but for the loss of him. Yet if she made herself recall *how* it had happened, that she'd neither asked for nor wanted it but that, once it had started, she'd been unable to refuse—then she wanted to weep for another set of reasons.

Weep, and rage. She would not remember the Elf King. Tomas, painful as the thought of him was, made for safer memories. Though they were tainted, because he had Elf blood. She was through with the Elves and with anyone kin to them. It was finished, that part of her life. It was over, and Ennis awaited her at the other end of it.

The men who took her said never a word, made never a sound. One moment she was moving at a good clip through the silent boulders, as if trying to outpace her own thoughts. The next moment a set of arms closed about her from behind, pinning her arms and stopping her mouth with a hard hand that smelled of onions and sweat. Someone else kicked the back of her knees and she stumbled, whereupon a third man seized her legs. Then they lifted her, squirming but unable to kick or strike out, unable even to speak, and began carrying her back towards the harbor.

They were slavers. They had to be. She bit the hand over her mouth as hard as she could, and heard a stifled curse. The fellow shifted his grip to free one of his hands and she was expecting his fist in her face, when someone said softly and icily in Norse, "Have you forgot the purse I offered you? It's more than you'd earn in five voyages. Have you forgot our bargain? No ill usage."

The voice was a light tenor, refined, sarcastic, and utterly certain of being obeyed. A lord's voice. What had brought a Norse lord to a Dubhlinn pasture full of sheep dung, and why was her person worth so much to him? There was a corrosive and ominous undernote to the voice that made her skin tingle and her breath congeal in her lungs. She was a Seer; she knew what that meant. Power. The speaker could wield magic.

"I want her in perfect condition when she arrives," said the voice.

Power and cruelty. Merely the tone would have revealed it, without the hasty manner in which the man who held his bleeding fingers over her mouth took his hand away, doubtless intending to replace it with the one she hadn't bitten. Before he could clamp down on her lips again, she turned her head in the direction of the voice and said quickly, "Arrives where, please?"

A slight redheaded man, unarmed and confident among the five or six massive Norsemen who accompanied him, met her gaze, then gestured imperiously that her mouth be left free. The redhead's eyes were a flickering, burning hazel, and shifted in a way that both commanded attention and provoked deep uneasiness. All the Norse kept their distance from him, and the arms of the two who carried Caraid grew tense as he closed alongside. His face was as sickly a white as if he'd spent his whole life underground. He moved with a demented, loose-jointed and eerily flexible gait, as though he had no bones at all. It was more of a scuttle or a strut than a walk, and it had no center of gravity. Watching him might have made Caraid dizzy even if she'd been upright when she saw him. His aura was ablaze: nothing but fire, not white-hot but a sullen and smoldering orange-red. Now that she'd glimpsed it, she couldn't block it from her Sight. He must want her to see it, then.

A tremor shook her. He wasn't a man. He wasn't an Elf. She wasn't sure that he was a god, either, yet he was closer to one than to anything else she could have named.

When he grinned, she closed her eyes before the concentrated ill will in his face. "When you arrive at the auction," he said cheerfully. In Irish, moreover, though she'd spoken Norse to him. "I'm frightfully sorry to keep you in suspense, but I don't know exactly where yet myself, you see. Someplace where Tomas the Rhymer will know you've been taken by slavers. I want him distracted."

Only then did it strike her, as sharply and undeniably as if she'd been slapped, and with all the horrible clarity that she knew for the Sight, that this was how she would die, after having seen Tomas and spoken with him six years ago. And this was why she would die, so that this being could use her death to hurt him. "Distracted from what?" she asked as steadily as she could.

"His life. His children. His Fate and theirs," said the ginger-haired man.

What children? This creature knew that Caraid would die, or he wouldn't be telling her anything. Perhaps he could be persuaded to tell her more. "Who are you?"

"I was Loki. Perhaps you've heard of me, during my recent stay in Asgard?" Beaming. Sly. "Now I have assumed the role of the Nazarene's Lucifer, and I am *the* Power in Midgard. Or will be."

Loki. Another tremor went through her, and she fought nausea. He'd not get what he wanted, even though she had no way to stop his using her for bait. "By Dana, you are not, nor shall you be," she said clearly.

"Dana?" He started to laugh.

Whom could she call upon who might impress him, this Norse godling? "And by *Freya*. I swear it." She raised her voice. "Loki shall not be the only Power in Midgard. Lady Freya, hear me!"

CHAPTER FOUR: A PASSAGE TO ELFLAND

"We're all traveling disembodied. Not in bird-shape, no matter what Nissyen said," Tomas told the pooka, and hoped his amusement didn't show. Nissyen must have wanted to see Aubrey's reaction.

The pooka looked relieved. Then, as the full import of Tomas's words sunk in, he flattened his ears and stalked off without a word through the lakeshore's frozen reeds, his retreating back stiff with indignation. It was all too easy to become accustomed to the Elves' inability to lie—and to forget the sylph's facility at it. Nissyen had doubtless noticed Aubrey's clumsiness in bird-shape.

Gillian had said her farewells the night before with Aud and Brubakken. Aidan and Jared were yawning, knuckling the sleep from their eyes. Standing at Tomas's elbow, Moira gazed out over the lake. Two Parcae hovered near her, holding the blanket-wrapped twins. Tomas blinked: surely his children had grown since the name-fastening? Moira noticed the direction of his stare and nodded. "Halfbreeds," she murmured. "They grow much faster than full blooded mortals."

Nonetheless it was uncanny: they appeared more than old enough to crawl. His chest tightened with a cold little knot that he slowly recognized as apprehension, not for himself but for the twins, though precisely what he feared he could not have said.

The rest of the Parcae crowded about Tallah, who appeared to be lecturing and was punctuating her speech with an occasional flap of her wings. Perched on a nearby stump, Nissyen was listening intently, its narrow green eyes alight with interest. Tomas had a hunch that the Elemental was trying to learn the Parcae's tongue, and a slightly uneasy feeling that it might succeed. Although the winged Elves seemed to mind neither the damp nor the chill, Aidan was stamping his feet and blowing on his fingers. The ravens were circling overhead; Aubrey returned, with his ears at half-mast when Nissyen gave him a gleeful little wave, and Tomas was past ready to go.

In order to guide the passage, he, Tallah and Nissyen would go free of anyone's touch. Travel between the worlds had become so difficult that the other Elves all gripped a Parca's hand. Hands and bodies alike would dissolve during the journey, a phenomenon that Tomas didn't entirely understand, though he'd grown almost accustomed to it. He caught Moira's eye, then Tallah's. Both Elves nodded: they'd maintain some sort of mindlink with him en route.

Closing his eyes, Tomas waited till he felt both presences in his mind, tenuous as a lightly held skein of yarn, too insubstantial for him to know what either Elf was thinking, only where they were. Then he visualized Moira's palace on its promontory overlooking the jade-green Elvish Sea. A round structure of weathered grey stone, the palace was built at one end of a long rectangular greensward cleared from an ancient and immense forest. At the other end of the green, a ring of hawthorn trees encircled a well. He'd drunk from that well; he'd danced on that green. Light shone from the great hall's double doors, carved of onyx, and from its lozenged windows. Somewhere in that hall was an airy room with a lofty ceiling and tapestried walls, a low bed piled with cushions, and perhaps the remains of two guttering candles...

"Let's be off," he said, aiming, focusing on the palace with his mind's eye.

When his facial skin felt drawn and tight, a current of energy began to flow from him, arcing away in a narrow stream. Suddenly every last particle of his body tingled. Aubrey snorted, and one of the Parcae let out a whoop that sounded more eager than frightened. The air turned bone-searingly cold. Next it began swirling around Tomas's body, slowly at first, until it gained enough speed to sing in his ears. Soon it grew so loud that he could hear nothing else.

A stab of pain at the base of his skull rocked him onto his heels. With it came a flash of light across the darkness behind his closed eyes, then another slicing pain. That shouldn't be happening; that should be no part of the passage. Now he'd lost contact with Moira and Tallah, and was alone with the wind that howled in his ears. Alarmed, he tried to call a halt to the departure, but he couldn't open his mouth. He couldn't even feel it; his lips were numb.

Abruptly there was silence. Next the air changed direction, or he did, because now he was swirling around it. And then he wasn't anywhere at all.

After a while the crowding images began to come and go.

His mother's face. The night he'd first played music with Linley. Moira: in Elfland, in Wessex, in Birka, her dark hair swept from her forehead, her eyes soft or pensive by turns. His flute master back in Vestfold. The twins. A puppy he'd had as a child. Dubhlinn harbor with its clean salt air, curraghs and dragonships moored at the docks, and the gulls wheeling overhead no greedier than the men who trod the plankways beneath them.

It was as if he were free-floating in time, and through it all he felt only the ravens nearby. He'd have to trust that Moira and Tallah were with him, since he couldn't reach out for them. It was all he could do to keep concentrating on Moira's palace—their destination—when so many images kept flashing before him.

He saw a shattered bridge, multicolored, glittering, stretching out over nothingness like a lunatic tumbler executing a backflip. Bifrost, or what was left of it. He saw himself as he once was, having recently stepped off that bridge, huddled on Asgard's plain with his head in his hands. And he saw Loki.

At first he glimpsed only the Trickster's approach to his own slumped form, but soon Loki's figure grew larger and overshadowed his. Then larger still, a half smile on the thin lips, the burning hazel eyes shifting this way and that. All about that still-expanding face a thin halo of smoke appeared, though Tomas couldn't smell it. He had no body and no sense of smell, nothing but awareness and this hodgepodge of visions.

Loki's head turned and his eyes narrowed—just before Tomas saw Caraid. His reflex to gasp was still there, but with no body it had no outlet. He didn't know if the others saw her, nor if any of them besides the ravens were still with him. The birds' sharply concentrated presence he could feel drawing closer, akin to the way he might have sensed the approach of someone behind him. He saw Caraid lying on her back, her arms at her sides with her palms turned up, fingers curled and limp. Her eyes were closed. Her clothes were torn and splotched with what looked like dried mud.

Not blood; please, not blood. Was she a bit older than when they'd last met? And when might that have been? How long had he been traveling?

Now he could make out a row of shapes on either side of Caraid, blurred figures who also seemed to be lying supine. He tried to make out the immaterial colors about Caraid that would tell him how she was feeling, but her form had no aura at all.

Panic tugged at him. It was only an image, not her actual body, he reminded himself. Then the entire scene grew streaky and darker and began to pulse. By the time it was rippling and billowing, he knew something was wrong.

Very wrong. Without warning he was surrounded by flames, as if someone had tied him to a stake and lit a pyre. There was no smell, no sound and no physical pain, but fire was everywhere, dancing and flickering. More than fire. It had an intent. Someone had placed it there as a—

Barricade. There must have been an exorcism. He'd seen them before, mostly as glowing bars of energy rather than flames. How this one had reached from Midgard to wherever he and his companions now were, he didn't know. Perhaps they were still in Midgard or close to it.

Picturing the Elves' hall, he moved his awareness forward until it struck something thick and viscous that slowed his progress. Some of the flames took the shape of the cross-Rune. Definitely an exorcism. He felt disoriented, weak, the way he did around iron. The ravens drew closer still, sending him a steady current of energy. He began pushing ahead through the fire.

Then Loki was back, huge, all out of proportion, towering over Tomas. The Trickster was leaping in the flames, dancing with them, not directly ahead of Tomas but off to one side. Loki was naked, his head thrown back in exultation. His ginger hair was ablaze, its strands stirring about his head as if they were alive, until it was hard to tell where they ended and the flames began. Sparks shot from his finger-ends.

Pass, by all means, Tomas heard in his mind. Loki's voice, unmistakably, a light tenor, overrefined and laced with sarcasm. *Go to Elfland. But can you return?*

Not a dream-voice. It was too clear, too close. And he could feel the ravens' wariness vibrating all about him like an echoing shout.

The way is guarded, and Midgard is mine.

Tomas's feet connected with broken and uneven turf. Gasping, he stumbled a few paces before recovering his balance. His eyes were streaming as if the smoke and flames he'd just seen were real, and his every muscle felt bruised. He heard a series of thuds as bodies of greater and lesser volume than his own smacked down onto the earth. The Parcae were chittering, and Aubrey gave a great trumpeting sigh.

Moira checked on the twins, then came to take Tomas's hand, her eyes dark with exhaustion and her mouth tight with nerves. This was no time to mention what he'd just experienced; all their attention must go to whatever awaited them here. They stood on the open greensward, but so drastically had it changed that he scarcely recognized the well to his left and the great palace to his right. The enormous trees closing in from all sides were unmistakable, however, although half of them were uprooted. The lawn that had been so lush was seamed with raw fissures, several so deep that he was grateful none of his companions had fallen into them. Around the well, most of the hawthorns were withered trunks whose dry and shriveled branches looked like claws against that sky of muted pearl.

Suppressing a shudder, Tomas began studying the hall. Over half of it had caved in. The stones that had once formed its curving walls lay about in cracked and tumbled heaps; all the windows were dark, and the onyx doors hung askew on splintered hinges. Moira was staring at the wing that overlooked the Elvish Sea. Most of it was no more than rubble. The rest had rolled down towards the water, and wisps of smoke drifted about that end of the palace like so many homeless ghosts.

Aidan had gone even paler than usual, and his brilliant blue eyes were stricken. He took a step towards the hall, but stopped when Jared put a hand on his arm. The Parcae were peering into the devastated trees and muttering amongst themselves, while Nissyen was watching Tomas. Aubrey came to Moira, dropped to his knees and, speaking Elvish, said something low-pitched and tentative. There was a peculiar glistening quality to his eyes, and his voice wasn't altogether steady.

"Get up," Moira told him in Welsh. Her voice was taut and deadly soft. Although her hand was shaking in Tomas's grasp, all her attention was fixed on the pooka, who scrambled to his feet with the whites of his eyes showing. "When you are in Tomas's presence, speak a language that he knows. Say nothing in his hearing that he cannot understand." She looked at the other Elves. "That goes for all save the Parcae."

"Your pardon, my lord," said Aubrey, his brow furrowed with contrition.

"Granted. You've been long away and found your home in ruins," said Tomas. "You must wonder about all you've not yet seen."

The pooka nodded then glanced aside, and his throat moved as he swallowed.

Moira was eyeing Tomas, not with disapproval. "The ravens could perform any survey you wish," he told her.

Her pupils dilated. She paid no heed to the two Parcae who'd come up to them with the twins, nor to the grim-faced Jared. Her color deepened as she looked into Tomas's eyes. It was a moment before he realized why. The ravens were the reason she'd compelled him to go to Asgard, and now he'd freely offered her the full use of them.

As if awaiting permission to speak, Jared was studying her. When she turned to him, he said, "A survey of Elfland is what I'd most need for the Guards. It may take more than my lord's ravens to do it, but they'd make a fine start." Aidan was wheeling about in a dazed circle where he stood, taking in the whole clearing. With a meaningful glance at the Seer, Jared asked, "Shall we begin by finding out who's close at hand? I'd have proposed getting the two of you installed in the throne room, my lady, and bringing all the folk we found to you there. But the throne room is gone."

At Tomas's suggestion, the company set up temporary quarters in what had been the Guards' wing of the palace. "It's built of stone; it's intact and you know it well," he told Jared. He didn't add, "And how to defend it," but Jared seemed to hear the unspoken thought, and nodded. His dark gypsy's face was closed and somber.

"I've a map you'll want to see, my lord," he said once he'd shown Tomas and Moira to their new rooms—he'd surrendered his own quarters to them. He unfurled a great scroll of parchment on the long austere dining table, then weighted the scroll's corners down with salt cellars, a wine jug and a heavy glass vase. Moira had reluctantly left to visit the twins who, to Tomas's stupefaction, had just taken their first steps. Nissyen drifted up to peer over Tomas's shoulder with Aubrey.

The map showed the entire hall. "Let's mark off what's fallen," said Jared. He began rummaging in the drawer of a sideboard made of ruddy close-grained wood, then looked a bit startled when Aidan walked in carrying two bottles of ink and three quill pens, which he handed to Jared with a matter-of-fact air. Tallah followed the Seer into the room and hopped onto a chair from which she could see the map too.

The captain lined through the areas that represented the collapsed sections and started labeling what remained. "There's the Guards' wing.

And your quarters." He pointed. They were housed at the opposite side of the palace from the part that had tumbled to the shore. Most of that fallen area had been Rhys and Moira's private wing and the best guest rooms.

"That's the armory. The kitchen, pantries and cellars, the dining hall, the fenodyrees' wing. The music room—that's gone now. The other guest suites. The hall of records. The Parcae's arboretum—no, that's gone too. Have a look at this, Aubrey. You too, Aidan. Have I omitted anything?"

They chose posts for the guard-sylphs who'd followed Nissyen to Elfland, and decided to send more sylphs to search the ruins, the green, the shore, the well and the immediately surrounding woods.

"Could your Elementals tell whomever they discover to come to you here?" asked Jared.

Although the captain's face was expressionless, Tomas didn't need his Sight to know he was being subtly tested. He didn't fault Jared for it; rather, the captain rose in his estimation. Jared had sworn fealty to both Moira and Tomas, and while his outward comportment might be scrupulously correct, he was someone whose full and heartfelt inner allegiance one earned. Tomas had only lately proven himself as a Magician, and not at all as a strategist.

Hoping he'd learned something about both statecraft and leadership from watching Alfred of Wessex, Tomas said calmly, "Moira and I will want to see any Elves who are found. However, I'd prefer that the sylphs stay invisible and shielded while they make a preliminary search, and then report to us as quickly as possible."

"Done!" said Nissyen. *Well begun, my Mage,* it announced down their mind-link, then vanished so fast that Jared suppressed a start.

"We'll want a royal herald," said Tomas, and looked at Aubrey.

"Yours to command. As herald?"

"I doubt it's your final appointment." Tomas smiled. "Rather than ask anyone to come to us, would you please tell them? Loudly."

"Indeed I would!" Ears atwitch and eyes narrowed, Aubrey started to pace. "I'll make a banner, shall I?" When he ruffled Tallah's hair in passing, she gave him a grin full of good will and incomprehension. "A right big one, with streamers. The Parcae could fly it over the—I know just the thing! You wouldn't happen to have a drum anywhere about the place, would you, Jared? A big one?"

A smile was tugging at the captain's mouth. "I do, actually. You may borrow it and welcome."

"And pen and ink?"

Wordlessly, Aidan handed the pooka an inkwell and a feather.

"I'll get right to it, I will!"

"Aubrey?" Tomas's tone was mild, but the pooka stopped bounding across the room with the quill in his teeth and snapped to attention. When their eyes met, the mischief slowly drained from Aubrey's expression. "Loudly, and as a matter of great gravity."

"Aye, my lord," said the pooka, blinking. What might have been respect flashed across his face, and those of Aidan and Jared.

In the names of Owein and Fraine, King and Queen of all Elfland, and in the names of their regents, the lady Moira and the lord Tomas, Aubrey issued a royal proclamation. The pooka moved with surprising dignity, Nissyen reported, and beat Jared's drum only when he wasn't speaking. Above him flew Tallah and another Parca, holding a fine linen banner lettered with the text of the proclamation. To the Guards' assembly hall they summoned every Elf that the sylphs had found in or near the green, the bordering woods, the palace or the seashore below.

"What of the remainder of Elfland?" Tomas had asked Moira privately. They were in the Welsh Elves' territory, and that alone included the Parcae-wood, some much wilder sections and, no doubt, many areas of which he knew nothing yet. There were also the realms of the Sidhe, the other Celtic tribes and the Norse Elves. He didn't even want to think about the rest, but he had to ask. As regent he had to know.

Moira looked approving, then grim. "First you and I and the ravens should survey it ourselves. Or as much of it as we can."

Now Tomas gazed at the crowd through a peephole in the curtain that temporarily hid a makeshift stage which he and Jared and Aidan had built. The Elves had seemed a trifle surprised at his offer of help but accepted it readily. Tomas had been glad to work with his hands; it reduced his tension. Nevertheless his stomach was sour with nerves as he and Moira stepped onto the stage before that sea of watching faces.

Hand in hand with the twins, Tallah and her sister Corrigan followed Moira. Tomas tried not to stare at his children. None of the Elves seemed taken aback by the unnatural speed of the twins' growth, so he was trying to ignore his unfocused misgivings. The only children in this part of Elfland, Fraine and Owein themselves had no way of knowing that they were unusual; why should he subject them to his anxieties? To his relief, their minds were keeping pace with their bodies. They were talking a bit now, and that in a hodgepodge of four tongues, Elvish, English, Welsh and Norse, which they got endlessly confused. He and Moira devoted every spare moment to their children, but the majority of their time was spent with their nurse or, to Tomas's pleased surprise, with the pooka. So far, Aubrey's patient attempts at keeping their languages separate from one another either frustrated or amused the twins, but Tomas knew they'd sort it all out in the end—he'd grown up speaking three languages himself.

They grow faster by the second, said Nissyen down their private mind-link. The sylph was invisible and shielded as well, though probably the whole of Elfland had heard of the unbound Lord of the Air who'd actually volunteered to become one of Tomas's mage-allies.

Moira's shield was up, as was his and, he supposed, that of every last Elf in the hall. His own shield felt like a layer of pulsating energy, about four fingers in width, that emanated from his solar plexus in a steady current and surrounded his entire body. As he stood at gaze with his head held high, glad of the ravens' silent weight on his shoulders, he hoped that the Elves before him had heard of Nissyen and more. Otherwise, besides the ravens there was nothing to remark about him: a tall Norseman who must seem no more than an unpracticed youth, long and coltish in the flanks; indeed, lacking considerable flesh for someone so heavy of bone, with unruly white-blond hair, a crooked nose and an increasingly grim and weary expression on his square-jawed face. Still, let the Elves believe him the most powerful mortal adept who'd ever set foot here, and the twins two more such to come. Let the Elves think he'd wrestled Loki alone and unaided.

He and Moira took their seats in two simple wooden chairs from Jared's dining room—the thrones were gone. Carrying a roll of parchment, Aubrey strode onto the stage and read the proclamation yet again. "Hail, Owein and Fraine," he concluded, and used the scroll to point at them. They were watching him, round-eyed and solemn. "The twins of the Parcae's prophecy. The King and Queen of all Elfland, and its hope of staying green. Hail to their regents, the lady Moira and the lord Tomas." He knelt. "Who have my fealty till the coronation."

"And mine," called Jared and his Guards in unison.

"And mine!" came a chorus of voices.

Elves were dropping to their knees. They had more supporters than Tomas had expected, but the meeting was far from over. Calmly, he rose to his feet. "The lady Moira is well known to you," he said, pitching his voice to carry throughout the hall. That part was easy; he was a skald. "And many's the tale you'll have heard of these ravens. It's I whom you may not know. I am called Tomas the Rhymer, and Thought and Memory are now my allies. When Asgard fell, they came with me."

Silence, abrupt and total. Two or three more Elves knelt.

"And I come to you now. I would serve you as these birds serve me: freely, of their own will and by their own accord. The ravens and I are a link to the other eight worlds. Together, we can prevent your drifting further from them."

Hope. Doubt. Bitterness. Agreement. Too many emotions in that hall of faces, and too many thoughts. He felt the Elves' ambivalence as a wave of pressure at his shield, a wave that issued from the audience at large and was no more an attack than was their breathing.

Then, like a fiery spear aimed at his chest, came a quick probing jab at his shield. He'd expected as much. He bolstered his defenses with an extra pulse of energy, and the attack fell aside, though not without tiring him.

That was done by the pale Elf at the back, near the right-hand door, said Nissyen. *A most ambitious fellow named Deverell. A Guard, until Rhys promoted him to some sort of personal trustee. He hates mortals and the Sidhe. He helped Rhys destroy Finvara.*

Tomas reinforced his shield a second time. From Moira's sidelong glance at him, she'd just done the same.

Using the most compassionate and measured tones at his command, he told the assembled Elves: "You have seen much sorrow of late. I offer you a Rune working that alleviates grief." It could also promote reconciliation. He raised his arms, more for effect than for anything else, since Brubakken had taught him to work without gesturing. The trick was to pick a specific point in the air and focus on it to the exclusion of all else—

Feel free to do so. I am observing the hall for you.

Nissyen was further down their mind-link and into his thoughts than he'd supposed. *I thank you*, he told the sylph mildly.

"Fehu!" he cried, then sent a tendril from his shield to his focal spot in midair. The sensation wasn't unlike a cross between sneezing and how he imagined a dog might feel as it shook the wet from its fur, except that he hadn't moved, and that the release of energy came from his midsection and was under his control. He shaped the tendril to the form of the Rune Fehu, then set it vibrating so fast that it became visible. Radiating great sparks of light, it floated above the crowd.

It was immaterial; it would burn no one below. Still, he heard a few gasps. It might have been easier to draw Fehu by commanding the Elementals bound to him and Nissyen to assume the Rune's shape in the air. But the Elves would know whether the bind-Rune above their heads was composed of Elementals or of Tomas's own psychic force. Brubakken claimed that Tomas was an exceptional manipulator of the energies, and Moira agreed, so they'd decided to showcase that particular strength.

"Shouldn't I hold something in reserve?" he'd asked her when they planned the Rune working.

She had given him a startled look and then, slowly, one of her more private smiles. "But you are. More than you know."

The Rune of Prosperity, Fehu was a power-sigil, and the first of the twenty-four Runes. A good place to start. He let it shimmer half a moment longer while he concentrated on the new blood he'd brought to Elfland, the new beginnings and the hope, his and that of the Elves.

Another attack at his shield, from the middle of the hall and a more aggressive source. Again he deflected it.

"Inguz!" He sent a second Rune-shape to dance with the first. Inguz meant fertility, wholeness and inclusion. It was sacred to the Vanir, gods of abundance. To the sea-god Njord, father of the twins Frey and Freya. Its shape, a helix, a lattice, oscillated above the Elves.

The second assailant stabbed at Tomas's groin and the small of his back, viciously and deliberately, but his shield held.

Drawing the deepest breath he could, Tomas willed himself to see the lattice of Inguz linking a united Elfland to Midgard, the new pivot-world. "Laguz!" he shouted as he projected the final Rune. Water-Rune; Rune of the heart's depths. Rune of women. Rune of mysteries. Moira said that the role of women needed healing in Elfland—and elsewhere.

Still, it was to Mystery and mysteries, those he had lived and those yet to come, that Tomas offered the working's last Rune. He stretched Laguz's fishhook shape to dwarf the other two Runes, then sent them spinning round it. May I be open, he thought. May I be flexible. May I be wise.

The bind-Rune shone like copper struck by the Sun. How many Elves in this hall had ever seen the Sun of mortal Midgard? Some of them stretched their arms towards the Runes; a few called out. Tomas kept his hands directed at the bind-Rune while its power snaked and coiled through the air.

"Pretty!" said Fraine suddenly. Scattered chuckles from the crowd. When he shot a glance at his daughter, Tallah grinned and ruffled Fraine's hair. Moira was sitting stark upright with her hands in her lap and her face an elegant mask. Then her gaze locked with his. The molten glimmer in her eyes was more than approval.

Gratified, focusing on the Runes above the crowd, he pulled the energy that formed them back into his shield. It felt like reeling in a sail that flapped in a high and capricious wind, for the bind-Rune had gained momentum and substance of its own. There was sweat between his shoulderblades and more sweat on his brow. He braced himself for another attack, but none came.

"The blessings of all the gods upon you," he said, when at last he regained his chair. Perhaps the working had alleviated some of his own sorrows; he felt calmer. And more spent, though he knew better than to show it.

There was cheering, loud and prolonged, and brighter faces than when he began. There were also some scattered hisses.

Shall I tell you who—

Later, please.

"I was your Queen. I am your regent now," Moira said, rising. Her briny, aromatic voice, her voice that had always reminded Tomas of the Sea, was hushed and intent. "Rhys took me prisoner, but I escaped with the aid of the Parcae, who remember their prophecy." She spoke slowly, swaying and holding her hands aloft, but not as Tomas had done. Moira's narrow fingers reached towards her listeners, moving, beckoning, summoning. Her voice was so soft that some of her audience, their palms cupping their ears, leaned forward the better to hear her. "I bring you this Mage and his ravens. I bring you our twin children."

She all but chanted the last words, and suddenly her eyes were ablaze.

Elves were born to the magic that Tomas was learning as fast as he could. One magical gift was provoking emotions and influencing the will; for that he'd needed Runes and all the energy he could spare from his shield channeled into them. Yet Moira was compelling this packed hall's attention with only her presence and her voice.

"The rulers of all Elfland, our children could be! Is that your wish also? Will you follow us?"

Before the stage stood Jared in a line of freshly reinstated Guards, less than half their original number. "Yes!" they shouted.

All their relatives are with you, said Nissyen. *So are Moira's kin and personal attendants. That bodes well, since they have noble blood.*

More cries of assent. Every Parca that Tomas could see was shrieking and leaping up and down.

"Will you follow us?" Moira called again.

About three dozen Elves shouldered their way through the crowd to kneel before her. When Tomas squinted, using his Sight, their auras looked like the one around the pooka: silvery and changeable and glazed with swirls of red. *Water Elves?* he asked Nissyen.

Every one, and many are shapeshifters. They are Aubrey's friends and kin.

The water Elves moved aside with alacrity to make room for others pressing forward. Tomas counted twelve of them. Tall and lean, the new arrivals had a great breadth of shoulder, powerful arms, and a layer of black hair on what could be seen of their chests and backs. They had dark hair, round black eyes and swarthy skin; some of their faces appeared more furred than bearded. They moved silently on splayed and padded bare feet, seeming to carry a disproportionate amount of their weight on their toes, which were oddly shaped—Tomas blinked. They had claws. When they reached Jared, they halted and gazed up at the twins. After a few seconds, Owein gave the strange Elves a solemn little wave.

"Lir, I am named. We have come from the Inner Reaches," said one of them in a low rumbling voice.

Jared, who had gone utterly still, was staring at Lir with dilated pupils. The hall was silent, as if collectively holding its breath. Only the Parcae looked unsurprised.

"We are honored," said Moira. "Why are you here?"

"On every path the game are fewer. Too many creeks run dry." Lir turned to Tomas. "And you called us."

When? Not at the name-fastening. These creatures were Elves, not deities.

Lir's eyes were steady. "You and the golden Lady," he said. "She who loves us."

Moira? But her hair was dark. When Tomas glanced at her, she moved one hand ever so slightly from side to side on the arm of her chair. No, she was telling him; she had not called.

"We will help you. We were bidden," said Lir with finality. "And you will bring the game back." He looked at Jared. A glance lengthened between them, black eyes meeting black. None of the tension left the captain's stance, and his breathing quickened.

There was a flash of something white and pointed as Lir smiled. "We would make you welcome at our campsites," he said in a voice so soft that it was probably meant for Jared alone, but Tomas had keen hearing. "If you would come, brother." Lir and his party moved to the side of the stage and, with a mixture of hunger and shock in his eyes, Jared watched them go.

A procession of Elves came forward and swore fealty, including a few indignant fenodyree, most of whose kin had abandoned their duties as palace staff and gone to live apart. Then came half a dozen silent, wary Elves dressed in leaves and bark, whose mottled brown and green skin changed color with their surroundings. They were followed by the entire Cooks' Guild and their apprentices—Moira looked surprised and touched. Finally all of the Parcae, including their men, marched to the front of the hall. A great murmuring arose: no one had seen the winged Elves outside the Parcae-wood for a very long time. After they'd help Moira escape from Rhys, the Elf King had put a price on their heads and, until Rhys had been forced apart, no one in Elfland had seen any Parcae at all.

An encouraging show of support, but there were more undeclared Elves than loyalists in the hall, and some of the crowd had backed Rhys.

"We will send word to the rest of Elfland, wherever it has scattered," Moira announced.

There was a hearteningly loud roar of approval. Someone was pushing forward through the crowd. His head was down; Tomas couldn't see his face. He carried something round and something pointed, and he was using his shoulders and elbows to clear his path. When Tomas narrowed his eyes and employed his Sight, the fellow's aura was flaming red.

"We will unite Faerie beneath the twins," shouted Moira above the cheers. "We will rebuild this hall."

Let him speak, Tomas mouthed at Jared, but watch him. The captain nodded. With Aubrey hard at his heels, he moved to intercept the advancing Elf.

"The twins and the Mage Tomas will weave bonds to Midgard that cannot be broken! You will see our trees in flower once more."

The Elf reached the line of Guards surrounding the stage. Of medium height, he was a solid mass of muscle where most of his kin ran to a wiry slenderness. An unusually handsome fellow even among the Elves: he had dark stick-straight hair cropped at the shoulders, large lustrous hazel eyes and milky flawless skin, apart from an angry spot of color high on each angled cheekbone. He carried a bucket and a withered hawthorn branch.

When he met Tomas's gaze, a knot began to work in the clean line of his jaw, and his slanting eyes turned cold and bright with rage. This must be the second and more aggressive Elf who had jabbed at Tomas's shield.

His name is Evan, said Nissyen. *The pale blond thin one coming to join him is Deverell.*

Before either Elf could so much as open his mouth, Tomas said calmly, "You may speak, Evan."

The Elf glared at him. "I need no mortal's permission to speak here." Too late: what might have been a dramatic moment was lost. He ignored a faint giggle at the back of the hall, though his nostrils flared. "It's you who need ours. It's you who brought this to Elfland!" He started to upend the bucket on the stage; Tallah hissed at him, wings outspread, and darted in front of the twins, and Aubrey slammed his doubled fists down on Evan's elbows. The bucket's contents landed almost entirely on Evan himself.

It was blood, most of it as red as Evan's aura, but some a drying streaky brown. Evan's cream-colored tunic was soaked. There was blood in his hair, on his face and hands, on the pointed toes of his boots. He rounded on Aubrey, who laid his ears back with a disdainful smile. Tomas could have sworn that the pooka's dingy yellow teeth had grown sharper.

Evan took a mighty breath and turned to Moira. "This is mortal blood, shed in Midgard and flowing here. It came from our well. Look at this branch!" He brandished it, ignoring Aubrey's watchful eye, then dropped it. "It's from the hawthorns around the well. Mortal blood is poisoning us. And mortal blood is what runs in his veins." He pointed at Tomas. "His and his children's. Why should we suffer their presence?"

The room was absolutely still. When Jared caught Tomas's eye, he shook his head: let the fellow have his say.

"Mortal blood is the reason we're dwindling." Evan kicked the hawthorn branch aside. "I'll not accept the rule of mortals any more than my lord Rhys would have done. Where is he? Deverell and I are his nearest kin; we've a right to know."

Deverell, a slender and anemically pale Elf with a remote, curiously confident expression, fixed his clear grey eyes on Tomas and nodded coolly.

Evan pointed at Moira. "You're full of fine words, but it's you and your Fool who brought us to this evil time. What's befallen my lord Rhys?"

"Isolde sent him to live apart. No one knows where," said Moira. Her voice was level and her face bland, but for the barest instant her eyes were the eyes of a hungry wolf cornering a deer. As intent, as determined, and as merciless.

Tomas let out his breath. *Nissyen, have Tallah and Corrigan take the twins to our quarters, please.* The two Parcae promptly slipped behind the curtain with the children.

Evan didn't look surprised at Rhys's Fate. Neither did anyone else; it was common knowledge and the question rhetorical. Evan hooked his thumbs in his belt and looked Moira up and down. How could he have missed the threat in her eyes? Hunger of a different sort crept into his face as he stared at her. Tomas felt his chest tightening, but it wasn't time yet. Not quite.

"You're still Queen," Evan drawled. "Not your children. You could retain your title once a kinsman of Rhys is crowned King. The throne wants a man's hand." He flicked a contemptuous glance at Tomas. "Not this mortal's. It wants *mine,* as Rhys's cousin—and I claim it!"

Scattered cheers from the crowd. Aubrey was standing on tiptoe with his fists knotted and his face a mottled shade of purple, but Jared was a frozen statue. The captain's breathing had slowed; his slitted pupils were fixed on Evan as if no one else were in the hall. Half of Lir's party began creeping to Jared's side, while the other half fanned out about Evan and Deverell. When Moira shot Jared a warning look, the Elves from the Inner Reaches halted where they stood.

"Deverell," said Evan, "take this mortal into custody!"

Tomas made no psychic attempt on Deverell's person. Elfin shields were different than mortal ones, and Brubakken had warned him not to waste energy trying to crack them. Instead he dropped the protective barrier that he'd placed around the dagger he'd brought from Birka, got its wooden grip in his hand and vaulted down from the stage to meet Deverell.

A sour acrid smell filled the hall. There was coughing, followed by gasps: "Iron! He has iron!"

Elves began scrambling out the doors that Tomas had ordered left open. One knife would hardly affect all of them, but he didn't see anyone stopping to think. They were probably too shocked. In Midgard they were prepared for the occasional proximity of iron, but that poisonous metal had never before come to Faerie. Moira had guessed that it might prove more deadly here, and she was right. Even Tomas, who had learned to control the iron-sick and was less susceptible to it than anyone in the hall, felt his nostrils stinging from the corrosive stench in the air.

The Parcae swarmed onto the stage and surrounded Moira, who was the only other person who'd known about the dagger, and who sat calmly watching the chaos. Panting, Lir went into a crouch, then made his way to Jared and Aubrey where they stood ready to defend Tomas. Aubrey's eyes streamed with tears and his whole body rippled in and out of focus as if he were fighting a reflex to change shape, while the captain had gone a dingy grey about the mouth and nose.

Slowly, ignoring Jared who'd eeled over to block the challengers' retreat, Evan moved towards Deverell. Deverell was staring at the blade in Tomas's hand. A crimson rash had broken out on the Elf's colorless skin, and he was perspiring.

"It can cut your shield," said Tomas softly.

Deverell's eyes widened. Tomas might appear not to suffer from the iron-sick, but all Faerie had heard of the true speech that he shared with the Elves.

"If it does, it will cut you." Even touching iron, for an Elf, felt like handling ice so cold it burned the flesh that adhered to it.

Evan gathered himself for a spring; Deverell stepped away and Evan hurtled himself at Tomas's knees. Tomas melted aside with the knife held low—

No, my Mage!

Tomas whirled—was Deverell closing in? But Deverell was frowning at Evan, who had unaccountably crashed to the floor and was grappling with something invisible. There were grunts, then a snapping sound, followed by an aborted groan from Evan as Aubrey reappeared with his teeth buried in Evan's arm. Jared leapt at Deverell but didn't even touch him before shooting backwards as if tossed by a giant's unseen hand. Tomas caught a glimpse of the captain's startled face as he curled himself into a ball before hitting the ground.

He rebounded from Deverell's shield. Its strength is unique among the Elves. And was held secret; I have only just learned of it.

Pushing a strand of sweat-soaked blond hair from his brow, Deverell turned a cold stare upon Tomas and took one slow step towards him.

Tomas didn't plan what happened next. He'd barely begun to form a desperate thought about shapeshifting his dagger, to try to get the iron in other than solid form past Deverell's shield—when something flashed out of the blade. Something like a darting sliver of patterned and shifting energy, something that Tomas couldn't quite focus on because it wasn't fully visible, as if it existed in more than the visible world. He saw it just long enough to tell that it had many colors, some of which glowed, although the hue that he would best recall later didn't gleam. It was the ominous sullen red of boiling quicksand.

He had no time even to blink before Deverell was on his knees, doubled over, clutching at his chest. Tomas hadn't thrown his dagger, hadn't used the Runes that fettered or confused a foe, hadn't consciously done anything at all. Yet Deverell's extraordinary shield was gone, while the iron-reek in the air had grown so strong that Tomas's stomach heaved.

With the whites of his eyes showing, Deverell slumped onto his side. Spittle ran from his slackened mouth; one leg kicked spasmodically.

My Mage! What did you do?

I don't know. Aloud, Tomas said quietly, "Deverell needs a healer." Suppressing a coughing fit, he replaced the protective barrier of energy about his knife.

"I'll have them summoned, my lord," said Jared, whose eyes were streaming. "For Evan too."

Three Guards, all white to the lips and moving gingerly, rolled Deverell in a blanket. Beside the fallen Elf stood Evan, nursing his bitten arm, with the pooka gripping him by both elbows. Evan's smooth ivory face was strained and he swallowed hard as Tomas met his gaze, just before Aubrey marched him off after the guards and their cloth-wrapped burden.

With their expressions blank and their eyes hiding their thoughts, what was left of the crowd parted to let the pooka and his prisoner go by. Elves were returning to the hall, though they carried themselves as if they were picking their way through a snakepit. More Elves peered around the doorway.

When Tomas rejoined Moira on the platform, she gave him a triumphant smile, but her brows were aloft. He let one shoulder rise and fall in the most unobtrusive of shrugs: he'd no idea what he'd just done. She stared at him for perhaps two seconds, then got to her feet and surveyed the assembling Elves.

When the hall was nearly as full as it had been, she said, "Are there any further challenges to the twins' throne, or to Tomas and myself as regents?" Her carriage was proud, her face relaxed and confident, her voice utterly calm. As if they'd planned Tomas's assault on Deverell. As if she knew what was happening.

The audience was silent, many of them open-mouthed and a few of them shivering. Tomas saw several headshakes. There'd be no more challenges—not now, at any rate. Then, by twos and threes at first, they began to kneel.

CHAPTER FIVE: IRON AND MIRACLES

Once Tomas and Moira, followed by a wide-eyed Nissyen, regained their rooms, Tomas described the energy that had left his shield and felled Deverell. Moira's face was calm as she listened, her hands relaxed in her lap, her expression reflective. He had no idea what her thoughts might be. Her shield was down and so was his, but he seldom tried to reach her mind when Nissyen was present. She'd give him her opinion later.

While he spoke, the ravens perched amid the knickknacks on the mantlepiece and preened their feathers. Nissyen flitted like a dragonfly about the room and rubbed its bony palms together. It kept up a barrage of questions: had Tomas felt a clicking sensation anywhere, or any heat? Had he been angry? Did the experience tire him?

All that Tomas could tell the Elemental, patiently and repeatedly, was that he'd just started to think about shapeshifting his blade to get it past Deverell's shield, though he hadn't been at all sure that was possible, when something had released itself from his own shield and Deverell collapsed.

"Could you do it again?" demanded Nissyen.

"I'll try. On a rock?" He glanced at Moira, whose expression didn't change. He opened a window, fastened its shutters back and scanned the broken boulders in the courtyard below.

Nissyen pointed. "That one."

"Half a moment while I put up a shield and uncover this knife." The ravens sailed to the back of an overstuffed old armchair near the window. He looked at Moira. "Will you mind the iron-sick?"

"Not enough to matter. I'll stay by the opposite wall," she said mildly. "And I'll do what I can to shield this room from the rest of the palace."

Although it took some experimenting, without a particle of help from the ravens he could soon shatter any boulder below merely by thinking of his blade. After a few attempts, the energy appeared to come directly from the weapon itself rather than from his shield. At that point he began to feel a peculiar snapping sensation at the base of his skull, something just shy of a twitching muscle. It wasn't unpleasant. Now that the energy no longer came from his shield, the snapping sensation was also the only way he could tell, other than seeing the rocks split, that the experiment was working. With a bit of practice, the rocks cracked just as easily regardless of whether the blade's protective barrier was in place.

The barrier was formed of energy first emitted from his shield and then separated from it. They had labored over that barrier, he and Moira, before he brought the knife to Elfland. "I'm learning, but I doubt I'll ever be as facile with magic as you are. So I'll be at a disadvantage, especially at first," he had told Moira.

"Not every Elf is so skilled as I," she had reminded him. "And you've very little left to learn about manipulating the physical energies, Tomas.

That's why you can travel between the worlds; your body is matter. Then there's weatherworking. It's a rare art and you excel at it. All the physical arts but healing, for that matter."

"Thank you," he said, trying not to sound exasperated. She was usually more sparing with praise. "I do have some strengths. But just now any Elf knows more than I. All of you know precisely what you can and can't do, while I'm still working that out. What good is power I've no idea how to use?"

She considered him. "Very well. I take your point." Slowly her eyes narrowed. "You want something. What is it?"

He took a breath. "To use the one advantage I know I have at the moment: I can handle iron more easily than anyone in Elfland."

For five seconds Moira's expression went blank. Lips parted, she glanced at the floor, then back at him, searching his face. Hers wasn't so much troubled as caught off balance.

When he was sure she wouldn't speak right away, he added, "Can we hide a dagger till I need it, if I do?"

He had been intrigued to learn that shielding an object, rather than his own body, wasn't so hard as he'd feared—or not so hard for him, when the object was his knife. Moira could conceal any other item in Aud's house faster and more easily than he could: the loom, the table, his harp. But she couldn't hide the dagger at all. Every tendril of energy she tried to wrap around it simply melted aside, and the effort had set her teeth on edge.

"But you can certainly hide it," she had concluded, when once again she was unable to detect any iron in the room. "Take it with you."

Now Nissyen made a show of propping its immaterial elbows on the cracked and powdering stone ledge of Jared's window and contemplated the shattered boulders in the courtyard below. "I can propose no definite theory about how you accomplished that, my Mage," it announced. It was bouncing up and down on the balls of its bare feet, and it sounded thrilled. Moira gave Tomas a long-suffering look.

"Though I have a hypothesis." It turned from the window and regarded him with slitted eyes. "I am wondering if your iron-sick has changed?"

"I still feel it," said Tomas. "I've just learned to overrule it."

Twirling a lock of its hair around one finger, Nissyen shook its head. Its imitation of mortal gestures was steadily improving, and now it was adopting them even in Tomas's presence. "You may have learned to deflect iron's influence upon you," it said, studying his face. "To make a weapon of that influence."

Tomas looked at Moira, who shrugged.

"Iron makes the Elfin part of you ill," said the sylph. Its voice was patient, but its eyes were gleaming and intent. "Its essence attacks you like a weapon. The mortal part of you, or the Mage in you, may have devised a way to turn that aggression aside, and in so doing made a weapon of it."

The Elemental started to pace. "What was a defense became an attack. Perhaps only halfbreeds can accomplish that, or perhaps only halfbreeds with your ability to manipulate matter." It pointed at Tomas. "I have never heard of the like. It may not have happened before." The sylph was beaming. "This is something *new* to me. Pray accept my congratulations!"

"Not at all," said Tomas helplessly, avoiding Moira's ironic eye. That was why they had to deal with an unbound Lord of the Air: it found him interesting. 'You are unique among Magicians, Tomas,' it had told him when they first met. 'Part mortal and part Elf. A bridge between the worlds, at a rare shifting in their balance of power.' Tomas glanced at the knife in its sheath on Jared's table. At least he'd turned one liability of his mixed blood into an asset.

Then an idea struck him. Simultaneously, Thought let out a single harsh caw from the ravens' perch on Jared's armchair. When the room flooded with the immaterial shimmering tints that came with his Sight, Tomas made a grab for Nissyen's shoulder and immediately yanked his chilled hand away. He'd forgot that he would grasp no more than freezing air, air that whirled with all the force of a gale but was eerily compressed to the sylph's illusory shape.

"Yes?" said Nissyen eagerly. "You have Seen something!"

"The bridge between the worlds. The bridge and the twins and I."

Eyebrows aloft, Moira was studying him.

"It's in the prophecy. About the twins," said Tomas, his words tumbling over one another. "They're 'trebly blooded, trebly fated: Elf, Mortal and Mage.' They're mortal; might they be able to manipulate the physical energies at least as well as I can? But they have Elf blood, so might they have more innate skill with magic?"

"Yes," said Moira, her face alight. "Yes!" When Nissyen started to interrupt, she made a peremptory gesture for silence. "This is important. Go on, Tomas."

"The prophecy says 'only if both twins and Mage so choose.' I'm needed, likely to teach them something of what I just did with iron. But why couldn't they build that way, as well as destroy? Why couldn't they build the bridge itself?"

Nissyen let out a whoop. "You have seen it! You have found it!"

Tomas picked up his sheathed blade. "There's a knife in the prophecy. It could signify what I just did with this one. 'A blade to cut the cord and bind the ties.'"

Moira crossed to the window and gazed at the rocky debris that Tomas had left in the courtyard below. "I believe you are right, Tomas—no, I am certain of it. Part of the bridge may be material. Or depend on Midgard, where matter is most powerful." Her expression was that of a climber at the foot of a newly discovered mountain. "We should start the twins' training in magic as soon as ever we can. She looked at Nissyen. "It's well our supporters are in the majority here. Who hissed after Tomas's Rune working?"

"Rhys's cousins," said Nissyen, graver now. "And a large faction who follows Evan. He named Deverell captain of his Guards. A platoon of them and most of their relatives are backing him."

A tap came at the door: one of their own Guards announcing Jared, who entered with his dark eyes cautious and a melancholy cast to his features. Once they all were seated, Jared said, "Evan has callers I've not let see him pending your instructions, though the healers would give leave. They say his bite wounds will mend nicely." He handed Moira a piece of parchment folded in quarters. "His visitors."

She glanced at the list and handed it to Tomas, who didn't recognize any names. "Admit them one at a time, with six Guards present. When Evan fares better, release him and bring him to us."

"What do the healers say of Deverell?" asked Tomas.

"To begin with, that he's worse off than Evan. He's very ill indeed. They'll allow him no callers." Jared's expression was sober. After a few seconds he placed his hands on the table with the tips of his forefingers touching. Since he'd just come from the prison, it was understandable that his shield was up.

Still, Tomas didn't lower his own. "Take your time," he said mildly, holding Jared's gaze.

The lines about the captain's eyes deepened. Not a muscle moved in his face, but there was tension in the hands he'd laid on the table. When he spoke, his tone was reserved and respectful, albeit with an undernote of inquiry. "The healers say we've not had so severe a case of the iron-sick since mortals first began using that metal, and we'd not yet learned to avoid it. They're consulting their chronicles and all they can do will be done, but it's a fair guess that Deverell will be ill for some time." He glanced at Nissyen and Moira, then back at Tomas. His expression was different. Speculative. Not doubtful; rather, appraising.

"You have questions," said Tomas. "Ask them."

"Thank you, my lord. They're not many." The dark face grew still and careful. "Since I'm charged with protecting you and your household, I must know something of your capacities. You have Elf blood, and the iron-sick generally accompanies it." An intent glance, just shy of probing. "There are attacks that can turn on the attacker—did you also fall ill?"

"No. I smelled iron. It stung my eyes and nose, made me cough and gave me some nausea. I've learned to control it to some extent."

"So have we all. Though it's easier when one knows it's coming," said Jared in the most neutral of voices. "Have you performed that manner of attack before? Or since?"

"Just now. On the rocks in the courtyard." Tomas pointed at the window.

The captain went to it and stood there for perhaps thirty seconds, during which he took hold of the frame and leaned far over the ledge. When he turned around, he kept one hand gripping the sill. Several questions moved across his face before he said colorlessly, "May I ask if that was easier or harder than Deverell?"

"Easier."

"Easier." Like a man who'd made up his mind, Jared nodded. "Very well, my lord. I'd thought to propose four to six bodyguards for you, but I believe we can make do with two." He looked at Moira. "And two for you, and two each for the twins?" A faint smile. "Though Aubrey says Owein needs at least three."

"Very well. You're not short-staffed, then?"

He shook his head. "Not so much as I'd feared." He did not quite glance at Tomas. "Not since the assembly."

Moira was starting to wonder if she'd have to order Jared and Nissyen out of the room. When they finally left, they passed Aubrey in the doorway, who was bringing a list of Elves who'd sworn fealty to the twins. No sooner had the pooka installed himself at Jared's table than one of the Cooks' journeymen, a stout Elf with dark close-cropped hair and an immaculate apron, tapped at the door. "My lord, my lady, I'm sent to inform you that the twins won't come down from the big oak near the well," he said respectfully. "You know it: the one with branches growing nearly all the way to the ground. Tallah showed them how to climb it; she's up there with them now. The nurse wishes to know if she should send someone into the tree with their supper, or should she insist they climb down for it?"

Aubrey chuckled, and Moira shot him a smile.

"I took the liberty of offering to rig a dumbwaiter and a pulley to haul the plates up," said the journeyman. He appeared to be stifling a grin. "The lady Fraine quite liked that idea, but the nurse sent me to speak with you."

Before either Tomas or Moira could answer, there was yet another knock at the door. "I'm from the healers, my lord," said the pale Elf who stood on the sill. He cast an uneasy glance at the silent ravens perched on Jared's armchair. "They have a few questions for my lord Tomas."

Tomas's face closed. To Moira's relief, he had the presence of mind to send Nissyen to confer with the healers in his stead. Moira temporarily dubbed Aubrey royal chamberlain and told him to deal with the twins' supper as best he saw fit, and with all other inquiries until further notice.

At last everyone had gone. Moira wanted to see her children so much that it was almost a physical pain beneath her ribs, but she wanted to be alone with Tomas even more. He'd flung himself onto Jared's sofa, leaned his head back and closed his eyes. He hadn't taken any supper yet either. She rang and asked the Cooks to prepare something.

Tomas held out his arms and she went to him.

"Most of them go in fear me now," he said after a while. "But you don't."

"No." She was sitting in his lap, resting her head on his chest. She could smell the wool of his jerkin and the soft airy fragrance of his hair, like cotton hung outdoors to dry. Beneath those odors was the scent of his skin, a little like a barrel of walnuts just at the point of ripeness. The smell of mortality. The longer he stayed in Elfland the longer it would be before she lost him. Yet lose him she would, for he was mortal, and that telltale nutlike odor brought a lump to her throat. It was mingled with something like freshly cut hay, sweat and salt, and with a musky undernote unique to Tomas. She liked the way he smelled. She could have picked him out of a hundred mortals in the dark. "You're coming into your own powers, is all, and I'm glad of it," she told him. "It was bound to happen. I take no fright at it."

His lips brushed her temple. "I'm glad of that." A long silence. "Do you understand what I did to Deverell?"

"No. And frankly, nor do I care."

He looked at her questioningly.

"It worked. You can defend yourself with it, teach it to the twins, and they can use it to help build the bridge. That's all I need know. Let Nissyen fret over the rest. I don't understand how I perform all my magic either."

He closed his eyes with what she took for relief, and said nothing for so long that she thought he might have fallen asleep; she could hear his heartbeat. Then he muttered, "That list of oath-takers Aubrey brought. I'd breathe easier if they'd sworn fealty out of respect than from fear."

That so many had sworn fealty at all approached the miraculous, but she said only, "It may be from both in equal measures for a time. Fear isn't necessarily hatred."

Another pause. "I suppose not."

"The oaths haven't all come from fear. Not Jared's or Aidan's or the Parcae's. Aubrey swore out of liking, you know, and he first of all."

Tomas grinned. "In some circles that wouldn't be a compliment." An insistent rap came at the door. "I'll get it." He sniffed the air. "The Cooks haven't been idle."

She eased out of his lap as the tapping continued. He rose to his feet in one fluid motion, more limber than she'd expected, and went to the door. "How quick you were," she heard him say. "Why, you've brought us a feast!"

Two fenodyree, one carrying a covered platter, the other a decanter, a pitcher and a bowl that held a pair of damp warmed towels, stalked into the room. Their faces were stern. Most of them had no use for mortals, and Moira had been agreeably surprised when they swore fealty. Still, just now the sullen gleam in their eyes might not be entirely resentful.

They set their loads down on Jared's table. With a determined expression, a pucker of distaste about her mouth and a hot towel clutched in her six-fingered hand, one of the fenodyree reached for Tomas's arm.

He sidestepped her neatly. "I thank you. But I don't require your attention tonight, and I'd prefer to wait on the lady Moira myself."

Her hairy little face suspicious, her steely eyes black and unwavering, the fenodyree scowled up at him.

Tomas flashed her a smile. "And no one need come for the tray till we ring, please."

For an endless frowning moment the small Elf considered him. Then she slapped the towel into the bowl and thumped the bowl down on the table.

Looking dubiously at Moira, who nodded, the other Elf followed suit. Neither fenodyree said a word, and they both looked as if they'd swallowed a spoonful of vinegar, but the first one made Tomas a small grudging bow as she closed the door.

He leaned his folded arms on the door above his head and rested his forehead against them. "Is my food poisoned?" His voice was tight with suppressed laughter.

"I doubt it. That's not their way," she told him, uncovering the platter. She did her best to sound serious. "They prefer to knife their victims in their sleep."

"How comforting." He was grinning.

"You did very well with them. Truly. They don't care for mortals."

"I gathered that," he said, eyeing the platter. "At least they'll not starve me."

Later, Moira was to remember that meal and its aftermath as one of her last perfect times with Tomas before all the trouble began. Perfect from far more than the food although, considering the impoverished state of the pantries, the Cooks had outdone themselves. There was warm golden bread fresh from the ovens, loaves braided into great rings and dusted with poppy seeds. There were roasted chestnuts, a marvelously subtle leek soup, and the richest plum pudding that Moira had ever tasted. Tomas said that not only had he never tried one before, he hadn't even known they existed.

She'd been braced for questions, reproaches, demands for information. In one way she'd not been far wrong: one shallow layer beneath the surface of Tomas's eyes lurked a thorny grey reef of questions. Much of their conversation caromed off that twisted reef or sank within it like a stone into a pit. She had a feeling what some of those questions might be. What was that Fool-into-Mage business? Would there be any attempt to bring Rhys or Finvara back from exile? What was Moira's past experience of Evan and Deverell? Would she and Tomas set off to explore the rest of Elfland, and what might they find there?

Legitimate queries all, though she'd no answer for too many of them. Instead, the night was one of wonders.

Tomas had frowned at Jared's austere mattress, more flat than narrow, though its sheets were scrupulously clean. "One moment," he muttered, then stripped off the coverlet, put a hand on the bed and shut his eyes. When he opened them, the mattress was sumptuously thick, the lean pillows had suddenly plumped out, and the bedclothes were a warm maple-brown shade of silk.

That was one miracle: physical magic worked not from necessity, but purely to please her. Another was the painstaking and reverent way he'd washed and toweled her hair, and a third was the sigh with which he'd welcomed her rubbing fragrant oil into the entire length of his body.

His skin was drier than she remembered, his bones more prominent. He lay on his back on Jared's transformed bed with his head turned to one side, arms crooked above his head, palms open and fingers relaxed. She hadn't touched him with anything approaching this level of intimacy since before she'd given birth. To make him the gift of privacy, she stayed out of his thoughts. Easy enough to tell from his muscles where his tension resided.

Waves of her slowly drying hair drifted over him as she worked. She found herself lingering at the soles of his feet, his inner elbows, the small of his back. He turned this way and that as she bade him, and twice caught her hand and kissed it. His eyes were closed, his eyelids violet with fatigue. To keep him warm, she put another two logs on the hearth, though he wasn't shivering, then dug her fingers into his shoulderblades. This time his sigh sounded as if it came from the bottom of his lungs. There was nothing but peace in his face.

"Sleep, love," Moira murmured at last, tugging at the conjured quilt. "Sleep and dream."

She'd thought him already adrift. But he sat up, his eyes soft and dark and hungry. "Not just yet," he whispered.

She wasn't quite healed. She didn't have to warn him; he did no more than caress her, touching her as if she might shatter beneath his hands. Once she reached for his mind, the better to let him know how much pressure she could tolerate and where, but he stopped her. "Let me guess," he breathed, kissing her throat. "Let me surprise you. There's no hurry."

Nor was there, and suddenly she thought that this time he might want to embrace her entirely as a mortal would and as he and she never yet had, with no melded awareness. So she'd closed her mind and abandoned herself to his touch until, much later, it was her turn again. After that they fell asleep, so entangled in one another's limbs that they might have been two corpses in the same shallow grave.

CHAPTER SIX: THE TWINS

Warm heavy weight of Moira's arm wrapped around him, one leg draped over his thigh. Her face was buried in his neck. Every time he moved, she moved with him and mumbled in her sleep. Tomas covered the toes of her extended leg with his; the Elf flexed her foot in response.

The pressure of her hips jolted him awake. Scenes leapt into his mind: how she'd held him last night, what she'd said. He rolled, catching her face in his hands and lifting her chin.

"Tomas," she murmured, softness in her eyes.

At that precise instant the hammering began at the door. It grew louder and more insistent, then more substantial, as if whoever sought entrance had tired of bruised knuckles and was using the side of a fist instead.

"Damnation," he muttered. Tossed the covers to the foot of the bed. Yanked his trousers on. Moira was pulling a gown over her head. The pounding continued. Where were the Elves and sylphs watching that door? Where was Nissyen?

Courtesy, he could imagine Brubakken saying; use courtesy at all times. Doubtless the old man had known a few times like this one. He'd damned well better have, before he gave such advice.

"Who's there?" Tomas shouted none too charitably. The hammering stopped.

"Owein," came a strained young voice from beyond Jared's triply reinforced and supposedly guarded door. The voice of a child of eight or ten winters. "I need to ask you something."

"And Fraine, " said someone else. "May we come in?"

"Half a moment, please." To Moira, in a whisper, "Is the door latched?"

She nodded. The latch was a simple bar-in-trough arrangement. Easy enough to unbolt: he sent a tendril of psychic energy from where he stood.

Moira squared her shoulders, took a grip on his hand and moved to his side. "No mind-speech and no shields," she said, very low. "Just as we are."

The bar thudded to the floor; he pushed it away. "Enter," he said.

Staring wild-eyed at the door, Owein was frozen in place. Fraine knew how he felt because she felt the same: nothing but nerves. Fraine shot a glance at Aubrey, whom the nurse had summoned when she no longer knew what to tell the twins. He'd done his best to counsel them to wait for their parents to waken on their own—but he was their subject, as Owein had reluctantly pointed out a few minutes ago, and the decision was theirs.

The pooka's expression was a shifting amalgam of guilt, empathy, resolution and anxiety. "Go in, the pair of you," he said softly. "I'll go with you, and I won't leave till I'm told."

Of that much, at least, Fraine was certain. Owein was still rooted to the spot, so she plucked up her courage, put the flat of her hand against the wooden door and pushed. She must have used too much force. The door flew open and banged into the opposite wall; Aubrey winced, and Owein made a grab for her elbow.

Stepping through the doorway, Fraine studied her father. He looked like Owein. They had the same long loose-jointed bones, thick pale hair and fair skin, and Aubrey said that Owein bade fair to be as tall one day. At second glance she saw their differences. Owein's face and hers were at once sharper and more delicate than Tomas's. All three pairs of eyes were the same shade of grey, but while Tomas's were less slanted, they were more piercing. There was curiosity in Fraine's own eyes, she knew. There was uncertainty in Owein's, and a tremor in his hand gripping her arm. But in Tomas's eyes she saw tiredness and pain, and several layers of feelings she'd no names for yet. Then she looked at the alabaster face of the tall Elf woman beside him. Moira. Her mother. No one's hair could be any more black. Her features were pointed, still more so than those of the twins, and not like Tomas's at all. Moira's mouth was Fraine's mouth. Her five-fingered hands were Fraine's hands. Although her eyes were that same tint of grey, they were more slanted—and *older.* Older than the eyes of anyone Fraine had met. They harked back so far and saw so much more than Fraine could see that she darted an involuntary glance over her shoulder in case someone else had entered the room. Only Aubrey was there, giving her a grave steady look. Moira's expression was soft as she studied her children, and welcoming. And apprehensive. Why?

"I want to know why we're mortal," said Owein. For the second time.

That was why he'd insisted on waking their parents. Now the twins knew what an emergency was, more or less, and that they shouldn't disturb their parents unless an emergency had arrived. The four of them and a very quiet Aubrey were finishing a light meal. Fraine had met two more Elves, the fenodyree who'd brought the food. They were small and hairy and sullen, and they'd eyed the twins the whole time they were in the room, though they seemed to be trying to hide their stares. Fraine didn't think that Aubrey had noticed, but she and Owein had. She wasn't sure that she liked the fenodyree. She wasn't sure that Tomas did either. He'd fallen silent and watched them till they left.

"Because I'm mortal, and I'm your father," he told Owein now. He didn't sound impatient. "That makes you a halfbreed. One must be wholly an Elf to be immortal."

"The way Moira is?"

Why did Owein keep asking? That was what the nurse had said and the Guards had said and the pooka had said. None of them could lie; they were all full-blooded Elves. Besides, there was so much more to ask about, not least of which was the fact that she and Owein were King and Queen of all

Elfland. They'd neither of them any real notion yet what that would mean. Why discuss mortality at such length? She sensed that there was nothing to be done about it and, which was puzzling, that Owein sensed the same.

"Yes," said Moira. "I have full Elf blood."

"How much do Fraine and I have?"

She glanced at Tomas. "More than half. We're not sure how much your father has."

"Why not?"

Tomas pushed his hair from his forehead, though it wasn't in his way. His jaw looked tense. "Because mine came from my mother, and she died before I'd learned enough about it to ask her any questions."

Fraine knew that something was wrong even before Owein went very still and the whites of his eyes showed, and before the air about his head turned a dark swirling crimson. She knew because there was an unfamiliar and unwelcome knot in her throat, followed by one in her chest. Something was wrong, and Owein was frightened.

"Your mother died?" he was asking. His voice was taut and higher than usual. "What does that mean?"

Tomas gave him a sober look. "That she lost consciousness. She stopped breathing. Her heart stopped beating."

"When will it start again?"

"It won't," said Tomas, very gently.

Owein shoved his chair away from the table. "Then where is she?" His voice had risen another notch.

Their parents exchanged glances. "Her body was buried in the soil of Midgard, many years ago," said Tomas. "In Vestfold, where I was born. I don't know where her soul is."

"What's a soul?"

Another glance. This time it was Moira who answered. "Mortals have souls. Souls...live in the body, but are different from it. When a mortal dies, the soul is eventually reborn in another body."

Owein swallowed, hard, twice. "Where is the soul between times?" he demanded.

"It could be many places." Moira's expression was calm, and very serious. "Calling it just 'the soul' is too simple. The truth is more complex."

"Then where's the dead body? What becomes of it?"

"It's in the ground, or wherever it was placed," said Tomas. His voice was neutral. "Decomposing. Dissolving. Sometimes it's burnt."

Owein blanched. "Does that hurt?"

"Not at all," said Tomas, quickly and reassuringly. "There's no feeling in the body once it's dead. As if it were asleep but not dreaming, and not waking again."

Studying Owein's face was like watching the tide recede—Fraine had learned about the tides when Aubrey took the twins strolling along the shore. Slowly and inexorably, something ebbed out of Owein's expression, and the strange red tint in the air around his head turned darker. Then a roaring, grinding noise began to fill the room. Very low it was, and seemed to have no source. It reminded Fraine of the Sea. After a moment she realized that she wasn't hearing it with her physical ears.

Owein's breath had grown shallow. He got to his feet, his face twisted, and stood looking at her. Suddenly he touched her shoulder with a cold hand. "Will Fraine and I die?"

"Yes. And so will I," Tomas told him, holding his gaze. "Though we'll outlive most of our kind by a great many mortal years, thanks to our Elf blood. We'll live longer still if we spend more time in Elfland than in Midgard."

"Why is that?"

"Because we age more slowly here than there. Time runs differently here."

Owein wheeled about to stare at Moira. "Will you die?"

"No," she said in a patient voice that didn't match the way she held herself, very stiff and straight in her chair. "I am an Elf. We are immortal. Our bodies may change, but do not die."

There was a prolonged pause, so tense that Fraine wondered if the air would shatter. Without warning a mottled rainbow of colors appeared around Tomas's entire body, and not one of them was the blackened crimson that hovered about Owein's head.

"Then it's better to be an Elf," said Owein.

"It is different," said Moira promptly. "We have no souls, and no opportunity to acquire another body. We cannot handle iron without pain, as mortals can. Except for Magicians such as Tomas, mortals cannot perform magic without study and great effort, but we Elves are born to it. You'll learn it; your mortal blood is Mage blood." She glanced from Owein to Fraine. "Midgard could not be more important to the Elves just now, nor Elfland to you. Aubrey's told you there are nine worlds? Elfland used to be the pivot-world round which the others turned, but that role has just passed to Midgard."

Fraine leaned forward. This was more interesting than bloodlines that no one could change.

"If Midgard remains strong and green and linked to Elfland and its magic, so will the other worlds. But if it's...unjust, and too distant from us for too long, it will wither. And so will we all." She folded her arms. "I've no idea how much you remember of your journey here. It's very difficult for most Elves to travel between the worlds of late, though it's easier for Mages. That's in part why we need you. You have roots in both worlds, and you can help keep them connected and alive."

"Then will we be immortal?" Owein's voice was strained.

"No. Not then or ever," said Tomas quietly, and put a hand on Owein's arm.

Owein searched his father's eyes. They were deepset and not slanted; from their shape Tomas's Elf blood couldn't be detected at all. Just now they were direct, and more understanding than gentle.

"What do you want of us?" asked Owein, turning to Moira.

"To build a bridge between Elfland and Midgard. It's been prophesied that you can."

Owein looked at Tomas, who nodded. His hand was still on Owein's arm. When Owein glanced at Aubrey, whose face was sober, the pooka gave both twins a nod and an uneasy flicker of a smile. Moira was studying Owein. Her face was poised and her hands relaxed, but something in her expression was immensely tired, and so sad that Fraine had to look away.

Though the room wasn't hot, Owein was perspiring, and the darkening air about his head looked clotted now. Aubrey's long horsey face was seamed with worry; Tomas's was taut, while something in Moira's stillness was more tense than all of them put together.

What could Fraine do, when she didn't even understand what was wrong? Owein was more than afraid, she realized abruptly. He was almost sick with fear.

Staring at Tomas, Owein blurted, "Why should Fraine and I bother ourselves about the nine worlds? We'll rot anyway and so will you!"

He bolted from the room, slamming the door so hard that it rebounded and swung on its hinges behind him.

Fraine wanted to go after him, but for a horrible moment she couldn't move; she couldn't even breathe, and everything seemed to stop. Tomas gripped the arms of his chair so tightly that his knuckles threatened to burst through the skin of his hands, and Moira's eyes went nearly black in the echoing silence. Suddenly Fraine caught a whiff of something bitter, an odor that wasn't physically there any more than the colors around Owein had been, yet the smell meant something...

Fraine inhaled slowly. The bitter odor about Moira meant *sorrow,* while the colors surrounding Owein had spelled anger and despair, and the pulsing lavender and indigo tints around Tomas's head came from some growing power. And that sharp clean scent, like the smell of the Sea, that began pouring from Tomas meant shock and weariness and determination, and something permanent and earthshaking was happening to Fraine that she didn't understand and couldn't control.

"I'll find him," muttered Aubrey, and got to his feet. He smelled like boiling cabbage, sour and dismayed and indignant, and just as plainly as Fraine had ever known anything in her short life, she knew that he shouldn't go after Owein at all, and especially not when he smelled slightly rotten and full of disapproval. Besides, she had a feeling about where

Owein had gone.

"No!" She shot into Aubrey's path before he could reach the door. The pooka almost crashed into her; she stood her ground, making him stop, making him teeter to and fro. Windmilling his arms to keep his balance, he gaped down at her.

"Please don't go after him," she amended, and looked at her parents. "I will."

With narrowed eyes and an odd look of concentration, as if half his attention were on Fraine and half on something else, Tomas was studying her. In Moira's face was relief and something akin to recognition.

"Go with our blessing," she said. "Bring your brother back, if you can."

Fraine found her twin where she'd suspected she would: on the shore. Lying on his belly in a crumbling layer cake of a sand dune, chin propped in his hands, frowning at the water as it tossed and foamed. The crimson tint about his upper body hadn't so much disappeared as turned grey, nearly the shade of the air. He didn't seem surprised to see her, and only mumbled her name as she dropped down beside him.

For a long time they both watched the Sea. Fraine wanted to live right here on the strand, in a great house full of windows that would all overlook that dark green water. It swirled and pitched and sang to her in a rough gravelly voice, and it smelled of salt and dreams and freedom. It smelled of many things, but so far those were all she'd been able to name.

"Sent you to find me, have they?" asked Owein, rolling onto his back. He sounded tired and doubtful.

"I came on my own."

"So I thought." He was staring overhead. "Are you going back?"

"Are you coming with me?"

At last he looked at her, and the skin about his eyes was taut. "Have you started...seeing things that aren't really there?"

"Around people's heads? Colors that mean something?"

He nodded.

"Yes. I think that's part of our magic. It must come from our Elf blood."

He was comparing their hands. The same shape, slender and pointed. Almost the same length. Nearly identical lines in their palms. He noticed them at the same moment she did, and bent her five fingers back gently, the better to study the markings. "Do you suppose Tomas sees such things?"

"I guess he sees quite a lot."

"Then do you think he..." Owein dropped her hand. "Sometimes I see pictures when people speak. Pictures of their feelings. And thoughts." His voice was stark. "I don't like it."

"Owein," she said, groping her way, watching the tension in his profile. "Owein," she began again, "I can *smell* what people are feeling."

His mouth twisted. "So can I."

"I don't like it either. But that doesn't change anything."

He looked her full in the face. "Then what do I smell like? What am I feeling?"

You smell of death, she wanted to say. Like the rotten plum that their nurse had sent back to the kitchen. Like death and sweat and brine, and that fish corpse at the water's edge. "You're afraid," she said neutrally. "You smell of fright."

"So that's our Elf magic?" His eyes were bitter. "That's all the use of it?"

"That's part of it. We don't know the whole of it yet."

"I know enough." He sat up. So did she.

"Come back with me," she said. "Learn with me."

He looked at her steadily.

"Of course you're afraid. So am I. Why let it stop us?"

"Not that long ago," he said in a small voice, "we couldn't even sit upright without help. I remember it and so do you. Then we took our first steps. Then we could talk. We kept growing and everything kept changing. It still is: now our *magic* is growing along with our bodies. They none of them know what's coming next, Tomas or Moira or Aubrey; I can see that they don't. None of them know anything save that our death lies at the end. How fast will it come? As fast as everything else has?" His voice had risen. "I don't *want* this! I want something I understand!"

"Do you think I don't want the same?" she shouted. "I'm in this with you and we're twins!" It felt good to shout, as if it released something. It made her feel powerful. "Running away won't help. It won't stop our magic growing. Better to learn all we can of it, I say."

He faced her, breathing hard and fast, hands clenched at his sides.

"I don't want to die either, nor a life I don't understand and that's passing too fast for me." She hunted for words, for thoughts she'd not fully formed. "I think I'll be happier if I have something to do. Something important. There are whole worlds that need us."

"Why help them?"

"Why not? Running won't keep our death away. You heard Tomas."

After a stark narrow-eyed look at her, Owein got to his feet, kicked off his boots and trudged to the waterline, where he halted at gaze and let the waves tumble about his shins. Soon his trousers were soaked to the knees. Once he crouched down for a brief examination of the dead fish on the strand, then stepped farther into the surf. He dipped his hands in the water, scrubbed them over his face. Fraine waited. She knew he'd not leave her, so when she found herself drowsy, she stretched out on her side, pillowed her face on her hands and closed her eyes.

Scattered drops of cold water struck her temples and her neck. She pushed herself upright, blinking.

"Your pardon; I didn't mean to splash you," said Owein, who was slapping sand from his lower legs. He put his boots on, made a face, took them off and used his sleeve to wipe his feet. Then he sat facing her, pale and strained but no longer angry: the crimson cloud had gone. "Maybe Tomas is wrong about our death."

"He can't lie. He has true speech and prophecy."

"I didn't say maybe he's lying. I said maybe he's wrong." Owein glanced aside. "He's a halfbreed too. With less Elf blood than ours, and Aubrey said he hasn't been a Mage long. Maybe there's a way around dying that hasn't been found yet."

"Owein..."

"Do you know for certain there isn't?"

"Of course I don't. But I believe what they told us. I believe that there isn't."

Owein shook his head. He was slumping now, staring at the sand. Moving slowly, he put his boots on.

"Chasing after a way out of it probably won't work," Fraine said patiently.

He shook his head again.

"Let's do something we know we can do. Learn about magic and Elfland. I don't want to do it all alone."

His eyes were dull. "I won't give up hope."

She wanted to shout, 'Look at yourself! You're giving up everything else!' She bit her lip instead. "You don't have to give up anything. Unless you want to." She pondered for a moment, decided to take a risk. "Why are you so afraid of dying? It makes you afraid of living, too."

His eyes blazed. He didn't hit her, but a sharp scent of burning charcoal told her that the impulse had crossed his mind. Then she watched him realize that she knew it. He covered his face with his hands. "I'm sorry."

She didn't like the smell of shame: old and stinking. Poisonous. "Don't be. You've done nothing." She put her arms around him. "I love you."

"Love you too," he said gruffly.

Silence. She liked holding him, though after a while it made her tense.

It wasn't long before he mumbled, "I want to take a walk. Alone. You'll wait for me? You won't leave?"

"I won't take a step away from this spot."

Fraine slept again, wakened, found herself hungry. How long had she been here? Owein was nowhere in sight, only a breathtaking green Sea streaked with foam. She admired it for a while, then stretched, found a pointed stick and practiced drawing the Runes that Aubrey had taught the twins.

She and Owein trusted the pooka. But he probably wouldn't know what to say to Owein; Aubrey wasn't mortal. Tomas might understand better.

She eyed the ruined hall atop the promontory. What if Tomas joined them at the shore?

When her belly tightened at the thought, she knew that if he appeared, she wouldn't ask him to speak to Owein. At first she wasn't sure why. Then a thought came to her: Owein might not listen to either Tomas or Moira, because they were the reason that the twins were born halfbreeds. And the reason they'd been born at all, but there her mind began walking crabwise in circles. She threw the stick down and turned her attention to examining all the different kinds of pebbles worn smooth by the Sea and hurled up on the strand.

Finally she spied Owein some distance away, moving towards her in long hurried strides. To her relief the crimson cloud was still gone from about his head and his face was less strained, although just as serious.

As soon as he came within earshot, she asked, "Are you in a muddle? Because I am."

He gaped for an instant, then surprised her by starting to chuckle. "Of course I am. Nothing about us, our birth, our parents, is—" He was laughing outright now, and smelled of flowers. "Is normal. At least I think it isn't."

"We haven't any idea what normal is. How could we? That's a problem."

Owein found that statement even funnier. "No, no, no." He sounded just like Aubrey teaching them the Runes, and that set Fraine giggling too. "It's *the* problem. Yours and mine."

After so much tension, it did her good to laugh until her stomach actually hurt. She hugged Owein and wiped tears from her eyes. When they were both calmer, she asked, "Do you suppose Tomas and Moira might be less confused than we are?"

"Probably." He drew away just far enough to look at her sadly; still, she got a faint smile. "You think we should let them teach us whatever they can, and try to build their bridge for them. Don't you?"

She nodded.

"Because they're all we have," said Owein.

"Not all," she corrected him fiercely. "We have each other."

She was almost crushed by his hug.

CHAPTER SEVEN: PLANS AND DREAMS

Tomas called Moira in halfway through the twins' first lesson because, he said, their innate shielding technique seemed more Elfin than mortal to him, and he wasn't sure how much more he could show them. Once he'd left, Fraine realized how patient he'd been. Moira brooked no questions. Moira expected them to get everything right the first time. And Moira was relentless, hammering at their fledgling barriers until Owein and Fraine both collapsed on the floor.

"On your feet," Moira told them, inexorably calm. "Try again." She knelt to offer each twin a hand. "It's for your own good," she added more gently. "You'd get no second chances from an enemy. You've the gift to be sure, but you're not concentrating."

"I'm ready," said Fraine. Still catching her breath, she watched Owein take a sudden experimental jab at Moira, who did no more than smile faintly. Owein couldn't have knocked Tomas down, but Tomas would definitely have found it harder than Moira did to turn that blow aside—the twins were near their full growth now.

Then, as if someone had slapped the side of Fraine's head, Moira's attack sent her sprawling. If she hadn't sensed that she'd best save her breath, she'd have groaned. She wasn't fully upright when Moira struck again.

"Are you trying to hurt me?" Fraine gasped.

"No." Moira smelled like sea water. That scent meant resolve, Fraine had learned, and deeper feelings which their owner might want to conceal. "I'm assuring myself no one else can." Her eyes were remote, her face a mask. "You're not angry yet, Fraine. No one has a right to assault you like this. Not Owein, not any Elf who lives and breathes..." A tremendous buffet at Fraine's ears made her stagger again. "And surely not your mother," Moira finished coolly. "Get up and fight me. Stay out of it, Owein; your turn will come."

Somehow Fraine was standing, hunched over, elbows on her knees. Sucking in great gulps of air. Letting the energy of her shield circulate, as Tomas had taught her, out from her solar plexus and around her entire body. Infusing it with as much strength as she could. It was all so baffling, and she wanted to think about what she'd already learned, not go further into unknown territory without a map—

A landslide fell on her shoulders; a tidal wave rocked her onto her heels. Something was squeezing her ribcage, crushing it. Hammering came from all sides. No time to plan, no time to do anything but react, not if she wanted to live.

"*No!*" she shouted, and pushed back. Her defense came from more than her shield or her body. It was a sheer effort of will that came both from the flesh and beyond it, though she was panting, though she was dizzy and drenched with sweat and queasy to boot. But most of all she was filled with a purely physical rage. She would not die. By all the gods, she would not die here before Owein's horrified face. Her heart was racing; her fists and teeth were clenched.

"No!" she shrieked again, pushing twice as hard as before. Every iota of strength that she funneled against Moira came back to her own defenses, so immediately and with such force that she almost stumbled again, and squeezed her eyes shut. She was weeping. She hadn't wanted it to be war, this learning of magic.

Five lifetimes later she heard Moira say, "Fraine. Fraine! At ease, my dear. It's over."

Panting, she peered at her mother, who appeared utterly unruffled, her shining black hair sleek against her shoulders, her expression serene. But her eyes steered a turbulent middle course between pride and speculation. "I don't know if you could crack my shield," Moira said softly. "But I'm virtually certain I couldn't crack yours. You did very well indeed."

Fraine sat on the floor, smack in the middle of the storage room they'd appropriated in Jared's former quarters. "Thank you," she said, saving her breath. She needed it to bear watching Moira's sudden attack upon the white-faced Owein.

Owein learned to fend Moira off—he had to.

Next the twins took some difficult but considerably less dangerous lessons from Moira about the least draining ways to maintain a shield, and the use of one as a warning device. Then Tomas taught them how to see Elementals, communicate in mind-speech, move objects and ward off the iron-sick. All of those skills they found easy. Using iron's essence to topple the dead trees in the woods near the palace was even easier.

"You're so quick at it that I feel like a deaf man teaching music," Tomas told them, smiling.

"What else must we learn to build the bridge?" asked Fraine.

They were passing the well on their way back from the forest. Tomas glanced into the empty trees, then motioned the twins inside the hawthorn circle. "I wish I knew," he said when the three of them were seated on dry turf. "Before we start the bridge, I'll take you both to visit Midgard and see what's to be learned there." He didn't look surprised when Moira and Nissyen joined them; perhaps they'd planned to meet here. Moira sat by Tomas, and Nissyen took a seat across from the twins.

Fraine was still making up her mind about Nissyen. Conversing with the sylph was a joy, because it never tired of the twins' questions and was more than ready with answers. Indeed, it seemed to know everything. The history of all the nine worlds. The biographies of every Elf, god and mortal the twins had ever heard mentioned. The varieties of magic.

Endless nuances of meaning for each Rune. Nissyen was canny about practical matters, too. The length of an ell: from the elbow to the outstretched fingertips. How the Cooks had prepared this or that dish. The names and growth habits of each plant in Elfland. How many dolphins were in the schools they saw leaping in the Elvish Sea. How harps were made.

But when Fraine wondered why and how she could smell emotions, and why she never sensed them about Nissyen, the sylph said only, "Magical gifts differ, and that is not one of mine." Tomas had already explained why Nissyen had no feelings, but that brief exchange was the first time Fraine really absorbed the fact. The Elemental acted as if it liked her and Owein, but since it had no feelings, could it truly care for anyone? Moreover, it never ate; it never slept, and it didn't even have a real body.

She didn't dislike Nissyen, but neither did she feel wholly at ease around the sylph. Neither did anyone else, she suspected. Everyone smelled too much like wormwood whenever the sylph came around, and wormwood, tarry and herbal, meant wariness.

"To visit Midgard?" asked Owein now. "What region of it?"

"Wessex," said Tomas. "One of you will work on the bridge from Elfland and one from Midgard. I'd just as soon you were among friends there."

Fraine and Owein exchanged glances: they wouldn't relish being parted. Still, they'd remain in communication. Mind-speech with each other had been ludicrously easy to learn and besides, most often they didn't even need it. Then she smelled mint. Owein was curious.

"Could I be the one to stay in Midgard?" he asked.

"I don't see why not," said Moira. She looked at Fraine. "With your agreement? In some ways it would be better. A young man would attract less comment and questions there than a young woman would."

Less danger, she meant. The twins had heard about the mortal realm's attitudes. Fraine nodded; she had no real preference.

"You'll both go there with me, then Fraine and I will return here," said Tomas. "You have need of some experience traveling, and you'll meet Rose and Linley."

He'd told the twins all about them, and his estate. It would be interesting to meet some mortals besides Tomas and Owein.

"I've another reason for taking you there before we begin work on the bridge," Tomas said quietly. "There may be some constraints about *when* Owein could work. Elfland isn't bound by Time, but Midgard is. I want Linley's advice on the matter. He's an astrologer, and he knows more about the cycles of mortal Time than Moira and I do."

"An astrologer?" asked Fraine.

Tomas looked blank for a moment, then started to smile. "A kind of soothsayer. Astrologers study the motion of the Midgard's Sun, Moon and stars, to discern their influence on mortal affairs." He darted a glance overhead.

So did the twins. The empty sky was as it always was: a uniform pearled color, matte and luminous at once. Milky yet dull, like the unwashed interior of an oyster shell. But the mortal world had days and nights, and vast blazing bodies to mark their courses and light the steps of those who walked there.

As soon as Tomas mentioned the journey to Midgard, Owein began sleeping fitfully, and his dreams grew troubled.

In one he stood at the mouth of a smoking fissure in the earth. He couldn't see within, yet he knew, in the sinking unmistakable way of dreams and dreamers in all the worlds, that Death lurked in that chasm. Moreover he knew that Death was aware that he, Owein, stood outside. Not that Death was in any hurry to collect him. His time had not yet come.

The horror of it was that his death *would* come, and he didn't know when.

"But I might," said a cool insinuating tenor at Owein's elbow.

He turned, trying to move quickly, but a dreamer's near-paralysis so weighted his limbs that it took an eternity. At last he saw the speaker: a slight young man with a lithe and supple carriage, chalky skin, ginger hair and the most peculiar burning hazel eyes. Owein couldn't read them; he could read nothing about this man. No scent, no aura, nothing at all. His eyes were sly and horribly intent, and power glittered in their depths. He was watching Owein, humming a little tune.

Owein's breath grew short. He looked at the chasm, looked away again. What had he just been thinking? He had no idea. He felt dizzy. Suddenly his dream-world had narrowed to this creature before him. Just as suddenly he knew that the creature wasn't human, though he had no idea who or what it could be instead. Nor was he sure that he wanted to learn.

"I might know when you'll die," said the redhead. "I might know a lot about Death in general." He smiled, intimately, appallingly.

Owein smelled smoke. He gathered strength for a scream, but no sound came.

"Including yours," said the redhead sweetly, and vanished.

He left Owein able to move at last. Bellowing, he struggled upright, fighting an oppressive something wrapped around him like a shroud—the bedclothes, he would learn when the Guards that Jared had assigned to him woke him from his shrieking fit, just before his sister and his wild-eyed parents burst into the room.

He had a second dream, then a third and a fourth with that same oppressive ginger-haired man and his talk of death, all riddled with hints and promises that left Owein feeling vaguely unclean and more than a little stupefied, as if his brain were full of rotten wheat. Finally he told Fraine about the nightmares.

They were at the shore. The seaside was their usual haven when they had a break in their various lessons, not only in magic now but also in the history and customs of Midgard. Tomas thought they needed to learn as much as possible about the mortal realm before their journey there. The Sea was calmer than usual and the salt air more still. Fraine paced along with her hands burrowed deep in the pockets of her tunic and a faint vertical line between her eyebrows.

"Have you mentioned these nightmares to anyone else?" she asked.

"No." He didn't bother to explain why. Fraine would guess that after his outburst about death, he'd be embarrassed to recount such dreams to their parents. It had been hard enough to tell her.

"Do you think they might be real, and not nightmares at all?" she asked.

"I don't know." The thought had never occurred to him. "Why, are you dreaming too?" They'd had so many parallel experiences...

She took his arm. "Not about your redheaded man. About a woman with golden hair."

"Like our hair?"

"Not very like. Hers is darker, a warm yellow like gold. It shines like gold, too." She glanced out to sea. "So does her skin. And she hasn't said anything about death. She says...I don't know. Encouraging things."

"What sort of things?"

A smile, then a shrug. "It won't seem like much. It doesn't to me when I'm awake. It's more the way she says it." There was a shade of reticence in her voice. "That I must be strong. That I *am* strong. That she'll help us."

They walked in silence for a while, watching the gulls and kicking up clumps of wet sand. At last Owein said, "You haven't spoken to Moira about her either."

Fraine shook her head. "Perhaps because it felt private," she said simply.

"I'm glad you told me." A pause, while they watched a dolphin jump. "I only wish my dreams were as pleasant."

"Pleasant? Mine are challenging. But yours sound worse, to be sure." When she turned to face him, her eyes were thoughtful. "Perhaps they'll change after a while. Or perhaps mine will."

[illegible] and [illegible].

They [illegible] shore. The seaside was their usual haven when they had [illegible] in their [illegible] lessons, not only in [illegible] in the [illegible] and customs of [illegible] [illegible] as much as possible around the [illegible] before their [illegible]. The sea was [illegible] and the [illegible] from [illegible] along with her [illegible] [illegible] and [illegible] between [illegible] eyebrows.

[illegible] she asked [illegible] [illegible] [illegible] that [illegible] [illegible] dreams [illegible] [illegible].

"Do you [illegible] [illegible] [illegible] nightmares [illegible] [illegible] [illegible] [illegible] [illegible] had so many [illegible] experience.

[illegible]

[illegible]

[illegible] "I don't know [illegible] things."

"What [illegible] of things?"

[illegible] [illegible] that she [illegible] [illegible] [illegible] the [illegible] and [illegible] [illegible] Moira [illegible] [illegible].

[illegible] [illegible] [illegible] [illegible].

"[illegible]" Moira [illegible] [illegible] to be [illegible] [illegible] [illegible] [illegible] [illegible].

CHAPTER EIGHT: REUNIONS

Somerset, late spring, 885 A.D., Christian reckoning.

In the loft of Limecliff's great hall, Rose sorted through the old clothes in the storage chests, searching for a garment to patch Linley's warmest tunic. The tear in it hadn't accompanied a wound, for which she was profoundly grateful. Linley had ripped the garment while helping hoist pallets of sick and injured men-at-arms onto the carts that would bring them home—those who survived the journey. He was bone-tired, as were all of Alfred's troops, after the hard road they'd had. One pallet and its occupant barely cleared the side of a cart, and rather than let the pallet catch on a splintered pole and jar the man, Linley had heaved it higher and torn his sleeve.

He was sleeping now in one of the bedclosets below. They'd only got home a few hours ago, he and Simon. Simon hadn't slept a wink; he was off tending the sick and wounded soldiers who were tenants of Limecliff, in an empty granary they'd commandeered for that purpose. With the redheaded Saxon cook Hroswitha, Matilda was preparing herbal poultices and infusions to Rose and Simon's specifications, and no doubt hoping for a spare moment to look in on the birds at the mews.

All of Limecliff was at sixes and sevens, but that was what came of war. At least Alfred had freed Rochester and taken whole shiploads of booty from the Danes. He'd made sail and got underway heavy-laden, Linley said, with every cargo ship's hull riding so low in the water that his own vessel had pulled far ahead of them—only to have another Viking fleet appear and steal all their own plunder back again. All but the freed former slaves so ill or mistreated they were likely to expire before arriving home: those ill-fated wretches the Norse had left with Alfred. They'd even made him a derisory present of several others whose contagion they no longer wanted on their own dragoncraft.

A great many of those unfortunate men and women had already died, and since the weather was more than cold enough to keep the bodies recognizable a while longer, Simon had offered to help identify them and notify their kin. How many more corpses would come to Limecliff before life returned to some semblance of normal?

Rose took an ancient woolen cloak from one of the storage chests, closed its lid gently, mindful of the sleeping Linley, and started down the ladder. As she reached the last rung, she heard a tap at the door.

Frowning, she hurried across the room. Who could it be? Anyone from the estate would have entered right after that perfunctory knock, and anyone off the estate should have been escorted and announced. She tucked her brown hair beneath her kerchief and smoothed her gown. With a finger to her lips, ready to ask the visitor to speak softly for Linley's sake, she cracked the door open a few inches.

She almost dropped the old cloak she was holding when she saw who waited patiently outside: Tomas the Rhymer, with his clear melancholy grey eyes and his gentle smile the instant he saw her. He looked not a moment older than when he'd left six years ago.

"Hullo, Rose," he murmured, then came inside looking all about the hall.

He was followed by two young adolescents who at first glance resembled him so much, with their long limbs and unruly pale hair and Northern prominence of cheekbone and temple, that Rose knew immediately they were kin to him. At second glance their gait was more graceful and their features more delicate than his, with wary tilted grey eyes and pointed chins, while both the width and the exquisite cut of their mouths reminded her of—

"Where is Moira?" Rose whispered, and groped for the back of a chair. Had the Elf survived her lying-in?

Tomas reached for Rose's elbow as if to steady her, and ended by giving her a hug. "She's well, in real health again. She sends you and Linley her greeting. These are our children, Owein and Fraine."

When he turned to them, they smiled and murmured Rose's name at the same instant, not shyly, yet the reserve in both faces reminded her of Moira all over again. So the Elf had borne twins.

"Welcome home," Rose said warmly, trying not to stare. For all their Saxon clothing, they looked nearly as alien as their mother. Beautiful creatures, both of them. Breathtaking. She found herself blurting her thought, "How comes it they're more than six years old?"

"That's how long I've been gone?" Tomas asked, so quickly that she guessed he'd been impatient to know.

"Yes." She kept her expression neutral. "Why—" There would always be plenty about Tomas that she'd not understand: he was a Mage. She let out her breath, squared her shoulders. "Never mind why. Time runs differently where you've been." It wasn't hard to summon a smile. "Tired and hungry, are you? We'll soon put that to rights. Linley will be glad to see you."

"He's here, then?" A world of relief in Tomas's voice. "Is he well?"

"I could hardly be better," said Linley, emerging precipitously from the bedcloset with his trousers on backwards and his chest and feet bare. "Welcome home!" He included Tomas and both startled twins in his embrace.

So far, Midgard smelled mainly of smoke.

How could anyone live in this stuffy hall with its two hearthfires? Fraine and Owein were coughing intermittently, and so was Tomas. Fraine could understand the need for fire; Elfland was never so chilly. But why could they not knock more smokeholes in the roof and put in another window or two? After a while Linley looked at her thoughtfully, exchanged glances with Rose, then propped the door open for a brief interval.

That act of consideration was characteristic of her hosts, Fraine decided. Except they weren't really her hosts, since the hall belonged to Tomas. She liked Rose and Linley. From the way Owein had begun to relax, she could tell that he did too. And Tomas clearly loved them both. He didn't smile so much around anyone but Moira, while he and Linley wasted no time in pouncing upon the lute and the harp that stood in the corner. After a troubling journey that had seemed to have no end, Fraine was glad of a chance to lounge in her father's high-backed wooden armchair and let a stream of melodies soothe her.

They hadn't traveled disembodied, since Tomas thought they'd only find it harder that way. She and Owein had each grasped one of Tomas's hands, and they sailed along through the 'tweenlands at a good clip with the ravens pacing them on either side. The 'tweenlands had been odd enough when they were trackless and featureless, just infinite empty space, uniform and grey, neither hot nor cold and without a breath of wind. At first it was unnerving to have no sense of direction, no up, down or sideways, until Tomas explained why, even without the ravens, he could always tell where he was bound. After he showed them how to cast ahead with their Sight to find Midgard and its iron, Fraine didn't feel so lost.

But when the first bars of streaky yellow light had appeared, she'd been confused all over again. The bars looked like the interior of a giant wasps' nest, while forcing her way through them was as painful as if so many invisible hornets were stinging her. Her eyes were watering and she was coughing, but it wasn't the iron-sick.

Then great distorted Runes began to drift across their path, all blazing a dark and angry red and all shaped more or less like a cross. They smelled of burning rancid oil and scorched almonds, and of smoke. They smelled of fear, and of something Fraine couldn't identify.

"Exorcisms," Tomas muttered grimly.

"It hurts," Owein gasped.

"That's because they won't accept us," said Tomas. "They'll not compromise. They're fanatics."

That was the marshy fetid smell that Fraine had been unable to name. Fanaticism.

At last they left that vortex of cramped and hostile energy and entered a new region of the 'tweenlands, one that Fraine found more to her liking. Rainbows of colored light spiraled about them in an interlocking network. As if intending to rest or observe, Tomas slowed his pace. They hovered motionless for a little space, during which Fraine gradually became aware of a sphere floating some distance ahead of them.

It was mostly blue and green, with every shade of melded malachite and lapiz, peridot and sapphire, aquamarine and opal, but stained with ominous brown spots and streaks. She squinted: was it slowly turning in place? Perhaps she was merely detecting the waves of energy that sheeted off its surface. When she sniffed the air, the iron-reek was strongest straight ahead, where the sphere lay.

Suddenly she knew what it was. The mortal world.

Owein nudged her and pointed: he had noticed both their destination and the discoloration among its tints.

"Midgard," she mouthed at him behind Tomas's back.

Owein nodded, pointed a second time and a third, and then again. Six or eight separate times, perhaps; she lost count but kept following the direction of his finger. And then she saw them. Spaced evenly well above the surface of Midgard, yet clearly in the 'tweenlands, were several amorphous and whirlpool-shaped centers of power. Or rather she didn't see them: they were clotted opacities in her field of vision, an absence of one manner of energy that created the presence of another, though what kind she could not have said.

As she examined one center, it seemed to pulse, to grow larger, even to stretch towards her like the end of an immense tunnel. Her skin prickled; her chest grew warmer. For an instant she thought she heard voices, but it could have been her own heartbeat. No, it was voices, singing or chanting. If she moved closer perhaps she could make out the words.

"Fraine," came Tomas's voice, low and steady. His grip tightened on her wrist.

The power center was definitely growing larger or drawing nearer, perhaps both at once, and spiraling about in a circle. She could see rayed lines within it now. She didn't know the chanted language. It was so faint that it must come from Midgard rather than within the center itself.

"Stay with me, Owein." Tomas again, more urgent now. "Fraine!"

She could have sworn she saw a long tendril of light arcing across the opacity straight out of that spiraling center. Like a finger, beckoning, pointing the way. What frightened her was the sudden ache in her shin bones. What was happening? Was she growing again?

"*Fraine!*"

One hand on her wrist, the other on her shoulder, Tomas shook her, not so hard that Owein released her other hand, but more than enough to shatter her reverie. She found herself staring into her father's deep-set eyes. They were blazing, and he gave off a scent like burning tar. He was warning her.

"Never enter a trance when you don't know what lies at its other end," he said grimly. "These are the 'tweenlands. What have you learned about them?"

Her teeth chattered. "I'm cold," she mumbled, surprised.

"That's because you were all but tranced." Tomas's ribcage heaved; a pulse jumped at the side of his throat. He released her shoulder but kept hold of her hand, then pulled her about until the three of them stood in a triangle facing one another. She was dimly aware of something black circling overhead—the ravens. Owein was pale, his hand clammy in hers.

"Root and branch, I've a mind to shake you all over again. What have Moira and I taught you about the 'tweenlands?" He stepped closer still; the grey eyes bore into hers.

"They lie between the worlds," she recited from memory, haltingly, straining after the words. "And touch all nine of them." She was shivering. When Owein moved nearer she pressed against him, grateful for the warmth. "Whether they contain the nine worlds or the worlds contain them, no one knows."

"Go on," Tomas ordered. His jaw was tight. A muscle twitched near the corner of his mouth, and his hand clamping hers was hard and relentless.

"Time and space," Owein breathed in her ear. Tomas flicked him an irritated look.

"No one has ever charted them. Their topography changes as the worlds change," Fraine said by rote. "Time and space behave as strangely in the 'tweenlands as mortal Time behaves in Elfland." She felt a bit stronger now. "They contain Hecate's crossroads. No one rules in the 'tweenlands, but She sometimes speaks to travelers or changes their routes."

"Good," muttered Tomas. "What else?"

"Rituals performed in one world to affect any other are all felt here," said Fraine, remembering the exorcisms.

Tomas scrutinized her. His mouth was taut, his eyes shadowed. Some of the rage was slowly ebbing from his expression, with worry taking its place. "Do you understand why I'm in a temper?" he asked very quietly, and released the twins' hands.

Fraine had already taken an experimental and surreptitious sniff of the air, and now smelled a mixture of plums and singed almonds about her father. "You were afraid I'd endangered myself."

He nodded. "By...?"

"By entering trance when I didn't know what lay at the other end of it," she said, feeling her own blood rise. "Here in the 'tweenlands, without telling anyone and without planning it."

He nodded a second time.

"I'll not do it again." She tried not to sound curt. "I'll go carefully."

"I'm glad to hear it." He rubbed a hand over the back of his neck. "What did you see that drew you so?"

She turned to look. The blue-green sphere was still there, and so were the centers of energy in the 'tweenlands that connected to it.

"Midgard?" Tomas raised his eyebrows.

"Partly. More those power centers."

He squinted. "Where?"

When she glanced at Owein he nodded. Of course he had seen them; he'd called her attention to them in the first place. "In the 'tweenlands," he said with remarkable patience, given the storm brewing in his face as he gazed at Tomas. "Eight of them. Linked to Midgard."

"Point them out to me," said Tomas, gripping Owein's hand. "Then I'll be able to see them henceforward." He sighted along the length of Owein's outstretched arm for a few heartbeats before his eyes narrowed, and he took a wondering breath. "That's nothing I've ever come across."

"What are they?" asked Owein.

Tomas shook his head. "Some kind of portal. But where they lead I don't know."

"To Midgard," Fraine said.

He shaded his eyes with one hand. "So they do. But we'll not pass through them on our way there. Another voyage, perhaps, once we've learned more about them." He looked intently at each twin. "If you come across anything else in the 'tweenlands that you don't understand, tell me. That instant."

After such a passage between the worlds, Fraine was glad to listen to music and to see Tomas's face soften a trifle as his hands moved over the harpstrings. She stole a glance at Owein, who had turned around on the bench to watch, his legs stretched out before him and his back propped against the massive wooden table. His expression was milder as well, and he was studying the lute with interest. Tomas had one just like it.

Once the instruments were set aside, they all sat down to the worst meal that Fraine had ever tasted: a cabbage-based slop with gritty bread and dried fish so salty it parched the mouth. Were all mortal Cooks so unskilled? Only politeness made her and Owein swallow as much of the stuff as they did, but Tomas either didn't notice or didn't care. He showed Linley the twins' nativities, asked Rose endless questions about the estate and its tenants, listened to a detailed description of Alfred's campaign in Rochester, and inquired after Linley's brother Simon, all with the same intense concentration that he brought to his harp or to the twins' lessons. Still, his eyes kept straying to the door.

Linley noticed those glances. "I've no end of things to show you," he said cheerfully, then looked at the twins. Politely, but with more than one question in his face. She and Owein must be the reason everyone was still withindoors.

Tomas was steepling his fingers. "I'll tell you why we've come."

Rose started to get to her feet.

"Stay, please." Briefly, he explained that they planned for the twins to build a bridge to Elfland, that Owein would manage the process from the Midgard end, and that they wanted him near Rose and Linley if possible.

Without the slightest hesitation Linley said, "Owein will need an identity, then."

"Precisely."

Both men looked at Owein, who was leaning forward, his eyes alight with interest.

"Your younger brother?" suggested Linley. "Visiting the estate?"

"That would serve... Better that than to say he's here in permanence. He may be called away a fair amount."

"Where shall we say you and Moira are?"

"In Vestfold," said Tomas. "Seeing to a disputed inheritance? That's common enough. Is anyone here likely to have been to Vestfold recently?"

Rose shook her head.

"Excellent. I've told Owein enough about it that he'll sound convincing should anyone question him."

"Half a moment." Linley shifted on the bench. A hint of color crept into his round olive-skinned face, and his expression was that of a man forced to ask a graceless question. "About sounding convincing. Do the twins have your true speech, Tomas? Or can they lie?"

"They can indeed," Tomas said, quietly and with such absolute gravity that Fraine nearly overlooked the mischief in his eyes. "I've reason to believe they might even attain my former skill at it."

Linley grinned, while the twins exchanged a sheepish glance. Fraine tried to look dignified, though she wanted to laugh. "Aubrey's been telling tales," Owein murmured in her ear.

"You and Rose can keep Owein informed about Limecliff," Tomas told Linley. "Doubtless there's much I forgot to say. The less communication he has with anyone but the two of you and Simon, the better."

"There's another consideration," Rose began. "Someone else lives here now."

"You've had children?" asked Tomas, warmth in his eyes.

"None yet. I was speaking of Matilda; we've grown to love her as if she were ours. She's Alfred's niece, Tomas, who's come to live with us. His brother's illegitimate daughter." She glanced at Linley. "Alfred's quite fond of her, and sees her as often as may be."

"Ah," said Tomas thoughtfully. "They'll meet Owein too, then. What age is Matilda?"

"Thirteen? Fourteen?" said Rose, shrugging. "Not a child."

"Alfred's not been to Vestfold, but he hears news of it now and again from visitors to court," Linley pointed out.

"You'll have to tell me more of it, then. You're a good storyteller," Owein said to Tomas, then flashed him a beatifically innocent smile. "Though not so good as I am."

At last the five of them took a roundabout path by some empty outbuildings and off to the woods. It was crucial that no one see Tomas, who was supposedly in Vestfold. He and the twins could have explored by themselves with far less risk of attracting any attention, Fraine knew, but Linley wanted to show Tomas as much of the grounds as possible in person. She and Owein, grateful for the fresh air, brought up the rear and tried not to let the strange new landscape distract them from the Saxons' conversation.

The first thing Fraine noticed was how *bright* Midgard was. She liked the Sun and the pale yellow fingers it stretched towards them from the west, while the earth rolled slowly away from it. She knew where the Sun was at every second, its light and its heat, and where it was moving, just as surely as she'd known that the portals in the 'tweenlands led to Midgard. She didn't glean this information from the Sun's heat on her skin. It was more from the pit of her stomach, effortlessly, rather like the way she always knew, as soon as she awakened and before opening her eyes, the direction of the door of the room where she'd slept.

The Sun certainly helped her see the land better than one could in Faerie. Even dotted with drifts of dirty snow that hadn't yet melted, it was beautiful terrain. She liked the alders and the copper beeches in particular, while Owein and Tomas kept lingering near the willows. All the trees were smaller than in Elfland, but far fewer of them were dead or uprooted. To judge by the relatively untrodden leaf mold, not so many mortals roamed the woods here as Elves did in Faerie.

It was strange not to sense any Elves about, though there were plenty of Elementals, mostly gnomes in the wooded areas, with undines by the creeks. It was even stranger how Rose and Linley didn't notice the Elementals at all, although Tomas said that Linley was half-Sighted. To get out of Linley's way before he trod upon their long twig-like toes, several gnomes dodged as fast as Fraine had ever seen them move, and muttered about his clumsiness. Once he seemed near to turning around or glancing over his shoulder but ended by doing neither.

"What is it?" asked Owein.

Tomas shot him a dark look.

"Nothing," said Linley. "For an instant I thought there was someone behind me."

When he moved a little ahead with Rose to scout out a shorter route back to the great hall, Tomas slowed his pace until the twins drew level with him. "Take no notice of the Elementals, please, or we'll just attract more of them," he murmured. "Nissyen's with us, and Nissyen draws enough Elementals as it is."

"Very well," said Owein, lowering his voice to match Tomas's pitch. Neither twin had known that Nissyen accompanied them. They'd had not a glimpse of the ravens since reaching Limecliff, but no doubt the birds were nearby as well. "Will we see the sunset? It's not long in coming." Owein pointed to the exact spot where the Sun would sink beneath the horizon. So he could feel it too, the Sun's motion and direction and pace, and the way all the weight of the Earth slowly turned from it.

Of a sudden he had Tomas's full attention. "Can you tell where the Sun will set?"

Owein nodded. When Tomas looked at Fraine, she nodded too.

"And when?"

"In twenty minutes," Owein said, and hesitated. "Can't you tell, then?"

"No," said Tomas. "But attunement to nature is a magical gift, and you clearly have a greater share of it than I." His eyes were bright. "That's marvelous!" He raised his voice. "Linley! Would you happen to know when the Sun will set?"

"On this day I would," said Linley, retracing his steps to join them. He looked apologetic. "I checked the astrolabe this morning. That's why I'm pushing on so fast." He glanced at the western sky. "The Sun sets in less than half an hour, I'd say, so we'd do well to be out of the forest and on more level ground by then." He smiled at the twins. "If we step lively, we'll just make it."

The sunset was beautiful—and began exactly when Owein had said it would. He and Fraine lingered at the edge of the woods nearest the great hall to watch. At Fraine's request, Tomas kept them company.

The changes were subtle at first. The earth wheeled inexorably along its track, while the sky's color slowly deepened and all the clouds began to glow as if so many torches were concealed inside them. Then the Sun changed from a blinding yellow-white to an orange that kept shading towards red.

By the time Tomas said it was safe to look directly at the Sun, the sky was streaked with carmine light. New shadows appeared and old ones lengthened, and before long Fraine couldn't see very far into the trees. All the tints about her darkened: the mud in the yard, the watering trough, the walls and roof of the outbuildings. When something small and white and pointed winked at her from halfway up the inverted indigo bowl overhead, although nothing had changed in the earth's trajectory, she made a grab for her father's elbow.

"What's that?" She pointed at the glittering pinprick of light.

"The evening star," Tomas said soothingly, and put an arm about her and Owein. "Soon there will be more of them."

And there were, sixes and tens and then dozens, so many that Tomas didn't even know all their names. A misty streak of stars started meandering across the center of the darkening sky. It was a miracle. Through it all the earth never stopped turning, and Fraine still knew where the Sun was.

Tomas waited until night had completely fallen before ushering the silent and bedazzled twins back to the hall. In the lamplight, Linley and

Rose were poring over maps spread out on the table. Beside the maps were Linley's copies of the twins' nativities, with a round object made of interlocking plates of open-worked metal.

"Hullo," said Linley without looking up.

"Ale?" asked Rose.

Tomas poured himself a mug. The twins politely refused; neither of them cared for it.

"Owein will stay with us, of course. But where will he be working?" asked Linley.

Tomas glanced at the twins. "We've not yet decided. Likely a place where he can lie hidden." He tapped the round metal object near Linley's elbow. "I wanted to ask about that. About when more than where, actually. Could you find some times that would suit?"

Linley pursed his lips and let out a long whistling breath. "Possibly." He looked at Tomas for the first time since they'd come indoors from watching the stars. "It would help if I knew a bit more of what you're about."

"It would help if we knew more too," said Tomas, with a smile that didn't reach his eyes. For a long moment he was silent. "Some of it I can tell you. I know where Elfland and Midgard are," he began. "And how to reach them. For full-blooded Elves, lately that takes more and more...resistance to iron, and to exorcisms. For halfbreeds it's easier. We can use our greater tolerance of iron to—" He broke off, glanced at Rose. "May we show you? That might be simpler."

"Show us what?" asked Rose.

"Nothing drastic." Tomas turned to Fraine; they'd discussed this beforehand. "Several objects in the loft contain iron. Would you fetch us a small one, please?"

Fraine wrinkled her nose, huffed the air. Overhead, five ells to her right, she caught the first whiff of something sour. Iron, though not much of it. She opened her mouth to deepen her sense of smell, suppressed a grimace at the way the stench made her nose and throat sting, and sent out a preliminary tendril of energy. The thing was the size of a small basket or a large bowl.

She performed what, for lack of a better term, she and Owein thought of as the reverse of the technique that Tomas had shown them with his iron knife. Reversing it was more difficult, because it took more concentration to maintain control and pull the object to her rather than push or shatter it. Her target wasn't entirely made of iron, but when the familiar snapping sensation at the base of her skull told her that the thing was moving, her nose prickled again and she stifled the urge to sneeze.

Whatever it was soared into the air. It wasn't heavy. She pulled on it slowly and cautiously, letting it clear the loft railing and soar down towards her as smoothly as possible. It was an old wooden bucket, bound with rusted iron rings popping loose from their rivets.

Tomas caught her eye, then waited for her nod before he plucked the bucket from its trajectory and passed it to Linley. The Saxon accepted it as if it might leap from his hands at any second.

"A mending job for the cooper?" Tomas asked with a smile.

Fraine rubbed her itching nose. Rose murmured a white-lipped agreement, but Linley's face was alight, and there was reverence in the way he set the bucket on the table.

"To build the bridge, then," said Tomas, "Fraine will work from Elfland, and to find Midgard she'll use its iron, the way she found the bucket just now. They might fix lines of energy—" He considered his round-eyed friends, changed his mind. "Owein will know where to find Elfland, because he'll know where to find his twin, and she'll be there."

Owein gave her hand a squeeze beneath the table.

"But we're not sure *when* he should work. That's not a problem for Fraine." He glanced at the smokehole in the roof. "The stars have something to do with mortal time, is my guess. Elfland hasn't any, and time is different there. Although Elfland's drifted so far from you even that's changing now.

He poured himself a mug of water. "On my last voyage here, I arrived in Birka eight days after Owein and Fraine were born." At the same instant, both twins gave him a smile. "At that point I could have returned to Elfland, then gone back to Midgard and arrived at any time I chose. I thought I'd learned how not to lose time on the journey." Frowning, he propped his chin in his hands, and the lamplight etched flickering shadows on the strong bones of his face. "This time I tried to arrive at Limecliff as soon as possible after Moira and I had gone." He looked gravely at his Saxon friends. "I hoped it might be only few weeks later, but it was six years instead."

Linley was fascinated. "Do you know why?"

"Not with any certainty. More exorcisms, perhaps. And other hindrances." A glance at the twins. "And something else: we three came to start work on the bridge, with all our Fates directly involved. I'd dare not guess how many others indirectly." He centered the water jug on the table, considered its position and moved it a hair. His face was pensive. "I was guiding the passage, but nearly all of my magic is learned, and guiding isn't controlling. And I'm traveling with people whose gifts are more innate and spontaneous, and still growing." A sudden smile. "Maybe we arrived not only *where* we most needed to, but also *when*." He glanced at his son. "Still, none of us wants Owein to spend six more years with you, so when he'll do the work is important."

"I see." Linley picked up the round metal plates that lay next to the maps. "That's where the astrolabe comes in."

"I've an idea," Rose began quietly. "It's said there are nights when the gates between the worlds are more likely to open. Those nights were celebrated once, and still are in some places. Moira came to us on one of them. All Soul's Night; that's Samhain."

Tomas was nodding. "I first met her on May Eve."

Fraine wanted to ask him more than one question about that meeting and, from Owein's swift enigmatic glance, so did he. But not now.

"May Eve is another such night, Tomas. It's Beltane," said Rose. "There are several others. Lammas, for one."

"And Imbolc," said Linley. "Candlemas, Simon would call it." He twirled a plate on the astrolabe. "Those four festivals fall at the middle of the fixed signs; I could pinpoint them for you."

The germ of an idea took root in Fraine's mind: something about the mortal feast days. She folded her arms and concentrated, waiting for the rest to come clear to her.

But just then Tomas frowned and said, "Half a moment." His head was tilted, his expression alert. "Matilda's coming." He turned to Fraine. "Into the loft with us both."

Fraine scrambled to her feet and across the room. Perhaps Nissyen had told him about Matilda.

"Is she likely to go there for anything?" Tomas was asking from halfway up the ladder. Rose shook her head.

"Why don't the two of you just—?" Linley began, but Fraine and Tomas were already in the loft.

Following Tomas's example, Fraine made a dive for the row of storage chests that lined the back wall, away from the ladder and the field of vision of those below. Flat on her belly, she looked at her father. His grin was so much like Owein's that she had to smile back. Then he pointed at something near his elbow—a good-sized open knothole in the wooden floor—and put his finger to his lips. She eeled towards him as silently as possible. They could both see something of the table below, but they'd have to be careful not to attract attention.

"You've had a long road," Linley was saying in a low, urgent voice. "You walked here from Axbridge so you could see the countryside round about, and you're weary."

"To the bone," Owein agreed, and slumped a bit on the bench; Fraine was proud of him. Then, after only the lightest of taps at the door, a girl holding a tallow lamp stepped across the sill.

Although Matilda was slight, she didn't look frail. She had some color in what Fraine took for a naturally pale complexion, and she walked with her head high and her shoulders back. Her hair was a rich shade of brown that caught what little light there was in the hall below. Fraine thought her eyes might be dark blue. They were definitely not tilted; they were mortal eyes, shaped like those of Tomas and his friends.

Matilda pointed at the scattered maps on the table. "Working half in the dark again!" she said affectionately. "You could go stone-blind, the pair of you." Then her step faltered. "Your pardon; I wasn't aware we had a guest." She sounded formal now, almost hesitant.

The bench scraped as Owein got to his feet. "My lady."

While Linley made introductions, Fraine positioned herself where she could better see Owein's face. His gaze was on Matilda. His eyes were very grey, and for a disoriented instant Fraine thought they appeared more slanted. Perhaps it was merely the odd angle from which she was spying. Yet surely he resembled Moira more than Tomas just now, with the shape and the sweep of his facial bones and the width of his mouth all showing his Elf blood, at least to Fraine's eye. She smelled something musky, not sweet but not unpleasant either.

Matilda, who appeared to be trying not to stare, had probably never seen an Elf and would likely not recognize one. Still, she looked mystified. "We trust you'll make a good report of us to your brother, my lord."

"Call me Owein, please." He smiled; his eyes softened. The musky smell intensified—from Matilda, who produced a tentative smile in return. Fraine caught the scent of apples.

After she moved to give Tomas a view of the scene below, she saw recognition cross his face, followed by a twinge of humor, then uneasiness, quickly suppressed. About her father she smelled something briny then, which was the scent that came whenever someone sorted through a private and convoluted set of feelings.

After Matilda left, Rose tried not to worry about the look in the girl's eyes, as if she were adrift in heavy fog. Clearly there was warmth between her and Owein, and both of them were about the age when a blinding infatuation could strike. But Owein was only six years old. No, he wasn't; he was a halfbreed: they grew differently. Just how old was the boy? Rose would have to judge by appearances; she could think of no other way. She cast Owein a sidelong glance; he had picked up Linley's astrolabe and was turning it over in his hands. She had seen Tomas hold his flute with just that unseeing stare.

She looked away and tried to think, and her gaze fell on Fraine, who was climbing down from the loft after Tomas. If Fraine weren't a halfbreed, Rose would guess her to be a bit younger than Matilda. But the height that Owein had inherited from Tomas could let him claim a year or so more than his twin. At least physically. Girls matured faster, but Matilda might not have learned that yet.

"Why did you hide?" asked Linley when Fraine and Tomas joined them at the table. "Why not just disappear?"

Fraine appeared puzzled for a moment, though not so puzzled as Rose. *Disappear?* The cold that had settled in her stomach began to reach into her limbs. What else had she and Linley agreed to take on with Tomas's halfbreed child? Still, there'd been no question of refusing to harbor Owein even had they not loved Tomas. They'd be landless if it weren't for him.

"I could have, but Fraine couldn't yet," Tomas said vaguely. "At least I think not."

"Aubrey says," began Owein, then intercepted a glance from Tomas and fell silent. Who was Aubrey?

"And it can be tiring." Tomas gave Linley half a smile. "Sometimes it's best to choose the simplest path."

Rose had just opened her mouth when Fraine spoke: "There are eight nights in the mortal year when the gates to Elfland are open."

Precisely what Rose had intended to say. She stared at the girl.

"So there are," said Linley, retrieving the astrolabe from Owein. "How came you to know that?"

Fraine's gesture wasn't quite a shrug. "You mentioned four. When I thought of them, I could sense the rest."

Owein was nodding.

"When are they?" asked Tomas.

"Exactly between the first four," said Owein, and turned to Rose. "You think that's when we should start building. Don't you?"

Rose agreed. After a moment so did Tomas, and there was pride in Linley's smile.

"You've found an answer for us, Rose, and I thank you for it," said Tomas slowly. "I believe that's exactly how we should commence. The eight points will be...the structure? The scaffolding?" His brow was furrowed and his voice so serious that Rose thought the exact phrase must be terribly important.

Owein and Fraine exchanged glances. "The ladder leading elsewhere," said Fraine, her eyes glinting, and pointed at the loft. Was there a hint of drama in the gesture? Owein grinned. A few seconds later Tomas did too, and Rose saw that the twins were having a bit of fun at his expense. For a moment they could have been any pair of adolescents.

But that they were not; they could make buckets fly. Rose remembered Matilda's bemused expression. "The festivals span a year's time. Will building your bridge take a year, then?" she asked casually. She'd intended the question for Tomas, but he glanced at the twins.

"Not if we begin at my end," said Fraine.

"You're right." Owein's face lit up. "If it's not started here, finishing it won't be subject to mortal time."

Fraine gripped his arm. "The portals we saw! Eight of them, linked to Midgard. We're starting the bridge from Elfland but most of it will be—"

"In the 'tweenlands," Owein finished. "The portals will anchor the bridge to the festivals here."

"With enough trance work, we could build the bridge in the 'tweenlands without spending a year at it."

Both twins looked triumphantly at Tomas, who appeared to have followed that exchange perfectly. But every bridge that Rose had ever seen connected two places and had two ends. This one would connect two worlds in eight places, or at eight times? And what were the 'tweenlands? She was completely at sea and, from Linley's nonplussed expression, that made two of them.

Tomas rubbed his knuckles through his beard. "Owein needs to be physically in Midgard to do his share. At least to begin it. But where he'll aim the working is in Elfland, or between the two worlds. Just as Fraine will aim for Midgard while she's physically in Elfland." His glance at Rose and Linley held both apology and a touch of embarrassment. "I'd explain more clearly, but I don't know how. Partly because we've yet to begin something that's not been done before. I suspect we'll all learn more than a little along the way."

Too much for Rose to understand, it was, and perhaps more than she'd wanted to hear. She appreciated Tomas's candor, but it was unnerving how much he himself didn't know.

Tapping the astrolabe, Linley said to Owein, "So you can sense *where* the eight gateways should be, even though our time of year in this world might not be at that *when.* That's how it works, is it?"

Owein and Fraine glanced at each other, then at Tomas, who in turn had been studying them. All three broad-boned faces reminded Rose of someone adding a long series of numbers in his head. The twins began to look frustrated, as if they'd lost their place in the calculations. After a moment Tomas lifted a shoulder and let it fall.

Owein shrugged, and Fraine glanced up from her folded hands. "So we hope. We can't be sure yet."

"Very well," said Linley cheerfully. "Then Tomas and Fraine will go back to Elfland, after which Owein will, ah, ferret out something here and communicate it to Fraine, I should think—"

Both twins were trying not to grin.

"But what if he can't?" Linley looked at Tomas. "Would you return?"

"Or send a messenger, more likely. Provided one could get through."

"The ravens?" asked Linley. "Or Nissyen?"

"Possibly."

Rose knew about the ravens, but who was Nissyen? Then Tomas surprised her by pressing her hand. "It's never my intent to mystify you nor to treat you like a simpleton, Rose. I apologize if you've felt for a moment that I have. I thank you for suggesting we begin at those eight festivals. May I ask you to take your questions to Linley?" He glanced at Fraine. "I've a hunch it might be wise to return soon."

"We'd like a few minutes to look at the stars first, if you please," Owein said respectfully, and took his sister's arm.

Twins, and closer than most, being halfbreeds, thought Rose with a pang of sympathy. And likely never parted before. This was the first time they'd seen the nighttime or the stars in it, though it wouldn't be Owein's last.

"Take as long as you like," said Tomas gently.

CHAPTER NINE: THE MIDSUMMER POINT

Elfland

Tomas and Moira sat amid the circle of withering hawthorns. Around them, silhouetted against a dusky mother-of-pearl sky, stood their silent and motionless Guards. The pooka roamed the clearing with his ears atwitch. Other than the rustle of his feet in the dry leaf mold, the only sound was the querulous muttering of the wind in the Parcae-wood. When Tallah and Aidan arrived, they took a seat within the hawthorns. The air was cool, and the rest of the company had been waiting long enough to feel the chill. Moira drew her heavy dark green cloak more closely about her, and caught Aidan's eye.

The Seer shrugged: he didn't know when Fraine would arrive. She was coming, of course; she'd not have changed her mind. Hands on his hips, his back to Moira, Aubrey stood at the edge of the clearing nearest the palace and stared down the path as if staring alone would summon Fraine. No one would hurry her. She'd appear in her own good time.

Someone touched Moira's elbow—Tomas, handing her a flask of water. She smiled as she met his eyes, and raised the flask to him. Then she poured a libation to the Powers. She had not a few reasons to be thankful. The respect that Tomas was earning from the Elves. Owein's rallying. Fraine's steady presence; the bond between the twins. And perhaps most important, their relative equilibrium in the face of a nightmare-swift coming of age.

The Parcae's prophecy claimed that a halfbreed Mage and his children could link Elfland to Midgard and keep both worlds green. Still, Moira had never imagined it might be done by turning the iron-sick to their advantage, and making that Elfin malady part of their magic and their attunement to the mortal world. She was glad of Rose and Linley's cooperation, and the protection they'd afford Owein in Midgard. Most of all she was grateful that Tomas had both reached Midgard with the twins and arrived home again with Fraine—and that they'd hammered out a plan. Might the Powers grant that it work. The libation completed, Moira drained the flask. When she lowered it, her daughter was walking down the path towards the hawthorn circle.

Fraine's gait was measured, her face still and inward, her gaze fixed directly before her. She wore a loose cream-colored gown beneath a pale cloak. Around her neck, from a leather thong, hung a small shell polished to a flat rectangular disc by the Sea. On the shell was inscribed a Rune. Moira narrowed her eyes. Kenaz, Rune of Insight? No, the left edge of the shell was ragged; it had been deliberately broken, and the Rune wasn't Kenaz at all. It was the right-hand side of Gebo, Rune of Partnership, whose entire form was shaped like an X.

Touching Tomas's hand, she asked in mind-speech, *Does Owein have the other half?* She hated to ask—far better to have no other magic in this clearing than what her daughter was about to conduct. But she had to know, and mind-speech was preferable to even a whisper that might break Fraine's concentration.

Yes. They made the necklaces before leaving Elfland, and exchanged them before Fraine and I returned here.

Moira blinked, once and quickly, with slightly averted eyes. No aura about the necklace. Not a talisman, then: rather, for sentiment. She found herself squeezing Tomas's hand. How much had it cost Fraine to part from the only other being who truly understood her unique birth and the tasks it had brought her? Still, though the pair was physically separated, they were linked in other ways.

Tomas spread his cloak on the ground so that Fraine needn't lie on the leaf mold. For that matter, what had it cost Tomas to leave his land and his mortal friends again?

After Fraine stretched out supine and closed her eyes, Moira covered her with her own cloak. She and Tomas took a position on either side of Fraine's head, with Aidan at her feet, Aubrey at her right and Tallah at her left. In one of Fraine's hands Tomas laid a stone knife, in the other his iron blade. It stank worse than the Parcae did. One grew somewhat used to them, but the iron was a constant assault on the lining of the nostrils. Aubrey wrinkled his nose, while Tallah scowled and Aidan set his jaw.

Breathe in, breathe out. Blink the tears away. Stifle the urge to cough; ignore the churning in the gut. Moira's throat burned. After what seemed a mortal century or two, with that sulphur-like reek growing stronger all the while, Fraine still wasn't in trance. When Moira cast a sidelong glance at Tomas, he shrugged.

"The working needs both of us," Fraine said tonelessly with her eyes still shut. "Owein's not ready yet. He knows that I am." Silence. It was perhaps five or ten minutes before her breathing slowed. "He's alone now. He wasn't before." Her fingers curled about the knife's wooden handle. A few seconds later her entire body went rigid, and she turned her head to one side so sharply that Moira feared she might wrench her neck and come out of trance. "Dagaz!" Fraine cried.

Dagaz, Rune of Midsummer. Would the twins build that point first? Tomas stretched out both hands till he nearly touched Fraine's shoulder. So did Moira, while Aidan did the same at Fraine's feet and the other two Elves at her hands. Moira's skin tingled as a current began to flow among their open palms: protection, support—but no guidance. Wherever Fraine's spirit-self was going, it would go alone.

Moira didn't know how much more time had passed when Fraine's body began to relax, though she was still tranced. She was immobile and as pale as a nocturnal moth's wings, her lips scarcely parted. The sight chilled Moira, and she wanted to smooth the hair from the girl's forehead, to take her hand., but she shouldn't be touched while in trance.

Had there been a way, Moira would have built the bridge herself. Such a tender age, such an unmarked face to bear all that it carried. In Tomas, though neither he nor his fellow mortals would ever see him as she did, she loved that untouched quality, that lack of years and memories all too apt to prey on her own mind. Now and again she felt them press close about her and drag at her steps like so many cold hands.

To Moira's thinking, there should have been an even greater contrast between Tomas and Fraine as there was between Tomas and herself. Compared to Tomas, even with Fraine's runaway growth she should have seemed like new-fallen snow, as fresh and unmarked and full of possibilities about to emerge. In a way she did: she was a font of questions, and encountering so much for the very first time, from the fenodyree to the mortal stars, cabbage to hearthfires, sunsets to her own menses. Yet the girl's Fate was hardly one of endless possibility—it was bound by a narrow and singular path foreseen mortal centuries before she took her first breath.

Moira looked down at her daughter's alabaster skin and blue-veined closed eyelids, at the glacier-pale Northern hair that Tomas had given her. What roads had Fraine's soul walked to bring her to such a Fate now? Perhaps that was why she had that air of gravity. There was little peace inside her, which wasn't surprising given that she ought to have been still a child in both body and mind, but there was more silence than Moira had expected.

Somewhat later Moira's palms began to itch, and the current of energy that pulsed among her and Tomas and the Elves grew stronger. The ravens had joined them. They were perched on Tomas's shoulders and he looked heartened by their presence; his color was better. Still, a line deepened between his eyebrows as he studied Fraine.

She might have been a corpse, waxy, hands limp at her sides and eyelids ringed with greyish mauve. Just as well that Owein wasn't here to fret over her. How had he fared in his part of the working, with no one in mortal Midgard to lend him strength should he have need?

Nothing for it but to wait. Aidan looked stoic, Aubrey worried, Tomas expressionless now. The ravens seemed alert and Tallah half asleep, though Moira knew better. She closed her eyes.

So quietly did Fraine come out of trance that Moira's only warning was the easing of the current of energy that warmed her hands, as if a pair of tight gloves were stripped away.

Fraine blinked up at Tomas. "No need to speak yet," he said.

But Fraine, looking more tired than dazed, and far paler than when she'd entered trance, was already propping herself on her elbows. Aubrey moved quickly to support her. With a sigh she settled back against the pooka, then accepted the water flask from Tomas. Suddenly she smiled at Tallah, who was studying her with a worried pucker about the mouth. Moira waited.

"You were successful," Aidan said at last.

"Yes. The midsummer point's done."

"I'm proud to hear it," said Moira warmly. She was gratified at the flush of pleasure in her daughter's face, and noted a hint of surprise there as well. "Proud of you both."

Relief flooded Tomas's eyes. "So am I." He touched Fraine's hand; she gave him a feeble smile. No need to ask if the work had been difficult; the strain in her face was answer enough. "The techniques I showed you..."

"They performed as you thought they would."

Tomas let out his breath.

"I'll try to describe what I did, shall I? Then I'll sleep."

"You needn't tell us—" began Moira.

"I want to," Fraine insisted. "From trance, I went to the 'tweenlands and found the place where we saw the eight portals, the gates. They were in a big circle at first. Then the circle lit up and turned into a spiral, and then something like a rotating sphere that was spitting out long tongues of energy..." She stopped, frowning, and shook her head. "It doesn't make any sense now; I understood it better then. Each portal connects to Midgard at one of its eight festivals. And to the other seven gates and to the nine worlds, all at once." She glanced from Tomas to Moira. "It's like the way the 'tweenlands touch all nine worlds and lie between them, and no one truly knows if they contain the worlds or if the worlds contain them."

She searched her parent's faces as though she expected them to contradict her. Moira certainly wouldn't; she'd heard far stranger tales than that, and as for Tomas, he merely nodded. After a moment Moira asked, "And then?"

"I looked for the portal closest to me. It was the midsummer one." She pointed at the knife that Tomas had laid in her hand. "I drew from that for the iron-essence to begin with, but all of a sudden I'd no need of it. It came out of my body and into my shield, and I sent it to Owein and he sent it to me and it—" She made a frustrated gesture. "It anchored us to Midgard on midsummer's day there. Now the portal's more of a point, and it looks like a big whirling pinwheel with long rays of energy that stretch all the way between the two worlds. At least sometimes it does. They aren't always lines, the rays, and they're reddish and glittery and I think they're made of bits of moving light—"

"Hush," said Moira, and laid a hand on Fraine's clammy forehead. "Don't tire yourself." She read anxiety in her daughter's expression, along with doubt of her success and eagerness to please, and the sort of bone-deep but nervous exhaustion that would heighten all her emotions. "You've done well; you could not have done better," she said reassuringly. "I'm proud of you. You and Owein have built the first point of the bridge. Rest, now. The working has fatigued you."

A shadow crossed Fraine's face. "Owein's tired too. He's content that we're done for the moment."

"And?" Moira prompted.

Fraine looked away. "He misses me." A heartbeat's pause. "I miss him."

Aubrey ruffled Fraine's hair, then wrapped his long grey-pelted arms more tightly around her.

She gave his knob-knuckled hand a pat. "We should have another go at it soon. It won't get much easier till all eight points are done. It may not even then."

Aubrey frowned; Moira shot Tomas a glance, and he gave her the slightest of nods. They were all agreed: both twins would need rest before their next effort.

"Can you communicate with Owein when you're not working on the bridge?" Tomas asked Fraine.

"In a way. I've always known where he is, and usually something of how he's faring." Her gaze fell. "You were right. I can't work on the bridge alone and neither can he. We each tried, but it takes both of us," she said in a small voice. "We can't work on it from the same world, either. He has to start from there and I from here."

Which answered what would have been Moira's next question.

"How is Owein faring at Limecliff?" Tomas asked.

"Well, I think. He performed this working in that willow grove the two of you like so much." She caught Tomas's expression and added, "Linley knew he was there."

"Is he out of doors all the time, then?" asked Moira, thinking more of the Elementals her tranced son might attract, or the ignorant humans he could encounter, than of any breach in Rose and Linley's hospitality.

"No, he prefers the out of doors. He's seen the entire estate, and he's lodged in the great hall."

CHAPTER TEN: DREAMS AND PREMONITIONS

Midgard

It was a particularly dark dream, and it had already lasted too long.

In that dream, Owein was surrounded by a featureless landscape of overcast yellowish grey. He had no way to tell where the sky met whatever horizon there might have been. He must be standing on something solid, because he wasn't floating and his body seemed to have both weight and a center of gravity. Yet when he looked at his feet, all he saw beneath them was that same greyish-yellow void.

Moreover he was completely alone and, worst of all, he couldn't tell where Fraine was. That was unprecedented. He always knew where she was, the way he knew the location of his limbs and, when he was out of doors, exactly where the Sun had progressed in its patterned arc overhead, and which way the wind blew. He kept reaching out: with his mind, with a tendril of energy from his shield, with his sense of smell. With what finally seemed to be his every pore, but he couldn't sense her anywhere.

They were separated for some reason. He could remember that, although not why. He tried walking in one direction for a time. Nothing changed; he sensed nothing and saw no one. He tried the opposite direction with exactly the same results. When he called out, his voice rolled away from him without even an echo, as if the saffron-grey emptiness had swallowed it whole.

How long had he been here? He didn't want to remain for so much as another second. He broke into a lope, then a run. Nothing happened; he arrived nowhere. Eventually he slowed to a walk, his chest heaving. He hated this. Detested wherever he was, and his inability to sense Fraine. And hated being alone. Although in one way he wasn't, not entirely. Panic was stalking him, not so much from without as within. So far he'd held it at bay but it was gaining strength, and if he weakened, if it succeeded in tightening his chest and rising in his gorge, he'd end by howling and throwing himself to the ground.

"Whenever you wish to converse with me, I'll be pleased to oblige," said a sly insinuating tenor that had spoken to Owein in more than one dream.

Heart thudding, he stood absolutely still. He'd neither heard nor sensed anyone approach. The skin on the back of his neck prickled; his palms grew damp. A subtle change came in the air not far behind him, then just at the back of his head. A presence.

He whirled in his tracks and saw no one, no ginger-haired man, only the same empty wasteland. Breathing hard, Owein turned in a circle. He might not see anyone, but he wasn't alone. "Who goes there?" he asked roughly.

"I'm not at all certain you're ready to talk," said the voice, as if musing to itself. It sounded regretful.

"Talk about what?"

"Death," the voice said fondly. "Yours."

That was when Owein tried to scream, but it was hard to muster enough breath to make any noise at all. Was he suffocating? Perhaps if he backed away from the voice, he could breathe. But now it was difficult to move, as if some invisible energy had wrapped itself around him, though his shield had given no warning. He flapped his arms, trying to break free. He scuffed his boots in the dust. Raising his arms over his head, he inhaled as deeply as he could, then forced out the loudest sound he could produce—a muffled gasp.

Like a choking frog. He sucked in his breath, braced himself, thrashed his arms as if they could pump air into his lungs, and screamed again. Not much louder, nor was the next one. But it seemed easier to breathe, so this time he'd let out a shout good and proper—

"Owein!"

Someone—the redhead?—gripped his shoulder and shook it. He jerked away, making a fist.

"Owein, wake up!" His fisted hand was seized. "You're dreaming."

Then he was breathing hard and blinking up at Linley. How had Linley come to this trackless yellow place? But the wasteland was gone now; it had receded, and Owein was back in that abominably stuffy hall where the Saxons lived.

He lived here now too. After he and Fraine had managed to construct the first point of the bridge, he'd returned from the willow grove so tired he could scarcely see, gone to sleep and dreamed of that ginger-haired man again. But the redhead wasn't kneeling by Owein's sleeping bench with his hair mussed and the skin about his eyes creased with sleep and the worry slowly ebbing from his face. Linley was. Linley, letting go of him now, sinking back on his haunches.

Owein sat bolt upright, then started to cough. Smoke, always smoke in Midgard, from the hearthfire and now from the tallow lamp that Linley must have lit, in its bracket on a post near Owein's head. Rose and Matilda, having emerged from their respective bed-closets and provided themselves with a precious candle each, were standing behind Linley.

What were they all thinking? Fighting embarrassment, Owein glanced past Linley at the women. He'd never seen Rose without her kerchief; he'd no idea her hair was so thick and heavy. In an oversized gown with fine embroidery at neck and sleeve, Matilda looked like a child, her acorn-colored hair falling all about her face and her eyes soft with concern, then with a sudden shyness that turned their indigo irises nearly black in the flickering light. Still, the smile she returned to Owein was spontaneous and unguarded and so warm that his breath wanted to stop in his throat.

"Slaying dragons?" asked Linley easily. He smelled like apples: that was concern. But Owein caught a whiff of honey, too: that was politeness. Linley would ask no prying questions, and no more fuss would be made of Owein's dream than Owein wanted made.

Talking about it was the last thing he cared to do. He smiled into Linley's measuring brown eyes and said, "The third dragon's always the worst."

Rose extinguished the tallow lamp. "I hope they'll not trouble you further." She wore much the same expression as Linley: carefully casual.

"Simon could mix you a sleeping draught," ventured Matilda.

"No, thank you," said Owein, a bit too quickly, perhaps. He liked Simon, his gentleness and perceptive silences. But the priest's bitter scent was so suffused with pain, his own and that of others, that Owein didn't care to be around him just then.

"My grandmother always said nightmares are worse when you go to sleep cold or hungry," put in Linley, a gleam in his eyes. "We might do better to consult Hroswitha than Simon."

Hroswitha invariably cooked more food than anyone at Limecliff could eat, though with Owein it was more a question of poor quality than excess quantity. "I'm never cold," he said, trying to be diplomatic and catching Linley's stifled grin. Suddenly he realized that he'd gone to bed nude and was sitting up bare-chested, the blanket haphazardly pooled about his hipbones, to converse with people whom Tomas had told him were more prudish than Elves. More susceptible to chills, too: Rose had thrown a woolen cloak over her nightdress. In spite of himself Owein glanced at Matilda, who didn't meet his eyes and who might even have turned faintly pink, though he couldn't be certain for the dark and the smoke. Then he intercepted another grin from Linley and took his cue from it: best to make light of the situation. "And Hroswitha never starves us," he added, yawning. "Do you know, I believe I could drop off again."

But he was lying. After the Saxons left him to his sleeping bench, he lay with his eyes open till dawn, straining not to hear the ginger-haired man's voice a second time.

Elfland

Tomas.

Farther away than he'd been.

Eyes closed, Moira reached out a hand that met nothing. After a moment she swept her fingers in an arc across the sheets. Tomas wasn't in bed, though he was somewhere in the room. She sat up and rubbed her eyes.

They'd gone to sleep tired, both of them, though not so weary as Fraine had seemed. Tired and vaguely troubled, at least on Moira's part, though she couldn't say why. The work was going well, according to Fraine, and that it should tire her was understandable.

Moira's eyes had adjusted to the low light. She could see Tomas's profile by the window now, the crooked nose, the tousled hair, the height and the ranginess of him and all the fatigue in the set of his shoulders. He was leaning against the sill as if he were gazing out through the shutters, which were nearly closed. Perhaps he harbored a mortal notion that opening them might disturb her, though the perpetual Elfin twilight was hardly bright enough to do that.

"You're not easy in your mind either," she said after she'd watched him for several moments.

"No," he said, unsurprised at hearing her voice. He opened the shutters and the window before he turned, but she had already climbed out of bed to join him.

She leaned her elbows on the stone sill and gazed down below, taking the air. The Guard looked up at the two of them questioningly, accepted their signal that all was well, then moved as far across the courtyard as possible. To afford them some privacy, Moira supposed. A fluid stride and a padded shape to the fellow's bare feet told her it was one of the newcomers, Jared's distant relatives from the Inner Reaches. He was as silent as the palace walls, as silent as the half-light in the courtyard. Only the shattered rocks spoke of the changes that Moira had brought to Elfland along with Tomas. She glanced at him.

"It's Loki," he said. "He's brewing something, but I can See nothing of it. Nor can Aidan."

She nodded: always, it was that way with the Sight, if Seers were too close to whatever they were scrying.

"Nissyen can't tell either, and Aud's too far away to ask." Tomas put an arm around Moira and she leaned against him. He felt so foreign. She savored it: a different musculature, more fragile and less flexible than hers, and slower reflexes. Not so strong as an Elf, though unusually so as mortals went; perhaps his gentleness had developed to balance it. A different temperature, too: his skin was always cooler than hers.

"There's danger in whatever he's plotting, but I can't tell for whom." His arm tightened about her shoulders. "I don't think it's for you, but how can I be sure that's not because I don't want it to be?"

"I understand," she said softly.

Silence. He put his lips to her hair. "It's for someone dear to us," he said at last.

She knew that too. She had a feeling it wasn't for Fraine, though she was less certain of Owein. What worried her most was that the danger might be for Tomas—but how did she know that was because she didn't want it to be?

He closed the shutters and started to kiss her.

CHAPTER ELEVEN: DEATH BY THE CARTLOAD

Midgard

Holding a broom, Rose opened the great hall's door to find her mother Susannah poised to knock a second time. She waggled a finger at Susannah's upraised hand, expecting an answering smile and a joke, but her mother's face was serious. On her cloak was a smear of blood.

Rose drew her indoors. "What's amiss?"

"Naught with me. Two more cartloads of wounded from Rochester just pulled in, with five men who died on the road. Simon sent me to tell you."

"I'll fetch Matilda," said Rose, putting on her heaviest cape. It was bitterly cold, unseasonably so for late spring. She drew the hood over her face and started for the mews.

Susannah laid a hand on her arm. "There are four women dead too, and more who'll not last much longer if our Lady is merciful. The slavers' leavings. Is it well-advised for Matilda to see—"

"She spent her childhood at court and she's a bastard," said Rose. "Her mother might pretend that Matilda's a sheltered flower, but I'd wager she's seen more than I had at her age." She squeezed her mother's arm. "More's the pity."

Matilda and Owein, who was carrying a cadge with a leather hinge that needed restitching, emerged from the mews. Owein was smiling down at Matilda, his height and pale Northern coloring and preoccupied charm all so like Tomas's that it was little wonder how easily they could pass for brothers. Yet as Rose drew nearer, she was struck by how much the poise and suppleness of Owein's carriage brought Moira to mind.

Susannah looked speculatively at him and then at Matilda, who was intent upon Owein, smiling up at him with her eyes aglow and her lips parted like petals and her face tinted with a deep uncertain color that, Rose suspected, had nothing to do with the unseasonable chill in the air. She hadn't noticed the older women approaching. Susannah glanced at Rose, who gave her a non-committal shrug: she was doing her best not to worry. She and Linley tried to let Limecliff's tenants and neighbors see Owein only from a distance whenever possible, for at close range he could stop a body in its tracks.

There was no keeping Matilda out of close range, however, for Owein was lodged in the great hall. Day after day Matilda got the full force of those slanting eyes, grey and dark and moody, with their thick pale lashes and unpredictable changes of expression. Owein's features, exotic and individual and wild as those of a fox, held equal measures of delicacy and intensity. Rose had never seen a man's mouth like his. It was as full as a woman's mouth—as full as Moira's, though unmistakably masculine. Rose could have sworn the boy had gained an inch in height since his arrival. To her mind, Owein couldn't have looked any less human if he'd had twelve fingers, twelve toes and wings, but then she knew the boy for a halfbreed.

Perhaps Susannah had guessed the truth. A relief and a wonder it was that she'd asked no questions about Owein. Indeed, she'd made no comments at all, beyond a hushed exclamation about his appearance the first time they'd met, though not before he was well out of earshot. "Hello, 'Tilda," she said briskly. "Good day to you, Owein."

Matilda started forward with an exclamation when she saw the blood on Susannah's cloak. "You've taken hurt!"

"Not I. More wounded have arrived."

"Has Simon need of us—"

"In the granary," said Rose. Susannah was already hurrying in that direction.

Owein's face closed. He fell into step beside Rose and Matilda. "More wounded from Rochester?"

"Yes. Soldiers and former slaves. Freed captives."

"Are they dying?"

His voice was so low that Rose glanced at him. There'd never been much color in his fine-pored skin, and now there was almost none. "Some of them already have," she said, trying to sound gentle. "And more of them will, in spite of all we'll do to prevent it." She saw concern in Matilda's eyes, and the way she was bracing herself for the hours ahead of her. Doubtless they all were, except Owein. He had no obligation to assist them: he was a guest, and their proprietor's brother.

Tomas would have helped tend the wounded. Tomas would know they'd want every pair of hands, and he wasn't squeamish. But perhaps Owein didn't care for the sight of blood.

Perhaps he'd never seen any. That would soon change. They hadn't even entered the granary, and groans could already be heard. Owein's eyes were wide and stark; his nostrils flared, and his skin looked tightly drawn over the prominent bones of his face. Susannah disappeared into the building, rolling up her sleeves.

Before the granary's doors stood two mud-spattered carts; from one of them the last pallet was being lifted. The wounded man who lay close-wrapped within was unconscious, black-haired but paler than Owein from loss of blood, with one battered arm strapped to his chest. The other cart was covered with a lashed-down tarp that did little to block the smell that wafted from it, and its horses were stamping their shaggy feet and rolling their eyes.

Looking relieved, the cartman hailed Rose with a travel-stained hand. Somewhat past middle years, he had the dark mournful face of a hound, with a puckered scar above one eye. She didn't know him, though she knew many of the thegnhood who came from these parts.

"Where shall I take the dead, my lady?" he asked. "We've not found all their names, but a record's been made of their goods."

Owein went rigid beside Rose.

"You've burnt no one?" she asked. "Some died on the way?"

The cartman nodded. "We'd no time. We'd the living to bring to their kin." He glanced at the granary, then back at Rose, and his eyes widened as his gaze passed over Owein. "And to the healers." His expression said he doubted how much use they could be.

He'd not met Susannah or Simon, then. Rose took a breath. "There's a place just above one of our fallow fields." She pointed to the northwest: higher ground, less likely to be damp. "Pass three sheep pastures and you'll see it. Climb the slope with two copper beeches on the ridge. There you'll find a stone cistern that's not been used in a century; it can hold the bodies until their kin claim them. We'll bury the others on the ridge." She found she'd been pleating her cloak in her fingers, released the folds of fabric. "I'll have men sent to help you. Have you eaten?"

"I've not been able to," the carter said, grimacing, then added more politely, "But I thank you."

"Go to the kitchen when you're ready. Tell them Rose sent you; you'll be served a hot meal."

"That's kind of you, my lady." He picked up the reins. "Where shall I take their belongings?"

"To the great hall. If it's locked, come and find me; I'll see that someone lets you in." She and Linley would go over the goods of the dead, restore to their families whatever objects they recognized and keep those they did not, in the hopes that other relatives might thereby succeed in identifying someone they'd lost.

The carter clucked to the horse. Rose glanced at Matilda, who was pale but composed. So was Owein, though he was staring at the retreating cart so fixedly that Rose couldn't catch his eye. "Owein?" she began.

Blanching, he turned to her and remained silent. His eyes were dark and unseeing.

"We'll likely be here for some time. Where will you be, should we need to find you?" Rose asked carefully.

He blinked down at her. "Why, here," he said with no enthusiasm and very softly. "Helping you." Then he bit his lip, as if he thought he might have presumed too much. "That is, if I could be of assistance."

Rose hugged him. By the Powers, he deserved it: he was more than reluctant; he was in some sort of pain yet staying regardless. She felt both the surprise and the tension in his tall lean frame, but he gingerly put an arm about her and patted her on the back. When she stepped away from him, he looked pleased, and Matilda gave her a grateful little smile.

"You could indeed," said Rose, and opened the granary doors. "We've no time to waste."

Invisible and well-shielded, on the off chance that the halfbreed child had more Sight than Loki had first judged, Loki sat on a grindstone outside a granary that now served as a makeshift infirmary on Tomas the Rhymer's estate. As he watched the halfbreed and the women step inside, he was far from pleased.

He'd got Caraid sold to the Danes who held Rochester, after satisfying himself that this particular lot didn't enjoy inflicting the sort of pain that could damage the Seer beyond recognition. There'd been no need to make her fall ill: harsh treatment and her own frailty would accomplish that on their own.

Nor, fortunately, had there been any need to interfere with the Danes' skirmish with Alfred. Informed by the salamanders, Loki had guessed well about the Saxon King's strength, which ships he'd likely take and what course he'd set for home. He'd guessed equally well about which Danes would then attack Alfred's fleet, reclaim their captured cargo and mockingly return their sick and dying slaves to him.

But Loki had forgotten how *slow* mortals were, and he still hadn't devised a way to lure Tomas here to discover what had befallen Caraid. The bridge was going up entirely too fast, and something had to stop it. Something had to get Tomas sufficiently upset that his status with the Elves and his guidance of the twins were both affected. Something had to rattle Owein, too. So far, all Loki's dream-appearances and talk of death hadn't disrupted Owein's work on the bridge.

If Loki couldn't incite Tomas to come to Wessex, then perhaps if he observed Owein long enough, he could find a way to weaken the boy instead. Or better yet, to afflict both father and son. Still invisible, Loki padded into the granary.

The smell was awful but no worse than he'd expected, and the groans rather less. A double row of bodies was laid out, mostly on their backs. Among them moved a few stooped figures. Loki could see as well in the dark as in full daylight, and the first person he recognized was the Nazarene priest, Simon, whom he'd encountered before. In Daniel's cave, when Simon had tended two wounded men who'd sought refuge there.

The priest's face was stark and white and tense, and he was sweating despite the cold. Sleeves rolled above his elbows, he moved from pallet to pallet, clasping the hands of the wounded, applying hot wet rags where bloodsoaked clothing had adhered to flesh, and speaking quietly to a man who followed him and made notes. About the priest's entire body glowed a yellow-white sphere of light, brightest at his hands, from which it streamed into the wounded as he touched them. The hotter the light that flowed from Simon's palms, the more dimly shone the aura about his heart.

The priest must be mad to tire himself in that fashion, although such power couldn't possibly be his alone. Squinting, Loki detected a current rising into Simon's feet from the earthen floor of the granary. But from the slowness of that current, and the way the priest didn't tap into it when the aura lessened about his heart, he must be ignorant of its presence.

In addition to the man at Simon's heels, his helpers included a few soldiers who limped as they chopped wood, built a fire, hung kettles to hang over the flames and began to cut bandages. Two of the women whom Loki had trailed here were grinding herbs and examining the wounded themselves, while the third one held a lamp for them. A whey-faced boy left in search of extra blankets, an assortment of herbs and more errand-runners.

As for Owein, he had the brittle look of someone whose every muscle was strained, as if the simple act of remaining in the granary lay nearly beyond his strength. He was white-lipped, his eyes enormous and shifting in the murky room, his nostrils flared like a horse who smells wolves. He didn't sense Loki, who was well-shielded. Still, from the way he was staring at Simon's hands, then at the wounded and back again, he certainly sensed more about the priest than the others did.

Rose sent Owein to bring in another load of wood, had him move several injured men on their pallets, then asked him to build a fire outdoors for heating stones to drop in the kettles or ease painful limbs. Moving as if he expected to be struck at any second, coughing intermittently, Owein obeyed. His mute stare kept straying to the youngest woman present: Matilda, they called her. She was watching him too. Her face was somber, but she didn't appear nearly so shaken by her surroundings as Owein did. When he left to build the fire, she made as if to follow him, but Rose gave her another assignment.

Loki slipped outdoors after Owein. He was standing in the middle of the trampled clearing in front of the granary, his face turned towards an overcast sky that was low and grey and quilted, like a filthy blanket, and breathing in great gulps of air. After a moment he eyed the firewood piled just outside the granary door, then surveyed the uneven ground.

"Stones," he said to himself, sounding tired. "Flint. And a shovel."

One of the soldiers limped outside just then and handed him one. "Mind you don't misplace it," the Saxon said, grim-faced. "The grave-diggers need them."

Without a word, Owein accepted the tool, and his knuckles were white against its handle.

The soldier took a closer look at him. At first the man appeared to be trying not to stare, but then his expression changed. "Lost someone, have you?" he asked more kindly.

"I—" Owein swallowed, rubbed the end of his nose. A decision moved across his face. Very quietly, he said, "I don't know."

"Ah," said the soldier. "Not knowing is the worst." His face grew pensive. "Let's hope you find out soon enough." He turned back to the granary. "Give us a shout if you need anything."

When the door shut behind him, Owein threw the shovel to the ground. His eyes closed; his nostrils flared. For a long moment he was silent and motionless. Then he walked over to the lowest-lying part of the clearing, frowned at a shallow depression in the earth, and retrieved the shovel. After overturning one great clod of dirt, he paused. Concentration narrowed his eyes. His jaw hardened; he glanced over his shoulder at the granary. After perhaps five seconds, he muttered something in such a low voice that Loki couldn't make out the words, though they sounded like a command.

Power flickered like heat lightning in the air about the boy and was gone.

Loki blinked at the pit that now lay where the depression in the ground had been. It wasn't a particularly wide pit, but it was over half an ell deep, more than adequate for heating stones. There'd been no Elementals about when Owein performed the working less than a moment ago, though a few small curious sylphs, drawn by the magic, were already floating into the clearing and pointing at the pit. Owein ignored them.

The boy had moved the earth on his own. More than tolerably well done: no wonder he was making such progress with the bridge. Now he was casting about for stones, gathering up several of different sizes and dropping them in the pit. With his hands, not by magic. The Saxons had built the granary on stony ground not fit to be planted, so rocks were plentiful. A few sylphs began to lose interest and skitter away. Next he carried wood and kindling from the pile by the door to the center of the pit. When he turned towards the granary, Loki decided that he probably intended to go inside for a brand of burning wood, or for flint and tinder.

Why not help the lad out a bit? Loki was a fire being, after all. And still perfectly shielded. Smiling, he pointed, felt the gratifying lick of heat as it left his index finger, and watched all the wood in the pit begin to blaze.

Whirling as fast as if his clothes had caught fire instead, Owein stared in Loki's direction. Loki put out his invisible tongue at him. Owein narrowed his eyes, using his Sight, but obviously detected nothing beyond the sylphs, who'd fallen all over one another to investigate this new use of power and were shouting suggestions at him. He paid no more attention to them than before and sniffed the air instead, opening his mouth as a cat would. Interesting: he must use his sense of smell much as he did his Sight. Loki grinned. He'd heard of all kinds of magical gifts, but second *scent*? Halfbreeds could be most entertaining.

But Owein could neither see nor smell Loki. Wary as a startled hare, quivering slightly, he was making a slow survey of the entire clearing. To judge only from his tension and the white that showed about his irises, he was shocked and frightened in equal measures, but Loki noticed those clenched fists: Owein was angry. He had some of his mother's fight in him—the dreams hadn't worn him down nearly enough. Should Loki merely let him wonder who'd started the fire, or should he speak? Something about flesh being flammable as well?

Then the granary door opened and the brown-haired Saxon girl appeared. "Owein?" she said, stopping short. "What's amiss?"

He turned a strained and colorless face to her. "Nothing." When his attempt at a smile failed, he pointed at the firepit. "Will that serve?"

"It's perfect. And fast work. The wood must have been very dry."

"So it was," said Owein. A new worry came into his eyes. Moistening his lips, he glanced surreptitiously about the clearing, no doubt still hunting for the source of the fire. Loki waved at him, gleefully and invisibly. Two sylphs were leaping up and down on the grindstone and shrieking at Owein, vying for his attention, while three more skirted the edge of the pit and discussed the flames.

Matilda obviously had not the slightest idea that the Elementals were present: she must have no Sight at all. She was searching Owein's face. "All's well, then?"

At the same instant, Owein moved towards the granary and said, "Aren't we needed within?" When she looked taken aback, he added quickly, "Do they need stones yet? Have they any fire tongs? I heard Rose ask for some."

"No. I mean yes," Matilda said, flustered. "We have great need of stones. Whether we have tongs yet I don't know. When Hrothgar returns, we can send him after some."

Owein cast an edgy glance over his shoulder. Loki was enjoying this: the boy was rattled, and wanted to take Matilda away from whatever had started the blaze. "We could fetch some tongs now. Only show me where they are, and I'll carry them."

A crease appeared between Matilda's brows. "We're both needed here," she began. Then Owein put a hand on her shoulder, as if to turn her towards the path that led away from the granary. Color came into her face at the touch. She took a hesitant breath. So did Owein. He moved a step closer, then slowly lifted his hand from her shoulder to her warm maple hair.

Footsteps echoed down the path before the Saxon boy Hrothgar came into view, panting and harried, clutching a load of blankets and an overflowing sack of herbs. "Matthew and Dagobert are bringing more," he called out. "Another cartload of wounded's to arrive, and I'm to ask Master Linley where to put them."

Owein's hand fell away from Matilda's hair, but not before Hrothgar's pallid face sharpened with interest at the sight of the couple—and Loki had an idea. It would begin with giving Plirok the salamander a few choice tidings for Daniel, but it wouldn't end there.

CHAPTER THIRTEEN: FRAINE'S DREAM

Elfland

Fraine was content with their progress on the bridge: three more points constructed in their entirety—but the work was extraordinarily tiring. Owein had been upset when they began their last session. Wounded and dying Saxons were being brought to Limecliff, he'd told her, and that he was helping tend them. And that Simon was a healer, and most of the Saxons very kind. And that he wasn't up to talking about it any more just then. Couldn't they just have done with it, so he could sleep? The wounded and his chores among them would all still be there on the morrow.

Fraine could tell how distressed he'd been at the sight of the dying, and that he wasn't telling her everything, neither of himself nor of Matilda, and not a word about some fear that had nothing to do with the wounded. But he sounded weary to the point of incoherence, and though Fraine wasn't sure he should be working on the bridge at all, she'd agreed. After they had finished, she'd wished him easeful sleep and closed her own eyes.

Now she was dreaming. She knew that, oddly enough, but not why she was uneasy. The golden-haired woman was always a welcome visitor to Fraine's sleep. Her skin was as radiant as ever, and the fine cloth of her robes and her exquisite golden necklace as shining and perfect as before. Still, this dream was different.

For one thing, the woman wasn't alone. She was accompanied by two sleek grey cats, larger and more muscular than any Fraine had ever seen, though they weren't lynxes or anything like. They were cats, and they kept pace with the woman as she approached, then stood at her either side when she came to a halt and stood at gaze, studying Fraine. This she did for a very long time, and her wordless scrutiny was somber and measuring.

Fraine didn't feel frightened or castigated, yet she did feel judged. And respectful. The woman was powerful, though after a different fashion than Moira. When Moira wasn't working magic, one could still sense her ability to use it, and her accompanying confidence and restraint. Those characteristics were particularly conspicuous when one first met her, like her black hair and her pallor. Fraine's awareness of them hadn't faded; rather, it had blended into her other perceptions of her mother. Age. Tenderness. Dignity, tension, impatience, sudden flashes of humor.

The power of the golden-haired woman in Fraine's dream was inescapable, what one first noticed about her, and one never lost sight of it. Power filled the pulse at her throat, the shape of her hands, the layers of awareness in her eyes. It hovered in the folds of her dress and moved with the cats at her side. She wore no shield at all. She didn't *have* power; she *was* power.

Yet as Fraine met her eyes, humbly, knowing that she was being judged by a being whose essence was far beyond hers, something about her dream visitor seemed increasingly odd. Not dangerous. Not even surprising, but something was different, not as Fraine had expected it to be, nor as she had first thought it was.

She waited. It was not for her to speak first, and besides, it afforded her more time to sort through her impressions. But what ailed her; what had she been thinking? She'd neglected one avenue of perception. She inhaled as deeply as she could without being obvious. And that was when she identified part of the anomaly. The woman had no scent.

Fraine tried not to show her surprise. All living beings had their own distinctive odor, at least to her senses, an odor that changed as their thoughts and feelings changed. This woman was real, not merely a dream figure; Fraine could not have been more certain of that. Both Tomas and Moira had taught her that sometimes the Sight came in dreams, and that sometimes one received messages in them. Yet this golden-skinned and unshielded being had no scent at all.

Or none that Fraine could detect. Was she alive, then?

"*Less so than before, perhaps*," said the woman in a vast and confident voice, looking straight into Fraine's eyes.

Fraine suppressed a start, not so much from having her thoughts read as from identifying another piece of the puzzle: as formidable as this woman was, she had recently lost power. A *great deal* of power.

Fraine swallowed. Her head was trying to spin. She chewed her lip, striving for clarity. This being bore her no ill-will. Of that much, at least, she was positive.

"*That is true,*" said the woman. "*Another truth is that you do well to remain strong.*"

Strong. Fraine's breath was growing short. In her weakened condition, this woman was so powerful that in her former state she must have been a—

"*So I was. And I alone of all the gods yet live,*" said the woman gently. "*We have spoken enough for the moment. Sleep.*" She pointed one shining finger at Fraine's forehead, and the dream ended there.

CHAPTER FOURTEEN: OWEIN AND THE BISHOP

Midgard

Rose found Linley on the ridge with the gravediggers. How like him, she thought, to include among all the duties laid upon him as Limecliff's reeve the hardest and most unpalatable tasks that followed Alfred's skirmish at Rochester—assisting the healers and burying the dead.

To a man, Linley's companions were somber and intent, straining to force their way through earth that, she gathered from their talk, was more frozen than they'd first judged. They passed about a flask of something hot, wiped their grimy brows, and took turns away from the shovels to stamp their feet and flex their fingers. Just now they were digging the common grave intended for the unknown dead, and would leave the linen-wrapped corpses in the former cistern until that job was completed. If someone hit a particularly stubborn patch of ground, every last one of his fellows came and helped him. Linley's example, that. Most of these men had known him from childhood and all of them liked him, lately met or no.

No one had noticed Rose, so she watched the digging for a while, dividing her attention between Linley's round and serious face with its shock of dark soft hair that would never stay out of his eyes, and the linear pattern that the copper beeches made against a uniformly leaden sky. The air was damp as well as cold, and very still; she was glad of her woolen cloak. They could yet have snow even this late in the spring, and she offered the Powers a silent prayer for fair weather. A bird sailed by overhead, and for an instant Rose's heart lifted—but no, it was a single bird, a raven or a crow, not a flock returning from wherever they wintered. Some scavenging bird on the prowl. She eyed the old cistern. Yes, it was securely covered.

Linley's turn for a rest had come: he straightened up, hands at the small of his back, stretched—and saw her. The man next to him, Alan, an old friend, took Linley's shovel and waved at Rose. She waved back as Linley came towards her.

He gave her a tired smile. "I'm too filthy to hug. In a muck sweat." She kissed him regardless. "How are you faring?" he asked. "All's well, I trust?"

She nodded. "It's a hard job you have here."

A shrug. "It's got easier, and we'll soon be done." He eyed her for a few seconds, then lowered his voice. "What is it? More wounded?"

"One cartload. Alfred brought them."

Linley let out his breath. "I'll be down directly. How is he?"

"Hearty enough, though not a little tired from the road. Washing up and catching his breath just now; I insisted as best I could." She ignored the amusement in Linley's eyes. "He wants to help identify the bodies, so he's coming here first."

"Half a moment," said Linley. He hurried back to the gravediggers and conferred with them briefly. Then he and Rose started down the ridge together. "After Alfred's done here, he'll go find Matilda and Simon, I should think?"

Rose nodded. "When he does, he'll meet Owein."

"Owein," muttered Linley. He glanced at the sky as if for assistance. "I'd nearly forgot him. How is he?"

"Not well, I should say."

Linley was trying not to frown.

"He was frightened." Rose tucked her hand in his elbow. "I wouldn't know any other word for it. He's terrified of pain and blood and the dying. I thought he'd faint clean away when he saw the first wounded." She squeezed Linley's arm. "Not like Tomas when Moira turned up half dead." Tomas had been angry and troubled, not frightened. "But he's no coward, that Owein, and he rallied. He's been a great help to us, nursing and fetching and carrying and digging a firepit and all." She drew closer to Linley, and he put an arm around her. "Though he's got less color than a snowdrift, and I doubt he's eaten for nigh on two days. He'll disappear for a few hours, then come back as dismal as a suicide's ghost and work just as hard as before." They were silent for a little space as they plodded on through the spring chill. Her shoes were filthy; the overcast sky had grown darker. She wished that she and Linley were anywhere but here.

"And Matilda?" asked Linley.

"I wish I'd an excuse for separating them," she said starkly, then put out a hand to forestall Linley's scowl. "It isn't anything untoward. He's done nothing; I'd swear it." She shook her head. "It's the way they look at each other. It's the tension... Not tension; it's the—"

"The feeling between them," Linley finished for her.

"Yes. And Alfred will see it. How could he not?"

Linley stared into a hazel hedge they were passing. "He'll see how different Owein looks, too." When he glanced at Rose, his pace faltered. "What is it?"

"The Bishop's here with Alfred. So is Daniel."

"Gods," muttered Linley. "Have you warned Owein?"

"As best I could."

Linley was shaking his head. "We must have lost our wits. Alfred will want to know why Tomas has sent him no word."

"But he has," said Rose. "Owein brought a letter from him." She shot Linley a small triumphant glance. "We wrote it in the loft an hour ago, Owein and I."

"Well done!"

"We haven't had it sent to Alfred because we wouldn't have known where to find him," she continued serenely.

"He's been at war and on the road," agreed Linley.

"And the letter wasn't urgent."

No longer smiling, Linley said, "But Alfred's questions for Tomas will be. Let's pray they're only about the Danes."

Rose knew that more than one motive prompted Alfred's visit. He and Simon were much of an age, had grown up together and remained fast friends. Alfred appreciated Simon's loyalty, kindness and discretion. And his healing ability as well, though Alfred rarely mentioned it, for that ability was the way the Sight manifested in Simon. Ever the devout Christian, Alfred preferred to call it a gift of the Spirit, yet everyone knew that Simon had possessed the power long before taking vows, and that it had waxed with the years.

In peacetime the grounds themselves were sufficient motivation for a visit, since they offered prime hunting and hawking with Alfred's boyhood cronies, Simon and Linley. Six years ago, the presence of Tomas himself had also drawn Alfred, to benefit from Tomas's knowledge of Norse ways and his far greater Sight, which Alfred deemed another gift of the Spirit. Of Moira's arrival and the uncanny events that had accompanied it Alfred did not speak, though he sometimes politely inquired if Linley had received any word of Tomas. Occasionally Rose wondered if Alfred's support of Matilda's presence at Limecliff stemmed not only from his genuine affection for the girl and his awareness of the dog's life she'd led at court, but also because she gave him still more occasion to visit—and to hear any news of Tomas as soon as possible.

There weren't nearly so many reasons for Bishop Werferth's presence. Certainly he knew of no misbehavior for which Simon merited reproach. Unknown to Werferth, six years ago Simon had given aid to an Elf—Moira—concealed the appearance of a winged Elf to Limecliff's cook, and failed to verify the attack of a whole flock of winged Elves upon the hermit Daniel. Nor had Simon vouched for Daniel's intimations of witchcraft against Tomas, and the hermit had reacted with such exaggerated vehemence that he only weakened his credibility. Afterwards, Simon had murmured a few words to both Alfred and Werferth about the hermit's affliction by the falling sickness, and how that malady was oftentimes preceded by strange fancies.

Rose had no idea what private opinion the Bishop might hold of Daniel or Tomas, but officially the hermit had lost that round. Werferth would not have come to Limecliff for an ecclesiastical pronouncement against its absent owner. Nor did any monastery stand nearby to prompt the Bishop's visit, though Alfred had plans to found one at Athelney. Daniel was still angling for one of his own, but Rose doubted he would ever get it.

There he was now, trailing after Werferth and Alfred towards the great hall, with his hands folded in the sleeves of his robe and his tonsured head held high. He wasn't sufficiently devout or charismatic to draw enough followers to start a monastery, as had happened time and again among the Irish. He possessed neither the wealth nor the land to build one, which was why he coveted Limecliff's charter. Some church lands were willed to the descendants of the abbot or priest who held them—celibacy was by no means strictly enforced, all the less so during the chaos that had overwhelmed church and state alike from the Norse invaders. But even had Alfred approved, Daniel was in line to inherit no such property.

Before he noticed Rose or Matilda waiting in the doorway, a fine conceit of himself gleamed in his eyes. A few paces behind him, Linley gave Rose a long-suffering look. Daniel had doubtless gathered that ties of the heart as well as of duty bound them to Tomas, and probably concluded that he himself was not welcome at Limecliff. Even without the King and the Bishop to accompany him, his visit would have been politely tolerated, yet from his triumphant expression he regarded it as a moral victory. Rose felt her back stiffen with distaste.

"Good day, my lords," she said as she and Matilda offered their guests two basins of hot water and some towels. "May I ask if you were able to put a name to anyone else on the ridge?"

She studied Werferth as Linley made the introductions. Of medium height, the Bishop was on the thin side, and would have been altogether unremarkable in appearance had he not possessed a long patrician face, rather pale and tight with fatigue just now, and prematurely silver hair. Habitual tension showed in the lines about his mouth, and watchfulness in his grey eyes. Daniel had no doubt spun him all manner of tales about Tomas, and how Rose and Simon had tended Moira during her stay here, but Werferth's expression betrayed neither judgment nor curiosity. It betrayed nothing at all; the man had the tightly schooled face of a diplomat. It fit what Rose had heard of him: that he was cautious, not a man of many words, and a better than average administrator.

"We recognized a few men, my lady," he told her politely. "Not the one I seek."

There was the reason for his visit. "Have you lost a kinsman?" asked Rose.

"I've not heard from a nephew," he said briefly, wiping his hands.

Likely as not that was the truth, since he was scarcely old enough to have a son in the thegnhood, Rose thought cynically, then chided herself. She'd heard no rumors about Werferth's virtue or lack of it. Nor had she wanted to hear any, but that was neither here nor there. She was letting her antipathy for Daniel affect her mood.

The hermit had given her a constipated smile along with his damp towel, then turned to speak to Matilda. The girl was no fool. Rose and Linley had said nothing against Daniel in her presence, but she could read the constraint in their manner, and she wore her most formal expression—until Alfred plucked her basin of water from her hands, gave it to Linley and enveloped her in a hug. She turned her head to one side, away from the surprise in Daniel's face.

"My dear," said the King. "How well you look! More like your father every day."

"I'm happy to see you, Uncle," she said softly. "Won't you come in and be warm?"

"Presently." Alfred released her, then held her gaze for a moment, smiling. "I've never seen so much color in your face. I knew it would do you good to come here." He transferred his smile to the gratified Linley. "I'll thank you and Rose properly later. Our cart should arrive at any moment. Is Simon with the injured?"

"Yes, in one of the granaries," said Linley. "Shall I take you to him?"

"If you please," said the King. "And Tomas's brother Owein, where is he at present?"

Rose didn't like the sudden gleam in Daniel's eye. "Assisting Simon," she told Alfred. "You can make his acquaintance there if you like, and he'll dine with us this evening."

Owein didn't relish helping Simon any more now than he had at first, but he'd realized something that made it more bearable: most of the men and the few women in the granary were at least as afraid of dying as he was. Moreover they had greater reason to fear. The smell of terror was overwhelming. It varied from one sufferer to the next but always held sweat and mustiness, with a sharp oily undernote like scorched almonds, and something as rotten and grainy as ale gone bad. He could smell sorrow, too, which was bitter, so piercing it was nearly corrosive, and could taint every other emotion that accompanied it. To Owein's amazement, not all the wounded smelled of fear, although every last one of them reeked of sorrow. He caught that scent from Simon most of all and, despite the priest's increasing exhaustion, more of the salt-water odor of resolve and self-control than he'd ever sensed from anyone save Moira. Perhaps that was why he made himself stay and assist the priest.

He'd been useful, too. He was stronger than everyone seemed to assume he was, and there was lifting and restraining to do. He helped keep the woodpile replenished and the fires burning, fetched and carried, did whatever he was asked and tried to anticipate what wanted doing next. Yet he soon realized that he could offer another kind of aid.

The first time he'd eased himself onto his knees beside Simon, who was tying splints to a broken leg, and asked for a private word, he wasn't sure if the priest would take him seriously. But Simon left the rest of the knots to Susannah, moved a little aside and raised his eyebrows.

Stooping, Owein mouthed next to the priest's ear, "We should move the dark-haired man who lies next to the west wall. He wants to kill the younger fellow beside him. He thinks that—" Owein hesitated, though Simon was listening with nothing but receptivity and fatigue in his face. The soldier's scorn had been so powerful and his urge to violence so strong that Owein had not only smelled sourness and charred wood, he'd also gotten an image: the younger man had panicked and broken ranks before the Danes' shield-wall. "That the fellow did something wrong, and others died of it."

The dark-haired soldier had such a bad facial injury that he couldn't speak coherently, while the youth had been unconscious since he was brought in, but Simon didn't ask how Owein came by his knowledge. The priest's eyes were tired, measuring, abruptly compassionate, and the nod he gave Owein was that of an equal.

Motioning Owein to follow, he headed for the western wall, where they lifted the dark-haired man's pallet and carried him over to the patients who were slated for transfer to another outbuilding. The soldier gave them a single glare, intent and burning and horrible above that ruined mouth, then grunted and closed his eyes.

It wasn't the only such incident that day. Simon appeared to sense where his charges' bodies hurt, where their bones were broken and, wretchedly, when the stream of energy pouring from his hands would do them no more good. But Owein could tell who was frightened, who needed to ask questions and who was desperate, before losing consciousness, to send word to someone far away. He could tell when a man loved or feared the person next to him, and who should be placed beside whom. Simon accepted all of Owein's murmured comments without question and acted on them immediately. To Owein's relief, the priest repeated nothing to Matilda or his other helpers. More than once he thanked Owein for the information.

Increasingly, with the strongest emotions he also perceived images, not so much visually but with a burst of insight, as if someone else's memory as well as scent had just entered his brain. He would know how this wound was received and whom that man longed to see before his last moment came. Once he knew who had abused a dying woman the most. That revelation was the worst, and not only because it provided no insight which Simon could use to help her. At some point in Owein's short life and insanely fast maturation, he'd guessed what happened between men and women, and Tomas had told him the rest—but that it was ever accompanied by such cruelty left him shaken. He fetched Susannah, for the injured woman was afraid of him and not entirely easy in her mind about Simon, either. Susannah squeezed Owein's hand and said he'd done right to call her; she seemed to know why without being told.

He didn't welcome these perceptions, for they came with a tidal wave of mingled scents that turned his stomach and more than once confused him to the degree that they drove him outside, where he slumped against the granary wall and took great laboring breaths of air until his head cleared. Still, each time he returned, he could sort through the odors and images a bit longer without being overwhelmed, and Simon was relieved to see him again. It didn't show in the priest's face, but the bitter odor about him grew less pungent.

Owein was heartened that Simon was glad of his presence. Though Linley and Simon were both half-Sighted, Simon was the only mortal Owein had met, besides Tomas and Fraine and himself, who actively used any power. Working with Simon made Owein less homesick. The priest must know that Owein was using the Sight, but most likely he didn't know how. For that matter, Owein didn't know how Simon sent forth that rivulet of healing force from his hands, nor whether Simon could see as well as sense it. To Owein's eyes, sometimes the power was so bright as to be all but opaque, though it often dwindled to a shimmer when Simon was approaching exhaustion.

Owein knew nothing about healing, for since neither Tomas nor Moira possessed that gift, they were unable to teach the twins anything about it. But he did know something about pacing himself. On one of the rare occasions when Simon stopped to catch his breath, Owein impulsively beckoned him into the clearing in front of the granary and said, "You might try stepping outside when you need a rest."

The priest regarded him calmly. "Why?"

It wasn't a challenge; it was a request for an explanation. What should Owein say? He might already have revealed too much about himself and his own Sight; Tomas had warned him to be discreet with everyone but Rose and Linley. Yet Simon needed help, and while he was the saddest man Owein had ever met and one of the most conflicted, he was also one of the best-intentioned. On the other hand, how Owein perceived Simon wasn't an easy thing to explain, especially when he had no idea how much the priest knew about his own Sight.

"I think you'd feel stronger if you went out of doors more often," Owein said at last.

Simon considered. He glanced over his shoulder, as if to make sure they were alone, then asked, "As a rule, or at present?"

"Both."

After a moment Simon gave him a nod. "I thank you." He started for the granary, but turned when Owein took his arm.

"And if you touched the ground when you did."

Now Simon looked wary. "Touched the ground? How?"

With your hands or your feet, Owein wanted to say. Preferably both. He cleared his throat.

"And where?" Simon added, looking about the clearing and into the neighboring trees as if he expected someone to appear there.

Owein whirled and saw nothing. His dreams of the ginger-haired man had left him almost as edgy as whoever had lit that fire for him. Simon was eyeing him. "No particular place," said Owein, frustrated. "Only touch the earth. Take off your boots if you can. Climb a tree; I don't know."

"Climb a tree? In my stockinged feet?" Simon's brows were aloft.

What else could Owein say? This talk was going badly; he shouldn't have begun it. But he had, and would take none of it back. Besides, suddenly the priest smelled of new-mown hay, and Owein knew that Simon was on familiar territory. However reluctant he might be to discuss it, he must have some idea what Owein meant. "Barefoot would be better," he said firmly, and pointed at the granary. "You'd work better within if you were unshod as well. What you do comes from..." He took a breath, feeling his way. "You're part of the earth. You come from it. It would help to—" The faint whiff of hazelnuts in the mingled odors from Simon stopped him as much as the priest's expression, which had turned wistful.

"To be reminded?" asked Simon. "Dust to dust. So it might." He studied Owein for a long moment. That wasn't what Owein had meant and they both knew it, but he had an uncomfortable hunch he'd best let it go at that. Then Simon surprised him. "I am of the earth. So are we all. Even you." His voice was hushed, and he cast another glance over his shoulder. "Though you belong to—another country, as much as you do to this one. I can tell you've drawn strength from it. As I should from mine?"

It still wasn't quite what Owein meant, but he nodded.

Three heartbeats went by before the priest said, "I thank you for your advice." Conviction mingled with the utmost gentleness in his face. "Will you be guided by mine? It would be best for you not to speak of that country save to Rose and Linley. Alfred and Daniel and the Bishop could be another matter, though Alfred's the best of men."

He'd meet them soon, Owein knew, having been informed of their arrival. "I understand," he said. But there was something else he needed to ask, and Rose and Linley were with Alfred at the moment. For all Tomas's warnings and Simon's reticence, Owein sensed that the priest could be trusted. "What of Matilda?"

Simon's face withdrew a little. "She's Alfred's niece." He studied Owein's eyes. "And a Christian, and so is he. Whatever you tell her could reach the King's ears," he said flatly. "And the Bishop's." They heard Linley calling their names in the distance. Simon gave an answering shout, then turned back to Owein. "Not only that," he began hurriedly, "I've seen your other country." His voice was a strained whisper. "Once or twice and only dimly, though I've sensed it more often than that. But Matilda has no awareness of such things, Owein. You'd only frighten her."

"She hasn't any Sight. I know that. That doesn't mean I'd frighten her."

Simon gave him an incredulous stare. Abruptly, Owein caught an odor like sour cabbage. Exasperation. Worry, too. "I beg of you, say nothing to her. It might lead to more harm than you know." He gripped Owein's arm and gazed directly into his eyes. His next words were very low, and came as if torn from him. "It could even end by driving your other world still further from ours, and all your hard work would come to naught."

The damp cold silent air swirled about Owein's head, pressed against his ears, and filled his lungs with such sodden weight that it was a moment before he could ask, "Who told you of my errand here?"

"Not a soul. I can see it," said Simon, after a wordless silence during which some uneasy resolve came into his eyes. "In and around you. You look—different than other men, and you're using your Sight in a way that exhausts you. Not in there." He gestured at the granary. "It's something else. Something physical. A kind of reaching."

"You see only the body, then," said Owein slowly. "You see wounds."

Simon drew a hand across his eyes. "Yes, I do. That much our Lord has given me to see. And sometimes how to ease them."

"You don't see feelings?"

"Only a little. Not as you can, I think." Of a sudden Simon looked exhausted, and cast a troubled glance in the direction from which they'd just heard Linley's voice. "Owein, you must not speak of these things with anyone but Rose or Linley. You and I won't discuss them again."

The scorched-almond smell was back. "There's no need to be frightened," said Owein with the beginnings of indignation.

"But there is," said the priest. His voice might have been bitter had it been less weary. Then his face closed; his spine stiffened. "Ah, here they are. Come meet Alfred and the Bishop." Like burning tar, a warning radiated from him. "And Daniel."

Alfred was of medium height, with an unusually erect carriage, oaken-brown hair and lapiz eyes the exact shade of Matilda's. She was accompanying him, and their resemblance was plain to see. The King moved like a man conserving his energy and one who'd been long on the road, yet there was an abundance of warmth in his voice as he greeted Simon. When he turned to Owein, for an instant his face went utterly still. His subsequent smile was genuine, yet he gave off an odor of sweat, pine and berries. Good will, curiosity, shock, and then a need so intense that Owein almost took a step backwards.

Instead he smiled, inclined his head and said, "Good day, your Grace. I'm well content to meet you at last, and to bring you greetings from my brother."

Alfred's eyes narrowed ever so slightly. That was the need: to hear from Tomas. "How fares your brother, up the North Way?"

"Well, thank you. Somewhat burdened just now with settling his inheritance."

"Has it been challenged?" asked Alfred.

Even without the momentary flicker of assessment in the King's face, and although his tone was light, Owein would have known what that question meant: how did relations stand between himself and his brother? The King had quick wits. How had Tomas, with his gift of true speech, contrived to deal with him? Fighting a stab of anxiety, Owein smiled a second time. "Never challenged by me, my lord," he said as calmly as he could. "Though we have kin for whom the ties of blood or loyalty are perhaps not so clear."

Owein had grown more or less accustomed to the way everyone in Midgard stared at him when they first met. No one here had features anything like his, though he suspected that if he'd been a full-blooded Elf, he'd have been far from the most striking among them. Some of the Saxons not only studied his face, they looked his entire body up and down into the bargain, generally when they thought he wouldn't notice. Alfred was subtle about it, but Owein could feel the appraisal in his gaze. "Would you be Tomas's half-brother?" asked the King.

"Yes," said Owein, glad of any explanation, however threadbare, for his appearance, and doubly glad that he could lie. The darker of the two newcomers whom he'd not yet met, the one who smelled like a poorly drained swamp, was frankly gawking at him. "We had different mothers."

"Perhaps yours came from the far East," said the silver-haired man unexpectedly, the one who stood next to Alfred. He must be the Bishop; his clothes were more ornate than those of the other fellow.

"I don't know, my lord Bishop," Owein said sadly, temporizing. The only scent he could detect was stinging nettles. Caution. Perhaps it came from his own body, he thought wryly. "She died when I was quite small. But I'm told she was very beautiful."

When Matilda's face softened with sympathy, Owein felt guilty. He met her gaze, calmly and briefly, because not to have done so would have made him feel worse, and he saw that Alfred noticed the glance.

Then he was introduced to Daniel, the dark-haired, tonsured man wearing plain robes, who at close range smelled even more like a marsh, and who had clearly disliked Owein on sight. The hermit's animosity was so strong that images came with it one after another: he was mistrustful and fearful of Owein, wanted him banished, wanted Limecliff, dreaded the reappearance of the Parcae—and wondered if Owein might be Tomas in disguise.

Let him wonder. The fellow was a Mage, Tomas had said, and also that he wasn't an adept and hadn't much Sight. And that he relied on fire Elementals. Yes, there was one now; Owein squinted just enough to see it without its noticing his scrutiny. A squat troll-like fiery body, webbed hands and feet, no neck and a lolling, sparking tongue. Little wonder some of that marshy reek was of sulphur.

Owein didn't like Daniel any more than Daniel liked him. Beneath the hermit's stronger emotions was a slyness, an anticipation and an air of secrets closely guarded that was puzzling in someone otherwise so distinctly hostile. It made Owein's gorge rise, that and the stench. Still, he was courteous, as it would behoove Tomas's brother to be, and he answered all of Alfred's questions as well and carefully as he could. When the King, Werferth, Daniel and Matilda went to the granary with Simon and Linley, he followed them all inside. He was grateful for the respite from the King's attention. That there would be more questions he had no doubt.

Once inside, however, it was Werferth who caught Owein's eye. The Bishop appeared calm, but all the while that he moved among the wounded, he cast unobtrusive glances down the rows of pallets. His scent had changed, first to wormwood, which was wariness, then to the sea water of determination and hidden feelings. There was a hint of evergreen too: he wanted to know something. He must be looking for someone.

Daniel followed him and offered small comments, though his gaze kept veering in Owein's direction. Alfred, on the other hand, was completely focused on the wounded, listening, taking his time, with an occasional question for Simon. He bestowed coin purses now and again, and smiles and encouragement everywhere. Matilda, making her way down the next row, came to an awkward halt by the woman who'd been abused.

Matilda's indigo eyes widened; her lips paled. Even without the odor of rotting fish that now came from the injured woman, Owein would have known what had happened. Without thinking he went to Matilda as quickly as he could, stepping nimbly over and among the pallets. Matilda turned a white face, not so much shocked as tragic, up to his and stretched out her hand. Owein took it, with an expanding pain in his chest, but she drew away almost immediately, her cheeks flaming.

The fragrance of nettles—of caution—hit him full in the face, and not just from Matilda. She was looking past him. Owein turned and saw Alfred, his expression sober, studying the two of them from a few ells away. Daniel was watching as well.

Simon gently pulled a blanket over the face of the corpse. "Rest in peace," he murmured. He rested a hand on Matilda's shoulder. "Would you please prepare her—"

"Yes!" said Matilda. With her face averted, she left the granary so fast that she nearly tripped, and Owein sucked in his breath. He was about to offer to carry the woman outside, but Linley motioned Daniel to help him do just that.

Not until the door closed behind them did Owein fully register what they were carrying. A body. A dead one. That wretched Saxon woman had walked and breathed and slept and eaten, just as he did. And loved: that he would do one day, too. Then she'd been captured and abused by the Danes, returned to her kin, and suffered and died in this close filthy hall despite all the power in Simon's hands.

Mortal hands. Would an Elf have done any better? But Elves didn't die. Matilda would die one day, just as that woman had. Matilda would die and so would he.

His head was swimming. All he could smell was rotten fish, as if he were drowning in them, his windpipe stuffed with carrion and brine. His breath had grown short.

Someone touched his arm, and he found himself blinking down at Simon.

"Go and wash, Owein, then come to the great hall," said the priest quietly. "It's nigh on time for the evening meal, and you've not eaten enough for days to do the half of what you've done here."

He swallowed hard, past the bile in his throat. Alfred and Werferth were moving down the rows of pallets again, with Daniel at their heels. "I'll leave when you do," said Owein.

After a moment Simon nodded. "As you wish." But have a care, said the priest's eyes and his tarry odor, as unmistakably as if he'd shouted the words.

Feeling as if he might lose his balance at any second, Owein went to join Alfred and the Bishop. They had just reached the last pallet beside the west wall, where the young man whom Owein had protected from his murderous neighbor still lay senseless. Alfred's face was a bit pensive as he gave Owein a nod, but Werferth didn't acknowledge his arrival.

The Bishop was gazing down at the unconscious man. Werferth's features were arranged to convey impersonal compassion, but that wasn't what he was feeling. Determined to master his light-headedness, which was aggravated by the jumble of scents from the Bishop, Owein set his jaw. He'd never smelled anything so complex before. The top note was something corrosive, which might have been regret or remorse. There was a distinct odor of scorched walnuts, but the whole granary smelled of pain. Then he caught a whiff of something different, earthier, musky, faint but undeniably present. With it came both a wave of sorrow and an image of the Bishop and the young man, a scene that Owein hadn't remotely expected.

He hadn't known that two men could love one another in that manner; he'd thought it was just men and women. Perhaps two women could do so as well.

He had a lot to learn and no time to complain about how quickly: he'd no choice in the matter. Werferth's was a personal grief; that must be why he was acting so remote. Death was fearful enough in and of itself—Owein struggled with a bout of nausea—and it must be still more terrible to lose someone whom one had loved. He didn't want to think about losing Fraine; he already missed her too much. Perhaps in time he'd understand why Werferth also smelled of wormwood, which was wariness.

"This man is done for, I fear. I doubt he'll regain his senses," Simon said quietly. "More's the pity, for I've no idea who he is."

Werferth's gaze shifted briefly to the priest. "I can tell you his name. He lived in my village." Relief flowed from him with the scent of fresh cream, then another current of grief.

Confused, still light-headed but most of all moved to pity, in his gentlest voice Owein repeated what he'd heard Simon tell the bereaved spouses of the dead: "You'll want to take the body home with you, of course. Do you wish to prepare him for burial yourself, or would you prefer that we did it for you?"

The Bishop's head snapped up. There was shock in the gaze he fastened upon Owein, with all the tarriness of warning and then abruptly something fetid, which meant shame. Slowly it was replaced by the odor of charcoal. Werferth buried his hands in the folds of his robes. He wanted to strike Owein, who smelled so much smoke that he coughed. Purplish spots of color burned high on Werferth's cheekbones: he was enraged. Why?

Then Owein noticed the piney scent—curiosity—from the other Saxons, and how it was increasingly mingled with the spoiled-honey fragrance that meant polite embarrassment. No one would meet Owein's gaze or that of Bishop. No one but Simon, who was giving Owein a white-faced stare. He'd made a mistake. A serious one. Werferth's eyes were livid as he glanced aside, and Owein knew he'd made an enemy, too. He could smell nothing but smoke now. Even more than that dark-haired soldier had wanted to kill the Bishop's dying lover, Werferth wanted to murder Owein. Suddenly he knew why, and why the odors of fear and awe were streaming from the others. It was more than the fact that Owein shouldn't have revealed his knowledge that the young man was the Bishop's lover, and more than the stigma that such relations must carry among the Saxons. It was that Owein shouldn't have known at all.

Werferth didn't join them for dinner, much to Owein's relief. He himself wanted sleep, not food, but not so much as he wanted to build more of the bridge. He was too tired for a magical working, but that was when he felt closest to Fraine, and sometimes they managed a scrap of conversation. His twin's absence was a constant ache, the way he'd once heard Simon warn an amputee that a severed limb could still be felt. Owein missed Moira and Tomas and the pooka. He missed Aidan and Jared, and the Cooks and their skill. He even found himself yearning for a sight of Nissyen and the Parcae.

If he didn't converse with someone who thoroughly understood him, and soon, he didn't know how well he'd bear it. He was bone-tired of smelling death all the time, and weary of the Sun and the merciless stars. How much longer could he watch his every word and gesture among the Saxons? Though he'd been as careful as he knew how to be, he'd made a dreadful mistake with Werferth. With a *Bishop,* after all the warnings he'd had about not alarming any Christians.

Despite his desires, he wasn't asleep; he wasn't working magic and he wasn't even alone. Instead he was seated at the right hand of the Christian sovereign Alfred and eyeing a bowl of some supposedly edible substance. It looked like vomit and smelled even worse. Steeling himself, Owein tasted a bite. Cabbage, mostly, with some onions. At least they might have been once. They were mummified now.

Linley kicked him under the table. The King had just spoken, was looking at Owein, was waiting. "My lord?" said Owein.

"I have read your brother's letter," said Alfred courteously, but with the air of a man repeating something. "I was glad to learn somewhat of how he fares. He speaks well of you, Owein. You must be dear to him."

The letter had been Rose's idea. A good one, it seemed: Alfred was smiling at him, albeit cautiously. So was Matilda. Owein gave them both a smile in return.

"Your brother's letter gave no intelligence of the Danish hosts. In the past, Tomas has been most helpful to me in that regard. Would you know anything of their intentions?"

Scenes from the granary flooded back to Owein. "They mean you harm," he said tiredly, then wrinkled his nose at the resinous odor he caught from Simon. Another warning. Well and good: he'd been showered with warnings, for all he'd profited by them. "I regret I can tell you no more, my lord," he murmured. "Tomas follows such matters more closely than I, and I came by way of Dubhlinn. Your attackers approached from the opposite shore of this island, did they not?" Or so Tomas had told him.

Alfred agreed that they had.

"If you were to write to Tomas, perhaps he could inform you himself," Owein said pleasantly.

For a long moment Alfred surveyed him. "It would be difficult for a letter to reach Vestfold before the Danes move against us, if such is their mind concerning me."

Owein opened his mouth to offer to send word more quickly—but that he should not say. He reached for what had been the water jug at last night's meal, smelled the ale before he poured it, and set the jug down again. Matilda passed him a pitcher of water without being asked, and he smiled at her.

"You don't drink ale?" asked Daniel suddenly. The question was almost the only time he'd spoken during the meal, though he'd stared hard enough at Owein. At Matilda too, though never when Alfred was looking, and in a way that made Owein uneasy. It had begun not unlike how the Bishop had gazed at that boy, but soon grew darker.

Owein looked directly at the hermit. The man's eyes were moist and overbright and didn't hold his for long. "I've never cared for it," Owein said. Nor for Daniel's brackish odor, Alfred's questions or the smoke in this hall. Even the water tasted of it.

"Temperance is a virtue," said the King. "So is prudence."

He was studying Owein. What was he driving at? Prudence meant caution. Owein assumed a replica of Moira's most cautious expression. But he was overtired, and when thinking of Moira made him remember Aubrey's imitating her to amuse the twins, he was hard put to stifle a grin. Then he missed Fraine all over again, with a pang that made him glance aside for an instant.

Alfred was still eyeing him. "So it is, my lord," Owein said quickly. When no one replied, he added, "Prudence. A virtue."

Matilda gazed at her clasped hands, Rose at the tallow lamp on the table. Simon, Daniel and Alfred were all contemplating Owein, who felt Linley taking in the whole scene at once. With an easy smile that didn't match his plum-like scent of concern, Linley started to say something, but Alfred spoke first.

"I shall write to your brother," said the King into the gathering silence. "Perhaps Othere or another trader is running ahead of schedule, and can carry a letter up the North Way sooner than we might think."

CHAPTER FIFTEEN: TALLAH'S HUNCH

Elfland

"Owein's weary in body and mind," said Fraine, trying not to sound as worried as she felt. "I would guess from helping tend the wounded. He's more distressed with each passing hour, but that's the whole of what I can sense. The last few times I've entered trance and searched where we work in the 'tweenlands, I found not a trace of his energy there."

She and her parents sat within in the circle of stunted hawthorns by the well, with Nissyen perched on its rim beside the silent ravens. They were never far from Tomas lately, and Fraine was glad of their presence. As for the sylph, it was quiet and attentive, without the gleam in its eyes that meant it was thinking faster than ever a mortal could.

"Owein and I can't communicate in any great detail outside of a working, and each one's been more difficult than the last." Fraine hesitated. "Shouldn't they have grown easier instead? Once he recovers from whatever ails him, we'll soon finish the eight points. We should decide what comes next." The admission came hard. "If more isn't added soon, I don't know how long what we've done will endure."

Moira and Tomas couldn't build the bridge, either separately or together. They'd tried, when Owein had stopped working. Nor could Fraine do it alone.

"Have you seen more barriers in the 'tweenlands?" asked Moira.

"Exorcisms, yes. Sometimes I've sensed a presence."

Nissyen joined them on the withering grass. "What sort of presence?"

Fraine darted a glance at Tomas: should she answer the sylph? When he nodded, she said, "Fiery. Hateful."

"A salamander?" asked Nissyen.

"I don't know. It could be a powerful one, perhaps."

"Is it male?" Moira wanted to know.

"That's the odd part. I can't really tell."

"It could be anything," muttered Tomas. "We've two enemies, the Christians and Loki."

"If it is Loki, I would not know, my Mage. He is well-shielded, more so than even an Elf. I have not sensed him since we last saw him in the realm of the Sidhe."

"I have," said Tomas. "Once in the 'tweenlands, when we first brought the twins here." He glanced at Moira. "Is there a way to shield the bridge from him?"

She shook her head. "Even one point is too large."

"What became of the gods when Asgard fell?" asked Fraine, thinking of the radiant woman in her dreams. "Did they die? Do any yet live?"

Tomas turned to Moira. Her face was calm and her bearing far from tense, yet something that wasn't quite pain moved in the depths of her eyes. "Gods do not die," she said. Then she lapsed into a silence and Tomas into a stillness that both deepened before she added, "Nor do the Elves. Once we were more akin to them. At this pass, that they could come more to resemble us would not astonish me." She pushed her crisp black hair from the widow's peak on her forehead. "They were diminished when Asgard fell. Beyond that I have no answers for you, Fraine. It is not known to me if any of the Vanir or Aesir save Loki were able to leave their realms, or who among them can now act with anything approaching the power they once had." Another pause. "Loki is not fully a god, so perhaps he was affected differently."

"He may become one if the bridge isn't finished soon," said Tomas.

"Then he and the Nazarene would be the only Powers in Midgard." Nissyen's patient air nettled Fraine, as if it found them all slow-witted. "Such is his goal. For him to move against the bridge would be consistent with that goal."

"Truly." Moira's face was grim. "I mistrust this withdrawal on his part." A glance at Tomas. "Still less do I care for Owein's frame of mind. We must learn what lies behind it." She drew breath. "Could you not send—"

"I prefer to keep them with me." His eyes darkened as they met hers.

They were discussing the ravens, Fraine knew. Neither for the first time nor freely, from the sudden whiff of sea-water in the air. Nissyen was studying them both, but Fraine looked away. She had no wish to sense any more than she already had; it seemed too private. Should she change the subject? The lone topic that came to mind was the golden-haired woman, but Fraine had no wish to speak of her dreams either; they felt too private as well. "Pray excuse me," she murmured, getting to her feet. No one looked at her, though Tomas waved a hand in her direction.

As she neared the edge of the wood, she heard Moira's voice, very low. "You have the iron-power."

"And that's virtually all."

"You've had little enough time for anything else."

"Nor will I, till the bridge is done."

Staying close to the hawthorns so that she could be readily called, Fraine picked her way among the trees and climbed over a few fallen trunks before she found enough moss to allow her to lie down at full length. With a sigh, she folded her arms beneath her head and gazed up into the netted branches. It was always dim here. She liked the yellowed softness of this low filtered light. The forest smelled of oak, ferns and crumbling humus, and various small animal presences, most of them not Elves, all going about their business in the underwood. Of desiccated branches too, and drying creek beds. Of decay.

Fraine inhaled through parted lips, flared her nostrils and turned her head from side to side. That musty hazelnut odor meant longing, though without much hope, and the wormwood scent, herbal and green and fresher than the others, spelled wariness. Whoever inhabited the dwindling forest was well aware that it was ailing. Still, it was restful here, safe, and in its own way soothing. Because it was home, perhaps. Perhaps because she preferred it to what little she'd seen of Midgard.

She missed Owein. What was troubling him? She couldn't smell him in the 'tweenlands, where her awareness and his both turned whenever they worked on the bridge. She couldn't smell him, but she knew where both his body and his consciousness were. She knew where to send her energy to entwine with his, and how something of that link would pass into the bridge. She couldn't see Owein either, but whether his awareness was in Midgard or the 'tweenlands, she always had an impression of what he was feeling, the way she might remember the fragments of a dream before they slid from her mind upon awakening.

Owein missed her, and he was haunted by the fear of dying: those were the two constants. And he was tired, from their work on the bridge and now physically. That was a change. So were the flashes of curiosity, satisfaction and affection, and the intense bursts of frustration and anxiety. All about him there was so much pain of late that it couldn't be entirely his.

Now was not the time to reach out to him again; she'd likely be asked to rejoin Tomas and Moira soon. She stretched from head to foot, fanned out her fingers and toes, and massaged a knot at the base of her skull. A prime spot for a nap she had found here. The moss was thick, if dry, and the wood was very still.

Too still.

Something gleamed in the branches above her head, something shining that wasn't bark, or leaves though it was green. Fraine stiffened. It was gone. No, there it was again, almond-shaped, with a faint liquid shimmer. A pair of eyes the color of malachite, oversized and whiteless in a small chestnut-skinned face, peered down at her. One of the Parcae. Feeling the tension melt away from her ribcage, Fraine sat up and waved.

Without so much as the faintest rustle, a lithe naked body leaped down from the tree to land beside her. The Parca's odor arrived before she did: rank and earthy, but companionable rather than challenging. All adult Parcae women looked alike; her visitor's matted black hair, the pouch slung across her bare torso, and her prehensile hands and feet told Fraine nothing. But the winged Elves' scents were entirely different. Inhaling, she tested the full mix of odors from the Parca. "Hullo, Tallah."

The wizened little monkey-face creased with approval. "Tal-lah," she agreed, tapping the sleek skin of her chest just above her sternum. Then she tilted her head, furrowed her brow in exaggerated inquiry, and said, "O-wein?"

"I don't know," said Fraine, and frowned to show her concern.

Tallah glanced in Tomas's direction. Muttering beneath her breath, she considered for a moment. Then she pointed at him, jutted her chin out like a beak, unfurled her leathery wings one at a time, and gave them a single mighty flap that lifted her a few inches from the earth.

"Not the ravens," said Fraine. "He doesn't want to send them to Midgard."

The Parca narrowed her eyes and gave off the scent of wild onions: she didn't understand. Fraine picked up a sharp stone, brushed the leaf mold at the edge of the moss aside till she found the earth beneath it, and drew two stylized birds in the dirt. "Ravens," she said, tapping the image.

"Ra-vens," Tallah agreed, looking hopeful.

Fraine erased the drawing and shook her head. "Tomas isn't sending them after Owein."

The Parca scowled. After perhaps five seconds, she pointed at Tomas again, whose blond head was bent close to Moira's dark one. From a little distance away, Nissyen watched them intently. Still pointing at Tomas, with her tongue protruding a bit from her small white teeth and her brow furrowed with concentration, Tallah scratched an oversized Raido, Rune of Journeys, into the dirt. Next she said something unintelligible, but Fraine would have taken her meaning even if she'd not detected Tomas's name in the hissing jumble of sibilants. "He could go himself," she said, shrugging. "Whether he will I couldn't say."

Arms akimbo, Tallah glared in Tomas's direction, said something peremptory and began stalking towards him and Moira. Curious to see how they'd weather the interruption, Fraine followed. So did Nissyen, its eyes slitted and alert. The Parca was rummaging about in the bag that hung from the strap on her chest. By the time Fraine caught up with her, she was clutching something in one small hairy hand and smelled of overcooked cabbage—she was exasperated.

Tomas and Moira fell silent and watched her. Fraine would have retreated before her mother's dark level gaze; it was tense and remote and fully armed. But Tallah marched straight up to Tomas, grabbed his hand, slapped something into it and said, "Rai-do! O-wein!"

She'd given him a small smooth stone from the Elvish Sea. A Runestone, carved with Raido. Tomas's eyes went wide then flared with annoyance, but so briefly that without that single whiff of sour vegetables from him, Fraine wouldn't have been certain he was irritated.

Then his face lost all expression. He might have been a statue. A mummy. Someone might have turned him to stone where he sat, like an unwary troll in the stories that Aubrey had told the twins, a troll struck by the Sun's rays. Now he smelled of rain, like the wet clean air of Midgard still charged with intensity just after a storm.

Was he conversing with Nissyen in mind-speech? Probably not: the sylph was hovering nearby, lips parted and hair askew, trying to catch his gaze. Moira, her manner cool, divided her attention between him and Tallah. The Parca was frowning. As the moments rolled by and Tomas remained wordless and motionless, she looked less sure of herself. When Fraine glanced at the ravens, they were still perched calmly on the lip of the well, and their eerily conscious gaze was trained upon Tomas. Perhaps he was communing with them, though his eyes weren't focused on anything. More likely it was his Sight. She took a seat beside her mother and waited.

She'd lost track of how much time had passed before Tomas uncrossed his legs and slowly got to his feet. The skin about his eyes was dark and taut with fatigue, but his gaze was no longer remote. He held out the Runestone to Tallah and said, "I'll go to Midgard. With the ravens." A frustrated gesture. "It was dim, the Sight, but Owein has some need of me, and I of the ravens while I'm gone."

That meant they couldn't send the birds after him, should Moira require his presence here. Fraine wasn't sure what need might arise—Deverell and Evan's factions were relatively quiet of late, though Evan had begun watching her when he thought she wouldn't notice. Still, she didn't relish this turn of events, nor the thought of relying on Nissyen to send word to Tomas in the ravens' stead, and she didn't quite know why.

Moira's expression was just as shuttered as before. She met Tomas's eyes and murmured agreement; whatever he'd Seen, she'd not question it, or not question it just then. No extra colors swirled in the air about anyone, and everyone smelled much as they had, mostly of wormwood and rain. Why did the skin between Fraine's shoulderblades feel as if a cold damp hand had brushed against it?

Tallah took the Runestone from Tomas, then gripped his hand when he started to withdraw it. His face went still. After a few seconds she released his fingers, and some of the tension left her bearing.

Tomas told Moira, "I'll speak to Rose and Linley while I'm there; I would have regardless." He glanced at the Parca. "Tallah has a hunch that I should, though she's not sure why. Perhaps to speculate about what comes after the eight points."

There was a darkness—a foreboding?—in Moira's gaze at him. His next words were too low for Fraine's ears, but she suspected they were an assurance he'd be careful.

CHAPTER SIXTEEN: DEATH AND THE SIGHT

Midgard

The following morning, Owein went with Rose and Matilda to help Simon in one of Limecliff's barns, empty of livestock for a few years but in good repair, where they'd taken Alfred's cartload of wounded. Susannah was managing the granary, while Linley was closeted with Werferth and the King. Where Daniel was, Owein neither knew nor cared.

The day bade fair to be warmer than any they'd yet had, which meant they should get the corpses to the ridge and into the ground as soon as might be. Owein didn't know how much progress the gravediggers were making. He didn't want to go near the cloth-wrapped bodies, nor join a crew of Saxon strangers who were likely to maintain an uneasy silence in his presence and stare and whisper behind his back. But since digging was the work that most wanted doing that day, he found Simon and offered to go to the ridge.

"Anyone can handle a shovel," said the priest. "You're of more use to me here."

Relieved, Owein stayed in the barn. If he'd gone to the ridge, he would tell himself later, firmly and more than once, it still would have happened. When all was said and done, Skuld had come to his name-fastening, his and Fraine's, and their Fate was what it was.

The barn's ceiling was higher than that of the granary and these patients had only just arrived, so the air within was more bearable. The pain wasn't. More slaves were in this cartload, and more women. As for the men-at-arms, several had less grievous injuries than those in the granary, and might have recovered had their wounds not festered so badly nor been so long neglected.

"If he'd reached us two days ago," Simon muttered as he drew a blanket over a lifeless face. "Even yesterday morning, if luck had favored him."

Rose squeezed his shoulder in passing. "We've no way to fight time," she said gently.

"None." Simon looked resigned. "Though it doesn't always work against us."

For perhaps an hour after that scrap of conversation, Owein made his way among the rows of pallets. It was slow going. He spoke to the wounded who were conscious, and reported their words to Rose and Simon. He applied hot wet rags to adhered clothing, offered water, fetched blankets for the shivering or bread and broth for the hungry. He moved pallets if Rose thought it best to do so, called Matilda whenever anyone was frightened of his Norse coloring, summoned the priest if someone wanted him.

All too soon he was weary, and the day had hardly begun. He ached to step outside to breathe and to rest for a moment, but he'd not yet spoken to a battered and gaunt woman who lay crumpled at the very end of the row where he'd been working. He knelt in the herb-strewn straw beside her.

She had thick curly hair which must have been a warm shade between brown and blonde when it was clean. He caught his lower lip between his teeth at sight of the yellowing contusions on her face. She was younger than he'd first judged, and she had been very badly used. Her head was turned away from him, her swollen eyes closed. From the unnatural angle of one of her arms, it was broken. She would die soon; she already stank of fish cast up on the sand. Owein swallowed hard; he would never get used to it. She also smelled sour and metallic—there was the iron, at her neck. A slave collar. She hadn't worn the collar long, for it had chafed the uncalloused skin of her neck till it was raw and oozing. Apart from the bruises and the hectic color on her cheeks, she was bloodlessly pale. Doubtless she was fevered; she was shivering beneath a stained quilt.

"Are you awake, my lady?" Owein asked softly, holding out a blanket.

He hadn't even finished the question when her eyes flew open and fastened on his. Hers were round, like her face, and very blue, and awash with sudden tears. "*Tomas*," she said in a choked whisper.

Seconds grated past before Owein stammered, "What?" She must be delirious. She couldn't mean his father; she'd mistaken him for someone else.

But she was staring up at him with a painfully lucid gaze, her expression reeling from recognition to questions and then approaching some horrified certainty. He couldn't sense what she was feeling; the scent of death was too strong. He should ask if she were cold, if she could take a little food, where she was most injured. At the very least he should ask for her name.

"You are not Tomas the Rhymer." She spoke as if it cost her an effort, and with a lilting accent he couldn't identify.

"No," he said, jolted, kneeling there like an idiot with a blanket clutched in his hands. He spread it over her. She did know his father. "Give me your name, please. Where are you from?" His questions sounded harsh, and he winced and glanced about to see if Simon had heard. Simon, his back turned, was near Rose at the far end of the barn, but Rose was looking Owein's way.

"Caraid," she said. That must be her name. When he nodded blankly, her brows drew together as if she'd expected a different response. "From Dubhlinn." That explained the accent. Her gaze felt like a pair of hands on his face, searching, testing. Suddenly she made as if to sit up, only to fall back with a stifled groan.

"Calm yourself," Owein said urgently. "You may be too injured to sit." From the corner of his eye he spotted Rose walking towards them.

"You're Tomas's *son.*" Caraid's voice had risen a notch; she sounded positive. And appalled. Now Matilda was following Rose. "His and the Elf—"

"Shh! I beg of you!"

The Elf Queen's, Caraid had almost said. She fell silent immediately, studying his expression.

"*Please,*" Owein whispered, touching her hand by way of apology. "I am his son. And Moira's." He gave a tiny jerk of his chin in Matilda's direction. "But she mustn't know. She thinks I'm his brother."

When Caraid closed her eyes, he caught a bitter whiff of grief which was almost immediately overridden by the stench of the iron about her neck, and most of all by the death that hovered close.

"This young man is called Owein. Our only intent is to help you, my lady," said Rose soothingly as she knelt down beside them. "This is Matilda, and my name is Rose. May I know yours? Where are your nearest kin?"

"She's called Caraid." Owein wanted to spare her the effort of talking. "She hails from Dubhlinn."

"My brother's there," said Caraid slowly. "Brendan O'Quinlan." She gave Rose an anxious look. "Where am I?"

"Safely in Wessex, where Alfred rules. You've come to the estate of Tomas Sigtryggson. Owein is his brother, and my husband Linley the reeve here."

Caraid moistened her cracked lips but said nothing.

"All we can do for your comfort will be done." Rose's voice was reassuring. "Be troubled by nothing. I'll have word sent to Brendan."

Caraid gave her a small grateful nod. She glanced at Matilda who stood a little apart, her expression sober, then back at Owein. So did Rose. "Fetch Simon, please—"

"Must speak with you," Caraid interrupted dully, addressing Owein. "Alone. About Tomas."

Matilda threw Owein a startled look. "Be quick about it," Rose told Caraid neutrally, though her face sharpened. "When you're done, we've a cordial that can ease you somewhat."

Owein didn't know what any of the three women felt; all he could smell was death and iron, and they made him frantic. "Can't we get this collar off?" he blurted.

They all looked at him, Matilda with an increasingly bewildered expression. "Not without hurting her," said Rose in a still, careful voice. "She's not fit to be moved."

Owein should have known that. He did know it.

Rose said to Caraid, "I should examine you—"

Caraid gave a feeble shake of her head. "I'm dying. Too broken to mend."

Rose laid a gentle hand on the Irishwoman's forehead, then got to her feet. "Poppy cordial," she said firmly. "Ask Simon for the dosage." Matilda glanced at Owein as if minded to stay, but both women left in search of Simon.

Owein could smell nothing but death; he had no idea what Rose was thinking. Probably that he should do nothing to distress Caraid, and call Simon as soon as possible.

In this crowded barn Owein was hardly alone with Caraid, but the three men closest to her were unconscious and the fourth nearly so. He supported her head as carefully as he could and gave her some water from his flask. Though he tried to avoid the slave collar, it grazed his bare wrist and forearm as he lowered Caraid back down to her pallet, and he couldn't have pulled his arm away without jostling her head. He set his teeth at the cold and the burn of the collar. Hard to credit that it didn't sear her flesh the same way.

She was studying him. "Iron-sick?"

He nodded, then unclenched his fists. "It's bearable," he muttered. It would have been more so if he weren't tired and unnerved. He took a breath that came near to choking him. He was miserable. He wanted to go home, not that he had one. He wanted Fraine. He wanted to spend a mortal Moon scrubbing the odor of death from his pores. Most of all, with a constriction of his chest that he dimly recognized as the dawn of a towering rage, he wanted to find Tomas and demand why he'd never spoken of this woman.

"Is Tomas here?" she whispered.

"No."

Her face withdrew a little. Surrendered. The cold hand in Owein's went limp, as if relinquishing her hold on the world. She turned her head aside.

"Speak your piece, please, so you can rest," Owein said, heartsick. Now that she had stopped fighting, the end would come quickly—that he had learned all too well in the granary. "I'll only listen unless you've something to ask me." The smell of putrefaction from her was so strong now that he could hardly smell the collar. He should call Simon. "Press my hand if you want the cordial."

It was the first time he had seen her smile, and so wistfully that he had to smile in return. "Purse at my waist. For Tomas. Take it, please."

Gingerly, setting his jaw at the sight of her scrawny arms and protruding hipbones, he pulled the blankets aside and cut the cord to Caraid's pouch. He looked at it curiously; it was made of silk that had once been blue. But for something flat and tined, it was empty. When he looked at Caraid, she nodded, so he opened it and took out a comb worked from fine jet.

"He gave it to me," she said.

A dozen questions rose in Owein's mind, but he silently tucked the comb and the silk into his own pouch, then glanced at Caraid. Her eyes had gone flat and glassy, her lips slack. Owein's heart startled him with a great racketing thud. He was about to shout for the priest when he realized that Caraid might be in a state approaching trance. He'd promised not to interrupt her, but trance was different. He had to know. "Are you a Seer, Caraid?" he asked in the lowest voice possible, taking her hand again.

She nodded.

Owein twitched his long legs against the straw-covered earth as much as he could without uncrossing them. Fleas were doubtless biting him, but there was nothing to be done for that now. The Sight was often long in coming, and Caraid's end was so close that he didn't know which would arrive first, her death or her Sight.

He took a quick survey of the barn. Rose and the priest knelt by a pallet halfway across the barn, but Matilda was nowhere to be seen. Running an errand, perhaps, or gone to help Susannah.

Caraid's eyes were closed now, her lips moving. She must have been pretty not that long ago, with a lushly modeled face and masses of dun-colored hair. Her voice might be softer were she not in so much pain. Perhaps she'd refused the cordial because she'd felt the Sight coming on.

She knew Tomas. She hadn't known about Owein, though she'd quickly guessed who his parents were. She must have met Moira, then. Was Tomas acquainted with the Norse slavers who'd beaten Caraid? Did he know her brother Brendan? When had Tomas given her the jet comb? Owein hadn't known that Tomas had ever visited Dubhlinn. For that matter, Owein knew where Dubhlinn was only because Tomas had taught him enough of Midgard's geography that he'd not say the wrong thing to the wrong person. Not that geography lessons had helped with the Bishop. Owein waited and tried to stop fidgeting, while still more questions swarmed in his mind and his chest tightened with mounting anger.

Though it seemed an eternity, it must have been only a few minutes before Caraid opened her eyes. They were still clouded, no longer with trance but with pain. Her fingers felt like stone claws in his.

"Matilda. In danger," she said haltingly.

"What?" He'd nearly shouted. He gaped down at Caraid.

"So are you. Beware of Loki. Tell Tomas."

The constriction in Owein's ribcage caught fire. "Tomas is a Mage," he hissed. "He can look after himself. What of Matilda? What should I do?"

"Remember the Fates." Caraid's eyes were huge, sunken, shadowed. Her voice was weaker. The scent of corruption from her body was so strong that Owein's gorge kept rising. Her death was coming, swiftly, and he could do nothing to stop it. "Ask the Powers," she breathed. "Your sister...may know. Loki doesn't."

"Doesn't what?" Suddenly Owein realized he was gripping Caraid's fingers so hard that he must be hurting them, but she didn't appear to notice. There was something black around her and within her, moving towards her heart. At the sight he began to shake, but the blackness wasn't aware of him. It wasn't even aware of Caraid. It was a force, as what flowed from Simon's hands was a force, though this darkness had no swirling patterns. It was heavier than that; it had too much density, too much mass. Owein didn't want it to touch him, but he was too paralyzed to drop Caraid's hand, then too ashamed of his fear to shrink away.

Caraid followed the direction of his glance—she saw it too, the dark energy stealing over her. "Don't fear it. I'll be stronger."

"Stronger?" And then, because he couldn't stop himself, "When you're dead?"

She took a few shallow breaths. Her gaze was growing dim. "Gifts. Skuld's and others."

The blackness had almost enveloped her heart. Her life was draining away, and with it her reason. Owein looked about frantically for Simon. Past time for the cordial; still, it was something he could offer, and then he found himself battling a crazy hope that perhaps Simon could help; perhaps it wasn't too late. "The cordial. Do you want—"

Caraid shook her head, then confused Owein with a feeble pressure from her fingers. He squeezed back, blinking hard, and lifted his other hand to smooth her grimy hair from her forehead. At the touch her eyes filled; her lips moved. Afraid he'd not be able to hear, he shifted his weight so that he could lean down to her.

Her voice was faint and thready, scarcely stirring his hair as he brought his ear close to her mouth. Still, she spoke clearly enough that he could entertain no doubt, then or ever, of what her last words were: "I wish I'd been your mother."

CHAPTER SEVENTEEN: THORNY CONVERSATIONS

The 'tweenlands

Tomas was spinning formless in the space between the worlds, where he was somewhat comforted not to have sensed Loki even once. The fiery blocks left by exorcisms were thicker than ever before. All the paths were twisted and appeared to have moved since his last journey. In some areas the energy was as turgid as congealing fat, and his progress was halting. He didn't want to arrive in Midgard either before his last visit or so long after it that Owein had already left. When he communicated his concern to the ravens, they were encouraging, but they also began guiding him into areas where he'd never have ventured on his own. Every time he declined their lead he got lost in the maze of paths, until he ended by following the birds without question.

At length they halted in some sort of nexus formed by interlocking spirals of energy, above and below and all about. Many were huge, others middling, and some so small that he sensed rather than saw them radiating out from where his consciousness hovered. The whole area shimmered with every color of light: flaming pulses, soft blue haze, streaks of iridescent green. The ravens were alert, turning slowly to observe the entire array. At first Tomas was glad of the chance to rest, and wheeled about with the ravens, studying the network.

Before long he became aware of vast tinted spheres in the distance, massive ones, so great and so far from one another and from him that he could make out only a fraction of each curved surface. He counted the spheres: there were nine. What could they be but the nine worlds? That green and blue one, tending in places towards a sickly brown, must be Midgard. The one behind him, the color of pearled twilight, would be Elfland. Perhaps that was Asgard, blackened and rayed with a dark and spiky light, and the one full of shattered white plains was Jotunheim of the frost giants. Was that Vanaheim, that blue and gold orb between Midgard and Asgard? Home of the Vanir, gods of nature, already ancient when the Aesir came. The colors of that sphere were tarnished, but Tomas glimpsed a pulse of light reaching from it towards Elfland and another to Midgard.

He concentrated, looked carefully at the space between his world and that of the Elves. Averted his awareness, looked again. And saw a thread of energy the color of bleached rust stretching between the two realms. The tendril was so fine as to be almost invisible, but it was there and it was strong, and it had a structure that might form part of—

The eight points. Like the radial spokes of a spider's web, he could just make out the sections of the bridge that Owein and Fraine had already constructed. That rusty tint meant they were built by mortal blood, red blood that could bear and contain iron. He could see the whole scaffolding they'd erected, but that was all: a scaffolding and a tenuous one, in need of more energy to anchor itself and coalesce.

Midgard was moving; Elfland was moving, while something about the bridge's construction had to keep pace with the one and allow for the other, and all of it had to happen as quickly as might be. That much he could sense but little else, nowhere near what Owein or Fraine would detect. The twins were more attuned to the mortal world and its motion than he was—they had built that scaffolding.

He had to find Owein, learn what troubled him and why his end of the work had come to a halt—an errand that would require patience. That Tomas hardly knew his children was a source of pain to him. For that matter, they scarcely knew themselves yet. Tomas's own awakening to the Sight and to magecraft had been difficult enough, but when his Fate had led him to Moira, he'd long since attained his full growth and done so at an ordinary pace. And he'd soon found magical allies. The twins had all the help he and Moira could offer in what little time was left for building the bridge, but beyond that, only one another.

Not to have spent years in childhood. Not to have had a gradual and long-anticipated awakening to adolescence. What would it be to catapult into physical maturity, with all the volatility and bewildering drives of youth, almost immediately after learning to walk? Even if the twins had grown at a normal rate of speed, they were further set apart as halfbreeds, far more so than Tomas was. More mortal than Elf, he'd spent years thinking himself wholly mortal. The twins had too much responsibility, virtually no opportunities for instruction, let alone finding an Elemental or an animal ally, and precious little time to waste.

No time, yet Tomas must use patience, a trait he'd never possessed in abundance. Why were he and the ravens stalled here? If this place were a crossroads between the worlds, then where was Hecate, She who ruled all crossroads and every turning point?

Well met again, mortal, said a calm airless voice in his mind. *Your companions may pass. All roads are free to Thought and Memory.*

He started, spun about in a circle, didn't find the statue of Hecate that he and Moira had seen on his first passage between the worlds. A statue with three faces: maiden, mother, crone. He saw no one. But he had heard Her; She must be present. Therefore he asked, *May I pass, too?*

You may, though you shall have but little joy of it... You will forget Me.

All the substance of Tomas's body returned. Bones and joints articulating his flesh, muscles aching with tension, dryness behind his closed eyelids. A familiar twinge of nausea before his sense of balance reasserted itself. He threw his arms out to either side and took a reflexive gulp of air. It was damp, and he heard the sound of water running swiftly down a shallow and stony bed. His feet struck grassy soil. He rocked to and fro, recovered his footing, opened his eyes.

He'd arrived in Limecliff's willow grove, as he'd planned. From the movement and softness in the air despite its chill, and the great white clouds scudding overhead, it was later in the spring than when he'd left.

Later in the spring. He'd been thinking about seasons, about timing. The journey here had been both uncommonly long and momentous. Why? He'd seen more energy left by exorcisms, but that was a permanent feature of the 'tweenlands. Something else had occurred. Had he and the ravens seen someone there? Spoken to someone?

It was gone. He shook his head, frustrated, then shrugged out of his satchel—he'd never call on Linley again without bringing his own instruments. As he stooped by the creek to wash his face, the ravens watched him from a willow branch. For a moment he squatted by the creek bed, enjoying the small liquid voice of the water and letting it swirl through his fingers. It was refreshingly cold.

When he stood, Thought took wing, landed on his chest and clung to the front of his jerkin with both feet. Neither raven had ever done so before. Tomas staggered back a pace from surprise and from the scraping of Thought's talons against his skin, even cushioned as it was by his shirt. "What tidings?" he demanded, shaken, staring into a pair of yellow, ancient and overwhelmingly conscious avian eyes scant inches from his own.

We too are bound by the Ørlög. We cannot always reveal what lies ahead, said Thought in his mind.

That I know. The pit of Tomas's stomach lurched, and sharp cindery specks began to whirl in the air. Something momentous was coming, something shadowed and dark.

We can tell you only that you must use your reason. Ask us for help if need be. Ask Nissyen.

It took an effort to will the blackness away, but his nausea remained. He glanced at Memory, who was still on the willow branch.

Use your reason, said Memory.

Thought released his jerkin and flapped back to the tree. Tomas put a hand to his chest, rubbed the grazes there. The ravens were gazing at him with an air of finality. *My thanks for your warning,* he told them. *Have you more to say?*

Not at present.

Wishing Nissyen were with him, he picked up his pack, reinforced his shield and warily started the trek to the great hall.

Tomas stood out of eyeshot of the hall, thanks to his position among the encircling trees—and to magic. He hated shapeshifting, so when Aubrey had assured him that invisibility was easy to assume but very hard to maintain, he went to Nissyen for aid. The Elemental had shown him how to become less noticeable without changing shape: he simply made the energy of his shield vibrate. Passers-by, particularly those without the Sight or who didn't anticipate Tomas's presence, would have trouble seeing him when he was in deep cover, for his image tended to melt into the shapes and colors of his surroundings.

The wood was fairly still apart from the air stirring high in the treetops. Although the condition of the courtyard betrayed an unusual amount of recent foot traffic, he'd seen no one for the better part of an hour, and it would soon be time for the evening meal. Very little smoke rose from the roof, so the hearthfires were banked to burn low. Weren't they planning to dine? Where was everyone?

It was his steading and he'd sorely missed it, but since he was supposed to be in Vestfold, he couldn't knock on his own door. He sent Thought to scout for him and watched the raven soar above the great hall and its outbuildings. Still queasy, he sat on a flat-topped boulder while Memory waited silently nearby.

It wasn't long before Thought returned, arrowing above the trees for all the world like an ordinary raven, then diving down to settle on a branch near Tomas's head. *Many people are going in and out of a granary and a barn. Inside are wounded men and women, and others caring for them. Alfred is here. So is the Bishop.*

Fraine had reported that Owein was helping tend the wounded, who must have been brought from Rochester to Limecliff. Wounded meant dying: that was doubtless part of Owein's distress. If the casualities were heavy, it would be difficult to find a pretext to leave long enough to work on the bridge. How had the Bishop reacted to Owein? How had Alfred?

"Hullo, Tomas," said an exhausted voice directly behind him. Owein's voice.

The boy had the Sight and knew Tomas; little wonder he'd not been misled by the vibration of Tomas's shield. Still, it had given him no warning of anyone's approach, which meant that Owein's shield was in place. Why? Tomas turned eagerly, but froze when he saw his son.

Owein had never looked more like Moira. His expression was remote and unreadable, the slanting eyes hard as flawed quartz, the generous mouth utterly without affect. He stood with his arms folded across his chest and his feet a little apart. Beneath his eyes, smudges stood out against his pallor like sooty fingermarks. His hair was a wild flaxen sheaf knotted at the nape of his neck, his cloak pinned unevenly and thrown behind his shoulders, his tunic damp in places and his sleeves rolled above the elbows. Bits of straw clung to his boots and cross-gaitered trousers. And he was very well shielded indeed.

"What's troubling you?" Tomas asked quietly.

A faint crinkling of the skin about Owein's eyes was his only answer. "I saw Thought flying back to you." His voice was a trifle hoarse. "What brings you here?"

"I wanted to see you." Tomas kept his tone mild.

Too swiftly to be identified, a series of emotions flickered across Owein's face. "Why?"

"Fraine says it's chancier to communicate with you, and that you're weary and careworn. She can't work on the bridge without you, and you've stopped, and we're wondering what's amiss."

"So am I." Owein's mouth hardened. "Though it's a bit late for that."

When it became clear that Owein wouldn't speak again before Tomas did, he put as much gentleness and neutrality as he could into his voice, his face, his entire bearing. "Would you care to tell me about it?"

"I'd rather show you," said Owein flatly, turned on his heel and started off through the woods at a breakneck pace.

Frowning to himself, Tomas followed. They were heading for the fields, most of which were probably under cultivation. Though it was full twilight now, they could still meet a tenant wending his way home. "I shouldn't be seen here," Tomas said.

Owein didn't look back. "We can keep to the wood all the way to the ridge. We'll meet no one there at this hour."

The ravens were flitting through the trees in Tomas's wake. He sent them a query.

Use your reason, they told him.

His nausea grew, turning him light-headed, and the specks reappeared: dark, thick, pressing in on him. He'd always had good night vision, perhaps from his Elf blood, yet he found himself lagging behind. Owein neither slowed nor turned.

Mind your temper, Tomas told himself. Have patience. Something serious has befallen him. Something beyond his experience, or what little he has.

A faint breeze sifted through the treetops as they passed one field, then a second, and began skirting the edge of a third. All of them were fields Tomas remembered and welcomed, like a favorite tune he'd not heard in some time. He could smell moss and evergreens, wet earth and clean damp ferny air, the scents of his very own forests. He wished that it were daylight, and that he and Linley could go hiking for no more reason than the pleasure of a stroll.

Soon they reached the ridge with the copper beeches and the old cistern that Rose used to talk about sketching one day. Perhaps she had, in Tomas's absence; he would ask her. A full Moon was rising in the east, lengthening the twilight and illuminating the long wet grass atop the ridge—and numerous tufts of uprooted grass, still clinging to raw overturned sod. Graves. Fresh ones.

"You've been burying the wounded here," he said to Owein, who'd at last come to a halt opposite the cistern. To Tomas's recollection it had never been covered before.

Owein rounded on him. "How did you know?" His face was bloodless, his eyes ablaze.

"The ravens. You're tending the wounded in a barn and a granary." Tomas refrained from adding that he'd seen graves before. "Were they brought from Rochester?"

"Yes." With Tomas at his heels, Owein plunged out of the wood and made straight for the cistern. "But why ask me?" he threw back over his shoulder. "Don't you know everything?"

Breathe. Don't raise your voice. He's still a child. No, he's never been one. "Indeed not," Tomas said levelly. "What ails you, Owein? Why are you in such a temper?"

Owein was heaving the cover off the cistern. They'd chosen an old barn door for the purpose, double-paneled and heavy and thick, yet Owein sent it sailing through the air as if it were no more than a wooden kneading board. Elfin strength. Tomas recognized it; he had some of his own. He almost said that Owein was a fool to risk displaying it where the Saxons might see him. He wanted to point out that the ground was so wet that the door would have dug a furrow had it landed edgewise. He wanted to say that it was a mercy Owein hadn't disturbed any of the newly dug earth, and had he never heard of grave-robbers?

Likely he hadn't. As the ravens flapped down to the cistern wall, Tomas caught Owein's elbow and said mildly, "Compose yourself. Self-mastery is the first law of magic."

They were much of a height, their eyes at a level. Owein's were molten silver almond-shapes beneath the Moon, and his breath was coming fast. He turned his head a little aside. With his free hand he pointed and said, "Look." His voice was pitched higher than usual and oddly strained.

Even without the smell, Tomas would have guessed that the cistern held bodies. Was Owein distraught over someone lying there? Matilda, perhaps? Feeling seasick, Tomas released Owein's arm, took a few steps forward and stood at gaze.

The Moon had climbed just far enough above the treetops to illuminate the pale bruised face that he recognized, the dun-colored curls and the abraded skin of the neck. All too well, he knew what those sores meant: after his father had freed him, it had taken considerable time for the callouses from his own collar to fade. She had lost an appalling amount of flesh since he'd last seen her, but he would have known her in any state. Her round blue eyes were closed. So was her mouth with its full lower lip. He gripped the cistern wall with both hands and stared down at her. She lay on her back in an open coffin, swathed in a freshly laundered sheet, but someone had painstakingly wrapped the cloth to leave her upturned face and neck free.

"Caraid," he heard himself saying. His voice trailed away.

For a very long time there was silence on the ridge, but for the wind that fingered the branches and shivered in the tips of the wet grass, while the air turned slowly colder and the Moon rose inexorably above the trees. When a lone cloud drifted past, the light on Caraid's face dimmed and returned. The cistern was old, the stone beneath Tomas's hands pockmarked and crumbling and rough with lichen. He was chilled, but he made no move to wrap his cloak more tightly about himself. An owl called, once, some distance away.

At last he turned to Owein, whose mute and stricken stare was quickly replaced by a version of Moira's expressionless look. But the boy's jaw was tense and his face a trifle too tight, especially about the eyes, which were less stony now. "You didn't know," he said, as if he'd been arguing with himself about it.

"I had no idea." Tomas made himself breathe. "She was wearing a slave collar?"

Owein nodded. "I had them remove it after she died."

"When was that?"

"This afternoon." A muscle twitched beneath Owein's left eye. "She was in the cartload of wounded that Alfred brought. The Danes gave him their dying slaves when they recaptured their cargo."

"To demoralize the Saxons," said Tomas bitterly. He'd seen the Norse do far worse.

"She wasn't Saxon! She was Irish." Owein's voice cracked, soared up the scale a few notes. Instead of blushing he turned nearly as white as the Moon. "How did the Danes take her?"

"I don't know." Slavers call often at Dubhlinn, he was about to add, and to ask that they cover Caraid's face, but Owein shook his head vehemently and edged closer to Tomas.

"She knew you. She mistook me for you at first."

The grey eyes fastened on Tomas's face put him in mind of a stalking lynx. With a distinctly Elfin slant, they were nonetheless the precise shade of Tomas's eyes, and just as deep-set beneath that mane of Northern blond hair. What a shock Owein must have been to Caraid, still more so than she to him. "You spoke with her?" Tomas asked slowly.

"How do you suppose I knew she was Irish? I've no ravens to tell me." Owein jabbed a fingertip at the silent birds perched on the cistern wall. "Yes, I spoke to her, and she to me. She guessed who I am."

"What?" Tomas wanted to sit. He stayed where he was, still grasping the wall.

"That I'm your son and Moira's. And I said that 'Tilda mustn't know, and Caraid never let on. She sent Rose away so she could speak with me."

The night was the color of smeared charcoal. "What did she say?" Tomas stared at Caraid's mute face. She might well have said that the fault was his, for it was. Why had he not left her Dubhlinn garden right away, as she'd implored him to do, instead of pressing her to come to Wessex with him?

"That Matilda and I are in danger."

Caraid would be alive if he'd left Dubhlinn immediately.

"That you should beware of Loki."

Or if he'd not gone there at all. Aud and Brubakken had cautioned him that Caraid wouldn't follow him to Wessex.

"And that I should remember the Fates and ask the Powers."

"Ask them what?"

"I don't know! She died before she could tell me."

She'd made no complaint of Tomas, then. Instead she'd tried to warn him and his halfbreed children. To help them, and that after losing him to their mother. With an effort, he lifted his gaze from Caraid and looked at Owein. His son's wide and supple mouth, so like Moira's mouth, was a grim line. In the depths of his eyes was the faintest of red tinges, like the one in Moira's eyes when she was enraged.

"She was in pain, Tomas, but she refused Simon's cordial until she had speech with me. Then she died before we'd even finished." His voice was taut. "I was holding her hand."

"Owein..." Gods above and below. He had a long struggle to master his voice. "I am sorry out of measure that this should come to pass, and that you should witness it." He clasped Owein's shoulder.

Nothing. No softening of Owein's features, no dimming of the crimson at the back of his irises. He was staring past Tomas as if he'd not spoken at all. Perhaps Owein was still seeing Caraid's death. His first one, and what he most feared.

What would Aud do, if she were here?

Make Owein talk about it.

Which was the last thing Tomas wanted to do. He wanted to lie hidden in the woods and deal with the guilt and the grief that were burning behind his own eyes. His head throbbed insistently. He drew the deepest breath that he could, past the ache in his throat. "I wish I could have spared you this."

As if from a great distance, Owein surveyed him. "She gave me something for you."

He handed Tomas a bag sewn from blue silk, grimy and frayed, but he knew it. He'd given Caraid a whole length of that silk, the color of loganberries crushed and stirred into fresh cream, on his last visit to Dubhlinn. On his first visit there, he'd given her the jet comb whose tines he could feel inside the bag.

If he'd nursed any remote hopes that this corpse might not be Caraid, that Loki was playing some horrible jest, they were gone now. Brendan had been with Tomas when he bought Caraid that comb. It should be sent to Dubhlinn along with her body, both for sentiment and because it would help prove her identity. She and Brendan had been uncommonly close and fond. Little would be worse for Brendan than questioning whether this corpse was truly hers.

"Caraid has kin in Dubhlinn. Her brother Brendan will want these things." Tomas wanted them himself. Aware of the ravens' uncanny yellow gaze, he reached into the cistern, placed the comb and the purse on Caraid's cloth-wrapped torso, and touched her hair gently by way of farewell.

"She asked Rose to send him her body." Owein's face was bitter. "The coffin's waiting to have the lid sealed on. If no one can be spared to take it soon, they'll move it to a crypt until the next trader bound for Dubhlinn stops here."

"I should take her to Brendan," Tomas said dully. "But I can't leave Elfland that long."

"I'll go," offered Owein.

"You've no boat." Nor any idea how to sail one, but that he didn't say. "And you're needed here for the bridge."

"Can't you send me through the 'tweenlands to Dubhlinn with her? You're an adept."

Tomas had never felt less like one. "Owein," he said, striving for patience, "even if I weren't obliged to return to Elfland immediately, a great many people saw Caraid here before she died, and I expect word's got out that her body's to go to Dubhlinn. It can't just disappear—"

"I said I'd take it!" Owein was scowling.

"How would Linley explain to Alfred and the Bishop that my brother had suddenly left to take a stranger's body to Dubhlinn?"

"You weren't strangers."

He would not lose his temper. "Caraid and I weren't. But she was a stranger to everyone here, including you. Who else heard her say that she knows me?"

"Rose and Matilda," said Owein, enunciating each syllable. He had blanched a bit at the mention of the Bishop. "They told Simon and Linley. Whether Matilda's spoken of it to anyone else, I couldn't say. I thought it might seem odd to ask her to keep silent about it, so I didn't."

"You did well." Pain stabbed at the base of Tomas's skull. "They must wonder how I knew her," he muttered.

"So do I," said Owein, very softly. His Moira-expression was back: shuttered and dangerous, though most of the red gleam had ebbed from his eyes.

"Owein..." The boy deserved an explanation. "This may not be the best place to speak of it." He had to get away from Caraid's silent upturned face, from that wealth of dun hair and memories. "Shall we cover her and talk elsewhere?"

"Why not here?"

"Gods above," Tomas hissed, abruptly and overwhelmingly furious. "We are conversing over an open coffin under a full Moon, and we've not always kept our voices down. We could be taken for witches or grave robbers at any moment, and I'm supposed to be in Vestfold." Rage had an unexpectedly bracing effect; he stalked over to the barn door that still lay where Owein had hurled it. The ravens took wing and began a slow circle above the copper beeches. "Cover her face. Or don't, if that's how you left her. I'm covering the cistern."

Looking as angry as Tomas was, Owein got out of the way as Tomas slung the lid onto the cistern and started for the woods. He had splinters, but at least he could think again after a fashion. Tallah could bring Aidan here to take the body to Dubhlinn. Aidan could pass for an Irish trader, and he'd sailed the Irish Sea as a mortal would at least once before now. Moira would lose her Seer for a time, but he could be more easily spared than Tomas and the ravens.

"Where are you going?" said Owein from somewhere behind him.

"Is there an empty lean-to on the estate?"

"There's mine. I gave Alfred my place in the great hall."

"We're going to yours, then. When we've done talking, you can fetch Linley for me."

The lean-to was virtually empty save for a jug of water, a couple of blankets tossed over a wooden frame filled with musty straw, Owein's few articles of clothing and a tallow lamp. When Tomas lit it, Owein grimaced and pushed the door ajar; he must not care for smoke any more than Moira did. He eyed the ravens warily as they nudged their way into the lean-to and hopped onto his bedding. From its threadbare look, it was the last that Rose had. Apparently Owein had inherited the enviable Elfin trait of being able to fall asleep anywhere and at any time, regardless of his accommodations. Still, from the circles about his eyes, he needed more rest than he'd got of late.

Tomas swallowed a long draught from the water jug. He'd best start what promised to be a thorny conversation. At least Owein wouldn't question what he said. Thanks to Moira, he couldn't lie.

"I met Caraid in Elfland, when I first went there with Moira," he said, looking directly at Owein.

The boy was very pale but his nostrils were flared and his chin held high, and he met Tomas's gaze without flinching. Still in a temper. They both were.

"On my way to get the ravens, I was shipwrecked in the Irish Sea. A dolphin brought me into Dubhlinn harbor on a day when Brendan happened to be there. By then Caraid had returned to Dubhlinn. Brendan told her of me and she guessed who I was, and gave me a few nights' shelter before I sailed for Birka. That's when I bought her the comb."

He'd mentioned neither the draug who'd appeared to the foundering ship, nor how he'd slain his half-brother Olaf in self-defense, in full view of King Ivar of Dubhlinn and his court. Nor would he need to: Owein was fixing him with the same wordless stare.

"After leaving Asgard, I returned to Birka and then Dubhlinn, where I saw Caraid and gave her the silk. Then I came to Wessex and accepted the lands Alfred had promised me. Moira found me here. I didn't know she was carrying you and Fraine until she arrived."

"Why not?"

"She'd not yet told me."

With no hesitation, Owein asked, "Why was Caraid in Elfland?"

"She was brought there as a Seer. The Elves needed to know when and where to summon a mortal who could fetch the ravens. Their own Seers were too close to the matter to tell, and Caraid was quite gifted." He didn't want to answer any more questions, but the glint in Owein's eyes clearly meant that more were coming.

"Who brought her there? Was it by her will?"

"No. Rhys took her. He was the Elf King before..." What should he say? How much did Owein know? "He was—"

"Sent to live apart," Owein cut in. "Aubrey told Fraine and me." He looked a trifle worried. "Because we kept asking him."

"I'm glad that he did," Tomas said carefully. In many ways, the pooka had been more of a parent to the twins than either he or Moira had. How did Owein feel about living apart as opposed to dying? He might well wish that Rhys were his father; he'd be wholly an Elf then. "Owein..." Tomas ran his hands through his tangled hair. "We've been remiss as parents, Moira and I. We've not done well by you and your sister. Events have moved so swiftly and with so much at stake."

Statements, not apologies. After a moment Owein nodded.

"We haven't taught you enough. We've not spent enough time with you." He held Owein's gaze. "I regret that. You deserve far better." He sipped at the water jug. "I'm certain you have more to say." He wanted to tell Owein that his journey here had been harder than ever before, that the worlds were still drifting apart and, this last with a terrible urgency he didn't fully understand, that construction of the bridge must continue, and quickly. That they should consult Linley immediately, then Tomas should return to Elfland while he still could, and while Tallah could still bring Aidan here. More than anything, Tomas wanted to be alone with his feelings for a space. But the gulf between him and Owein was too great. More than one bridge needed building.

Owein took a swallow of water, watching Tomas all the while. He seemed calmer, but his eyes were haunted and dark. He put the jug down, corked it and wiped his mouth. Then his expression changed; he was bracing himself. Like twin bolts from a crossbow, the tilted grey eyes bore into Tomas. "Was Caraid your lover?"

Every bone in Tomas's ribcage seemed to split clear to the marrow. His heart twisted against the walls of his chest. Then his shoulders tensed; his fists started to clench. The ravens stirred a little on Owein's blankets, and Tomas bit back an outraged reply: the boy knew no better.

"Yes," Tomas said tightly, once he trusted himself to speak with any civility. His voice was composed and level, but the constraint in it could be heard nonetheless. Watching him, Owein turned two shades more pale. "That's a highly personal question, Owein. One that Moira's never asked me. If I weren't your father and you'd not seen Caraid die, you shouldn't have asked and I wouldn't have answered."

To Tomas's surprise, Owein's gaze fell. "I know." His tone was subdued. Then he gave Tomas's shoulder a fleeting touch, much the same gesture that Tomas had recently used with him. "I thank you for telling me. I—" He plucked straw from his boots. "I apologize. I needn't even have asked, really. I'd guessed as much." A great intake of breath. "She said she wished she'd been my mother."

Tomas put his head in his hands.

CHAPTER EIGHTEEN: DEPARTURES

Elfland

Moira waited with Fraine and Tallah in the hawthorn circle. Since Tomas had returned to Elfland and they'd heard his report of Owein, the twins had recommenced their work on the bridge, albeit slowly, and Fraine had been very quiet. Always a keen observer of her surroundings, she was if anything more watchful than before, yet seldom spoke unless asked a direct question. Tallah was studying the trail that led from the palace, her wings folded tightly to her body, her bare prehensile toes splayed and their claw-tips sunk ever so slightly into the earth, as if she were reluctant to leave Elfin soil again. She touched Moira's hand and pointed.

Someone was walking down the path towards them, a tall and limber man with a long stride. For a moment Moira dared to hope—but his gait was too lithe and assured for a mortal. Tomas moved more cautiously in the Elfin half-light. And this man's hair was dark.

It was Aidan. She steeled herself against the disappointment, loathe to let him read it in her face.

"My ladies," he said with a softening of his features that wasn't quite a smile. In his eyes was a cautious warmth, but no pity. Moira suppressed her relief along with everything else. No feelings. Not yet.

Fraine gave him a smile and said nothing. He bowed to Tallah, who returned the bow with one of her own, so deep that her matted hair brushed the ground. She could be unpredictable in her partialities and prejudices, but she liked Aidan.

So did Moira. She studied the Seer she was about to lose for a time. She and Nissyen had worked out the general outlines of Aidan's story, and although Aidan could no more lie than could the rest of Elves, he was quick-witted, and possessed more than enough Sight to know whom to avoid. His black hair, rather delicate fair skin and extraordinarily blue eyes would all help him pass as a Norse-Irish merchant. For his clothing, Aubrey had conjured up the sort of garb that might be favored by a prosperous trader scouring Waleis and Wessex for potential customers. Cross-gaitered trousers, looser-fitting than those that Tomas habitually wore. A better pair of boots with far thicker soles, their leather treated against the wet. A tunic of good Frisian cloth, and a very fine belt to which was fastened a well-filled purse. Over the centuries, the Elves had brought plenty of coins back to Faerie. Here they were of no value, but one never knew when one might have need of them in Midgard, and Aidan must buy passage for both himself and a coffin. Hanging from his belt was also an empty sheath where an all-purpose knife might go. His stout woolen cloak was fastened at the shoulder by an oversized and ornate silver ring-pin that a trader might wear to display his affluence. Nissyen's suggestion, that.

Sometimes the Elemental was quite useful. It had even drawn sketches to help the pooka get Aidan properly kitted out.

"You look perfect," said Moira. "I shall congratulate Aubrey and Nissyen. Are you ready?"

"I am," said Aidan thinly, and reached for Tallah's hand. He would need to maintain contact with her during the passage, since she'd be guiding it.

Tallah gave his wrist a pat, turned to Moira and said in her own language, "Foot."

Sometimes Moira wished she'd not tried to learn the Parcae's speech. "Aidan," she began, "Tallah thinks you would fare better if you held her foot instead. I expect she wants her wings unencumbered."

"Her foot," muttered Aidan. He looked at Tallah; she looked gravely back. "Now?"

"Yes."

"How does she propose to get aloft with... Pay me no mind." To Fraine he said gently, "I'll give Owein your greeting, my lady." He held his hand out to Tallah again. With her back to him, she looked over her shoulder and daintily pressed her hairy foot into his palm. "Go now."

Moira put up a shield breachable by Tallah alone, then closed her eyes. She'd provide all the assistance she could for the departure, although she was merely a passive source for Tallah to draw upon should there be need. Fraine had offered to help but didn't know how to make herself a source for anyone but Owein, and their connection was innate, not learned. It was harder to erect a partial shield than a full one, and Moira had no time to teach her.

They had so little help, her children. For all of Rose and Linley's desire to be of assistance and everything that Linley's astrolabe could tell him, Tomas reported that they 'd been able to make no suggestions about what part of the bridge to build once the eight points were done. If Tomas had any insights, he'd not offered them. The twins themselves had decided to proceed with whatever section seemed easiest, wherever they could make the most headway.

Moira had confidence they would choose well. At any moment of any mortal day, the twins knew where the Sun would set, where the Moon lurked above or beneath the horizon and where the stars would tiptoe next. Linley needed an astrolabe to divine such things, but the twins could sense the pace and motion of the mortal world and its time-bound matter. More importantly for the bridge, each twin could also sense the direction of the other, within the same world or across two.

"I've no idea how," Fraine had said once, frustrated, when Aubrey pressed her for an explanation. "I can tell, that's all. How can you tell that your feet are on the ground and how steep a hill you're climbing? And that left is left and right is right and which way the wind blows?"

How indeed, thought Moira now. Tallah and Aidan were gone, not without some draining of Moira's energy, for her joints felt momentarily stiff and her mouth was dry. Without a word, she and Fraine made their way back to the crumbling palace. After a silent embrace they parted company, and Moira turned her steps towards the wing that held Jared's former quarters.

Tomas wasn't where she'd last seen him, sitting on Jared's sofa and cleaning his flute with painstaking slowness. Now the flute lay in its case on the gaming table, while his harp stood in a corner by his satchel. She lifted the cover and ran a hand down the harpstrings. In perfect tune. Perhaps he'd been playing. That would be a welcome change.

"Tomas?" She opened the door to their room. The silk coverlets he'd given her gleamed upon the empty bed. His clothes were folded on a chair in the corner, his new boots tucked under a rung. The air was stuffy, for Jared insisted that the windows remain closed and barred. The entire room looked untouched since the fenodyree had last cleaned. So did the austere bath and the pantry and the surprisingly well-equipped kitchen. She'd never have guessed that Jared enjoyed cooking.

Tomas often left his harp here in their quarters, but he and his flute were virtually inseparable. Where would he have gone without it? She didn't want to use magic to find him. Not now. Not when he was dealing with a mortal death, and she was an Elf and immortal. Was he wishing he'd left with Aidan? And remembering the Irish Sea and the draug that had declined to take his life with the rest of the Vestfold traders, all drowned now, with whom he'd set sail for Dubhlinn? Perhaps he'd gone to the Sea, down to the shore below the palace. If he had, he'd not want to get sand in his flute.

From a peg by the door Moira took her old green cape, noted the absence of Tomas's cloak, and set off for the shortcut to the water. Not by magic, but through the tunnels under the palace. With luck they'd not all collapsed. She wanted to call no attention to herself, and she wished to meet no one on the way.

The tunnels were passable, although two were nearly blocked by rubble and fallen earth. By the time Moira forced her way out of doors, her cape was dusty and her hands and hair streaked with grime. Breathing the salt air, she stood for a moment on the splintered promontory just above the strand. Below her the water was a foaming green cauldron, and a hard wind caught the spray and snatched the cobwebs from her hair. The Sea was rougher than when she'd last walked here. It would grow rougher yet, she suspected, the farther that Elfland drifted from the mortal world and its Moon.

At first she didn't see Tomas. She'd expected to find him trudging along the shore, perhaps, leaning into the wind, heedless of the spray. Instead he was sitting on a flat untrodden stretch of sand a little above the waterline, where the eddies curved and bubbled nearest the promontory. The ravens had taken a position at the foot of a nearby cliff and out of the wind. Tomas's hair was a snarled mass of witchknots, his cloak bannered like a sail, his chin in his palms and his boots soaked. He seemed intent on the crash and thunder of the waves. As she drew closer, she saw irregular splotches of moisture rimed with salt upon his clothes. He'd been there for some time. If he noticed her approaching, he gave no sign of it till she was almost upon him. Then he turned a masklike face in her direction and made an effort to smile. He was very pale, but for the taut hollows of his eyes.

"Aidan and Tallah have gone," she said neutrally.

"Without my seeing them off." Moving like a marionette with a tangled string, he rose and made a perfunctory effort to stamp sand from his boots.

"Fraine and I did."

He didn't seem to know what to do with his hands. "I'm sorry."

"For?"

"For not being there with the two of you," he said, missing a beat. His eyes were nearly as turbulent as the Sea behind him. "How is Fraine?"

"As she was. I can't speak for Owein."

Tomas shoved a lock of wind-whipped hair from his face. He was looking at her, meeting her eyes, even, but he wasn't seeing her. Too many thoughts lay in between. After a moment he appeared to realize she might expect him to respond. "His work with Fraine will likely go faster once Alfred and Werferth have gone."

"When might that be?"

"I couldn't say."

She kept her voice calm. "Could you not guess?"

"What?" His gaze remained caught somewhere in the past, spiraling in upon itself like a swift-running stream that had just been dammed.

"Tomas," she said in a still, careful voice, "we have just sent our only remaining Seer to Limecliff. It's well that the twins have started working again, and that they have no more than a point or two of the eight left to build. But they must complete all the rest of the bridge too, and as soon as possible. Have you not noticed the condition of the Sea?" When she pointed over his shoulder, she saw a vague acknowledgment in his face, but he neither spoke nor turned to look. "You and I are too close to events at Limeciff to employ our own Sight. You are better acquainted with Alfred than I, and know more about how Bishops behave. Would you please hazard a guess about how much longer the pair of them could be housed there?"

He let out his breath slowly. "Alfred would want to stay for another night or two. His niece is there, and he can quiz Owein about my doings." His brows drew together. "But Werferth might prefer to leave immediately. Owein's shaken him badly and he's lost a lover."

"Did you and Owein discuss his future demeanor in the presence of Alfred or the Bishop?"

Tomas studied her for a few seconds, his eyes wide and dark and flickering. "No. Linley did."

"What did he advise?"

"I wasn't there."

"Where were you?"

He met her gaze. A muscle along his jawline moved. "In Owein's lean-to."

Had Owein seen Tomas so distraught that he'd not been able to counsel his son or his friend? His friend who'd taken risks for them and who'd been—not implicated in *maleficium*, not yet, but certainly compromised by his association with Tomas and now with Owein. Although Alfred had appearances to maintain, he meant neither Tomas nor Owein any harm. Daniel, however, most certainly did. Owein had just shamed and frightened the Bishop before Alfred and the hermit, and no doubt provided Daniel with all manner of fuel for a campaign against him.

How much guidance could Linley have offered Owein? Linley and his brother Simon were fine men, and Moira had formed a deep affection for them. But they were mortals, full-blooded and only half-Sighted, one bound with constrictions from Alfred's Church, and both of them scarcely more qualified to keep Owein from further blunders than Matilda was. While Matilda herself could provide ample occasion for another kind of misstep.

"Did you ask Owein what Linley had counseled him?"

"No." Tomas's mouth tightened. "I would guess it was not to betray any knowledge he'd gained by the Sight." His voice was strained, but he looked her directly in the eye.

Which made it harder to say what she still felt that she must. "What are your intentions, Tomas?"

"My intentions?" His brows were aloft.

"When you've returned from the funeral."

He stared. Waves tumbled and sang behind his back; the salt air stung her skin, stung her eyes. "I've not gone to it, Moira. Nor will I."

"Then *be present.*"

A spark, faint and sullen, kindled in his gaze. "Where do you think I am?"

"Somewhere in your past." Tomas's liaison with Caraid didn't trouble Moira; nor did his pain at the Irishwoman's demise. Were he not grieved, Moira would have thought less of him. But what mattered was that he was with her, Moira, now, and had been since long before Caraid's death. What mattered was that Moira had need of Tomas, his magic, his Sight, a show of strength from him as her fellow regent—and that his children needed him still more. How well would they adapt to their mixed blood and the unique tasks required of them, if the only other halfbreed they knew were to crumble in the face of death? Not that the death had caused him sorrow, but that he'd allowed the sorrow to stop him. Owein in particular should not see Tomas in that state, and Owein might already have.

What made it all the more difficult was that she loved Tomas, a feeling that she hadn't expected, had originally fought against and that was still growing. She wished this sorrow hadn't come to him and that, having come, she could lessen it. Later, she hoped, she could tell him so. If he came back; if he went forward. But not as he was now. All the more reason to shock him into the present.

Hands on his hips, his expression grim, he was studying her. "My past is why Caraid died as she did," he said, dropping the words like stones. "Dubhlinn's no tiny hamlet for slavers to raid with impunity, and she was wary of them. There's a very dark reason they managed to take her, but it's too close for me to see." For half a moment he sighted across the water as if he expected the wind to drive a ship with bare poles over the horizon. "The fault is mine," he said with finality. "Caraid's Sight told her that if she had anything further to do with me, she would die not long after."

Moira kept her face neutral. "She and her Sight also told you to beware of Loki, and that Owein and Matilda were in danger. We should honor her counsel. It means that we've work to do—"

"Has it all been about work for you?" Tomas interrupted. "The Elves kidnapped her for her Sight and me for an errand boy. She'd no recourse against you." His eyes were hard. "But with me you got more than you bargained for. Fool into Mage."

"You are not conducting yourself like one now," she said levelly.

"A Fool or a Mage? If there's a difference between them, you've not bothered to explain it. She wouldn't have died if I hadn't been both. But that doesn't seem as important as your bridge."

"I'll explain whatever you please, Tomas. Have you bothered to ask? And it's our bridge and our children. They need you now, at your best. Don't they matter to you?"

"Of course they do! So do you. Do I look to you so uncaring?"

She took a breath, but he cut her off: "I don't know if you can't understand how I feel, Moira, or if you won't. You've observed mortals long enough to know how difficult a death can be. Particularly if we bear any guilt for it, regardless of whether an—attachment is broken." He sliced at the air with one hand. "Surely you should understand that sort of loss, even though it doesn't happen to Elves."

Later she would realize it was at that moment she had lost her temper, so fast that she had no rising irritation to let her know she should mind her tongue. She had no warning at all.

"How dare you tell me what I should understand about loss," she said in a soft and deadly voice. "I have lost Rhys."

Tomas went stone-still, as if he weren't so much as breathing, as if he'd never move again. He gave her a haunted stare from white-rimmed eyes.

"Where Caraid's soul is now I could not say, but in time it will enter another body and forget all that befell her in this one," said Moira. "While everything that was Rhys, all our history together—"

Tomas flinched.

"—he is fully aware of and will remain so." And likely remain as crazed as he'd been when he was sent apart. Rhys had hurt her beyond bearing and beyond pardon, and in too many ways that wound was still raw, but nonetheless she'd almost prefer his madness to his regaining sanity wherever he was now. "He'll stay trapped in whatever tree or rock or clod of earth where Isolde sent him. Only she knows where, and Loki burned her so badly that it could be mortal millennia before she's any more than cinders."

"Moira," began Tomas, low and intent.

She ignored him, smoldering, all the words rolling out of her like lava. "You know the Parcae's prophecy as well as I. If we do not complete this bridge quickly, Midgard may become cinders too. All its magic gone, all its greenery withered—" She jabbed a finger at the Sea. "And all its water poisoned. Gone with its link to Elfland, and we Elves no better than mummies, yet as aware of their condition as Rhys is. Are those the two worlds you want for our children?"

Pale as lichen, he gave a single shake of his head.

"We should heed Caraid's warning. I've no idea what Loki plans, but I know he wants to be the only Power in Midgard. So do the Christians, and I will bargain with *neither* of them." To her mortification she started to tremble. "I see no compromise. Either we finish that bridge or we are lost, and Midgard with us."

His expression was grim, his eyes unreadable.

"The twins need you here and now. Your Sight; your knowledge of mortals; your ability to travel and manipulate iron. They need you as regent. Evan's not done challenging us and there could be other rebels." She took a breath, striving for calm. "Root and branch, Tomas, I neither challenge nor object to anything you feel, and I'd not wish an end like Caraid's on anyone. But I beg of you, don't let it paralyze you. She's dead, but your son and Alfred's niece are alive and in peril, and they need you able to *act*."

His face shifted, grew inward. He turned a little aside and stared at the boiling sea again, squinting against the spray. Some of his anger seemed to have ebbed though by no means all, no more than had hers. Fatigue weighted his gaze. Along with his grief, still there in abundance, she saw another kind of pain and suspected she'd caused it.

She waited. She'd spoken her piece, and he was turning something over in his mind. Digging her heels into the sand didn't stop her trembling. She might have lost him. She wrapped her cloak about her body and studied his rigid profile while the wind shredded her hair into broomstraw and gibbered in her ears.

She was weary. She wanted to fling herself down on the sand and carve out great gouts of it with her fingers, but she remained standing. Tomas hadn't moved and neither had the ravens. Aubrey had come to the promontory and left as soon as he spotted them. Nissyen had appeared on the cliff and departed promptly too. Some time later Jared had arrived, staying on the promontory only a bit longer than the pooka had, which was not a good sign. Still, the bodyguards that Tomas and Moira had eluded weren't sent back to them, not even to lie hidden some distance away. Moira extended a tendril of energy to check, but didn't put up her shield.

Nor did Tomas. A succession of thoughts moved across his face like the phases of the mortal Moon: full to overflowing, waning, dark.

It was a long wordless time before Moira recognized that she'd lost her temper.

After a while, she realized that although she might have erred, she'd take none of it back.

When she remembered that Tomas's mother had died a slave, she wanted to touch him but made no move to do so, deeming it wiser to wait, to let him be, to let him speak when he was ready.

She would come to understand that in doing so, she had definitely erred.

"Moira," said Tomas, turning to her at last. She caught her breath: he looked ten mortal years older. "You and our children have a claim on my aid, and you may call upon it at any time. You have my word." A low, calm voice. A bard's voice, trained and expressive. He'd said much the same to her in Wessex, when she'd found her way, pregnant and so ill she could hardly stand, to his doorstep, and he'd taken her in before the unnerved Saxons. But then he'd spoken with a raw voice and a hungry face. Now he was a courteous stranger. "What seems most important at present is that Owein and Matilda are in danger. How can we best determine its nature?"

She gripped his arm. "Tomas." He didn't move. He always responded when she touched him. Even when he tried to suppress his reaction, she could sense it, like a tide flowing towards her. Now she might have laid her hand on a stone. "Tomas, don't."

No change in his face.

"Don't cast me out." She was shaking again. "I've hurt you. I regret it. I'm truly sorry to see you grieved."

Nothing altered in his expression, but he put his shield up. He'd never done so when they were alone.

"I'm no threat to you." For an instant she wondered if the sand beneath her feet were quaking along with her.

"I can either act or feel at the moment, Moira. Not both," he said very quietly. "The twins need me to act, and I will." For a few seconds he gazed at her, completely here now, not struggling with a past that could no longer be blamed for the barricades in his face. "If you yourself want anything more from me, you've not mentioned it—"

"*Want* anything? I want *you*!"

"—and I am not prepared to discuss it just now."

"Tomas!" She dropped his arm, reached for him with both of hers.

He took a step backwards, into the Sea. A churning green wave broke over his shoulders and soaked him to the skin. Almost gently, he said, "Please don't press me. When I can speak of it, I will."

She stared at him. Water swirled about him and tugged at his knees.

"When I'm needed, come find me," he said. And turned, narrowing his eyes against the spray, and was gone.

CHAPTER NINETEEN: ROSE'S VISITOR

Midgard

When the tapping sounded at the door of Limecliff's great hall that afternoon, Rose had just drifted over the edge of unconsciousness. Simon and Susannah had sent her to rest, and when the pair of them joined forces they would brook no argument. The bedcloset door was open and Rose turned her head, uncertain whether she'd been dreaming or had truly heard a knock. Then it came again, brisk but light, a shade on the tentative side. Most likely a stranger.

She was alone in the hall, but the grounds were overrun with Alfred's men, who would have questioned anyone suspicious. So would Linley, who had better instincts about people than anyone Rose had ever met. "Half a moment," she called. Sighing, she rubbed the sleep from her eyes, finger-combed her thick brown hair and tied her kerchief over it.

"Good day to you, my lady," said the smiling and well-dressed young man whom she found on the doorstep. An Irishman, from the lilt in his voice. He certainly looked it. Spectacular blue eyes with dark lashes. Well-defined, symmetrical features, a bit on the sharp side. Rather a handsome man, actually. Thick black curls, slight frame, good posture. But it was his long pale whimsical face and the diffident humor in the set of his mouth that she found herself liking immediately.

"Rose, is it? Your husband Linley said you had a sweet face and brown eyes. He sent me to speak with you. My name's Aidan; I'm traveling through Wessex on my way to Dubhlinn." He hesitated, keeping his gaze on hers, but she knew he'd noticed her rumpled shift and stockinged feet. "I've not disturbed you now, have I? It would be no trouble for me to return later. No trouble at all."

"Come in," she said without hesitation, stepping aside. Linley had sent him.

Aidan ducked through the doorway—he was taller than she'd first judged. His nostrils flared ever so slightly as he glanced about the hall. The herbs on the floor were musty; everyone had been too busy to change them. She gave her guest a tankard of water, waved him into Tomas's high-backed wooden armchair, pulled a bench opposite and asked what she and Linley could do for him.

"It's more what I could do for you, truth to tell," said Aidan, looking sober. "Your husband tells me that a young woman by the name of Caraid died here recently, and that her remains and belongings want transporting to her brother in Dubhlinn, one Brendan O'Quinlan." He rubbed the bridge of his nose. "I've offered to take them to him."

She'd suspected as much. "I thank you," she said quietly. "You're very kind."

"Not at all. As I've business there myself, it's no bother at all, I assure you." He lowered his voice. "Linley and I have made arrangements for the coffin. He says that the young lady's belongings were stored here?"

"I'll fetch them." She went to the loft, took Caraid's purse of blue silk and its comb from a trunk. When she reached down to give them to Aidan from mid-ladder, his face went strangely blank for an instant before he tucked the silk in his shirt. He offered her his hand before she reached the last rung but she shook her head, smiling. What manners. He was likely a merchant. "Are you far from your ship?"

"I haven't one in your waters at the moment. I've gone on foot all this trip, seeing whose acquaintance I might make and what goods they might have for me." He flashed her a smile so full of good humor and dimples that she had to smile back. No doubt he'd made friends along the way. "From here I'm bound for the Saefren, and there I'll book passage to Dubhlinn. I'll find the poor woman's brother with no trouble. I know Dubhlinn town well; I've lived near it most of my life."

"We're much obliged to you, and we shan't forget it," Rose said. "When you return, I hope you'll bring your wares our way. What do you trade?"

Aidan's brow puckered ever so slightly. "Now that is a very good question. On this trip at least, I've mostly traded information." A sneeze, loud and sudden. "Your pardon!" He rubbed the bridge of his nose.

"Granted," she said, amused. Every craft had its secrets. Perhaps he hoped to become the only source for some bit of custom or other. "You're not taking cold, I hope?" He did look rather pale. "Would it help you to stop here with us for the night? You'd be welcome, and you could be on the road directly after we hear Mass with the King in the morning." When Alfred was at Limecliff, Mass was celebrated at dawn, and everyone on the estate who could attend was politely expected to do so.

"I think not, though I thank you most heartily, my lady," said Aidan. "I'd best refuse your invitation and be on my way. I'm needed at home, you see. Shall I have word sent here once I've delivered the remains?"

An odd question. Almost as odd as passing up an opportunity to meet Alfred, with whom any merchant would want to establish a friendly acquaintance. Surely Aidan realized that Rose was offering him one good turn for another.

If she hadn't suddenly grown suspicious, she might have remained caught up in Aidan's charm and never noticed the pointed delicacy of his features, his graceful narrow hands, balanced carriage and the slant of those breathtaking long-lashed eyes. They were reddened now; he was suppressing the sniffles. Not only that, there was a pained set to his jaw, as if his teeth had been on edge since he'd entered the hall. Something in it was plaguing him.

Perhaps Aidan wasn't an Irishman with the manners of a young lord and twice the looks of one, though nothing that approached Owein's beauty.

Perhaps Aidan was an Elf, and was fighting the iron-sick from Rose's cookware and her visitors' weapons. Another Elf beneath Tomas's roof, or at least another halfbreed. Still, Linley had doubtless guessed what Aidan was and Linley had sent him here, so there was no cause for alarm. Gently, to show that Aidan was trusted, Rose said, "I don't believe that will prove necessary, unless you've a wish to send word. Let's leave that up to you, shall we?"

From the easing of tension in Aidan's face, he'd seen that she guessed his secret and that she would keep it. The warmth of his smile caught her unawares. "I've something to ask you then, Rose. And something to tell, before I'm on my way," he said, holding her gaze. All the artfulness had left his voice, though the lilt remained. "First, will you please have a care for the lady Matilda?"

"Is she in danger?"

"Not from Owein," said the Elf mildly.

Rose felt her face growing hot. She'd no idea she was so easy to read. Linley said she wasn't, and Linley should know.

"I couldn't say from where. That's the trouble. So would you please be mindful of her?" Another incandescent smile. "As you are now, I'm sure."

She gave her promise. The Elf stood for a moment looking down at her with his dark head tilted to one side. "Never fret that you haven't the Sight, my lady." Were his voice any softer, he would have been whispering. His eyes were piercingly blue. "You have a perceptiveness that's uncommon even with the Sight and twice as rare without it, and a strength that will grow. Fare you well."

CHAPTER TWENTY: Beltane

Midgard

At last there remained of the eight gate-points only Beltane for the twins to construct, and Owein was in a fever of impatience to get on with it. They would perform the work that very night. Beltane night. That Beltane should be the last point made little sense to him, since Rose said that in ancient times it was Samhain, the festival opposite Beltane on the great wheel of the seasons, that ended one year and began the next. But nothing made much sense to him of late.

After the evening meal, Owein set out for the willow grove, circumventing all the bonfires and ignoring the inviting pair or so of feminine eyes that studied him from the hedgerows. None of those eyes belonged to Matilda, who'd been tongue-tied in his presence throughout the day. Everyone else seemed in a good humor, yet he thought that Rose was observing him a bit more closely, and had been during the weeks since Aidan had come and gone.

He felt vaguely guilty for not having seen Aidan off, but he'd wanted to go to Dubhlinn too badly to trust himself not to plead. He wanted to know more about Caraid. Like Simon and Linley, she was a mortal who had the Sight. If she'd been Owein's mother, he might not have belonged to two worlds at once and fully to neither. Might not have been answerable for the bridge, or smelled the despair about Tomas when he spoke of Caraid. Despair hadn't much of a scent, the way a stone hadn't. It was hard and cool and dense and leaden, and frightening because it seemed so irrevocable.

Then again, from what Aubrey had told the twins, a unique pairing of parents produced a unique offspring. If Caraid were Owein's mother, Fraine might not be his twin, and that he could not imagine. To be separated from Fraine temporarily was one matter, and more difficult with each passing day. But never to have known her at all was unthinkable.

She was in Elfland now, where she missed him, where she was experiencing some disquiet at the moment, where she was waiting for him to enter trance and the 'tweenlands for their next working. Because he existed, so did Fraine, and they lived and moved in a kind of rhythm with one another, the way the mortal Moon drew and released the seas. That predictability was one of the few things he liked about Midgard.

It was warm for early May, but cooler in Limecliff's woods. Tomas's woods. They smelled of moss and ferns and running water, reawakening sap and tender new bark, small feathered and furred presences and their patchwork of disputed boundaries. Earth Elementals stirred at Owein's passing, craning their chunky necks to peer up at him from the roots and boulders where they sat, then returned their enraptured attention to the surging green plantfire all about. More alert than alarmed, deer in their nests of flattened grass swiveled their ears towards the sound of his footsteps, and their flanks quivered as he went by. They smelled of grain and sweat, sweeter than horses, ranker than cows. He caught a more pungent scent as two exuberant fox cubs nearly left their den to stalk him. Once a badger melted into a thicket at his approach, and a motionless young owl scowled at him from a nearby branch. He knew why; he might startle the game: the mice, the shrews, the voles.

He liked the forests of Midgard and its sleeping hills, small rushing streams and brown rivers, its hazel hedges and profusion of wildlife. He liked Cheddar gorge and its limestone cliffs, the marshes to the south and the fields of his father's estate. He particularly liked the stars, the Sun's blinding fire on its daily visit and the moody cyclical light of the Moon. As long as he could be out of doors, he didn't resent being in the mortal realm quite so much, though he wished Fraine were here with him.

The land began to slope now, down towards the creek and the willow grove, and the air held more moisture. Owein relished the taste and the softness of it after the smoky hall. The creek was full, the water running high after the recent rains, the willows tingling with pale green buds. Heedless of the damp, he stretched out on the matted grass and closed his eyes.

The ginger-haired man was there again. Some distance away, floating in the 'tweenlands. A slight mocking twist to his mouth. Hands clasped behind his back, wide-eyed and silent, watching Owein.

The man had been there for the last few points, although only until Owein made contact with Fraine. To Fraine the redhead paid no attention at all; he simply faded away. So did Owein's memory of having seen the man again, which was disquieting for the brief instant he was aware of what he was about to lose.

It was always the same in the 'tweenlands, always the same before a working.

Fraine? Owein thought at her, when a faint and agreeable warmth in the center of his sternum told him that her energy was near. The warmth increased slightly, an acknowledgment, while the tightening of his facial skin meant an inquiry: was he well?

Yes. I miss you.

More warmth, with an ache at its center like a small chunk of bone. Then his chest tightened—she wasn't easy in her mind. After a moment he got an image of Tomas, features drawn and white, head turning away now, cloak enveloping his shoulders. Troubled. And another picture: Moira, also distressed, tight-lipped, eyes frozen, looking in the opposite direction.

Then an image of the unfinished bridge appeared, so abruptly and with such solidity that Owein recoiled a bit. Insistence from Fraine, felt as a churning beneath Owein's diaphragm. She wanted to begin.

So did he. The sooner the blasted thing was done, the better. He slowed his breathing.

Out, above, in the open air. His body motionless in the long wet grass below. Stars ablaze on their paths, the earth curved and turning her face from the Sun. The Moon was up now, near the full, wheeling towards the top of the eastern sky. Shimmering lines of force all about, from the Moon, the unseen Sun, the Pole Star and, more faintly, all the other stars as well. Let the power gather, the images grow. Sort through the lines of energy. He could so easily lose himself without the strongest line of all, the one that told him where Fraine was.

It was longer than usual before he saw the bridge. Not the sort they had in Midgard, all clumsy wooden slats with a disturbing tendency to crack and give way, so badly did the weather use them. This bridge was formed by long spokes of light, not wood, a coppery light fading to an anemic saffron in too many places—Fraine was right; they had to work faster. This bridge didn't cross anything. It wasn't even a straight line, more of a rayed spiral stretching in several directions at once. From some angles it was a helix. He always got the uncomfortable feeling that more of the bridge existed than he could see at any one time or from any particular vantage point. And it was made of far more dark and animate air even than of light, or of space or time.

Owein waited, turning, impatient for more of the structure to wheel slowly into view. There was the spring equinox point, light and dark in equal measures, the light just beginning to grow. It was connected to the fall equinox by whirling lines and the tethered gaits of earth and Sun. Yes, he could see the fall point now, dark and light in parallel with the dark just waxing, and red sputtering out here and there along its rays of energy. All the points, all the lines were moving, turning, breathing as the earth breathed, and they all led to one another.

Now he saw the Imbolc point, a wilderness of sparks in the empty space between the winter solstice and the spring equinox. And the Lammas point, the first harvest, hot and fiery, exhaling with the inhalation of Imbolc opposite. He and Fraine had been born near Imbolc. The feast of candles, lighting the return of the Sun that began at Yule, the winter solstice. At Yule, the rebirth of the light from the depths of winter. From the Yule point Owein turned and considered its opposite: midsummer. The summer solstice when the earth was awash with light, yet the return of the dark began.

Light and dark, waxing and waning. Sun and Moon in their patterned dance about the earth, with all the stars to mark their steps. Light and dark, life and death. He looked at Samhain.

He and Fraine had built it last, that point. Just before Caraid died, there in Midgard beneath the rule of time. Samhain, when the earth was dying. Samhain, the descent below, of seed and husk and all things spent. Owein had seen some entities and sensed many more, of both good and ill intent, crowding about for that particular working. The Samhain point had taken the most power to construct, culling something like the essence of iron, something that in some wise ran both within and beyond his blood, and hurtling it across the 'tweenlands to show Fraine where to aim what she was hurling at him in turn.

It was a kind of anchor, iron. A kind of arrow, too. And it meant here, *and* now, *and* this rather than that, *in a way that Owein sensed was foreign to the Elfin part of his nature. Iron meant direction. It was of the earth, iron, and it helped moor the bridge to Midgard.*

Every time he and Fraine built another point he felt depleted, craved rest and silence. With every working the fatigue that followed it grew worse. He hoped that the Beltane point would be easier to construct. If Samhain was death—and the door between life and death and whatever walked there—then Beltane, its opposite on the wheel of the year, must be life. And that which created life.

He wasn't surprised that the energy he sent unerringly towards his sister came more from the groin of his tranced body than it ever had. What startled him was the sudden image of Tomas that flashed into his mind. Of Tomas with Moira on a river bank one mild evening. Owein blocked the picture, but not before he understood that particular evening had been Beltane too, and the night when he and Fraine were conceived.

Conceived at Beltane, born near Imbolc. With that thought came the realization that something of Tomas's essence reached both forward to his son and backward to his father. Another image appeared, a grim-faced man of middle years, a man with strong Norse bones, a nose not quite so crooked as Tomas's, pale hair like Owein's own, and no softness in his expression. With a petrified brown-haired girl, perhaps Matilda's age, who had Tomas's eyes and hands. And a slave collar—

Owein blotted out the picture as fast as he could. Slowly and carefully, like extending his fingertips and stretching his arm a few millimeters past its habitual reach, he aimed another tendril of energy at Fraine. Are you seeing images? *he asked. He got an affirmative, faint but definite.*

When another vision began to form, he knew it would be of his own son. But that one he positively did not want to see, because it would show his son's mother and the conception, and because he was finding it so difficult to ignore his body and its urges in Midgard that such images might make it worse. He stared at the bridge as single-mindedly as he could but the picture came anyway, relentlessly, only he wouldn't look at her face, he wouldn't he wouldn't he wouldn't, and it was sweet and heavy and unbearable and overwhelming and one compressed perfect universe of pleasure with him at its center but all too brief, and then when he did look at her face, when he could, it was blurred.

Relief, immense and immediate. And disappointment, which made no sense. The cord linking him to his body twitched. He was losing concentration. He had to finish and he'd barely started; from now on he would look only at the bridge until he was done.

The Beltane point was a whirlpool of soft light, not blinding at all. It was beautiful, the only point to have so many colors and whose energy carried such a definite pulse. And it was finished! How could that be?

Something exploded all around him.

He was falling. No, it was he who had exploded. He couldn't breathe. But he wasn't in his body—

"Owein!"

He was now. Painfully, arching his back, gasping for air as if his ribcage were crushed. Willow branches reeled and thrashed above his head. He let out a groan.

"Owein?"

Someone gripped his elbow. He heaved himself upright.

"Dear God, should I fetch Simon?"

He found himself staring at Matilda's tear-stained face. There were dead leaves in her hair, a streak of grime on her forehead. She wore a falconer's glove on one hand, and she smelled of sweat and burnt grain and fear.

"No, no," he said in threadbare voice, both embarrassed and glad to see her. "No need for that." His clothes were soaked with sweat and dew and he was freezing. In his mind's eye he could still see the Beltane point. "What brings you here, 'Tilda?"

Her chin quivered. "I must have been careless closing the outer door of the mews. I was working with Trevor." Trevor was a raw young goshawk, though already more tame than wild, at least with Matilda. "And he got away."

Owein pulled his cloak about his torso and levered himself slowly to his feet. The skin at the base of his spine was prickling so strongly that it almost stung. Something odd was going on. Matilda was more careful than anyone about securing the doors to the mews. Besides, he felt watched, and by more than the forest dwellers whom he and Matilda had just startled into flight. He sent what energy he could spare to his shield. He wasn't as tired as he'd feared he would be after the working, but he was disoriented. He'd come out of trance far too roughly—and made a spectacle of himself in front of Matilda. "Did you come after him alone?"

"Yes." She sounded defensive. "I know I shouldn't have, but he'd only get farther away while I wheedled someone into bearing me company." She glanced aside. "And I didn't want to disturb Rose and Linley."

So he was alone in the woods with Alfred's niece on Beltane night, and she'd not told anyone where she was going or why. They should return as soon as possible, but she'd never abandon a bird if there were the slightest hope of catching him. "Have you any idea where Trevor is?"

"Not now. I followed him as best I could and I brought a lure, but he had the start of me and he stayed well ahead. When I lost sight of him, I kept on in the direction he'd been taking. Then I tripped over you lying here, and you came stark upright screaming."

Small wonder he'd been jolted back to his senses. He was grateful that she probably couldn't see the color flooding his face. If he could help her find the hawk, perhaps he wouldn't look such a fool. Suddenly he could smell wormwood about Matilda, and it gave him a pang. Never before had she been wary of him.

"Are you certain you're well?" she finished in a small voice.

"Quite well," he said firmly, trying to suppress his shivers. He didn't like the sound of her story, as if something had driven the hawk towards him. Wouldn't an escaped bird have cleared the treetops altogether and put as much distance between itself and the estate as possible or lain hidden somewhere till dawn, rather than fluttering from tree to tree in the dark?

Matilda must have decided not to ask what he'd been about, but he should probably offer an explanation. "I went for a walk and stopped here a while; I'm fond of these willows, you know. I suppose I fell asleep."

She nodded. Doubtfully. "Perhaps you had another nightmare."

It was an offer, and he accepted it. "I think perhaps I did." He managed a grin. "Something about a mad falconer attacking people in the woods. It was dreadful."

"Don't," she said, coloring, but he got a tremulous smile. "A fine falconer I am. I just lost Trevor."

Damn the goshawk and whatever had sent it this way. "You should go home, 'Tilda," he said as gently as he could. "Perhaps I can find Trevor for you. You'll only catch the grippe out here."

She stared at him. "It's not cold."

Nor was it; it was he who couldn't get warm—he who seldom if ever felt chilled. How many more mistakes would he make before he got her back to the great hall, or a hue and cry was loosed after the pair of them? Alfred's visit was over, so any search would fall to Linley, but the King could get wind of the matter nonetheless. "They'll be in a fret when they find we've gone," he said, trying not to sound blunt.

Her face went still, more from embarrassment than fear. And from something else, too: disappointment, perhaps? Then came the sweeter, muskier smell he'd been half craving and half dreading. "Tonight especially," she said, a little breathless.

Silence. He shouldn't touch her; he was still too close to the Beltane point.

Had Matilda turned rather pink? "I hope we can find Trevor," she said, avoiding his eye.

"So do I." He shouldn't let her return unescorted, which would make it harder to do what little he could to locate the hawk. He didn't have Tomas's affinity with birds, but his nose could certainly tell him if there were any goshawks about. Stifling a sigh, he said, "Would you give me the lure, please? I can see a bit better than you in the dark."

Full of resolve and nagging images of the bridge, he set off for the great hall and barely suppressed a start when Matilda took his arm. A normal enough gesture on her part: he'd just said that his night vision was better than hers, and her skirts were cumbersome. But his nerves were on edge; the touch felt warm through the cloth of his sleeve, her hair looked thick and soft, and he'd best think of something else. Alfred, for example.

They passed an owl and a badger, an elderly one from the dank note to its scent, then a rabbit warren. Owein might need more than scent to find the hawk, so he sent a long searching tendril out from his shield. Nothing. Nor could he tell who was still watching them, though the sensation had faded ever so slightly, as if their observer had withdrawn a little.

"Owein?"

"Mm?" Still no goshawk.

"I hope you're not out of sorts with me?"

"Not in the slightest," he said, startled. "Why would I be?"

She was gazing straight ahead. "Because I disturbed you, and now you're occupying yourself with Trevor and me." A pause. An awkward one. "You might have preferred to be alone."

After a moment he realized she meant that he might have been waiting for someone. "I prefer your company, 'Tilda."

"Thank you." A flickering glance. "I prefer yours."

Two deer, three field mice. Then, some distance ahead, he saw half a dozen Elementals squatting like stumps in the dark. Saw them, not smelled them. If they had a scent, it was indistinguishable from the odor of the soil and the woods all about.

One of the gnomes swiveled its knoblike head in Owein's direction. "Fair evening to you, halfbreed," it said, so quietly and in a voice so low and guttural that hearing it was like sensing the faintest of rumbles in the earth. Owein glanced at Matilda, who was intent on not stepping at fault in the leaf mold. No change in her face. She'd heard nothing.

"Greetings," he mouthed at the Elemental, then thought a salutation at it for good measure, though he'd no idea if the gnome could understand him. Usually it was sylphs and not gnomes who spoke to him or more often about him, pointing and jabbering; they traveled in packs. He ignored Elementals unless he was alone, and returned a greeting only when failing to do so would be rude. The sylphs never spoke directly to him when he was in mortal company, and an Earth elemental had never addressed him before. Had this one been watching him?

To his consternation all the gnomes were lumbering to their feet, their joints cracking like so many dead twigs. Now what had he done?

"We see your work upon this night of power," said the one who had spoken. All the others were melting away into the woods; he'd no idea they could move so fast. "To link our home to Elfland helps us. We thank you."

Owein gave the gnome a smile and a small courteous nod, then stole a belated glance at Matilda. Still concentrating on the path or rather the lack of one, she bent a low-hanging beech branch out of her way and appeared not to notice his scrutiny.

"She cannot hear me. You need not answer me. You help us; we help you. Eight trees ahead, hawk sits. We send him to you."

As the wind shifted, Owein scented the goshawk: gamey, a bit salty, warm dry feathers, topnote of meal or grain from the mews. Undernote of something more fleshy. Hot fast-coursing blood and hollow bones. It was probably hungry, which would help.

"Hold!" said the gnome.

Owein stopped in mid-stride and gripped Matilda's arm. "Shh. Have the hood and the jesses ready."

She complied, albeit with a puzzled look. The dead field mouse on the lure was no longer quite fresh enough to attract a well-fed hawk, but Matilda's nose couldn't tell her that. Owein swung the lure. A rustling in the trees, a flash of great pinioned wings. Matilda sucked in her breath. Trevor came soaring towards them, dipping his head when he scented the mouse. He circled, began to stoop, then veered away.

"Damnation," muttered Owein beneath his breath.

But the goshawk came back: a gnome had risen in his path. Owein was still swinging the lure. Trevor didn't dive for it this time either. Instead the goshawk startled at something else, another Elemental most likely, and took stand in an oak sapling just ahead.

From somewhere near Owein's shins came the gravelly mutter of a gnome: "Hawk hungry. Wait."

Owein managed not to respond, not even to look down. They waited, Owein nervously, with a silent curse for the passing of still more time away from the great hall, Matilda with her face radiating something between hope and awe.

"How on earth did you know Trevor was..." she whispered at one point.

He shrugged. "Luck, I suppose."

She was too much of a falconer to make further conversation. Otherwise she and Owein were silent, standing motionless and a little apart so as not to impede the sweep of the lure, letting the goshawk grow calmer and his hunger increase. From time to time his head bobbed as he eyed the mouse. What if a live one happened by? Perhaps the gnomes were patrolling to keep mice away. Owein counted seven earth Elementals ringing the oak.

At least Matilda wasn't holding his arm any more, and the bird gave him an excuse not to look at her. He kept expecting to hear Linley's voice. How would the Saxon react if he discovered they were both gone? Surely he realized that as much as Owein liked Matilda, he had sense enough not to creep away with Alfred's niece on any night, let alone this one, and that Tomas, before leaving Owein here for the first time, had advised him to mind his step.

Though Tomas appeared to have had his share of trysts. If he'd chosen Moira over Caraid, why were he and Moira both so upset? Hadn't they all done as they pleased? But Owein couldn't do likewise because of that confounded bridge.

Blast the Parcae's prophecy and his part in it, and blast the goshawk as well. He relished the fresh air and all the hushed calls and rustlings that animated the soft May evening, but it was hard not to fidget. He couldn't ask the gnomes to tell him if anyone were approaching. He couldn't ask them for a fresh mouse. He couldn't ask them anything at such close range without upsetting Matilda, who'd witnessed more than enough strangeness about him for one night.

Her head drooped, spilling her warm brown hair over the lowered hood of her lightweight cloak. As she stifled a yawn, for half a moment she appeared very young and vulnerable. She caught him looking at her, abandoned her hipshot stance and gave him a smile. When he smiled back, her face softened.

An instant later she glanced aside. "I wish we knew the hour."

"Past midnight." He could have told her more precisely, from the position of the stars he could see and the Sun he could sense, but he let it go at that.

"Hawk come now," announced the gnome nearest Owein. The bird stretched one wing and foot, then the other, and ruffled his neck feathers.

"Off we go," murmured Owein, and swung the lure in a narrowing arc.

The hawk left the branch and stooped in mid-flight; Owein held out a wrist. The air was a blur of wings and beak and outthrust talons and whirling lines and then it all came together; the miracle happened, and the bird flapped to Owein's wrist and seized the mouse. Matilda drew the jesses deftly about Trevor's unoccupied foot. That took courage, and Owein shot her an admiring glance and a smile, though it was still chancy; they could still lose the hawk. When Trevor dropped the mouse, Matilda presented her gloved hand and the bird hopped onto it, likely associating her with fresher food. Owein slipped the hood over the goshawk's head, made the jesses fast to Matilda's wrist and rubbed his own, more from relief than from the pinch of the talons that had just been there.

Glowing, Matilda ran a finger lightly down the hawk's back. He muttered within the hood and lifted a ridge of feathers, but stayed quiet on her glove. "Owein, thank you!" The luminous face that she lifted to him made him happier than she was. "I wish we had the cadge."

"So do I. But it's no great way to the mews now."

Owein went a little ahead to thank the gnomes, who gave him a silent nod and stumped off into the trees. Clearing the way as best he could, he coached Matilda along whatever path where a misstep would be least likely to agitate the goshawk. Noise didn't matter so much now, but they kept their voices down nonetheless. Matilda's eyes were alight, and she spoke to Trevor more than she did to Owein, but he was too relieved to mind. He'd redeemed himself after shrieking in front of her.

When they reached the mews, she asked Owein to take the key from the pouch at her belt. He fished it out as deftly as he could, all too aware of the faint odor of musk that drifted from her. They should probably go straight to the hall, but she wanted to get Trevor put away first. Besides, he told himself, Linley wouldn't have let her leave the mews unescorted at night.

While she lit the torches, Owein fastened the outer door, then followed Matilda to the inner chamber and wrinkled his nose at the closeness of the feather-scented air. A sleepy bird or two stirred, and a sparrowhawk stretched a leg and a wing, but there were no squawks. Matilda settled Trevor on his bark-covered perch, changed his water, and cast an admiring glance about the room before she withdrew.

"It's the finest mews I've ever seen," she whispered to Owein as she bolted the inner door.

"Tomas fitted it out well."

"So I've been told, and that he's a rare hand with birds. I'd like to meet him. The two of you must go hawking often in Vestfold."

Owein had never been there, and of Birka he had no memory at all. He was growing weary of this ongoing pretense with Alfred, and with Matilda he'd long since come to hate it. He pressed his lips together and nodded.

"A marvel you knew Trevor was close. You must be good with birds too."

"Not in the same way." He took a step towards the outer door.

"Do you resemble your brother?"

"So I'm told," said Owein uneasily. "Why do you ask?"

"That Irishwoman thought you were Tomas at first. Alfred likes him, and I've heard no end of tales about him." She wasn't quite meeting Owein's gaze. "None that made him appear the sort who'd mistreat a slave."

"He isn't; that was the Danes. And Caraid wasn't. Not one of ours, I mean," he said, flustered. How had Matilda learned that Caraid had mistaken him for Tomas? Owein had been close-mouthed about it. Who'd been gossiping?

She was eyeing him dubiously.

"Tomas hasn't any slaves. Not like that." He fought back a chuckle at the thought of the fenodyree and the Cooks, who were not only free but couldn't be less oppressed; everyone in Moira's household went in terror of offending them. Then he remembered there might be bondmen and women at Limecliff.

"I see nothing amusing about it," said Matilda, her face closing, and started for the door.

Now she was vexed, and that was the last thing he wanted. He reached for her elbow. "There isn't," he said earnestly. "There's nothing amusing at all about the way Caraid died." It was hard to say her name. "A different thought just jumped into my head; I've no idea why." Wanting to see Matilda's expression, he circled around in front of her.

He was expecting the sort of measuring look that Moira or Fraine would have given him, but to his surprise there was apology in the girl's face. "I know her death troubled you. That's why I thought you might have known her before."

"I'd never set eyes on her."

Matilda's voice wasn't entirely steady. "I can't fathom you, Owein. You'd never met, but her death grieved you. You knew something about the Bishop—" She stopped, reddening, then added quickly, "When I found you tonight, at first I thought you had died. You didn't even stir till I shook you; then you seemed to have some sort of fit. You can see in the dark better than anyone I know, but I still can't think how you knew where Trevor was. It was a miracle."

"I guessed," he said, caught between apprehension and pride.

"Sometimes you're the kindest person I've ever known, but then you turn round and ignore everyone. More than once you've shown less sense than a child, and—"

"Have I ever been rude to you?"

"No!" Exasperated. Trembling a bit. "And Alfred likes Tomas and I want him to like you," she blurted, as if it were some sort of confession.

How was that relevant? What was troubling her, if Owein hadn't been rude? Several seconds passed before he thought of something to say. "I'm confused."

There was a small choking sound. "So am I." A tear spilled from one dark blue eye. She turned her head aside, but he'd already seen.

"Root and branch, 'Tilda, don't cry," he said helplessly. He draped an arm around her shoulders. Awkwardly: he hadn't the faintest notion what else to do, and it was what he'd have done with Fraine. When Matilda took a step towards him instead of drawing away, he put his other arm around her too.

After five seconds he realized that holding his sister had never felt like this—perhaps because they'd not let it, but from that thought he veered away. His head was full of musk; there was heat in his chest, with more heat and a pulse and a stirring in his groin. Breathing as if she were fighting back sobs, Matilda leaned her head against his chest, and he found himself touching that sheaf of maple-brown hair, drawing his fingers through it as lightly as if it were cold running water. She swayed towards him a little. Then she was looking up at him so expectantly that he decided to risk trying what he'd wanted to do since he'd first seen her. First he kissed a tear at the corner of her eye, then another near her earlobe, then her mouth.

Apart from salt, it didn't have much taste. He felt clumsy; his lips seemed thick. He wasn't sure that he knew how to kiss. He wasn't sure that Matilda did either but she wasn't pushing him away. Instead she put her arms around his waist and her mouth began moving with his and he liked it, and then he was holding her tightly and he liked that too. Liked the smoothness and warmth of her face, and how her breathing was changing, and the taste of her neck, and the way that the curve at the small of her back felt beneath his hands, and the shape of her hips—

"Owein," she mumbled. "Stop."

"Why?" He found her mouth again. He might be drowning. He didn't care.

"Please," she said, trying to twist away. "You're frightening me."

The quaver in her voice reached him. "I don't mean to." He let go of her. "Your pardon," he said at random, though he wasn't sure what he'd done wrong. Surely she'd invited him to kiss her. Her indigo eyes were dark and troubled, her mouth a healthy carmine and looking fuller than usual, her breath coming fast.

So was his. "You're so pretty," he heard himself say. "I've wanted to kiss you for weeks on end."

"Thank you," she whispered. Her chest was heaving. "Owein, you...I've never seen anyone like you. You don't even look human. Everyone says so. You look like an angel."

He felt his face closing.

"What's wrong?"

"I'm mortal," he said heavily.

The hot color began draining from Matilda's skin. "Of course you are," she said in a high nervous voice. "I don't care what they say."

"What who says?" he asked sharply. No answer. Her hand crept to her mouth. "What do they say, 'Tilda? Tell me."

She stared at him. "That you— That Tomas..." There were tears in her eyes. "Nothing of any account."

Owein put his hands on her shoulders. "What do they say?"

"I don't believe any of it!" The dark blue gaze was very close, wretched and tremulous, but meeting his squarely. "And Alfred won't either. He doesn't want to."

Owein had intended to demand an accounting from her, but something about her sudden intake of breath drove the thought from his head. Their eyes locked. Her lips were parted; her face lifted towards his. She let him kiss her again.

They were lying in the straw and Matilda was helping Owein wrestle her shift over her head when the tap came at the door.

"Miss Matilda?" asked a sleepy Saxon voice. Hroswitha, the cook. "I saw torchlight under the sill. Is that you within?"

"Yes," said Matilda, eyes closed, arms and legs tensed, tears seeping from beneath her closed eyelids. How could she sound so normal? Owein's heart was thudding and his whole body was in an alarming state. "A goshawk escaped, but I caught him."

"Master Linley and Mistress Rose have been worried," said Hroswitha. Politely, but with a foreboding undertone. "Been looking for you for hours, they have, and for Master Owein too."

Matilda pushed him aside and picked up her outer gown. Grinding his teeth together to keep silent, Owein reached for his trousers.

"All's well," said Matilda. "Owein's here with me. He helped me find Trevor. We were just going back to the hall. Would you please tell Rose I'll be along directly?"

A grunt from Hroswitha, followed by a mumble of assent, then retreating footsteps. Owein turned to Matilda, but she was scrambling to her feet.

"Wait," he said, reaching for her.

Her jaw clenched, she shied away. "Let go of me." She wouldn't look at him.

"What's wrong?" he demanded, alarmed. What had he done?

"Stop," she said with a stifled sob. "It's all ruined. How can I be such a simpleton?"

"What's ruined?" Could he put it to rights? He had found her the hawk. He took her elbow, turned her to face him.

"Us!" she half shouted. "This!" Tear-stained. Defiant. "You nearly tumbled me right here on the floor. It didn't happen but that's no thanks to me. You'll never ask for my hand now. My mother was right all along."

What in the nine worlds was she talking about? "Your *hand?*"

"You'll never marry me! Why should you? I've been no better than a whore!"

"'Tilda," he said, staring. He'd never been more bewildered. "You want to marry me?"

Her chin quivered. "Yes!" she wailed. "No! Not any more! What's the use? You'll despise me!"

Gingerly, he put his arms around her. When she fought him, trying to hide her face, he leaned down and said next to her ear, "'Tilda. Matilda. Listen to me." She was weeping. He didn't know what to say. "Don't cry," he began. "I don't know anyone who's married in—where I come from." Not Tomas and Moira, certainly, nor Moira and Rhys. In Midgard plenty of mortals were lovers without being married: Tomas, Caraid, the Bishop. Still, it seemed important to some of them. He wasn't sure what marriage was, but then he wasn't a native here. No more than he was in Elfland. What if he and Matilda went there, where it didn't matter so much?

"You're not Christians, then," said Matilda, low and breathless. She shrank away from him a bit. "I didn't want to believe... But wouldn't even Norse pagans have some sort of handfasting—"

"I don't think you'd like it there," he broke in. He couldn't tell her the first thing about Elfland, let alone take her there. It wasn't fair. "I don't despise you. I love you as much as I love my twin sister." Differently, of a certainty, and Matilda would never understand him as Fraine did, but that he had just enough sense not to say.

Matilda gaped at him. He wasn't at all sure she was pleased. "You...have a twin?"

"I do. She's called Fraine." Probably he shouldn't have mentioned her. "I don't hate you. I love you," he said, more confused than ever. "I feel terrible. But that's as much my doing as yours."

Matilda was staring at him as if he had three eyes and five arms.

"We should go find Linley." He couldn't bear to hold Matilda much longer, but he probably shouldn't mention that either. "I don't want him angry any more than you do," he told her instead.

"You are more than a gentleman. Pagan or—" She choked back the rest of what she'd been about to say. Her eyes were damp. She let out a great sniff, and followed it with a hasty swipe of her hand across her nose. "I love you, too. Like as not you are an angel."

She pressed the key into his palm and darted out of the mews, not looking at him, leaving him to brush the last of the straw from his clothes and lock the door.

Birds called to one another beneath a pale eastern sky as Owein stood breathing fresh air and debating which route to take to the great hall. The mews lay where the edge of a field ran up against the woods. Crossing the field would be faster than circling around through the trees, but would also provide more opportunities to happen upon some tale-bearing Saxon. Though the tale could reach the whole estate in no time as it was. Why had Matilda told the cook that he was in the mews too?

Matilda didn't mind that he was odd, at least not very much. She wasn't full of warnings and assignments. She loved him enough to want to marry him, whatever that meant. It made being here easier. In some ways.

Perplexed and frustrated but giddily happy nonetheless, he set off through the forest. It was nowhere near as lush as Elfland's, though Aubrey insisted that theirs was fading. But it was still a forest and a beautiful one, with trees and moss and ferny air and all the underwood to tramp through, with birds' nests above him and flower faces to watch for and young rabbits crouched in the brambles, and all the greenery of the season unfolding. He was always contented here. Matilda seemed to like the open fields more. He liked them too, though not so much as the woods.

He was wondering why he'd not seen any more earth Elementals when he smelled sulphur, and an elegant tenor voice behind him drawled, "Young love is always so touching."

Owein whirled. The ginger-haired man that he'd seen in his dreams was lounging against a ivy-covered treetrunk. He was dressed like a well-to-do Saxon: trousers, supple leather boots, a belted tunic, a pouch, a sheathed knife. No beard and no cape, though, and smooth dead-white skin. He was neither short nor tall, and so slight that he could have been called frail. Moreover, he wasn't a man. At least he wasn't human. Mortals didn't have eyes like that, flowing and burning, red-flecked and crazed and full of sullen hazel light.

Owein fought a wave of dizziness. He wasn't dreaming; this time the man was really there. And was, he realized abruptly, the same man who'd been watching him in the 'tweenlands. "Who are you?" he said past the terror that was closing his throat. There was something he should do, now, immediately, but he couldn't remember what. More than one thing, actually, but he could recall none of them.

The amber eyes narrowed. "You don't know me?" He wasn't pleased. An impulse flickered across his bloodless face and was gone. "Who I am doesn't matter as much as what I can do." Watching Owein closely. "What I can do for you, and what you can do for me."

He was after something. If he got it, would he leave? "What do you want?" Owein whispered. His shield: that was one thing he'd forgot. He put it up as fast as he could.

The man smiled a little, then made an airily tolerant gesture. "Let's discuss what you want first, shall we?"

Owein didn't agree and didn't even nod, but the redhead grinned as if he'd done both. Then he fixed Owein with a smoldering stare that made his head spin. Half expecting the space between them to be set ablaze, he staggered back a pace.

"That was wise," murmured the redhead. "I can hand your little Saxon girl over to you."

"Don't touch her!" A shudder went through Owein, followed by a burst of protective rage. This creature would *not* hurt Matilda.

"Of course not, my friend. I don't want her." A poisonously sweet voice. Satisfaction flared in the amber eyes, as if he'd won a small wager. "But you do. Don't you?"

And Owein did, with a sudden redoubling of all his frustration in the mews. His hands twitched at his sides; his breath burned his throat.

"Indeed you do... I'd enjoy giving her to you. No one would ever know, and no one could find you if you didn't want to be found. You'd have her all to yourself for as long as you wanted her." A peculiar gleam in the hazel eyes. "Lucky girl. Think well upon it."

Owein could think of nothing else. Matilda's mouth. Her scent. The feel of her hips beneath that last undergarment.

"Now for what I want," said the redhead confidingly. "Or what I don't. It's very simple, Owein, really. I want you to tear down that bridge."

His body was still mired in images of Matilda and his thoughts still fogged, but the sound of his name caught his attention. The ginger-haired man knew who he was.

"I rather think you'd like to stop building it. We have that much in common, don't we? Perhaps more."

The fellow had been spying on him. For that matter, he had pursued Owein for months. Followed him into his dreams. And, Owein remembered with a jolt, had harassed him in the 'tweenlands. The redhead was strong and unscrupulous and he didn't like the way it looked at him, nor the way it spoke about Matilda.

Matilda, nude, alone with him. Reaching for him with a wide lazy smile—

No. Her expression was wrong. It wouldn't be mocking.

And her eyes weren't hazel.

The thing was in Owein's *mind.* Abruptly he was so petrified for both Matilda and himself that he could scarcely breathe, and his heart knotted into aching fibers in his chest. The creature must have got into his thoughts before he'd put up his shield. Sweat began trickling down his face, the back of his neck, between his shoulderblades. Who was this man who could invade his mind so easily? Not an Elf. Something more powerful. Something, perhaps, not far from a god. Owein might never have known he was there, but he'd given himself away.

Or, which seemed more likely, he was toying with Owein. Whoever this being was, he was evil. Owein could smell that along with the sulphur.

The redhead was smiling at him, intimately. Playing cat and mouse. He must know how badly Owein was frightened, but some core of stubbornness made Owein refuse to show it. He wouldn't give the creature, godling or not, the satisfaction of seeing him cringe. Whatever the man wanted he wouldn't obtain, nor would he hurt Matilda. Owein doubted he could expel the thing from his mind, but he'd try to block it from reaching any further than it already had. When Tomas had told Owein about his partitioned link to Nissyen, he'd shown Owein how to build walls to hide his thoughts. It was done with strong feelings.

"What do you say?"

Owein would have to work fast. Have to guess, too. He found the image of Matilda leering at him, and summoned up all his rage. Rage at the ginger-haired man. Fury at being separated from Fraine. Bitterness at leaving Elfland. Wrath at whoever had brutalized Caraid—and anger at Tomas, who'd hurt her in other ways. Anger at Tomas and Moira both, because Owein was a halfbreed. Resentment of the damned bridge. Anger at Daniel for tale-bearing and meddling.

Once Owein had started there seemed no end to his rage, but the redhead was beginning to eye him dubiously, and he might not have much more time. He hurled the whole weight of his anger around the Matilda-picture in his mind's eye, then retreated from it. "The bridge stands," he said flatly. "Leave us alone."

For two seconds the redhead gaped at him, slack-jawed, then doubled over with laughter. When Owein started to back away, the man straightened up, still sputtering with glee, and grabbed his elbow. Owein flinched as the grip burned through his sleeve, but some dim instinct warned him not to resist.

Demented hazel eyes bore into his. "You are worse than a cretin. Did you actually think that would work?"

Owein was shaking too hard to conceal it, so hard he could scarcely stand. But suddenly he had a flash of the Sight—it could accompany great danger—and he knew that the ginger-haired man wouldn't kill him. Because if the fellow had been able to destroy the bridge, he'd have done so himself long ago. Which meant he needed Owein alive to destroy it for him.

The realization didn't make him any less frightened. The man was laughing again, not hysterically this time: a low insinuating chuckle that was immeasurably worse. "I so love an innocent. A pity you won't stay one for long." His fist swung back. He might not kill Owein, but he was going to hurt him.

"Owein! Will you answer me? Where are you?" Linley's voice, wrathful and out of breath, and accompanied by a great thrashing in the underwood some distance away.

"Here!" shouted Owein, not that Linley could help. The next thing he knew, he was tasting blood and he'd fallen to his knees. He'd been slapped across the mouth so fast that he hadn't seen it coming. When he looked up, the ginger-haired man had disappeared.

Not completely. "I've not done with you yet," he hissed in Owein's ear.

Linley was crashing through the trees towards him. "Hullo," Owein said weakly, getting to his feet. His lower lip was already beginning to puff. "I'm glad to see you."

"Not as glad as I am to see you," Linley snapped. "Have you taken leave of your senses, to be all snugged down with Matilda on Beltane night?"

"Nothing happened—"

"Prithee tell me another tale, milord. She's still a virgin, is more the truth of it. Probably. Though I'd wager a kingdom the fault's none of yours." Hands on his hips, Linley glared at him. More troubled than angry, the Saxon smelled of burning tar and plums, of scorched walnuts and sweat, and his round secretive face was pale with strain. "Assuredly something happened to your mouth. Did she hit you, then?"

Owein shook his head. Best not to mention the ginger-haired man. "I tripped over a root."

"I wish she'd clouted you, so I do." He gauged Owein's expression. "Don't misunderstand me, now. I don't care tuppence if you cut a swath through all the other girls in Wessex and Mercia combined, but for pity's sake don't go bedding Matilda. There are too many whispers about you as it is, and she's Alfred's niece! Find some maid in Axbridge to your fancy instead. Find a dozen; I'll help you look." Linley folded his arms. "It's a mercy Alfred wasn't here last night. You could have been—"

"Killed?"

"No," said Linley, exhaling. "It isn't treason, and even if she were Alfred's daughter, he's in no wise so unfair. But the pair of you could put him in a position where you might have to be sent away, Owein, possibly even outlawed. If you got Matilda with child, her mother would move heaven and earth to have someone marry her, quite possibly you, or to—"

"Matilda wants to marry me now."

Linley stared for three heartbeats, then clutched his head in his hands, took a slow careful breath and let it out again. "Of course she does," he said, measuring each word. "She thinks you're in line for a Norse earldom or something like. For all she knows, Tomas could give you Limecliff, and she could chase after goshawks with you all night and day. Save your breath; I know that part's the truth." He glanced aside for a moment and ran his fingers through his unruly soft hair. The sudden smile he gave Owein was both wry and direct. "You're a handsome thing and so's 'Tilda. Little wonder if you're both smitten." He clapped Owein lightly on the back, but his eyes were dark with warning. "Have a care, please, my friend. You're far from slow-witted, but you don't know our ways and you've enemies here. So does Tomas. Ask me about anything that puzzles you. Anything at all."

There was too much that Linley wouldn't comprehend any better than Owein did; still, he nodded and murmured his thanks. Linley meant nothing but good by him.

The Saxon turned towards the hall but stopped in mid-stride, frowning and disconcerted. "Were you burning something?" He pointed at the ivy-covered tree where the redhead was lounging when Owein first saw him, and where a pattern of scorched and shriveled leaves now marred the tender green vines of early May.

CHAPTER TWENTY-ONE: SAD TIDINGS

Dubhlinn

Brendan and his family, with Ennis and his three nearly grown children as guests, had just finished their evening meal when they heard a knock at the door. A light tapping, so the visitor was an easy-going man or a child. Or a woman. When Ennis turned, the quickly concealed hope in his face gave Brendan a pang, for he'd not abandoned hope yet himself. Doubtless they were both idiots.

"Brendan, my dear," said his wife Kate, "will you see to the ale? We may need another cask. And Ennis, would you answer the door, please? If I burn another pudding you'll show me no mercy."

She was one of the best cooks in Dubhlinn, but no one contradicted her. Ennis's sons rushed to fill the silence with chatter, and Brendan's eldest daughter Maeve went to help Kate. With all eyes upon him, Ennis opened the door.

The young man on the sill was slender and tall, with luxuriant black hair and pale skin. Well-dressed, too, though more like a trader or an affluent craftsman than a courtier. When he smiled at Ennis, Brendan caught an icy-clear flash of blue eyes. No telling if the fellow were Norse or Irish, nor what his errand was, till he opened his mouth. He carried a satchel of middling size on his back, but from his belt there hung no more than a pouch and a small sheath. Brendan set the ale cask by the table and joined Ennis at the door.

"Good day to you and your family," said the young man in fluent Irish. A Dubhlinn accent. He could still be a Norseman born here in town, but Brendan found it unlikely. So did Ennis; a little of the tension left his face.

"I've not disturbed you at table, I hope? My name's Aidan. I'm looking for Brendan O'Quinlan."

"You've found him," said Brendan, smiling. "Come in and tell me what you want with him."

Kate handed Aidan a basin of warm water and a towel. He refused her offer of food, saying he'd just eaten at the harbor, but accepted a mug of ale after he'd washed his hands. He showed no sign of wanting a private audience, though he coughed a few times while he made easy small talk with Ennis and Brendan, who hoped that no ailment had come indoors with him. And he was indeed a Dubhlinner; his mother's people had lived near Fahey's wood for generations.

Although Maeve cast a few owl-eyed glances at their guest, the other children promptly lost interest in him. They clattered and clumped about, ostensibly helping Kate clear away the supper leavings, but hindered one another with scouring the plates and moving the benches, and laughed and chattered and made such a racket that Kate ended by banging two pots together to get their attention and ordered them all outside. Brendan caught the quick glint of amusement in Aidan's eyes, and decided he might like the fellow.

Kate joined the men at the table. "We can hear ourselves speak! A rare thing under this roof."

"A fine family," said Aidan with what appeared genuine interest. He coughed. "Are they all yours, my lady?"

"It feels that way," said Kate, warming to him. "But the three dark ones belong to Ennis here."

"I'm betrothed to Brendan's sister," said Ennis quietly.

"Ah." Aidan's expression turned somber. "May I ask what her name is?"

"Caraid," said Brendan. A weight began forming in his chest. "Why? She's gone missing, you see."

"Have you any word..." Ennis's voice trailed away. His face taut with misery, he ran a hand through his greying hair and stared at Aidan.

"I fear I bring you sad tidings." Aidan pushed his mug aside, steepled his hands on the table and looked at Brendan. "It grieves me to tell you that your sister Caraid died in Wessex, in the realm of King Alfred. She was well cared for in her last hours, and she requested that her body be sent to you. I was traveling through Wessex on my way here, and was asked to take you her coffin and a few small belongings."

"Caraid asked you this?" said Ennis.

There was a world of compassion in Aidan's long mobile face. "No, Ennis. She died before ever I reached the estate. She'd made a request of the Saxons who were nursing her. They put it to me and I accepted it."

"Whose estate?" asked Brendan. "Where?"

"In Somerset. It's called Limecliff," said Aidan. "It belongs to one Tomas Rhymer, who's not in residence there at the moment."

Brendan got to his feet. "Where is the coffin?" he asked roughly. "I'll send for it. Give me her things."

Speechless, Kate gaped at him—Aidan was a guest.

Aidan gave him a wary look. "The coffin's with the harbormaster." Moving slowly, he removed a small bag and a comb from his pouch and set them on the table.

Brendan drew his knife, not aiming it but clearly prepared to use it. Aidan froze, staring at the blade. His nostrils flared; his mouth was a tight line, all its affable humor gone. Ennis scowled and set a hand to his belt. Brendan said, "Hold, Ennis," and to Aidan: "Give me the rest."

"I am unarmed, sirs," said Aidan in a remarkably calm voice. "This is all your sister owned when she died." This time his cough came from deeper in his chest.

Brendan knew that comb, carved from fine black jet. He'd watched Tomas choose it for Caraid from one of the booths near the harbor. Tomas had reimbursed Brendan the price of the comb that same evening, once he'd collected a fee for a poem from Ivar, the Norse King of Dubhlinn. Brendan recognized the blue bag, too. Caraid had sewn it from the silk that Tomas had given her when he came back to Dubhlinn and asked her to go to Wessex with him. To whatever estate would be granted him by the Saxon King, Alfred. After sending Tomas away, she'd poured the whole tale into Brendan's ear. "She sent us no message?" he asked.

"To the best of my knowledge, she did not. I was given none for you."

"I'll not shame my hearth by laying hands on you under my roof," said Brendan. "And you will not abuse your position as our guest by lying to me."

"Indeed I won't," said Aidan quietly.

"Did Tomas kill her?"

"No."

Did Ennis even know who Tomas was? A fine time to explain, but Brendan hadn't much choice. He glanced at his friend. "Tomas is—"

"Caraid told me about him. And I've heard stories in town," said Ennis, absolutely expressionless.

Brendan turned back to Aidan. "How did she come to his lands? And how did she die?"

"She was ill-used by Norse slavers," said Aidan, studying both men. "You may have heard that the Danes gave their dying Saxon slaves to Alfred after the battle of Rochester?"

Brendan nodded tightly. Dumped them like so much rubbish, the stories went. Ennis's eyes hardened.

"Caraid was among them, and among the wounded and dying who were taken to Limecliff. There are healers living nearby." Aidan's face was guarded, but his tone was gentle. "When she arrived, she was too far gone for them to do any more than try to lessen her pain, though they said she was quite brave about it. I'm certain they could ease her suffering, Brendan. They're most skilled. One's a priest, two are midwives and all three are herbalists."

Ennis made an almost inaudible sound at the back of his throat.

"The slavers who took her, did Tomas send them here?" demanded Brendan.

Aidan looked him straight in the eye and said, "No."

"You learned nothing of how they came to capture her?"

Aidan shook his head. "The healers told me that by the time she came to them," he said patiently, "she was too spent to say much more than ask that her body be sent to you."

"Do you know who the slavers were? Some of them winter in Dubhlinn," said Ennis in a voice so controlled that it sounded remote.

"No. I wish that I did."

Brendan believed him. Believed every word. He tossed his knife to the far end of the table, slumped onto the bench across from Aidan and put his head in his hands. In the echoing silence that followed, he heard Ennis sit down as well, and Kate let out a troubled breath. The fire crackled in the hearth; it probably wanted more peat. Aidan's cough came again. At least they now knew what had befallen Caraid. They could stop wondering. Anything was better than that.

Perhaps Caraid should have gone to Wessex with Tomas. Staying in Dubhlinn had made her no safer from whatever Fate her visions told her that her affair with Tomas would bring to her door.

Perhaps Brendan should have drowned Tomas in Dubhlinn harbor on the day when a big snub-nosed dolphin had carried him in half-dead from the Irish Sea. If Brendan had suffered any premonitions about his sister's Fate after she'd crossed paths with that quiet fey Norseman, with his harp and his flute and his soft-spoken ways and his damnblasted Sight, just like hers—then Brendan might have done just that. But he'd been visited by no such forebodings. He had no Sight at all.

A little while later, Kate touched his knee beneath the table, and Brendan lifted his head from his cupped palms. They had guests; he had responsibilities—and he could open his heart to Kate once their visitors had gone. Ennis sat erect and unseeing, his mouth set in grim drooping lines and his arms folded, but Aidan was watching Brendan. His gaze, reflective and fatigued and full of impersonal melancholy, could have been that of a much older man. While he didn't seem offended, neither did he appear particularly at ease, and there was wariness in his bearing.

Brendan couldn't fault him for that. "I beg your pardon," he said, heartfelt, and extended his hand. "Though I fear I'm unpardonable."

He got a shrug—and to his surprise, a clasp of his hand. "Not by me." The fellow's grip was uncommonly warm. "You've lost your sister, and I'm a stranger to you," he said, stifling a cough. "You have my pardon. I'd have wondered the same things in your place."

"But you might not have asked them the same way," Brendan pointed out. From the corner of his eye he could see Kate shake her head: why must he always say exactly what he was thinking?

Aidan's eyes glinted. "Perhaps not," he said gravely, and got to his feet. He gave Kate a smile. "I thank you for your hospitality, my lady. If our interview's done, I'll leave you to your family now."

"Thank you for coming," Ennis said dully, and pressed Aidan's hand.

"I'll bear you company as far as the harbor, if that's where you're bound," offered Brendan.

Aidan made no objection. When they stepped outside, he gazed at the overcast sky and took deep breaths of the penetratingly damp air. Mist in it; it was a soft day. Likely it would rain. It usually did. The two men strolled in silence along the muddy plankways for perhaps fifty ells. Aidan worked a kink from his neck, flexed his hands and shoulders. He gave

Brendan a sober glance. "I wish I'd brought happier tidings."

"So do I," Brendan said heavily. "Still, I thank you for them. If she had to die among strangers, that they were kind ones was a mercy. And that we know it is another one."

There was a slight pause. "Tomas has been told, should you be wondering."

Because Brendan judged it best not to speak of Tomas in front of Ennis, he'd postponed asking whether Tomas knew until Aidan was clear of the house. "As well he should have been," began Brendan with some heat, then remembered that Aidan might be acquainted with him. Tomas wasn't a bad fellow as the Norse went; Brendan had quite liked him when they first met. Certainly he'd been genuinely fond of Caraid. Tragic, it all was. As though if Aidan were thinking along the same lines, his expression was dark, and Brendan, wanting to be alone with his grief, asked him no further questions.

CHAPTER TWENTY-TWO: ILLNESS AND JOURNEYS

Midgard

Fraine hadn't told Owein she was planning to visit. She hadn't even told Moira. Just Aubrey—because someone should know her whereabouts and the pooka wouldn't try to dissuade her, at least not very hard—and Tallah, who would guide the passage. Fraine had been worried that the Parca might refuse to leave for Midgard again so soon after she and Aidan had returned from there. Instead, after Aubrey explained what Fraine wanted, Tallah had given her a shrewd look from those whiteless black eyes, and a single nod. Fraine had a feeling that Tallah understood why she wanted to go.

The two of them had barely recovered their footing when Owein burst into the willow grove at a dead run and caught Fraine to him in a grip that nearly lifted her off her feet. He'd grown a bit taller since their last meeting. There was a stringy new layer of muscle to his arms and shoulders, and he smelled of violets. Likely they both did; she was equally glad to see him. From the corner of her eye she saw Tallah grinning at them. Owein stepped back, gave Fraine another impulsive squeeze, kissed the top of her head with a resounding smack and tousled her hair with both hands.

Their eyes met. "I missed you," they said together, then laughed at the same instant too.

Owein greeted Tallah, who chirped something cordial, then flung himself onto the long grass beneath the sweep of willow branches. His eyes were still soft but his face was serious; he knew that Fraine wouldn't have come all this way just to see him. Tallah gave him a doubtful look and pointed to a thick stretch of underwood. To tease her, Owein heaved a theatrical sigh, but they both knew she was right. What if some unknown Saxon happened upon them?

They followed Tallah into the forest and straight into a bramble thicket. Ahead of Fraine, Owein muttered as the thorns tore at his legs. Still, it lessened the likelihood that a stranger would come strolling by. Even goats would be disinclined to force their way through these brambles, yet Tallah cuffed the snaggletoothed branches aside as if they were no more than ferns. That chestnut hide of hers must be tougher than leather.

Owein and Fraine let the Parca clear a relatively thornless circle. When she began tramping down the leaf mold with her bare six-toed feet, they helped her. Then the twins sat cross-legged in the space they'd prepared, facing each other, their knees touching. Fraine took Owein's hand.

"What's amiss?" he asked before she could speak, searching her face. "At first I thought Evan had done something, but I can see it's worse. Is it Moira?"

She shook her head. "Tomas. But it pains Moira too, and Evan's not been idle."

"Is Tomas ill?"

"That's partly why I've come. I don't know. I thought perhaps Linley would. He's Tomas's friend. He has none so close in Elfland."

"He didn't come with you?"

"I didn't ask him. I doubt he would have. Apart from Court business, he's scarcely spoken since he left here, and I rarely see him. He holds aloof and apart most of the time."

"What is Moira's view?"

Fraine bit her lip. "They seem to have had a falling out."

"Ah," said Owein, frowning. "That's part of the trouble." He took a stick and carved a small deep furrow in the earth near his right thigh, then another. He smelled of cypress, which meant sorrow.

"I couldn't very well ask them what it's about. But I can ask you anything." Fraine put her other hand on his, and the stick stopped moving. "What happened here, Owein? I heard only snippets of it from Tomas."

She got a raw measuring look that gave her a pang, for it could only mean that he'd spent too much time being guarded of late. "Happened to Tomas or to me?"

"Both. Starting with you. I wanted to ask right away, but you up and—"

"Asked about you first," he said with almost his old smile. A squeeze of her fingers. "It's hard to know where to begin."

After he explained the Saxons' work with the wounded and the part that Simon's Sight and his own abilities had played in it, he recounted his blunder with the Bishop and finally arrived at Caraid. How she'd mistaken him for Tomas. How determined she'd been, despite her pain, to warn Owein of danger to him and Matilda. How he'd watched death creeping towards her heart, and the way that she'd died.

"Holding my hand," he said tightly. "As you're holding it now."

She nodded. "I can see she engaged your liking, even in so short a time."

"That she did. She said she wished she'd been our mother." He let out a heavy breath and looked away. "I asked Tomas if they'd been lovers. He said yes, but that Moira had never put that question to him and I shouldn't have, and that he'd not have told me had I not been his son and Caraid not died in my presence." He glanced narrowly at Fraine. "And, I suspect, if he hadn't felt guilty. After that he didn't speak for a very long time. So I left him to his thoughts and went to consult Linley about the bridge." Owein studied Fraine's face. "Ever since the Beltane point, you're the one dragging your feet, not I. We've done a fair amount since then anyway, but we should have done more. How have you been faring? And Elfland?"

"I'll get to that." She took a breath. "I don't think Tomas is at fault, though I can understand why he might feel guilty. But why do you?"

"I don't." Owein's eyes were downcast. "Well, perhaps I do at that. I feel badly; I just don't know quite how." He frowned at the bramble thicket. "If Caraid had been our mother, we'd be fully mortal and not saddled with any of this. Midgard would be our home." An attempt at a smile. "Smoke and terrible food and head-blind Saxons and all. Yet if we were her children, we wouldn't be ourselves. I suppose I'm in a muddle about why..." He shook his head. "About how we came to be who we are." Silence. Twice he started to say something, changed his mind and finally ended by asking, "You say Tomas and Moira are both out of countenance, but he chose her, not Caraid. Does he love her?"

"Yes. And she, him. Of that much I'm certain."

For a long wordless moment Owein studied her, and Fraine saw it again. The distance. The change in him.

"How are you so sure? Have you ever loved anyone?"

"You. Aubrey. Our parents."

Owein looked dissatisfied.

"Not as they love each other."

Something flickered in his eyes.

"Why, have you?"

"Perhaps," he said, very low. "Matilda."

So that was the reason for the privacy at the back of his gaze, the infinitesimal new reserve in the way that he'd held her.

"Does it pain you?" he blurted, clamping down on her hand.

"No," she said slowly. "You're my brother. We can't share everything." Wistfully, she touched the side of his face. "If she loves you too, then I'm glad of it."

"And if she doesn't?" The grey eyes very steady on hers.

"Then I suppose it will grieve you, and I don't want you grieved." There was something else, though, and it came out in a rush. "Does she know about me? Would she come to like me?"

Owein smiled. "I told her I have a twin sister." He turned her hand over and compared their palms. "She'll like you; be sure of it. I expect she fears you won't care for her."

"I can't meet her yet."

"Of course not."

She braced herself. "Owein, do you see a way I could meet her at all?"

His chin lifted. "We'd say you're Tomas's sister and mine. You could be here..." He rubbed the side of his neck. "Women don't travel through Midgard alone," he said at last. "I'd have to pretend to leave and fetch you."

"When could you do that?"

"When the damned bridge is done." Heat in his voice.

"'Damned'?"

He blinked at her. "Oh... That's a Christian word. It means something like condemned."

"Condemned by whom?"

"Their god, I think. They use it to swear with." He glanced away. Irritation crossed his face, followed by that new softness, a growing uneasiness and finally something like resignation. The fragrance of cypress was stronger. "I can't take Matilda to Elfland," he said tonelessly. "Would you come here?"

"Would you *stay* here?"

He swallowed. "Root and branch, Fraine. It's difficult enough now that she's more cautious with me. How can I answer that? I'm all at sea."

"Why?"

He told Fraine, sketchily, about his time in the mews with Matilda, and that no one was keeping her away from him except Matilda herself. She'd been more confiding, but also, intermittently, more wary. They took rambles across the open fields now rather than through the woods. Linley had sent them to Axbridge together once or twice on various errands for the estate, and there'd been plenty of evenings around the hearth with him and Rose. Whenever Owein managed half an hour alone with Matilda, not long after his pulse was galloping she'd pull herself away and, more often than not, ask a timid question about Vestfold. It was painful. And he kept dreaming about her. Sometimes he woke up almost as frustrated as he'd been in the mews.

"She took a chill or something a few days ago so she's been resting, and I'm amazed how much I miss her after even that short a time. Leaving her for good would be difficult. So would staying." He shook his head. "The worst of it is I can't explain myself to her. She's as Christian as Alfred and has no Sight whatever. She'd think me some sort of monster." He put his head in his hands. His voice was muffled. "Maybe I am."

"You've been here too long if you believe that," Fraine said levelly, touching his hair.

"Freak, then."

"Halfbreed. It's what we are, Owein. Nothing more or less." She took a breath. "Not even Mages yet, though I expect that will come."

He almost shuddered. "I expect I don't want it to. Look where it's got Tomas. And Daniel's horrible, for all he's a cretin." There was a weighted silence before he met her eye and said, "The ginger-haired man was here. I wasn't dreaming. I saw him. He offered to give me Matilda if I destroyed the bridge. When I refused, he said I'd not heard the last of him."

He threw a glance around their small clearing and beyond the bramble thicket. So did Fraine. Tallah had perched high in an elm tree a few paces away, but otherwise they were alone with the late afternoon Sun that was lighting pale sparks in Owein's hair. Not for the first time, Fraine wished that Moira or Tomas had taught them better shielding techniques. Neither twin could shapeshift, but weren't there other ways to be less conspicuous without taking to the trees like the Parcae? She'd have to ask Aubrey or Nissyen.

"The ginger-haired man uses magic, and he's much more powerful than an Elf. I'm glad you didn't see how his eyes burn," said Owein, lowering his voice. He glanced over both shoulders. "He might have been Loki. Caraid told me to beware of him."

"I'm almost certain he was."

Owein inched closer to her and said still more softly, "Caraid told me to ask the Powers, and that my sister might know but Loki didn't. Know what, Fraine?"

She would have given almost anything to be able to answer him. She shook her head. "I've no idea what she meant." Not yet, though the shiver that ran through her told her that she might soon find out. She added uneasily, "I'm not a Seer and neither are you."

"You just came through the 'tweenlands. Is the bridge—"

"Standing? Yes, the eight points and all we've done since. You're right; it should have been more."

He looked abashed. "I shouldn't have said that. I've been talking too much. What's happened that's kept you from working on it?"

"Well," Fraine began, "as I've told you, Tomas is distant and Moira's gloomy, and much of her attention is elsewhere. They're the regents still, but more of their work has fallen to me. It's so much to learn that I feel overwhelmed most of the time, Owein. If it weren't for Aubrey and Nissyen I don't know what I'd do." Fighting a sudden lump in her throat, she started counting the tasks on her fingers. "What land to try to salvage or clear, despite the drifting. Search parties and emissaries to be sent wherever they can still pass. Ambassadors from other tribes who've come for an audience, those few who've found their way to us. Endless disputes to settle; Aubrey says he's never seen such short tempers. Evan's faction complaining about everything. Ill will towards the shipwrights; even the most seaworthy boats are shredded to kindling of late. Not that the shipwrights are at fault; Aubrey says we've never had such rough seas. Trying to keep the Cooks content when all their gardens are failing—"

"Tell them I miss them," muttered Owein.

"I won't; they're already insufferable." She suppressed a sigh. "More work would fall to you too, but you're absent. That's another matter."

A crease appeared between his eyebrows.

"Evan's faction is lodging formal protests that some decisions should require both you and me, or both regents." There was no easy way to tell him the rest. "And Evan is paying court to me."

"What?" Owein's face darkened.

"Paying court to me. Pretending to woo me. Telling me how much help he could be, offering advice, suggesting I make this or that judgment. Hinting that he loves me."

Since Evan couldn't tell any outright lies and Fraine could, from time to time it had been almost amusing—until he'd found her alone by the well and tried to kiss her. She'd succeeded in bloodying his nose, mostly because he had no idea she'd try such a thing. She took his attempt as a warning: he didn't love her any more than he loved his worst enemy, but his designs on her were serious. Elf women weren't very fertile, but she was a halfbreed. If he got her with child, he must reason, his chances of having himself declared consort would be so much the better.

Aubrey was greatly put about when he heard what had happened. He'd already given Fraine many a lecture about slipping away from her Guards and leaving herself vulnerable, but she'd been desperate for a moment alone. She might not have another one for a very long time: apart from this trip to Midgard, Aubrey or the Guards now accompanied her everywhere. Not long after Fraine's confession to Aubrey, Evan had turned up sporting a black and puffy eye which both he and the pooka refused to discuss. Following Nissyen's advice, Fraine began returning Evan's letters unread and, no matter what he proposed, interrupted coolly and told him to bring a formal petition to Court. When he did, she quietly ordered them moved to the very end of the docket, which was growing bottom-heavy.

"I thought he wanted no mortal blood on the throne," muttered Owein.

"Nor does he. He thinks to manipulate me."

Owein shook his head, with his face full of pity and a gleam in his eyes. "A most unobservant Elf."

She put out her tongue at him. It felt good to laugh.

"How is Deverell mending?" asked Owein.

"Very slowly. The healers are pleased he's mending at all. But Evan has other sympathizers. Jared can hardly arrest them for questioning when they've done nothing as yet. Nor can we require loyalty oaths, or jail Evan for courting me."

"He'd never have begun if Moira and Tomas weren't distracted. I should go back," said Owein, scowling.

A moment ago he'd wanted to stay here with Matilda, and Fraine to join them. "Not yet," she said neutrally. "The bridge isn't—"

"I know, I know." He dug two more furrows in the earth and glared at them. "Wait until dark. I'll bring Linley to you."

Fraine sat in one of Limecliff's sleeping lean-tos. Owein had been its most recent occupant but left no impression beyond a faint familiar scent. For a bed, straw filled a wooden frame on the bare earth, but there were no blankets and no water jug; the transient residents must bring their own. From the hall Owein had borrowed a tallow lamp, but Fraine didn't care to light it until Linley came. She could see more than well enough to sit and think, and listen to the quiet outside.

Unusually still, this night. The air was summer-soft and very clear. She longed to leave the door open, but that might attract attention. No one save Rose or Linley must see her. Tallah had balked when the twins went to the lean-to, then planted herself at the edge of the forest and hissed at them from the cover of the wood. When it became clear they weren't going to join her, she'd shinnied up an evergreen, where she was probably still fuming.

Owein had left over three hours ago. Surely he should have returned by now? Perhaps Linley had gone into Axbridge with Rose. He could be conferring with Simon, who had moved to the estate until the last of his patients was well enough to travel. Owein said the estate was still housing eight or ten of them, including a man who'd lost his memory and a woman whose mind was dazed, though her body was mending.

Owein seemed to have learned rather a lot about healing. Neither Tomas nor Moira could teach the twins anything of that art, for neither of them possessed it. At first Fraine had been inclined to envy Owein the experience, until she realized how little he'd relished it. Nor was he any more at ease about dying; he could barely speak of Caraid's passing.

At last she recognized his footsteps, light and balanced and in rather a hurry, and Linley's heavier ones.

"We're here, Fraine," said the Saxon in a low strained voice.

She unbarred the door, took a grateful breath of night air and reluctantly lit the lamp. Linley was pale, though he met her eyes squarely and gave her just as affectionate a greeting as when they'd last met. He smelled of wormwood. So did the tight-lipped Owein, and of cinders, too. He was carrying a bundle of cloth and a wide-mouthed leather bag full of sticks, and he heaved them into the straw-filled frame where they landed with a muffled thud.

"What's amiss?" asked Fraine when they were all seated on the floor of beaten earth.

"Do you remember my telling you that Matilda caught a chill? She's much worse now," said Owein darkly. "Simon's tending her."

"She could be no more than tired," said Linley patiently, as if he'd said it before. His gaze at Fraine wasn't quite level and he didn't look at Owein at all. Were they having a quarrel?

"What are her—" began Fraine.

"I'll explain later," said Owein, fidgeting. "We haven't much time. Linley's expected elsewhere."

"Some wrangle among the tenants," said the Saxon easily. "Tell me about Tomas, Fraine." His gaze was trained on her face throughout her description of Tomas's behavior, and he never once interrupted. He was paying attention, too, not merely pretending; she could tell by the shifting nuances of concern in his expression. She found herself revealing a bit more about Aubrey's vigilant attendance upon her since she'd struck Evan, and about the coolness between Tomas and Moira than, in retrospect, she'd planned to relate. When she mentioned the pooka, Linley's brow furrowed with a kind of unnerved recognition, though he said nothing.

When she came to the end of her tale, Linley thought for a moment, rubbed his hands through the shock of dark soft hair that was always falling in his eyes, and looked hard at both twins. "What exactly are you asking me, my friends?"

"Whether Tomas is ill," said Fraine.

"That I can't say for certain. It sounds like sorrow to me." A minute hesitation. "I'd wager he's taken a bad shock."

That they all knew. Owein's nod was bleak, his hands knotted in his lap.

"Is he sleeping?"

"Not well, by the look of him."

"Is he speaking to you and Moira?"

"When we see him."

"And he's eating?"

"Less than before."

"Better than I am, I'll warrant," Owein muttered under his breath.

Fraine nudged him with one foot. "What might we do to help him?" she asked Linley.

"Not a great deal, I fear," said the Saxon after a barely perceptible pause. His voice was gentle. "Grieving takes its own road. Let him know you care for him. He's fortunate that you do and it will help him, though he may not seem to respond." A half glance at Owein. "Don't press him to talk, but listen well if he does. I expect he won't, though, not to you. Not for any want of trust, but because—"

"Because we're his children," said Fraine. "Not his peers." She'd just learned that word from Nissyen.

Linley blinked, and she saw both surprise and reassessment in his eyes. It might not be the right moment for what she'd come here to say, but there might not be another one. "Would you consider going to Elfland to speak with him?"

"Would I consider..." Of a sudden Linley grew very still. So did Owein, who was all but gaping at her. The Saxon moistened his lips. He wanted to go; he smelled of oranges. And of wormwood, so he was still wary, but whether for Tomas or for something else Fraine could not have said. For a long moment she watched the struggle in his face. "Rose and the estate need me here," he said very quietly. He'd always treated Fraine with respect, but now he spoke as to an adult of his own years. "If Tomas should ever have more need of me there, I would go—if I would find Rose and Limecliff as they now are when I returned." His throat moved as he swallowed, holding her gaze. "I can't lose seven years in Elfland, Fraine."

"You needn't," she told him. Then hoped she was right, given the drifting and the blockaded passage she'd just endured.

"Is Tomas poorly enough that you think I should go now?"

"No," she said slowly. Had to say. "I just.. I don't want it to come to that, Linley." She made a frustrated gesture. "For you to leave here when it would worry you. But I want Tomas restored to himself." Needed him, and so did Moira. But that she would say to no one save Owein.

"Of course you do," said Linley, warmth in his voice.

A sudden worry struck her: had she just done something that Tomas would find hard to pardon? "Please don't tell him that we—that I asked you...."

"He'll not hear it from me." Linley patted her arm. "Give him some time, but if you think he truly needs me, tell me straightaway, my dear. I must be off now, though; I've no choice." He looked at Owein. "Don't fret over 'Tilda. A proper rest should set her to rights."

"I don't believe Simon thinks so," said Owein bluntly, gazing straight at Linley. They must have had some sort of tiff.

"Perhaps he doesn't. Let's hope he's mistaken then, shall we?" Linley got to his feet and held out his hand.

Owein looked at it half a beat too long before taking it. "In that regard."

Linley's jaw tightened. "He's never wrong about the other." A smile at Fraine. "Give Tomas my greeting, and Moira too." Then, meaningfully, to both twins: "Have a care for yourselves. Good evening to you both."

She waited till the door had shut behind him before asking, "What was all that about?"

But her brother grabbed the bundle of cloth he'd tossed onto the straw, and thrust it into her arms. "Put this on." It was a long hooded cape. "Hide as much of your face as you can. You're coming to see Matilda."

"I can't—"

"The whole county round's full of woodcutters and peddlars, and you can be one for half an hour. You're selling kindling and herbs and trinkets. Don't talk much, and when you do, let on you're simple-minded." He picked up the bag of sticks. "Rose and Simon know you're coming. That's why I was so long getting Linley here. Arguing it all out with them."

"Simon doesn't know I exist," she reminded him as she shrugged into the cape.

"He does now," said Owein grimly, adjusting her hood.

She could smell his resolve, like sea water. Her pulse quickened. She would meet this half-Sighted healer, this priest. She knew how Moira felt about the exorcisms that abetted the drifting and all the blocks in the 'tweenlands, but Simon had been more than kind to both Moira and Owein, while Owein believed that Simon knew more of the Elves than he would say.

Fraine would meet Matilda, too. "What ails Matilda?" she asked.

"I'd rather you saw for yourself." Owein gave her a sudden rough hug; she saw worry in his eyes. "They say it's one thing and I say it's another, and I want to know what you think. What *you* think, not some purblind mortal."

"Very well," she said. They were mortals themselves, but no matter. "Is that why you and Linley were out of sorts with one another?"

"Partly." He reached for the lamp, but she put a hand on his arm.

"And the other part?"

"He wondered at first if Matilda might be with child. Simon told him she wasn't; he can know that sort of thing without asking." Owein's jaw was tight. "I told him she wasn't, too, but I could tell he didn't fully believe it until Simon saw her." A dispirited note crept into his voice. "He wasn't accusing me, not in words, but I don't like being mistrusted." He shook his head. "We don't fit in here, Fraine. We don't belong here at all."

"That we don't," she said, sighing. Nor in Elfland. How long would Owein keep rediscovering and resisting what she'd more or less accepted as soon as she'd learned of it? "Linley doesn't understand you as well as I do."

"No one does." She got another fierce hug. "Wait, you're not fit to go out yet." Now he was giving her an impersonal scrutiny. "I wish we could get you all sooty."

"Why not?" she asked, amused. She scraped up a handful of earth and rubbed into her face and hands and, for good measure, her hair, though it was so like Owein's that it ought to stay under her hood.

"Perfect. And some more on your boots and the cape? Here, I'll help you." He was starting to smile. He felt it too: this was their own small adventure.

"Shall you go first and I'll come after?" she asked when she was sufficiently grubby and Owein was wiping his palms on his trousers.

"I'll walk with you till we're almost there, as if I'd fallen in with you on the road. I'm following you the rest of the way. I want to watch your back."

First the twins had to placate Tallah, which was accomplished only by agreeing to let her flap along after them through the trees and stay just at the edge of the clearing by the great hall. She wanted to perch by the smoke hole on the roof, and dissuading her took a lot of vehement hand gestures and sketching in the dirt by all three of them. Then the twins had worked out a different sort of voice for Fraine, disagreed about her acting simple-minded, and discussed everything that Owein could remember about any woodseller or tinker he'd ever met between Limecliff and Axbridge.

Still, Fraine didn't feel quite ready for her performance as she rapped for admittance. Not that she was particularly bothered about that. She oughtn't to be enjoying herself, not with her parents wretched and Matilda ill and Owein's nerves strung tighter than the Parcae's wing leather, but enjoying herself she was.

In the doorway Rose greeted her. "We've firewood a-plenty, my good woman," she said briskly and rather too loudly. Her high-colored oval face was strained and her brown eyes wide, and she darted a few glances over Fraine's shoulder into the yard. Looking for Owein, no doubt.

"But I've herbs too, my lady." Fraine kept her voice soft and mysterious. "All manner of them. Febrifuges and tonics, chamomile and tansy—"

"Hullo, Owein," said Rose as he came up beside Fraine.

"—nor would I forget your cook and her pantry. Good evening, young master."

Holding a tallow lamp aloft, Rose studied Fraine, taking in the soiled cloak and overstuffed leather bag, the grime on her boots and her hands and what could be seen of her face beneath her hood. Disbelief, then approval and even a flash of what Fraine took for unwilling amusement, all moved across Rose's finely modeled features. "Enter, then, and welcome," she said, and swung the door open wide. "Show us all your tonifying herbs. We've a young lady who's feeling poorly."

Simon wasn't remotely as tall and confident as Fraine had pictured him. Instead he resembled Linley, rather below average height, sparely but sturdily built, with much the same round face and soft dark hair cut shorter than that of his brother. His eyes were just as brown and just as kind as Linley's but far more melancholy, and his expression and the set of his shoulders betrayed a chronic and controlled tension that Linley didn't harbor at all. Here is a man who carries a weight, thought Fraine. Who carries secrets and burdens, and more than his share of woe.

Without being obvious, Simon was studying her too, and his quick up and down scrutiny told her that he was reading her physical form. She didn't mind. She spread the leather bag's herbs on the table. They were from Rose's own stores, borrowed by Owein for a prop. While Rose and Simon discussed the plants—rather woodenly, but perhaps Matilda was too ill to notice such nuances—Fraine glanced about the room. Linley was absent, still with the tenants, most likely. One hearthfire was lit, burning low on this relatively warm summer evening, and one of the two bedclosets was shut. Did Matilda lie within?

Owein caught the direction of Fraine's gaze and gave her a tiny nod. He was frowning again; all the mischief and banter of their walk here together had left him. Fraine looked at Simon. "If I might see the young lady, I'd be better able to recommend something for her. I know what soil these plants grew in, and when they were picked and how they were dried." Pure fabrication, but Owein had told her what criteria the Saxons used to select herbs. "About the patient I know nothing at all, though."

Rose and Simon exchanged a glance. They smelled wary, but they'd agreed to this masquerade. "Very well," said Rose slowly.

The main door opened just then and Linley slipped in; he was slightly out of breath. Rose's face brightened with relief. She gave him a perfunctory explanation about the woodseller who also dealt in herbs and wished to see Matilda. Linley's eyes widened when he saw Fraine in her dirty cape, and all the greenery on the table. He said something in an undertone to Rose, then greeted Fraine civilly—and tipped her a wink.

Bless the fellow; she liked him more and more. Owein actually produced a half-hearted grin.

Simon turned to Fraine. "Speak her gently," he said in such a mild tone that it was impossible to take offense. The sudden smile that he gave her made him look more than ever like Linley. "Not that you need telling, I suppose."

She joined him by the bedcloset, with Owein at their heels. Simon looked tempted to ask Owein to stand clear. Instead he tapped softly on the bedcloset wall. "Are you awake, 'Tilda? We've an herbalist here to have a look at you, and Owein to bid you good-night."

A fatigued voice said, "I should be glad to see them both."

More a woman's voice than that of a girl. Fraine shot Owein a puzzled glance, but he was gazing through the bedcloset's open door at a woman who must be Matilda, and who was giving him a tired smile in return. She had nondescript brown hair and very dark blue eyes, and she was alarmingly pale. She wasn't old but she was certainly no longer young. The skin about her eyes was thin and taut, while some lines were beginning to appear both there and at the corners of her mouth. Why, she could be older than Rose, who might not be thirty yet. Moreover, she smelled of rotting meat—and of something that Fraine had never encountered before, something faintly sulphurous that stung her nose and made her eyes water. It wasn't the iron-sick. She had a strong impression that it involved magic. Whatever it might be, it wasn't Matilda's own scent, and neither was that odor of decay. When Owein folded Matilda's other hand in both of his and gazed down at her with mingled tenderness and concern, Fraine caught the glance that Rose and Linley exchanged behind his back.

Fraine was glad of the hood that hid her face. "How do you feel, my lady?" she asked as soothingly as she could.

"Weary." Matilda's chin wasn't entirely steady.

Fraine took her pulse, not that she'd any idea what it could signify, but Owein had told her that Rose and Simon did so. Matilda's hand showed rather a lot of veins and tendons, and the flesh of her neck betrayed a loss of elasticity that had nothing to do with youth. "When did that feeling begin?"

"A few days ago." She looked from Owein to Simon, standing quietly a little distance away, then back at Fraine. "It's kind of you to bring us herbs."

There was sweetness in her smile, and timidity, but very little curiosity about the odd figure that Fraine feared she must cut. Either Owein had coached Fraine well, or Matilda was too tired to question anything.

"I'm glad to be of service. Tell me, are you sleeping?" Linley had asked the same about Tomas.

"I do little else."

"And how is your appetite?"

"Not what it was."

Fraine made a few more inquiries, smiled into Matilda's trusting and exhausted eyes, and pretended to confer with Rose and Simon. She agreed with whatever they proposed, named a few herbs herself and mentioned sources for others. None of it meant much to her and no doubt she'd got many details wrong, but it set a more plausible scene. That Rose was worried could not have been more clear—she smelled of plums, and her brow was furrowed. When Simon returned to Matilda, Owein remained with them, but Fraine sat by the hearth to watch Rose brew an infusion.

The Saxon woman held each herb and considered it carefully. Some plants she bruised, some she ground, and some she cast whole into a kettle of water brought to a boil with hot stones from the fire. She put one mixture to steep and began another, taking just as many pains. Once or twice her lips moved, as if she were praying.

Fraine edged closer, but "by the Mother," was the only phrase she heard clearly. Wasn't Rose a Christian, and didn't they have just one god? Was there more than one kind of Christian?

Owein managed to catch Fraine's attention just then, and glanced pointedly at Simon. When Fraine looked too, she almost gasped. The priest was sitting next to Matilda, holding her hands. Both pairs of eyes were closed. A multicolored river of light radiated from Simon's heart, pulsated down his arms and streamed into Matilda's palms. The air about them smelled as if it had just been washed clean by a hard rain. As Fraine watched, the priest's face slowly grew pale, as if the energy he sent Matilda took some of his blood along with it.

Fraine turned to Rose and said, pitching her voice low, "Simon should rest."

"It does tire him. But he'll not stop while he can give her any ease."

And Matilda's color was a bit better, her face more relaxed.

"I'm preparing a separate infusion for him," said Rose. There was good will in her glance, and concern, and more than a little fear. But not of Fraine. "Why have you come?" she murmured. "Is something amiss?"

"Not with me. Tomas is..." She thought she could trust this woman. Linley certainly did. And wasn't it Rose who'd suggested that the twins build the eight points of the bridge first of all, and hadn't it worked? "He's not himself, since that Irishwoman's death."

"I've been praying for him."

"To the Mother?" asked Fraine. "Who is She?"

Rose stopped stirring the kettle and gave Fraine a searching look, punctuated by a swift look in Simon's direction. Fraine watched her make up her mind about something. "There's no end to that question," Rose said at last, very quietly. "It's almost as old as She is. My own mother, Susannah, traveled a bit in her youth, and she talks to every tinker and bard she meets. She thinks that the Mother has as many names as there are peoples. Brigantia. Danu. Ceridwen. Eriu. Tomas's kin might call her Freya or Frigg."

"But who is She?"

"Our Lady. Our Goddess. She rules the earth, whence we come and where we return. Some say She is the earth itself, or its spirit." Rose was eyeing Fraine closely, as if ready to fall silent the moment she saw an ambivalent reaction. "She can give both life and death. Both joy and grief. Most of all, to me at least, She is a mystery." Another glance at the white-faced priest. "Do not speak of Her to Simon, nor to Matilda and Alfred."

"Why not?"

Rose was silent for so long that at first Fraine thought she wouldn't answer at all. She chopped more herbs, removed a kettle of simmering water from the flames and poured its contents over a basin of macerated plants. She set another pot to boil, laid out a pile of clean rags and punched down three batches of bread dough. All the while she kept her eyes lowered and her thoughts to herself, her lips folded.

Finally she took a seat across the table from Fraine and said just above a whisper, "Not all Christians are easy with any mention of the older Powers, especially any of Her faces." A level look, gentle but direct, and full of gravity. "I expect you've gathered that neither Linley nor I feel as they do, or Tomas will have told you." She gazed at her flour-speckled hands. "Simon chose a different path, and for different reasons. You'll find he's more accepting than his fellows—but in listening only, Fraine. I would advise you not to ask more of him than that. Nor of Alfred."

"I understand," said Fraine quietly. Though she didn't, not about the Mother, not entirely. And Simon seemed to her less rigid than Rose painted him. Yet clearly the Goddess should not be mentioned to Alfred, and therefore not to Matilda. Fraine glanced at the bedcloset. "Matilda..." she began.

Rose shook her head. "Is Alfred's niece. Have a care with her. Tell Owein to mind his tongue."

Fraine looked at her and nodded. After a moment color burned in Rose's face. "Your pardon. I needn't have said that. It's just that I'm—"

"Concerned for him," murmured Fraine. "So am I."

White and mute, Simon came to join them, drained his infusion without a word, then slumped into the high-backed chair that Rose had left vacant for him. When Fraine accepted Rose's offer of a lean-to for the night, Owein said he would escort her there. After he took his leave of the Saxons, the twins left together, with Owein walking so fast that Fraine was hard put to keep up with him, so fast that she'd no time to erect a shield.

"Well?" he demanded as soon as they got beyond earshot of the hall.

"Matilda is ageing," Fraine began carefully.

"She's dying. I know that smell. And it isn't just death, it's—"

"Magic," Fraine agreed.

Owein stopped and leaned against a chestnut tree. They'd taken the long way through the woods to the lean-to, but so far Tallah hadn't caught up with them. "Someone's killing her," he said hoarsely. "Loki? Does he cast spells?"

"He's a god, Owein, or near to one." Fraine was breathing harder than he was; he'd learned his way about these woods and had set a breakneck pace through them. She put her bag by her booted feet and flexed her arms. "For all we know, he could age Matilda without any spells at all. Moira says that he wants to be *the* Power in this world, and that the less influence we have here, the more he does."

Her brother's eyes were nearly the color of the moonlight, his face tight and strained over the pointed Elfin cast of its bones. "What's to be done?"

"Have you told the Saxons what ails Matilda?"

"Yes. That is, I've told Rose and Simon and Linley." Owein swallowed and glanced aside; he smelled of cypress again. "I'm not sure they believe me. Simon might, but I've not spoken to him alone yet." He ran his hand across the trunk of the chestnut. "What could he do against magic?"

"I don't know."

Owein frowned at the stars caught in the leaves overhead. "I want to talk to Tomas. The sooner the better."

Had he forgot why Fraine had come? "Why not talk to Moira instead?"

"He's faced Loki. If she has, I don't know it." Owein's glance was raw. "And she's not mortal, but Tomas is. He'll understand—"

"Just now I wouldn't count on his understanding anything beyond the pit he's sunk into," Fraine said bluntly. "I'd rather convince Linley what the trouble is. He'll at least speak of it, if Simon won't. I'll consult Aubrey and Nissyen when I return."

"What of the ravens?"

Fraine pushed her sleeves above her elbows; the cloak was warmer than the night warranted. "They're never far from Tomas. What would I say? 'Your pardon, but may I converse with your ravens while you're of no use to us?'"

"Damnation." Two spots of color burned high on Owein's cheekbones. "We need him! Matilda is dying."

"So I've seen," she said, of a sudden exhausted. Had his voice just cracked? She came to his side. "And so I'll tell Tomas as soon as I may. That I can promise."

"But not what he'll do about it," said Owein more quietly, responding to the fatigue in her voice. He moved away from the tree just far enough to put both arms about her. "Only he can do that." He held her tightly. "I'll speak to Linley again. Before you leave, I hope."

She didn't want to leave either Owein or this sheltered space beneath the chestnut branches. Even the thought of the lean-to was stifling. "Must you return to the hall tonight?" she asked after a while, and rested her head on his shoulder. "Couldn't we just sleep here, you and I?"

Somewhere above them, the tree shivered as if from a light impact, and Tallah let out a faint hiss. They ignored her.

"I wish we could," said Owein. "But Linley might wonder if I'd gone back with you." He heaved a sigh. "Not only that, Alfred and possibly the Bishop are coming in the morning; at what hour I don't know. It would look odd if I weren't there to greet them, and worse if I wandered in after having been away all night."

"Worse than that, if they learned you'd bedded down with a tinker lass out in the open."

"That too." He slipped a hand into her hood to tug a lock of her hair. "And such an ugly one."

She couldn't suppress a giggle. Then a small green chestnut struck her shoulder with sufficient force that it must have been thrown, and Tallah hissed again.

"Ouch," muttered Owein, shielding his eyes with one hand and glancing overhead. "Why's she in such a temper?" He sniffed the night air. "No one's about."

No one they could smell, which didn't mean they were alone. When Fraine put up her shield, she felt the faintest of tremors in its energy, as if a being who used magic were near. It wasn't Owein; he was closer than whatever she'd sensed. So was Tallah.

Fraine stepped away from Owein. "My shield," she began in a whisper, but he nodded. He'd put his up as well. Lackwits, they'd been, not to have done so before. But this was Midgard, and no one here used magic save Simon and—

"Daniel?" she whispered.

Owein shrugged. He pointed at Fraine's hood and satchel, then towards the lean-to. She drew the cape over her face and followed him.

CHAPTER TWENTY-THREE: A CONFERENCE

To Rose's mind, there was only one mercy touching the conference with Alfred and the Bishop. Just before it began, Owein told her that Fraine had left Midgard. He'd got in late the previous evening, white-faced and taciturn. Rose was beginning to recognize those barricades in his eyes. Unfortunately he could hardly have chosen a worse moment to return: half an hour after the arrival of Alfred and Werferth, who weren't expected till the following morning. They had already seen Matilda, and the Bishop had Daniel in tow.

"Confounded hermit looks like a bitch who just whelped," Linley muttered in Rose's ear.

And Daniel did, sallow face smug, dark eyes glittering, a quarter smile tugging at the corners of a mouth bracketed by lines and folded shut with secrets. He paced unctuously after the Bishop, moved a chair for him without asking leave and, with a great display of furrowed brow, wiped a perfectly clean tankard. Rose longed to show him the door but hospitality forbade her, even had Daniel not appeared to be back in Werferth's good graces. Moreover, she knew Alfred well enough to see how he treated Daniel with a worried neutrality rather than the polite tolerance he usually showed the hermit. And Werferth was icily correct. Some current had shifted among them all.

Owein hung up his cloak, then stopped short at the sight of the Bishop ensconced in Tomas's best wooden armchair. It was the first time the pair of them had seen one another since that uncanny moment in the granary, when Owein had divined that unconscious and nameless lad had been Werferth's lover. Now the brief stare that the Bishop gave Owein was cool and deadly. Rose saw hatred there, vengefulness and calculation, yet in the back of Werferth's eyes there lurked fear and uncertainty as well. Whatever he and Daniel were plotting against Owein, Rose concluded, was by no means guaranteed to work. Which was a small comfort, but the only one she had.

Owein greeted Alfred, then turned to Daniel and the Bishop. "Good evening, sirs."

They answered in monosyllables. Owein might be too inexperienced to understand how discourteous a response they'd made to him under what was supposedly his own brother's roof, but he was sensitive enough to read faces, and his own closed still further. After a more cordial exchange with Alfred about the weather and the continued lack of word from Tomas, Owein lowered his voice and asked Simon how Matilda was faring.

"Worse, I fear," murmured Simon. "Alfred is much troubled for her sake. We're about to retire for the night, to leave the hall quiet for her."

"I shall take a lean-to," said Owein politely.

The hall could have housed him that evening, but Rose made no demur;

she knew he'd be happier away from Werferth. "We'll see you in the morning, then," she had said, rising to find him some bedding.

At Alfred's invitation, Rose's mother Susannah joined them for the morning meal. Owein took Rose aside on the pretext of sending for more bread, and told her that Fraine had left Midgard. When they returned to the table, Alfred announced that he and Werferth wished a conference with Linley, Simon and Rose, and that Daniel might attend if he so desired. With quiet courtesy and a face that betrayed nothing of his thoughts, Owein took his leave.

When Susannah, who'd just finished clearing the plates away, began her own goodbyes, Alfred stopped her politely. "We're to meet in Limecliff chapel, my lady. Would you be so good as to keep Matilda company while we're gone?"

Rose's throat tightened. It was for Alfred to decide who sat with his niece, yet Owein could have done so if they'd not adroitly got him dismissed before asking Susannah.

In silence they walked to the small chapel, refurbished under Simon's direction but still austere. Simon led the way, followed by Rose and Linley. After them came Alfred, bareheaded and alone. Werferth and Daniel brought up the rear, side by side but a few ells apart, both men's arms folded in the sleeves of their robes.

The dew was gone from the grass and the sky was a rare and lucid blue, dotted with puffed clouds. Within the chapel it was cool and dim, and the damp seemed to have settled into the simple wooden benches, leaving them faintly slick to the touch. Dust motes drifted in the morning air. When Simon propped the eastern door open, light fired the beaten earth floor to the shade of warmed clay. He and Linley arranged three benches in a rough triangle. The King took one bench, Werferth and Daniel another, and on the third Rose sat between Simon and Linley.

"This is not a formal accusation," began Werferth calmly, looking at Linley. "However, the Church may have reason for attention, if not concern."

"Go on," said Linley. He sat straight, hands relaxed on his thighs but shoulders tense beneath his jerkin.

"Moreover, it does not come from the King, although the Church wonders if his niece may be affected."

Rose wanted to huddle into her cloak but held her chin high, though not so much as to seem defiant. Werferth must be referring to Owein. Daniel's hands were still clasped within his sleeves, his features arranged to convey humility and respect, but his eyes, intent upon Linley, were hot and black. If only he would make a mistake, overstep himself somehow, and in a worse way than whatever was about to be said of Owein.

She glanced at Alfred, who was pale, his expression neutral. Because she knew him well, she saw that his indigo eyes, so like those of his niece, were suffused with foreboding. Since seeing Matilda, he'd said not two words that protocol or manners hadn't required. There'd been no way to hide the age in her face from him or from anyone else. Did Matilda herself see it in her hands?

If only Tomas were here. Linley said he'd been crushed by the Irishwoman's death, but they had need of his Sight to preserve Alfred's good will and protect Owein. Tomas had done no scrying for the King in far too long. Perhaps Owein could do it in his stead, but it might be too late for that now.

"Know you the nature of Matilda's ailment?" Werferth asked Simon.

"No, my lord." So the priest had said before. Face grey with fatigue, he looked steadily at Werferth. He'd lost flesh in his ongoing effort to heal Matilda; it showed in the more prominent bones of his wrists and the hollows about his eyes. Selfishly, Rose was glad that Linley's own portion of the Sight had given him no such power to heal.

"You have found no mark upon her?" asked the Bishop.

Simon's brows drew together. "What manner of mark?"

Daniel's gaze flickered ever so slightly towards Werferth, who nodded almost imperceptibly. "As from an arrow," said the hermit. "A small one."

Simon shook his head.

"Have you examined her?"

"Several times."

Again a glance, a minute assent, passed between the hermit and the Bishop. Simon's jaw tightened.

"Thoroughly?" murmured Daniel with a patient air that didn't match his intent black eyes.

"I've not asked her to disrobe, if that's what you mean," said Simon calmly. "It hardly seemed necessary."

Daniel turned to Rose. "Perhaps you or your mother..." A delicate pause. "Elfshot is not always easy to detect."

"Elfshot?" repeated Simon, his face wary. Some ills of the body were said to be caused by tiny invisible arrows shot by Elves. No such minute puncture wound would be found on Matilda, yet any mole or freckle might be made to serve Daniel's purpose.

"Elfshot," said Werferth firmly. "By your own account you don't know what ails the girl. Can you rule it out?"

"I have never seen an illness caused by it," said Simon, measuring each word.

"Then how would you know one?" Triumph in the Bishop's voice. Simon grew very still. They all did.

It was Alfred who stirred first. "How would any of us?" he asked gravely. "Elfshot implies an agent. It implies *maleficium.* Who would be accused?"

He'd addressed no one in particular, and now glanced at each of his listeners. For a long moment there was no answer, while the sun burned dust motes to sparks before their eyes.

Then Daniel said, "Perhaps we progress too quickly. It would seem that first the young lady must be examined. A place struck by an arrow would likely still be painful."

"Examined with what cause?" put in Simon, whose eyes were beginning to kindle. "What would you have her told?" He ignored Werferth's scowl. "She should be caused no further distress. Her malady is no better."

"It is worse," said Werferth coolly. Then to Alfred, "There are cures specific to elfshot, my lord."

"Dock seed and Masses," began Daniel.

"If that's what ails her." Simon's round secretive face was taut now, his mouth hard. "I question the wisdom of frightening her over something that cannot be proved."

"Whereas I wish to do all I can," said Werferth, as if pronouncing a judgment.

Silence. Linley shifted on the bench. Simon was exchanging a prolonged glance with Alfred, troubled on the King's part, level on that of the priest. "Are you not content with my care of her, your Grace?" Simon asked quietly.

"I have no complaint of it whatever."

Another, weightier pause. When Rose caught herself holding her breath, she let it out with as little noise as she could.

"It would seem," said Alfred, his eyes dark with strain, "that to warrant a closer examination of Matilda, feeble as she is and whatever she's told of the reason, that there should be sufficient grounds to conduct one."

"Rumors of uncanny circumstances linked to this estate have circulated for many a year, my lord," said the Bishop without hesitation. His face was smooth, his voice reasonable, his hands folded in his lap. "Some of them Daniel has made known to your Grace, but perhaps you would allow him to list them for us all?"

A rather more detailed roster of events followed than Rose had expected; Daniel must have conducted a lot of interviews. There was Tomas's mysterious appearance in the well-patrolled marshes near Alfred's camp more than six years ago. Tomas's sensitivity to iron at that time. His unexplained ability to lay the Danes' plans before Alfred in detail. Tomas's conversing with invisible beings in the kitchen of one of Alfred's estates. Moira's arrival at Limecliff during an eclipse on All Saints' Eve, just after two men were set upon by a dark-haired demon who was with child—certainly Moira's appearance was extraordinary, and Tomas had acknowledged the babe that she carried. The winged creatures who'd attacked Daniel near Cheddar gorge, yet spared Tomas. His departure with Moira not long after. Then his brother Owein had appeared, looking scarcely more human than Moira did and, like Tomas, privy to facts he had no way of knowing.

At this point in Daniel's recital, everyone glanced away from Werferth, and the hermit continued with no pause for breath. Owein spent at least as much time in the woods as Tomas did. The boy had shown a marked preference for Matilda. He'd been seen all but kissing her outside the granary, and that with wounded men and women lying within. The pair of them had disappeared together for most of one night and been found closeted in the mews, shortly before Matilda fell ill.

Alfred's brows drew together; this last fact was new to him. The cook, Hroswitha, would never have mentioned it. Matilda must have been talking to the kitchen girl; they'd been thick as thieves before Matilda was taken sick.

And finally, Owein had been consorting with a tinker woman, just the sort of gypsyish ne'er-do-well who might be able to advise him how the Elves could be persuaded to loose their arrows at a mortal. A tinker woman, moreover, who appeared to be in communication with Tomas.

"That is an extraordinary claim," said Alfred in a quiet, careful voice. "Would you care to elaborate upon it?"

Rose shifted a little closer to Linley. He flicked her a sideways glance and a small encouraging smile, but the skin about his eyes and mouth was creased, and she could see the tendons of his throat. Simon's back had stiffened.

"Last night I was out walking, alone with my thoughts," began Daniel. "My path took me across Limecliff estate."

The hermit never hunted, so he wasn't poaching. Nor trespassing: the local landholders had given him leave to walk where he would, save at plowing or harvest times.

"I wondered if the Bishop might come early, and I directed my steps towards the sleeping lean-tos to see how many seemed occupied," said Daniel. "As I approached the great chestnut tree that stands near them, I saw Owein and the tinker beneath it."

Alfred watched him, motionless. Rose kept her gaze on the hermit. So did Simon. Werferth, head slightly bowed, was contemplating the altar.

"She wore an old ragged cloak, torn and stained with earth, and carried a bundle of sticks. Her face I could not see; it was hooded. Just as I noticed them, she stepped so close to Owein that she must have known her proximity would be welcomed. She said, 'So I'll tell Tomas as soon as I return. That I can promise.'"

Alfred's face withdrew a little. Before Rose's eyes dark speckled stars began to swim, and her left temple gave a painful throb.

"Owein embraced her," said Daniel, his mouth pursed in distaste. "And he said, 'But not what he'll do about it.'"

As if carved from twin blocks of ice, Simon and Linley sat frozen on either side of Rose. Light from the chapel's open door fell in a long rectangle upon the ground before their bench. The entire left side of Rose's skull hurt now, and her temples were pounding in rhythm with her pulse.

"Then Owein said, 'Only he can do that.' And, 'I'll speak to Linley about it again, before you leave, I hope.'"

Werferth gave Linley a long, grave look. Other than a deepening of the lines about his mouth, Linley's expression didn't change. He kept his gaze, steady and neutral, trained on Daniel.

The hermit's eyes narrowed a trifle. "The tinker asked if the pair of them couldn't sleep beneath the tree. Owein told her he wished that they could, but that Linley might wonder if he, Owein, had gone back with her. Gone where, he did not say."

Alfred's eyes were enormous, his face immobile, but there was fire in the depths of Simon's gaze. Don't let him lose rein on his temper, Rose prayed.

Daniel half closed his eyes, as one communing with himself or his God. Lips compressed, Werferth regarded the ceiling. At last Alfred asked, "Is that all?"

"No," said the hermit, faintly, as if it pained him. "No, your Grace, I fear it is not. Owein said that King Alfred and the Bishop were coming in the morning, and that it would look odd if he weren't at hand to greet them, and worse if he wandered in after having been gone all night. This, while still holding the tinker."

Rose tried not to fidget.

"Then the woman said, 'And worse than that if they learned you'd bedded down with a tinker lass out in the open.' And Owein was familiar with her."

Alfred said, very low, "How, familiar?"

"He put his hand inside her hood and said, 'And such an ugly one.'"

Rose wanted to laugh, wanted to cry. They should never have agreed to that masquerade with Fraine.

The hermit was still speaking. "Then he looked up at the chestnut tree and said, 'Ouch,' and, 'Why's she in such a temper? No one's about.'"

"In a temper? Whom did he mean?" asked the Bishop.

"I don't know," Daniel told him. "*I* saw no one. Then the tinker said, 'My shield.' They let go of one another and began walking towards the sleeping lean-tos."

Silence, thick and pressing. Daniel and Werferth studied Alfred who, head bent, was turning a ring about on his finger. When Rose stole a glance at Simon, he was breathing harder than before, and the low-burning spark was still in his eyes.

Resolve came into Linley's face. "A tinker woman came to Limecliff yesterday evening, before the three of you arrived. She had firewood and herbs," he said in a matter-of-fact voice.

Alfred glanced up; was that hope in his expression?

"She conferred with Rose and Simon about Matilda. Whether Owein knew her I could not say, but we could ask him." Linley looked at Daniel. "We could have asked him last night. Or this morning."

"What are you implying?" asked the hermit after a moment, a hint of strain in his voice.

"Nothing," said Linley with an easy smile. "Rather, it's what you are."

"We have said this is not a formal accusation—"

"Then why are we having this conversation without Owein present, do you think?" asked Linley, calmly and pleasantly.

Nonetheless he'd interrupted Daniel, whose eyes blazed. "I think," he said in a sharp, haughty voice, "that the King's niece is sick unto dying, and should be examined for elfshot. I also think there is ample evidence of something uncanny about Owein. Tomas's *brother*, and a guest beneath your roof when Matilda fell ill."

"Evidence?" asked Linley in the same tone as before.

"To mention only one piece of it, some of your tenants tell me that the boy's grown since his arrival here. It's unnatural."

Linley produced a tolerant smile. "He's of an age to grow. How old were you when you reached your full height?"

"I don't remember," snapped Daniel. "How old is Owein?"

"I don't know." Linley turned to Rose, as if it had just occurred to him that Owein might have told her. "Do you?"

"I've no idea," she said smoothly. "I'd wager that Owein hasn't either. It's my impression that the Norse don't keep as close an accounting of their birthdays as we Saxons do."

Alfred, ever curious about other cultures, was nodding.

Daniel switched tack. "Then there's the conversation I heard between Owein and the tinker."

"Was it heard by anyone else?" Linley asked.

"No," Daniel snapped.

Linley turned his whole torso, not just his head, to glance at Simon.

Two heartbeats went by before Simon looked at Alfred and said, "Nor did anyone else see the winged creatures that Daniel claimed attacked him."

Since Hroswitha the cook had seen one, though she'd voluntarily sworn secrecy in that regard, Simon had just told a boldfaced lie. And told it brilliantly, as if embarrassed to say anything that might compromise the hermit. The reluctance came, Rose knew, from the effort it cost Simon to lie at all, let alone to Alfred, his childhood friend and now his King. That Simon had done so was a measure of how much he loved her and Linley, and how fond he'd grown of Tomas and his children. Now he fixed a level and earnest gaze upon Alfred.

As the chapel filled with a silence laden with Daniel's suppressed anger,

Werferth's hostility and everyone's pent anxiety, Rose kept her face still and her hands quiet in her lap. Alfred might not care to hear that Owein had been shut in the mews with Matilda in the wee hours of the morning, but almost the only uncanny act that Owein had performed in front of more than one witness was his recognition of that dying young man as Werferth's lover. Which was hardly something that Daniel would spell out in front of Werferth, or perhaps even beyond his hearing. When Rose dared a glance at the Bishop, his face had turned waxen, and Alfred was studying him.

It all turned upon Alfred, devout Christian that he was, and upon his respect for the Bishop's office if not his person. Or did it? Alfred needed Tomas's second Sight.

Which Tomas wasn't here to provide. But Owein was. Remember that, Rose thought at Alfred as hard as she could. Remember that Owein has gifts of his own.

What most worried her, what knotted her stomach and left her throat parched, was that from all appearances Matilda was dying. Werferth and Daniel could quibble about elfshot all they pleased, seek to implicate Owein, scheme to get him and then Linley as his host turned out of doors, and Limecliff given to Daniel—and none of it would help Matilda one whit. If only Owein possessed healing powers along with his Sight; if only Tomas did. Or Fraine, who seemed wiser than her age. In Rose's opinion the girl took after Moira to an astonishing degree. Yet there was a calm observant intelligence, a detachment and a gravity to Fraine that were all her own. Moira's was the more complex and passionate character.

Linley took Rose's hand: Alfred had just turned to the two of them.

"I will think on these matters," said the King. His expression was mild but remote, with a shifting and reflective layer of wariness that forbade questions. He glanced at Daniel and Werferth. "My thanks for bringing us your concerns. Please convey nothing of this discussion to anyone beyond this room." A pause, during which the lapiz eyes filled with intensity. "Is that clear?" he asked very softly. There were murmurs of assent all around.

Alfred looked at Simon. "Will you continue tending Matilda for me?"

"Willingly, my lord."

"Rose and Linley, may I impose upon your hospitality for as long as she's ailing?" By rights Alfred could command it, yet he was asking.

"Now and at any time, your Grace," said Linley.

The King got to his feet. "I thank you." He didn't smile. "Now I shall go sit with Matilda. Please don't disturb us unless a crisis requires my attention, or unless you, Simon, want to see her for any reason. If Owein wishes to pay her a visit when I'm done, he may, but I request that someone else be present until I decide otherwise." Without a backward glance, he walked out of the chapel. Air and sunlight streamed through the door he'd left open behind him.

CHAPTER TWENTY-FOUR: AN APPARITION

The 'tweenlands

Fraine wasn't asleep when it happened, so she could not have been dreaming. She was returning from Midgard, had only just left the small stuffy lean-to and the willow grove. And left Owein, whose loss tore at her as if she'd swallowed powdered glass. She was spinning through the 'tweenlands, studying the eight brilliant points of the bridge and how they were threaded together by the beaded lines of scaffolding that she and Owein had slowly built among them, so few lines and under so much strain that a few of them quivered like bowstrings.

Without warning, a woman's voice said, *"Fraine."*

Not Moira's voice. Deep for a woman, it was hollow, full of echoes rather than Moira's peculiar resonance, a soft voice but by no means a gentle one. It not only compelled Fraine's attention but commanded her respect, for it held the shadow of power, as if it were a husk of the voice it once had been.

"Fraine," it said again. *"Daughter of Moira, hear us."*

Fraine turned about in a slow circle until she saw the golden-haired woman of whom she had so often dreamed, tall and regal, her skin suffused with a glowing honeyed tint. From her throat hung a breathtaking necklace worked of hot yellow gold. Beside her stood two immense sleek grey cats, their eyes more molten than the necklace. The power that Fraine had always sensed about the woman brimmed in her hazel eyes and exuded from her pores like a scent. She had no real scent whatever.

But the other woman who stood shivering two paces to the left of the radiant one, the gaunt woman with filthy hanks of dun-colored hair and bloodless lips and abrasions on her wasted neck, the woman whose round blue eyes were fixed on Fraine—the second woman most assuredly had a scent. She smelled, overwhelmingly, of death.

She was a corpse; she could be nothing else. Her body was wrapped in pale linen, with only her bare feet and arms free of it. One arm must be broken; it hung at an unnatural angle that set Fraine's teeth on edge. There was awareness in the gaze she bent upon Fraine, with grief and longing and something like hope.

Torn between horror and pity, Fraine whispered, "Who are you?"

She'd addressed the corpse, but it was the gleaming woman who answered in that vast echoing voice, *"I am Freya."*

Fraine couldn't speak. She stared at the golden being, at the cats whose flanks grazed her sides.

"Or I was. Yet I was also, in other ways, Dana, Ceridwen, Brigantia..." She drifted closer to Fraine, who was too paralyzed to retreat.

Freya, the love goddess. Who had yellow hair and a spectacular golden necklace: Brisingamen, it was called. Tomas had told the twins how Freya had won her neck-ring from its craftsmen, four dark grubby dwarves with bulbous eyes and grasping hands, by sleeping one night with each of them in their cavern beneath the earth. Freya rode in a carriage drawn by cats, her sacred animal. The woman who stood before Fraine could be that goddess, or could once have been. Freya, whose falcon-skin cloak granted her passage among the worlds. Freya, who claimed half the bravely fallen dead.

For a long reverent moment, Fraine bowed her head. It took several attempts but, looking directly into the purple-ringed eyes of the corpse, at last she managed to ask, "And who are you?"

"I was called Caraid," whispered the corpse, with even more effort than it had cost Fraine to speak. She huddled into her shroud and drew its folds more tightly about her with puckered fingertips. "I knew Tomas. Your father."

Fraine couldn't suppress a small breathless gasp. The dead woman's voice didn't echo. It held no power and was barely audible in its hoarseness. But it was immediate; it was *there,* directly before Fraine. The goddess, or the essence of what she had once been, might not be wholly in the 'tweenlands, although her power and her attention both were. But Caraid could not have been more present. Fraine could have reached out and touched that greying skin.

The reek from it was growing steadily worse. "Your name is known to me," Fraine said slowly. Her stomach gave a small ominous heave. "My brother Owein was with you when you died." The recognition in Caraid's nod made Fraine stifle a shudder. Only then did she notice that she'd stopped moving through the 'tweenlands, had in fact stopped some time ago. They were motionless, the three of them, when Fraine had to reach Elfland with all speed. She began to feel light-headed. "Why have you come to me?"

"It was my doing," said Freya. *"Caraid called upon me, and I answered as best I could."*

"Why?" Spots of black and brown and purple swarmed before Fraine's eyes.

"Many reasons." A slight pause. *"Both dark and light. Can you not guess, child? Skuld came to your name-fastening."*

She would not collapse. She would see it through, this apparition, whatever it might portend.

"We mean only to help you," Freya said gently. *"Although we can do little but warn you, and in some small way offer counsel and strength. Your enemy is moving against you. You may call upon us. You must."*

"Call upon you," said Fraine weakly.

"And upon the old Powers." Freya moved forward another pace and fixed Fraine with those radiant hazel eyes. *"Upon the Earth."*

"Upon love," Caraid whispered. She was shaking. "And upon me."

"Call upon you?" Fraine could scarcely look at her, the yellowing bruises, the puffed and mottled skin, the terrible awareness in the decaying face. "But you're not alive."

"Not wholly. Neither am I entirely gone." A brownish tear rolled down her cheek. "A boon has been granted me. And granted you, Fraine. While it lasts, I will aid you all I can. I have not lost the Sight, and I am not wholly in the realm of the dead. Not yet." Her lips blue, shuddering with a cold that Fraine didn't feel in the slightest, she glanced at Freya. "Thanks to our Lady."

For a few seconds Freya bowed her head, as if to witnesses whom Fraine could not see. *"And thanks to you,"* the goddess told her. *"You have not only heard. You have listened."*

Fraine tried to think. She had listened. Might she be permitted questions? "How can I keep the bridge standing?" she blurted. "How can Matilda be cured? And..." The most important thing was the hardest to ask. "How can I help Tomas?" She recoiled from the wealth of mud-colored viscous tears that began rolling down Caraid's cheeks, then felt guilty for flinching. The woman must have loved Tomas in life and love him still, but the putrefaction that wafted from her was beyond bearing.

When Freya moved towards Fraine, the cats kept pace with her, muscles gliding beneath their sleek grey hide. A rumble reached Fraine's ears: they were purring. Freya held something in one closed fist. Slowly, she extended it. Waves of power flowed over Fraine with the gesture and set her to trembling.

"Call upon us," said Freya. *"Listen to us. And remember—this."*

She reached for Fraine's hand and pressed something into her palm. A small tremor ran down her spine at the touch. She held a handful of earth.

Grave dirt, she feared at first, and almost dropped it. But the soil in her palm was warm, while Caraid was shivering so violently that her teeth chattered. Fraine studied the loamy earth in her hand. Rich, dark soil. It was moist. It smelled like rain. It smelled of spring and roots, of orchards and earthworms. There was one now, wriggling between her fingertips.

Her eyes began burning, then slowly filled with hot tears. When she looked up, her visitors were gone and she had begun to move again, or the 'tweenlands had.

CHAPTER TWENTY-FIVE: AN EYE FOR A BARGAIN

Midgard

Rose and Susannah were folding bed linen in a storage shed when Alfred tapped at its open door. Pale and somber, the King was alone. "Might I persuade you to take a walk with me? The kitchen garden's a rare sight this morning."

Ten minutes later the three of them were seated on a bench opposite Hroswitha's riotous patch of mint. Bees with small black shining wings droned in the mild air. Upon a stepping stone amid the herbs, a calico cat lay trustfully sunning its belly. A tabby spotted Susannah, who adored all cats and fed them indiscriminately, and began picking its way towards her along the topmost rail of the fence. Rose composed her face and waited for Alfred to finish his pleasantries about the weather and the lemon balm. Yesterday's conference left her in no doubt of his errand.

The King was studying a clump of lavender. "I came to ask the two of you to examine Matilda's person for any sort of mark that a small arrow might have left," he said at last. "It would be well if Hroswitha were present also, but not told what you seek."

Susannah, who knew nothing of the conversation in the chapel, shot Rose a puzzled look.

Alfred saw the glance. "Or left by some other such weapon," he said to Susannah as the tabby jumped into her lap. "I will tell you only that the question of elfshot has been raised. It was not good hearing, and should be addressed."

"Of course, my lord," said Rose, and Susannah nodded without speaking. Her face was quiet, her eyes reflective, fastened unseeingly on the herbs now. She'd have guessed that Daniel or Werferth might be at the root of this request, and that Alfred didn't care for it but would comply with the Bishop nonetheless. Susannah knew how much Daniel wanted Limecliff, and that with Tomas gone and Owein a cipher, only Rose and her husband stood in the hermit's way. All of this Susannah would understand, and how and why to hold her tongue. She'd taught Rose most of what she knew about the old deities, and how the seasons revolved around them. And all that Rose knew of discretion.

"When we've done, shall I come directly to your Grace?" Rose asked as guilelessly as she could. At all costs she wanted to bypass Daniel and Werferth with her findings, but neither did she wish to make it obvious that such was her intent.

Alfred gave her a look of piercing comprehension and, unexpectedly, a smile. "Yes, please." He touched her hand, a rare gesture for him, then reached to scratch the tabby beneath its fawn-and-white chin. "Matilda never wearies of telling me how kind you've been to her. You have all my thanks for it."

"It's easy to be kind, when she's so dear to us," said Rose. "How does she feel this morning?"

"I've not seen her. Last night she was tired to the bone. I rather think she was hoping for a word with Owein before he turned in, but she fell asleep almost immediately."

The King said Owein's name easily enough, though his voice was low and without affect. When Rose got up, Susannah set the disappointed cat down by her feet and stood too, her face calm.

Rose wanted no interruptions while she and Susannah were with Matilda. "Are the Bishop and Daniel..."

"In the chapel," said Alfred. "Still sleeping, is my guess." The pair of them had spent the night there.

"I'll find you once we've finished, my lord," Rose promised, taking Susannah's arm, and turned to go.

"Rose?" Alfred said quietly.

She stopped in her tracks, saw the sun full in his face and the darkness in his eyes. "Yes, your Grace?"

"If you should see Owein, would you please send him to me?"

Owein found the King where Rose had said he would be, sitting on a bench in Hroswitha's kitchen garden and staring moodily at a small spiky thicket of lavender. Owein was in a foul humor. He'd not seen Matilda since night before last and likely wouldn't see her this morning, now that Rose had sent him here. But an audience with the King took precedence; there was nothing for it but to go.

When Alfred glanced up at him, Owein was startled at the change in his face: white and shuttered and taut with grief. "It was good of you to come so quickly. Pray be seated." The King pointed at a spot on the bench beside him. A gracious gesture, and with it all the trappings of his habitual courtesy were in evidence, but his expression was pinched with wariness. Moreover he smelled so strongly of wormwood that Owein could hardly tell they were in an herb garden. Keeping his face grave, he waited.

"Can you tell me anything of Matilda's ailment?" asked the King.

"I am not a healer, my lord—"

"By your own account," said Alfred, holding his gaze. The lapiz eyes were dark and the brows lowered, but not with accusation. Far more than the face of a King, and despite its reserve, it was that of a man troubled for his niece.

Owein warmed to him for it. "Indeed I am not, your Grace, yet I know she's very ill. From what cause I could not say." Trying not to sound blunt, he added, "I fear for her."

"As do I," muttered Alfred. He propped his chin in his hands for a little space, then straightened and turned to Owein. There was no hope in his eyes; he was grasping at straws. "Have you any advice about her care? Any at all?"

At that moment Owein would have given anything he possessed for a fraction of Simon's powers. "Nothing, my lord," he said wretchedly as his gaze fell to his boots. "I only wish I did."

When he looked up, Alfred was nodding slowly to himself, as if he'd expected no better. He gave Owein a measuring glance. "She is dear to you, is she not?" he asked in the gentlest of voices, one at odds with the watchfulness in his eyes.

"Yes."

"Tomas is...different," murmured the King.

It might have been a change of subject, but Owein thought not. He made himself breathe.

"And so might you be," said Alfred. "Yet in friendship I've never found your brother wanting." He fastened his indigo eyes upon Owein, a searching look full of assessment and laced with an undernote of confusion. He smelled of grief now, of cypress and ashes. Bees crawled among the lavender; a calico cat, on a flat stone amid the herbs, sat up and began to wash. "Have a care with her," Alfred said quietly.

"So I have, my lord," Owein told him after swallowing a much sharper retort, with the King scanning his face all the while. He took a breath. "So I will."

There was a taut silence before Alfred let out a barely audible sigh and turned his head away. Owein knew better than to assume the interview was at an end. Perhaps half a minute later the King asked, "Have you any word of Tomas?"

None whose source Alfred could be told. Owein shook his head.

The King's shoulders slumped. He drew a hand across his forehead. "Might you be able to advise me as he did, Owein? About the Danes?" There was desperation in the mixture of odors that wafted from him now, an acrid scent, pungent and clinging.

Owein sensed that a great deal might ride on his answer. He had some Sight, though not so much as Tomas did. Still, did he know that for certain? Neither he nor Fraine had yet learned the extent of their gifts. And what he couldn't glean himself, surely he could have Fraine ask someone to scry out for him? Nissyen, perhaps?

Thanks be to the gods that, unlike Tomas, he could lie about it. Though he feared he might have waited too long to answer, he kept his face perfectly calm and said, "I believe I might, your Grace, given enough notice." And, daringly, "What do you most wish to know?"

"Let me think upon that," muttered Alfred. A keen look at Owein. A look that was rather doubtful. Of both of them.

Owein assumed a dignified air. "I know what manner of task I'm taking on, my lord." He didn't, not entirely. He only knew that Alfred was starved for reassurance. Though at that moment he thought it was merely about the Danes.

Perhaps an hour later, when it was clear that Rose and Susannah would take so much time closeted with Matilda that noon might well come and go before Owein had any hope of seeing her, he changed to his sturdier boots and set off for the willow grove.

The day was warm, the grass green and shining. The Sun had wheeled almost to the top of the sky but the Moon was down, nearly at the full, and invisible. Owein could feel it tugging at him like a slow airless wind, yet it was only one pull among many. Elfland wasn't like Midgard. With his eyes shut, he would have known which world held him. In Elfland there were no great burning weights and measures whirling in the dome of sky above and below his feet. Save his link with Fraine, in Elfland nothing pulled at him at all. It was a world adrift.

Swallows darted about the last barn that Owein passed; for a moment he stopped to watch them. Next came the fallow fields and the ridge where the Saxons had buried the unknown dead. He averted his gaze from the tumbled earth beginning to settle about the lone marker that Linley had placed there. Caraid's remains should have reached Dubhlinn by now, and Aidan should be back in Elfland.

Fraine was not. Owein knew by the way that his link to her was slightly tenuous, like a well-tied but elderly rope, and the way its direction kept shifting. It was an odd sensation, rather like how one's stomach felt when hanging upside down, as if the center of the earth had unaccountably moved. Owein didn't care for the feeling. It meant that Fraine was still in the 'tweenlands, and that the passage between Faerie and Midgard continued to grow harder despite all they'd built of the bridge.

When he reached the woods, he took in several lungfuls of fresh smokeless air scented with humus and ferns and the resinous tang of sap. There was the foxes' den, not far from Owein's favorite hazel hedge and a fallen beech. Flexing his shoulders, he found himself smiling, more at ease than he'd been since he saw Fraine. They should have spent the night under the chestnut tree; they'd both have been the better for it.

He spotted cloven tracks: deer had come this way recently. Perhaps three of them, likely a doe and her fawns. Next he passed the great oak with its squirrels' nest. Everywhere the lush deep green of new growth called to him. He spied baby birds overhead, then a lone grey owl, dozing in a coppice, who opened one slitted yellow eye as he passed.

When the ground began to slope and the air to hold more moisture, he knew he was nearing water and the willows. There he would stretch out on his back and try to remember all he'd ever heard of scrying. All that Moira or Tomas had taught him, all that Nissyen and Aubrey had said. Then, while concentrating on Alfred, he'd enter trance and see what could be learned—

No, he wouldn't. Not right away. Frowning, he halted and stood at gaze.

In the middle of the willow grove, his back to Owein, sat a man. He wore a lightweight jerkin and the sort of boiled leather cap that many Saxons favored. A farmer from off the estate? Something about him didn't seem right. He was more slender than most Saxons, but that wasn't it. Why would a farmer be idling in the woods? He wasn't kitted out for hunting. He had no dogs, no falcons—and bore no arms. Now that, among these iron-loving mortals, was exceedingly odd.

Owein put up his shield, which quivered as it locked into place. The fellow used magic, then. He wore no shield of his own, so he wasn't expecting company, was foolhardy, or so powerful he needed no protection. Owein took a cautious and silent step backwards, then another.

He needn't have bothered. The man stood and whirled to face him; he was bonelessly agile. He whipped off the leather cap and revealed a head of ginger hair.

"Loki," said Owein as soon as he could speak, and with as great a show of calm as he could feign.

"Indeed." Even at this distance, perhaps fifteen ells, the hazel eyes burned like some rare and costly oil. "I've been expecting you, Master Owein." He came closer, his soundless walk nearly a glide.

Owein stayed where he was. He didn't want to give Loki the satisfaction of seeing him run and besides, he doubted he would get very far. Without much success, he tried not to clench his jaw or his hands or his knees.

Loki stopped three paces away. "Have you considered my offer?"

"Offer?" It was difficult to meet that smoldering gaze. Owein's stomach churned. He should concentrate. Loki had made him an offer. But the ground wasn't quite steady beneath his feet, and— "Matilda," he said slowly, remembering. "No."

The ginger eyebrows shot upward. "You've no eye for a bargain?" A small sound that might have been a snicker. "Hard to credit, from your mother's son."

Owein's spine stiffened.

A drop of spittle appeared at the corner of Loki's mouth. "I should think again if I were you. I'm offering your Saxon maid for that bridge you've been cobbling together."

"No," Owein said with an effort.

Loki's teeth gleamed. "As she was, of course. Not as you'll find her at present."

The ground was tilting ever so slightly. If he tipped his head sideways to follow its list, perhaps he'd grow less dizzy. But he didn't, nor did his shield stop tingling. If anything, the tingling increased: he was in danger.

Loki gave him a dazzling smile. "A lovely full-blooded young thing," he said softly. "Just like you."

But he wasn't full-blooded; he was more than half Elf. Though he'd die like a mortal. Like— "Matilda," he said slowly. He loved her.

"Of course. Unless you'd prefer someone else?" Loki asked solicitously. "She's not what she was."

Owein shook his head violently, as if clearing his path through a swarm of gnats. "It's your doing." Pain stabbed at his temples. "You're murdering her."

Another smile, this one modest. A desultory wave of a hand, as if deflecting praise. A giggle, high and thin and disconnected. Then all the mockery left the hazel eyes. Narrowed to slits, they stabbed into Owein. "And you know how to stop me."

Stop him. Was it possible to kill him before he killed Matilda? Owein tried to take a step forward but only swayed where he stood, his breath coming thick and fast.

"You have only to tear down the bridge, and she's healed and she's yours." Loki's mobile face was patient now, his voice soothing, as if he spoke to an idiot or a child.

"And if I don't?" Owein managed to ask past the bile in his throat.

"Then she'll die. You know what death is. You saw enough of it on this estate not long ago."

Remembering the wounded, remembering Caraid, Owein knotted his fists.

With a satisfied air, Loki was studying him. "Matilda won't die in pain, as Caraid did," he said as if granting a boon. "But she'll die nonetheless. All that beauty withering away. A pity."

It was so hard to concentrate. Owein made a vast effort. "You know about Caraid's death," he said heavily.

"All about it." The ginger eyebrows were aloft. "Why do you suppose that might be?"

Owein tried not to goggle at him. Gods above and below, *Loki* was behind what had befallen Caraid. Tomas hadn't been able to stop him. Tomas hadn't even been aware that Caraid was in peril, and now Loki was after Matilda. But Owein knew what was afoot. He knew, and he'd not let Matilda be taken in the same trap. He eyed the smirking face before him. Clever. Loki was clever, and his very presence was dangerous: Owein knew quite well that he was confused. He thought as hard as he could.

"How do I know you'll keep your end of the bargain and let Matilda live?"

"An excellent question, my friend. A question worthy of your father's son. You don't know." Loki laughed, a high thin mirthless cackle. "But if you don't destroy that bridge, you do know that she'll die." He pointed a long finger at Owein, who felt a flash of heat across his neck as if a flying ember had struck him. Smoke filled his eyes. Gasping, he clutched at his throat but found only unmarked skin. When he could see again, Loki was gone.

There was no time to waste. Sprinting, heedless of the uneven ground, Owein set off for the great hall. An owl took wing; the foxes crouched in their den. His dizziness had faded, yet he tripped once or twice from the sheer speed of his gait.

Branches whipped at his eyes, across his face. Soon his legs began to ache, but he ignored their fatigue and tried to move even faster. He sailed over two low stone walls. Careened across the ridge and past the copper beeches. Pelted through fallow fields. Passed a barn and another, and a third. His breath burned in his lungs. Once a ploughman called after him, but he kept running. Mud from his last fall coated the knees of his trousers; dirt was ground into his palms. He held his breath when he passed the smithy at the edge of the estate; he could smell the corrosive iron reek long before he drew level with it. Next came the mews and the granaries. The sleeping lean-tos. The stable, the pantry, the kitchen, the courtyard and at last the great hall.

Still moving at almost his top speed, Owein slammed his outstretched hands into the door. It thudded against the opposite wall as he leaped over the sill.

Simon gave a great start, as if expecting a blow. Linley jumped to his feet and made a grab for his scramasax, then stayed his hand when he recognized Owein. He and Simon and Susannah had been sitting near the hearth, their dark heads close together as they pored over a sheet of parchment. Owein pulled up short beside Rose, who'd been grinding herbs at the table and now stood gaping at him.

"I must see Matilda," he said, panting. "Now."

Rose looked at him for perhaps two seconds. "You may, if she's awake."

Simon gripped Owein's elbow. "Have you learned anything—"

"It's what I've told you," gasped Owein; he'd not yet caught his breath. "It's Loki's doing. He's ageing her. He's nearly a full god now, at least in this world. Calls himself Lucifer, and—"

Simon cut him off with a peremptory slashing gesture, then pointed at the second of the hall's two bedclosets. "Alfred's in there," he mouthed.

Owein yanked his arm away. He'd no time for the King, no time for Simon's fears.

"Is there a way to stop the ageing?" whispered Susannah, her face urgent.

"I was going to ask you that very thing."

The Saxons exchanged stricken glances, but Owein had expected no better. *In the midst of order, chaos,* Skuld had said at his name-fastening.

He guessed, with a cold grinding pain like a fistful of icicles in his belly, that with the bridge he'd destroy more than his attempt at ordering the connection between his two worlds. He'd betray his parents' trust in him. And damage his link to Elfland, his realm that should have been. And—if Skuld showed no mercy; if the Ørlög weren't kind—his bond with Fraine as well as with the Elves.

But maybe the Elves were wrong. They didn't know everything: none of them had foreseen what had happened to Caraid. Maybe the prophecy was wrong, too. It said nothing about Matilda, nothing about the sacrifice of a mortal girl so the bridge could be built. For that matter, could it be rebuilt once Matilda was healed?

"Let me see her," he said hoarsely. She was real, not some cobwebby poem. He'd kissed her. She'd lain in his arms. With both his hands and his mouth, he'd felt for her heartbeat beneath the warm smooth skin of her breasts. Still, Owein had to know she was dying, dying like Caraid whom his father had been unable to save, before he could begin to wreck what he and Fraine had worked so hard to build.

After a silence fraught with worried glances, Simon took Owein's arm. "Say nothing to distress her," murmured the priest. He opened the bedcloset door and smiled down at Matilda. "Here's Owein come to visit you."

It was worse than he'd feared. An elderly woman with thinning grey hair looked up at him. The skin about her mouth and eyelids was creased, while the skin of her neck, of her hands, was crumpled and papery. She'd lost flesh, seemed to have collapsed in upon herself, while the scents of both sulphur and decay about her were far stronger. "Hullo, Owein," she said feebly, smiling. Her voice was thready, yet almost the same.

The back of his throat burned. He knelt and clasped her hands, felt the looseness of their bones and knotted joints. Icicles climbed from his belly into his chest. "I've wanted to see you," he told her.

"I wanted to see you, too."

He searched her face, cast a quick glance at her feet beneath the quilts. No swirling blackness lurked there, nor in the corners of the bedcloset. Still, he knew death was coming: Matilda smelled fetid. He was choking on it; he could hardly catch his breath. Apart from the additional reek of sulphur, it was like watching Caraid die all over again.

In the midst of life, death.

He pressed Matilda's hand to his lips, was both gratified and guilty at the blaze of incredulous warmth in her dark blue eyes—and in them he saw the girl who'd nearly made love to him in the mews. He wanted to weep.

Behind his back, Simon stirred, said something that ended in "my lord." Alfred was awake; Owein had best speak his piece quickly. "I must leave for a while," he said softly. "Keep well, 'Tilda. Let them care for you."

She nodded. Within their drooping pouches of skin her eyes were wide, and there was a suspicious mobility about her colorless lower lip.

"I"ll come back," he said rashly. Anything to wipe the dread from her face, the fear of loss.

"Soon, please," she whispered, and gave his hand a feeble squeeze before she looked past his shoulder and said, "Hello, Uncle."

To avoid questions and counsel, Owein slipped out while Alfred was speaking with Matilda. Anything the Saxons could say to him would be useless, no doubt, even Linley with his astrolabe. Where Owein was bound, he'd no need of one.

CHAPTER TWENTY-SIX: FOOL INTO MAGE

Elfland

Since Tomas's return to Faerie, the ravens were never far from him. While he paced by the Elvish Sea, his boots soaked with spray and his feet wet to the skin, they soared nearby. A few times they lit on his shoulders, and he felt their talons through the cloth of his cloak and jerkin, stiffened though it was by the salt and the damp. He kept his gaze resolutely out to sea, on the shifting horizon and the tumult of the foaming green surf. Whenever he stopped to rest in the shadow of the cliffs, the ravens fluttered down to the sand by a tidepool or perched on the rocks near his head. If he slept in a sheltered nook out of the wind, Thought and Memory were the first things he saw when he awakened: two great black birds hovering just out of reach, their wild ancient eyes focused on him, silently demanding recognition before he was fully conscious.

What is it? he asked them more than once. *What do you want?*

Use your reason.

He craved oblivion. Numbness. So much fatigue of the body and the mind that he'd tumble into the black welcoming arms of a sleep where no memories or thoughts lay in wait for him. But there was nowhere to hide from Caraid, from her murmuring voice, from the fear he'd ignored in her eyes when he tried to take her to Wessex with him. "Stop, Tomas," she had pleaded. "You'll be the death of me." There was nowhere he didn't see the gaunt sightless face and abraded neck that Owein had uncovered in the cistern. The gravelly crash and echoes of the great-throated surf didn't drown out her words. "Tell me it's over, that you're through with Moira, in every way. Can you say that?"

He could not, thanks to the true speech and prophecy that Moira had given him. She was, as Caraid had once said, very thorough.

So he trudged along the sand and wrestled with shadows, and slept only when his legs threatened to buckle beneath him. Once he considered ducking under the surface of those towering waves and drawing their light-raddled green into his lungs. A few full breaths, maybe more, and the draug who'd spared him in the Irish Sea might come back for him, if draugs sailed Elfin waters. But when he waded into the surf up to his knees, something besides the shrieking of the ravens prevented him from going farther. The twins might still need him. Aud and Brubakken might never learn what had become of him. He didn't know where his soul would go, what might await him there, what gods were left.

And then there was Moira.

At first the thought of her—the slanting eyes, the heated touch, the self-contained face she wore in the world, the private abandon—was something he tried to shove to the back of his mind. It was Moira who had watched the Nornir drop his thread from their loom, and called him to this Fate. He was a Mage now because of her.

No, he was not: magecraft was in his nature, and in time he'd have come to that realization with or without her. Who had told him that?

Moira had.

Eventually he realized that not only was he unable to direct his mind away from her, he'd thought of little else since the last time he'd slept. And that had been some while ago.

Stopping his aimless trek, he stood and thought, catching his breath. His clothes were damp. Thought and Memory flapped to a landing a few ells before him. In an effort to stabilize himself, he stared down at his boots. They were soaked, and covered with an uneven layer of fine yellow sand. There was no sun here, yet in the pearled unchanging half-light of Faerie, beneath his feet the sand winked and glittered like a living thing. Like a soul in fragments.

Caraid's soul wouldn't be trapped on these shores. An Elf who'd gone to live apart might have become sand, though, either here or in Midgard. Or an Elf forced apart. Where had Rhys gone, and would he ever return? Was that what Moira had wanted all along, and he, Tomas, been fool enough not to see it? He ground the heel of his boot into the sand.

Fool into Mage. Was he needed to bring Rhys back?

Was that another reason for the construction of the bridge?

His mouth was dry. He had questions for Moira, and both the asking of them and their answers were long overdue.

Tomas made his way up the path from the strand to the palace, leaning into his gait and ignoring the ravens even when Thought gave a loud croak above his head. His shield was in place and when it quivered, alerting him to the presence of someone else who used magic, he glanced up and saw Moira descending the trail a little distance above him.

A small start of recognition traveled through him as their eyes met. Hers were icy. He thought she'd stop and wait for him to reach her. Instead she increased her pace, heedless of the uneven ground. A small spray of pebbles shot out from beneath her feet.

At a bend in the path, they finally came face to face. He was panting a bit from the climb, but she wasn't even slightly out of breath. He caught her lean-muscled arm and searched her expression, in which everything was rigid and unreadable but her eyes. They grew colder as she studied him, and the wind whipped her hair to shredded black ribbons.

"It's past time we talked," he said quietly.

"Not here. In our rooms."

The palace was warm and dry, and its air was still and held no tang of salt. Instead Tomas smelled food and dust, spices here, candle wax there, and everywhere mortar settling. The floor was hard and even, and with each step he took, the sand that he'd tracked indoors crunched beneath his boots. He felt naked without the ravens; they'd not followed him inside. He and Moira met no one in the corridors.

Once they arrived at Jared's former quarters, Moira rounded on Tomas before he could open his mouth. "Fraine has gone to Midgard." She flung her cloak aside and stood facing him, her every muscle taut, her face bloodless and her eyes dark and narrow. She had already begun the conversation on her own terms. As usual.

"Why?"

"To speak with Owein, Aubrey says. They've stopped work on the bridge again."

"Before or after Fraine left?" Tomas was shivering. He was, he realized abruptly, wearing damp filthy clothes that clung to him and made his skin clammy. He was so tired that for all his acrimony, he could have fallen asleep where he stood. And his feet were frozen. He crossed to Jared's dining table, dropped into a chair and began pulling off his sand-streaked boots.

"Before," said Moira, following him. "They've done more than the eight points, to be sure, but there's half the bridge left to complete."

He tried not to glance at the door of their bedchamber where, he hoped, his dry clothes were still stored. Fraine had left Elfland. "Has she gone to see Owein?"

"I doubt that was the whole of it."

Both their shields were in place. He studied Moira's expression, thought he detected fear beneath her anger, fear that he shared. Fraine had left Elfland. What had become of her?

Moira was eyeing him. "You're cold, aren't you?" Mouth tight and hard, struggling with her own irritation. "Wait here." She marched into the bedchamber. The way that she shrank into herself tore at him, as though the room's air held something she didn't want to touch her skin. He heard a few thuds and an exasperated mutter before she returned with an armful of his dry clothes and his other boots, which she slapped down on the table.

"My thanks," he said to her retreating back; she was already halfway to the bath. She brought him a basin of water, a square of soap and a towel, went briefly to the pantry and then to the window overlooking the courtyard. There she stayed, her back rigid, working a comb through her hair and gazing out through the shutters while Tomas stripped and washed. The water was lukewarm and its quantity not nearly enough, while his tunic and trousers fit more loosely than before.

When a tap came at the door, Moira said without turning, "I sent for a meal." She raised her voice. "You may enter."

A fenodyree nudged the door open with one hairy foot, deposited a covered tray on the end of the table nearest Tomas, bowed to Moira and left without a word.

"Again, I thank you," said Tomas. The smell of food made him ravenous. "Will you join me?"

Moira shook her head. He ate in silence: fresh bread, stewed apples, a soup of carrot and leek, and a small plate of hard crumbling cheese. Moira remained at the window, her hands gripping the sill, and said nothing. He finished the water but left the wine untouched; he wanted his wits about him.

When he pushed the tray aside, Moira took a seat opposite him. Her face was carved of brittle colorless stone, her eyes guarded and perilous. "Evan has been paying court to Fraine," she said. "For all I know, there was another incident that figured in her leaving."

"She gave no reason?"

"No. Nor told anyone save Aubrey that she would go."

"Then how did you learn—"

"I went to Aubrey. He ended by telling me."

A warning, in that coolly uttered phrase and glittering stare. Tomas felt a twinge of sympathy for the pooka. He was still tired, but the meal had steadied him. He tilted his chair back and laced his hands behind his head. And he was still angry, at least as angry as Moira. So Evan was after a regency if not the throne, and had decided that Fraine would make a better pawn for him than Moira would.

"Evan doesn't know Fraine has gone. If you care to hear any more tidings, the Norse Elves just sent us an envoy. How he ever got through the 'tweenlands is a miracle, even though there are fewer exorcisms up the North way." She drew a hand across her forehead. "The Norse have declared for us. Thanks in large part to Gillian, is my belief."

He nodded.

"The Bretons have sent word they stand for us also, and the Scots and the Picts. But from Cornwall and Galicia all we hear are hard questions. My guess is they're backing Evan. Your Nissyen agrees."

Tomas hadn't seen Nissyen since he began tramping along the shore. So that was where the Elemental had been. Counseling Moira. A more unlikely pairing of advisor and advisee he could hardly imagine. Not from Nissyen's end: the sylph must have found Tomas and his feelings both incomprehensible and boring of late. Rather, he'd thought that Moira couldn't stand so much as the sight of the sylph.

"The Sidhe are in disarray," she said tightly. "I've no idea how they'll regroup, nor what they'll elect to do."

"Perhaps they're waiting for Finvara."

She stared. "Are you in jest?" She laid her palms flat on the table. "Isolde sent him apart. No one knows where."

"So they say." Tomas studied her eyes. "No more than you know where she sent Rhys."

The skin about Moira's mouth tightened, but her gaze never wavered from his. The air between them sang with tension. "I have no idea where Rhys is," she said after a few seconds. "Did you think that I had?"

"I didn't know," he said quietly. "I do now."

Color flooded into her face; she drew herself upright. "I can wait no longer for your help, Tomas. Aidan's unable to See what the danger to Owein and Matilda is. Why Fraine's gone to Midgard isn't clear to him either, other than it's something to do with you." She leaned forward. "The prophecy says you're part of what's unfolding between Elfland and Midgard. We're at another standstill with the bridge, and it *must* be completed." Her hands were still pressed on the tabletop—to keep them from shaking, he realized. "You've been so long at the shore that you've not seen how many more trees have died. I can't reach the twins, and Owein at least is in danger." She exhaled slowly. "Will you please use your Sight?" She held his gaze. "I believe it can get us through this impasse."

"That's what you want of me?" he asked after a moment.

"Yes." A strained, careful voice. When he was silent, she added, "You told me to find you when I wished to do something about Owein." Her eyes, that had gone from cold to guarded, were suddenly volcanic. "They're your children too," she said, biting off each word. "Abandon your quarrel with me long enough to help them."

"I will. As I promised."

"I thank you," she said bitterly, and got to her feet. "We've no time to lose—"

"*You* have all the time that will ever be," he interrupted as coolly as he could, and reached for her wrist. "But they don't, and neither do I. Your Fool and your children are mortal."

She stared down at him, motionless, though she could easily have yanked her arm from his grip.

"I'll do your scrying, though I'm not sure I'll See any more than Aidan did. But I'd like some answers first." He released her wrist. "Will you sit, please?"

Like a snake coiling into itself, Moira sat.

"Have you any plans to use my Sight or the twins' to locate Finvara or Rhys?"

She flinched. "Never." Slowly the rage began to drain from her eyes, revealing what he suspected was hurt, just before all expression left her face. "Even if it could be done."

"The Sight can be compelled," he said, remembering Caraid.

"Not yours. You're too well shielded."

"Or bribed."

She shook her head, dully but with finality. "Never, I said." A leaden pause. "Why have you asked me that?"

For several reasons, the most charged of which was mistrust. "Because I don't understand the transformation of Fool into Mage that was worked on me." He rested his forearms on the table, then reached for the water jug. It was empty. "I don't know if the same will be worked upon Fraine and Owein, or by what agency."

The look she directed at him came from a weariness like a deep and ancient well, with a thin new layer of pain on the surface. "By me, are you implying?"

He nodded. The center of his chest began to ache.

"It was not I who caused your transformation. If anyone did, it was you."

He opened his mouth to argue.

"I was a catalyst, but only one of many," she said colorlessly. "Your nature matched my summons, and you didn't flee from me."

Another flash of pain in her eyes. He felt an answering grief of his own, tinged with guilt.

"You came to Elfland. You accepted my errand." She twined her hands together in her lap. "At every step, you chose a path that moved you closer to your true nature rather than away from it. You formed a bond with the ravens. You sought out a teacher. Sometimes you chose the only step that allowed you to live. Yet they were still choices, and you made them." She searched his face. "When you think on those decisions, are there any you would change?"

He would still have responded to Moira. Impossible not to: he was fighting his response now. He would have communed with the ravens, found Brubakken, gone to Wessex...

He wouldn't have hurt Caraid. Yet she was no part of what had made him a Mage. Rather, that was why he had hurt her and why she had died.

"Not in regard to you," he said. "Or to my nature." He studied Moira's eyes; they were veiled and reflective now, and impossible to read. "The Fool remaining a Fool as well as a Mage—that's not part of it?"

"Some Fools remain so," she said gravely. At his frustrated gesture, she added, "Tomas, we are speaking of mortals, and they differ from one another far more than Elves do. Some Mages know or are told early on, like the twins, that such is their nature, and they strive to develop it. Others start out with no notion of their true selves. Yet something about their own natures may draw them down that path, till they've gone so far there's no turning back." A hint of impatience crept into her voice. "Mind you, not every common fool is a slumbering Mage, and not all Fools who could grow to Magicians ever perceive that possibility." Meeting his gaze. "Nor was every Mage once a Fool, yet an awakened Fool can make a most powerful adept. That's why the Elves summon them."

He'd heard more than enough. "I believe I understand now." He shoved his chair back, got to his feet. "I'll call the ravens before I begin scrying."

"Tomas." With a lowered brow she came round the table towards him. "I'll not summon another one."

Had he not been so tired, he might not have said it. "I'm glad I've proved satisfactory. Can we—"

"Why?" She grabbed his arm. He didn't know when she'd dropped her shield, but it was down now and his with it, so her pain and stung pride struck him like a blow to the throat. "Why must I constantly prove that I love you?" Her face was dead white, her eyes blazing. "I do." Her grip tightened. "And I loved Rhys, but if I'd all my own choices to make again, I'd have chosen you over him. May the Powers take pity on me." A long forced breath. Her chin came up; she loosened her grip. "You make me wonder if you'd say as much for me."

"*Yes.*" When he caught her to him, she went rigid in his grasp. "Yes," he said into her hair, against her temples. "I choose you." She raised her hands as if to push him away, but ended by putting her arms around him with a muttering sound that was harsher than a sigh or a sob. He kissed her, hard, on the lips. "I love you," he said against her mouth. Kissed her again, ran his hands down her back, felt her breathing falter and deepen. When he said her true name—only the second time he'd ever used it—her face softened.

Fiercely, she gave him a single kiss, the first one she'd initiated rather than merely responded to, though she'd been responding. It was followed by a rough impersonal shake. Startled, he rocked back on his heels.

She'd kept hold of him. Her face was flushed, her mouth full of hot color. "You will help us?" she demanded, low and intent.

He'd already told her he would. He only just prevented himself from shouting. Aroused, fighting his temper and exhausted all at once, he gave her a level stare and a nod.

"We've so little time," she said. As if he'd forgot. It made him angrier, despite the hint of unsteadiness in her voice. Then she gasped and turned towards the door. In almost the same instant someone began pounding on it.

They hadn't barred it when the fenodyree left, and now someone was opening it. Tomas flung himself between Moira and the doorway. At the same time, he slapped his shield into place and extended a tendril from it to force the door closed.

"Wait!" Moira cried.

Fraine leaped over the sill, her eyes widening when she perceived the energy cannoning towards her from Tomas. She dropped to her belly, half sliding and half-rolling aside as Thought and Memory darted in after her. A split second later, with a reverberating boom, Jared's heavy door slammed shut and left a single black feather whirling in the air before it. For an instant Tomas gaped at his daughter's travel-stained Saxon cape and tangled white-blond hair, before he and Moira rushed to where her prone body had struck the table and now lay motionless.

Gasping, Fraine turned onto her side, still clutching the earth that Freya had pressed into her palm, and found herself gazing at a leg of Jared's dining table. No carving, no froufrous, just a sturdy and serviceable and clean-lined column of wood. Surely those birds were out of place beneath such a table. Two big black ravens, not ornaments but alive, and regarding her intently.

They were Thought and Memory. Her father must be nearby. A good sign: he'd come in from the shore at last.

A hand, long and warm with narrow gentle fingers, was laid on Fraine's shoulder. "Are you injured?" Moira's voice.

"No. Breath knocked out of me." Fraine propped herself on one elbow and blinked up at her mother's deceptively soft ivory face. And her father's worried squarish one with its crooked nose and utterly human eyes, deep-set and not in the least slanted. Always graceful, Moira squatted easily, her heels flat on the floor, her gown a rivulet of peach-colored silk flowing round her ankles. Her eyes were huge and drawn and turbulent, as well they might be after what Fraine had just overheard. She'd hesitated too long by the door before knocking, and some of what was said by the raised voices within had been impossible to miss.

Kneeling beside Moira, Tomas touched Fraine's hand. "Have you just come from Midgard?"

Fraine nodded. Tomas's clothes were clean but the same couldn't be said of his salt-roughened hair. The lost expression that he'd worn when Fraine last saw him had disappeared. Instead, at the back of his eyes there lurked an impassioned mix of pain, anger and fraying self-control that made her regret intruding upon him and Moira. Driven by the memory of Matilda's greying face, she'd been waiting impatiently for Tomas to leave, but when it grew clear he'd not do so any time soon, she'd come in rather than risk being barred from the room. There was so little time, and she had to tell her vision of Freya and Caraid.

To tell Moira—Fraine didn't care to mention it before Tomas. She sat up, refusing his offered arm with a small shake of her head.

"How is Owein?" asked Moira.

"Frightened." Best to have it said and done with. "Matilda's ageing. She's dying. It's Loki's work."

Scowling, Tomas shifted from his knees to a cross-legged position facing Fraine.

"The Saxons know that Owein's been partial to Matilda and she to him," Fraine said. "He frightened them when he could See that the Bishop had a boy for a lover. Werferth hates him now and Daniel still wants the estate—"

"They'll accuse Owein of bewitching her," said Tomas, his eyes nearly black with foreboding, his hands clenched. "If she should die and they can't put Owein to death for it, they'll come after Rose and Linley for harboring him. And Simon for not healing Matilda, when I'd wager he's half killing himself in the effort."

Fraine nodded. "He's a fine man, that Simon. Christian or not, he couldn't have been more gracious to me."

"He's hardly a common one," said Moira curtly. "Don't judge them by him." Her tone said she'd brook no further discussion on that score. She tapped Fraine's closed fist. "What have you here, love?"

Without thinking, Fraine put both hands behind her back. "Nothing."

Moira's eyebrows went up; Tomas's went down. The two of them exchanged a long glance, wry on her part and simmering on his. A whole dialogue in that scrutiny, and not all of it to do with Fraine, she suspected. Neither of them looked at her.

When Moira finally broke the gaze, she turned to Fraine, who said awkwardly, "Nothing I care to speak of at the moment." Not with Tomas present.

Tomas glowered, though not at her or Moira, then clamped his jaw shut, folded his arms and looked away.

Moira gave Fraine a long cool glance. "As you wish."

"What's to be done?" muttered Tomas. "I'm no healer. I don't even know Loki's whereabouts. Last time he came to me."

Fraine didn't know there had been a last time. No one had told her of it, and from the raised drawbridge in Moira's face, no one would tell her of it now.

Tomas was eyeing Moira grimly.

"Don't," Moira told him. "You're needed here."

"How do we know I'm not more needed there?"

Pale, her every muscle tense, Moira stood and gazed down at him. "We'll know precious little till you've done some scrying."

He shot to his feet. "I told you I would," he said tightly. "Now. Bar the door."

Something black flapped past Fraine's face. Her heart tried to leap out of her body and she ducked, shielding her eyes but keeping her fist tightly shut.

"It's only the ravens," said Tomas. Given his frame of mind, she was surprised at how gentle he sounded. He patted her shoulder. "Will you stay?"

She nodded, then sat at the table and watched as Tomas removed his boots and lay full length on Jared's sofa. The ravens perched on the arm of the couch nearest his feet; Moira bolted the door and took a chair at his side.

Fraine had entered many trances of her own, during what magical training she'd had and while building the bridge. She'd witnessed more than a few trances in others, but she'd never seen anyone sink like a stone beneath the surface of his awareness as Tomas did. All his muscles went limp; his lips slowly turned white, and for a horrified moment she wondered if he were still breathing.

Using just a fraction of her Sight, she perceived that the ravens were sending him strength. So was Moira. It funneled from the birds in a multicolored and particulate stream like so many illuminated dust motes, tumbling and whirling about the soles of Tomas's bare feet, then disappearing into them. Fraine could sense the aid from Moira rather than see it, as heat can be discerned in a landscape where one hasn't set foot. From the center of the Elf's sternum, a vast thick flow of energy rolled inexorably to Tomas's forehead, chest and groin. Another such stream issued from Moira's solar plexus to coat the walls of the room like a shield.

Fraine lowered her eyes, reined in her Sight. She compressed Freya's earth and slipped it into a side pocket of her pouch. To send and receive such aid must take a depth of intimacy and a level of trust at which she could only guess. Perhaps her parents would resolve their quarrel yet.

She waited, dividing her attention among the silent and motionless ravens, Moira's still white face and Tomas's masklike one. When Fraine grew thirsty, she got up as noiselessly as she could and refilled the water jug that stood on the table. Once or twice she heard footsteps in the corridor, brisk and businesslike, but never any voices. She settled back in her chair, propped her feet on the table and tried not to fidget.

She must have dozed off. Without warning she was struggling upright in her chair and gripping its arms.

Bolt upright upon the sofa, Tomas was rigid, his eyes squeezed shut. "No!" he shouted.

Had been shouting, Fraine realized, and that his voice had awakened her. She hurried to her mother's side.

"Don't startle him," said Moira softly, erect in her chair and intent upon Tomas; she didn't spare so much as a glance for Fraine. The flow of energy from her to Tomas was dwindling. "He'll waken on his own."

The ravens were still perched on the arm of the couch. Thought was gazing at Tomas, but Memory was preening a wing feather as calmly as if no one else were in the room. A shudder took Tomas from head to toe. When it passed, he slumped a bit and put a hand out to steady himself. Moira took it. He opened his eyes; they looked rather glassy.

Moira flicked a sidelong glance at Fraine. "Would you fetch him some water, please?"

She brought Tomas a full cup and the pitcher. "Thank you," he murmured, touching her hand. His expression was troubled. "Loki's in Midgard, near Limecliff. Daniel's promoting an exorcism for Matilda."

Fraine winced: the passage there could grow still more tortuous.

"I could find Owein nowhere." Tomas looked at Fraine. So did Moira, just before she closed her eyes and dropped the shield she had placed about the room.

Pain twisted beneath Fraine's ribcage, sharp and hot; then the tugging began. She dropped the pitcher she'd been holding. Shards of crockery skipped across the floor; her boots were splashed. She scarcely noticed. It was all wrong, that pull; she felt it everywhere. The base of her skull. The tops of her toes. Her left hip. Sickened, she staggered and grabbed the back of Moira's chair. It was Owein. And he wasn't in Midgard. Or he was, but everywhere at once, or she wouldn't feel his presence draining her, globally, irresistibly, as if her life force were being drawn through her pores. It was hard to breathe. Tears started in her eyes.

"Where is Owein?" demanded Moira.

Fraine couldn't speak. All at once the air was full of the tug and spin of whirling weights, very distant, that didn't belong here in Elfland. That tugging could only come from a place beneath the rule of Time. The burning wheel yanking at her heart was the Sun; the fire that stabbed at her solar plexus must be Mars, and they were all threaded together and linked to Elfland, to this room and to Fraine herself. But they couldn't be, not unless they were linked to Owein and the bridge too, and not unless Owein was—

"Fraine?" Tomas's voice, his hand on her arm. "What is it?"

She must not have felt anything from Owein before now because of Moira's shield around this room and around Tomas's trance. "Have to find Owein," she blurted. She wasn't sure if he was in Midgard or the 'tweenlands, nor if she could locate him anywhere in his current state.

"Wait," demanded Moira. "Tell us what's happening!"

But there was no time. Fraine had never traveled to Midgard alone and wasn't sure she could do so now, but a tunnel had just opened in the reeling chaos about her, and from the way the pull increased, as if it could strip her skin from her flesh, she knew that Midgard lay at the other end of the tunnel. If she didn't step through it just so, *now, immediately,* it might not open again.

CHAPTER TWENTY-SEVEN: EXORCISM

Midgard

Rose would get through the next hour or so as best she could. Her fingers twined in Linley's as she stood at his side. Susannah was at their left, Simon to their right. All of them were grouped about the foot of Matilda's bedcloset, whose hinged walls were completely open to the great hall. Both hearthfires were blazing to keep her as warm as might be, and ruddy light played across the faces of everyone present.

To Matilda's right, Werferth presided over a makeshift altar. On it were arrayed the Scriptures, a chalice of holy water, the Host on a paten inscribed with Gospel verses, a dish piled with plants that Rose and Susannah and Simon had been hard put to find—dock seed, fennel, hassock, cristalan, disman and zedoary—a chalice of wine, and a censor. Beside Werferth stood Daniel, his lips and hands folded primly, but the febrile look in his eyes and the sweat on his forehead made Rose vacillate between nausea and rage. To Matilda's left Alfred waited, his gaze distant and troubled, holding his niece's withered hand.

At the end of the preparations that had rolled and eddied about her, she'd given Alfred a feeble smile, closed her eyes and sunk back into whatever twilight realm she inhabited these days. She shouldn't be put through this long and complicated ceremony. She ought to rest, tranquil and easy, with no one to trouble her, and Simon nearby if she should prove wakeful. It had been tiring enough for the poor child to be unclothed and searched for evidence of elfshot, even though Susannah had provided the excellent pretext of a bath.

She and Rose had found nothing, of course. Alfred had vetoed Daniel's proposal of a second search with him and Werferth present, yet hadn't forbade subjecting Matilda to this lengthy ritual. After a fashion, Rose understood why. As Bishop, Werferth was considered the spiritual superior of both Alfred and Simon, although Simon was the King's confessor.

Daniel handed Werferth a small brass bell with a wooden handle. Instead of promoting this exorcism, the hermit could have accused Owein of *maleficium*, of witchcraft with intent to harm. But in order to prove the case clear as noonday, he would need to produce far more evidence than he had. Such as eyewitnesses, along with the costs of their travel and housing at court. Or some tangible proof from about Matilda's person. A manikin dipped in blood. Parchment scribbled over with spells. Vomitus with nails in it.

Should Daniel be unable to prove the case, he'd pay a hefty fine, if not risk imprisonment should his accusation be judged as motivated by anything but an honest mistake. Moreover, in the interests of fairness and at the whim of the judge, Daniel could be jailed along with Owein at the very moment the complaint was filed. In the absence of more proof, Daniel might be ordered to undergo single combat with Owein or, which seemed more likely, a contest between their champions might have been arranged—if anyone willing to champion Daniel would come forward.

But Owein could not be found; they'd sent out search parties who'd uncovered no trace of him. Daniel had lodged no accusation against the absent young man. Instead, Werferth would conduct the rite of exorcism upon an ailing girl too weak to mount any protest; indeed, since Owein's abrupt departure, she seemed scarcely cognizant of her surroundings. Not that Werferth's ritual would prove efficacious against the displaced Norse fire god whom Owein insisted was behind Matilda's ailment. Not any more than all the prayers in all the monasteries in Wessex and Mercia and Éire had succeeded in repelling the Norse marauders who'd overrun those lands for nigh on a century.

Rose felt her mother's warning gaze, lowered her chin and tried to assume a reverent expression. It was an outrage, this choreography of incantation and gesture over a wretched girl too ill to know what was happening, and all of it meant to appease one lone god whom Rose wasn't sure Daniel and Werferth truly followed. One, out of so many others that his worshippers were trying to ignore and discredit and demonize. Simon knew better; Simon was different, but his hands were effectively tied. And it was all happening beneath Tomas's roof, and Rose and Linley were powerless to stop it.

The ceremony began. Rose bowed her head, and struck her breast along with the appropriate responses. When the others knelt, so did she. Werferth commenced an interminable prayer above Matilda's greying head. Rose didn't understand much Latin, just enough to tell that the Bishop was adjuring someone to depart, probably whatever spirit they fancied was preying upon the girl.

Simon had already heard Matilda's confession. If she had said anything coherent, Rose suspected that it had amounted to little more than an entirely understandable resentment of her mother and a few kisses from Owein. Not that either counted for a sin in Rose's eyes. If Owein hadn't succeeded in bedding the girl, then in Rose's opinion he should have. Fey and naive he might be, but there was nothing brutish about him; he'd have treated her kindly. Likely he was even more of a pleasure to touch than to look upon, and the poor girl might have known a small portion of sweetness before she died.

Beside Rose, Linley stirred a bit. She cast a sidelong glance at him; they were still on their knees. Pale, his expression uneasy, he was studying Werferth. From the motion of the Bishop's hand above Matilda's head, Werferth had progressed to what Rose took for a blessing. As Linley's eyes followed the gesture, a small shudder went through him. The Sight, it must be, and Linley was witnessing something that Rose couldn't detect.

She flicked a glance past him at Simon, but the priest wasn't watching Werferth. Instead, his brow furrowed and his hands fisted at his sides, he stared fixedly at Matilda. Rose didn't need the Sight to know that he was sending the girl all the healing energy he could without touching her. She lowered her gaze, then peeked at Susannah, who appeared tired and grieved but composed. Praying for Matilda, from the concentration in her eyes. Rose said a prayer of her own, to the Lady.

Daniel took up Rose's hard-won plants and handed them to Werferth, who dipped them in the holy water and used them to wipe the writing off the paten that held the Host. After holding it aloft, he poured the consecrated wine into the remainder of the water.

Rose stole a glance at Alfred. The King was making all the proper responses to the service but gazing only at Matilda, whose eyes were still closed, who lay motionless and mute. It was past time for an infusion, were she awake. Rose tried not to frown. Werferth had moved ponderously into another entire Mass, she thought.

Two masses, five psalms, the Credo, the Gloria, some litanies and a Paternoster later, Werferth blessed the water and wine mixture, and Daniel awakened Matilda.

Simon scowled as the hermit touched her shoulder, as if hard put not to start forward and pull Daniel away. But the hermit was holding the chalice of consecrated liquid to her lips, and Simon stayed where he was.

"Drink," intoned Daniel as she blinked up at him.

"Drink it all, my dear," said Alfred, kneeling at her side. "It's to help you mend."

Matilda glanced hazily at Simon, who nodded, then sipped till the chalice was empty. Meanwhile Werferth had begun swinging the censor, and perfumed smoke billowed into air already hazy from the hearthfires. Rose was coughing. They all were. The Bishop rang the bell that Daniel had given him. Nine times: Rose counted.

Finally the last prayer was said, the last blessing given, Alfred's thanks made, and he and Werferth and Daniel all filed out to their lean-tos. Linley shut the door behind them, leaned against it, heaved a long bitter sigh and raised a hand to his eyes. When Rose went to him, he pulled her into the circle of his arm and murmured, "The rite had an effect."

"It helped her?" Her heart gave a wild leap in her chest. "Is that what you Saw?"

"Nothing about 'Tilda. I think it moved us farther away from them." His glance was despairing. "From the Elves. From the bridge and the twins." He was whispering. "And from Tomas."

Rose hugged him as hard as she could, until some of the tension left his shoulders. She wanted to settle the two of them into the other bedcloset or up in the loft, hold him and smooth the unruly hair from his forehead, while they debated where Owein might have gone and what was next to be done. But she should help tend Matilda first.

When she turned, she met Susannah's gaze over Simon's bowed head. The priest had taken a seat on the edge of the bedcloset, folded Matilda's unconscious form in his arms, and was holding her. Not the way Rose had just embraced Linley, more as one cradles a sick kitten. Matilda's eyes were closed; her head hung limply against Simon's upper arm. Susannah stood at his side with a hand resting gently on his shoulder. Her expression was so laden with sorrow that Rose and Linley both started forward, Linley uttering a small groan.

Simon looked up at them and shook his head. "She lives," he said with an effort, his face grey. "But she's so cold. Would you please put more wood on both fires and fetch all the blankets you can spare?"

CHAPTER TWENTY-EIGHT: ATTACK AND SUPPORT

The 'tweenlands

Fraine was spinning and alone, she who had never before traveled between the worlds by herself. Spinning and lost. She kept dodging the awareness that she was frightened. Owein's essence still tugged at her from everywhere at once. She wasn't confident he was in Midgard. Yet he most certainly wasn't in Elfland, and where else save the mortal realm could he be?

The harder she tried to locate him, the more confused she became and the more images crowded in upon her. Matilda, greying and frail. Simon's hollow-eyed face. Once, clear as the full Moon and twice as bright, she caught a glimpse of Owein in a rage and reached out for him frantically, but no sooner had the impression come than it was gone.

There were odd bars of energy, hot and barbed and fiery, that hurt to cross. There seemed no pattern to them; she never knew when they might appear. They were left by exorcisms, Tomas had once told her. With that memory came a stab of vibrating energy that she sensed was from Tomas's Sight. He and Moira must be searching for their daughter. Fraine reinforced her shield. If they found her they might try to stop her, and she had to locate Owein.

Not that she knew where he was. She might have been worse than an idiot to leave Elfland alone, but she'd taken the only chance she had to reach Owein. Of that she was still certain, though not that she'd succeed. She might spin here forever.

Pushing her fear aside, she cast about for something she knew, some fact with which she could counter the panic that kept rising in her throat. She was somewhere between Elfland and Midgard. The 'tweenlands lay among all the worlds, not just those two. Sooner or later she'd come across one of them, or something that led to one. Those glowing bars left by exorcism must emanate from Midgard; perhaps she could trace them to their source. Better yet, maybe she could locate part of the bridge and follow it there.

She'd not yet tried to look for the bridge. Slowly she stretched her awareness, turned about in a circle, tried to see something besides mist and darting fragments of images. There should be, somewhere, eight fiery points linked with a network of pale crimson lines thin as spiderwebs and beaded with light—

Something burning raked past her eyes. With a gasp, Fraine threw up an arm to shield her face, just as whatever it was made the narrowest of hairpin turns and whipped even harder in the opposite direction. Brief images of Midgard followed: a spring evening in a patch of woods with all the trees clothed in green and a brown lazy river murmuring nearby. Small firepits, burning low and well-tended in the twilight. Processions of men and women, laughing, wreathed in flowers, playing a drum, a fiddle, a flute. Dancing, swaying in circles. Her father's face alight and very close; her mother's eyes. Each picture flicked by faster than the last. They grew distorted, stretched, seemed about to shatter into whirling splinters, yet held intact.

Beltane. It was the Beltane point of the bridge, and something was attacking it.

Pain closed a fist in Fraine's groin. Another line of energy careened past her, tumbling, unanchored. The Beltane scaffolding held, but like a snake gone mad, the line between that point and another one was whirling loose in the 'tweenlands. Who was trying to destroy what she and Owein had built?

Owein was.

Groaning, Fraine clutched at her midsection, doubled over as much from certainty as from pain. Overwhelmingly she smelled iron now, but the iron-sick wasn't what hurt. Something was hammering at her, at her groin for Beltane, at her heart for midsummer, pounding at her everywhere. With each blow she could sense Owein, frantic, hurling all his energy and iron-laden mortal magecraft at the eight points. *Why?*

Dripping with sweat, she was shivering, light-headed. An invisible vise was closing around her ribcage. She should have traveled disembodied, but she didn't know how; Tomas hadn't taught her and Moira never traveled in that fashion.

Fraine gasped as something struck the base of her spine: Owein was attacking the Samhain point. She staggered, recovered her balance. All at once she realized that she'd entangled her psychic and physical energy with the bridge in order to locate it. Now she must disengage from it before Owein injured her any more than he already had.

Owein! she shrieked in mind-speech. *Stop! You're striking me along with the bridge!*

No answer, no glimmer of awareness. Nothing. Just another blow, this one to her knees. Fraine stumbled, flung her arms out but couldn't stop herself from floundering through space. Now he was pounding at the winter solstice point. Why? How could he launch this attack without hurting himself as much as he was hurting her?

She had a spell of dry heaves; if there'd been anything in her stomach, she'd have ejected it. There wasn't any gravity, no up, down or sideways. Only the bridge, everywhere, nowhere, burnt into her bones. They were all still intact, but for how much longer? She didn't want the bridge to fall. She didn't want to die. Didn't want to die at all, but especially not here in the 'tweenlands. What if she remained here forever, slowly rotting like Caraid?

Caraid. Freya. They'd told Fraine to call upon them.

She'd hardly mouthed their names when they appeared before her.

Air displaced by their arrival struck her in the face, and with it the smell of corruption from Caraid. They were eyeing her, Caraid at once wistful and urgent, Freya with an intensity of purpose and a blindingly luminous face that would have terrified Fraine if she could have been any more frightened. Close by Freya's sides stood the two great cats, silent and watchful, their ears pricked forward and their molten eyes fixed upon Fraine.

They gave her a point of reference: up was up and down was down again. Slowly, she managed to lower her feet to the same level as those of the goddess and the corpse. Fraine's heartbeat slowed; her breathing deepened. And something had changed. "The pounding stopped! Owein's given over attacking the bridge."

Freya shook her head. "*No, my daughter. I have severed the link that made you feel it.*"

"But I must find him!"

"He is in Midgard, though partly in the 'tweenlands. I have not severed your link to him, only to his attack upon the bridge. Was that not what you wanted?"

"Yes." Fraine was cold, winded and felt bruised, as if she'd been the victim of a stoning. "You have my thanks for it." She was shivering uncontrollably.

"Be warmed," said Freya, and pointed at her. The goddess's face blazed like a thousand Moons at the full, dazzling, unbearable.

Fraine cried out and shielded her eyes with her palms.

"You have naught to fear from me." Very soft, that cavernous voice. *"How do you feel?"*

"Warm," said Fraine, hearing her own disbelief. But it was true. The shuddering fit had passed and with it the dizziness. She was still taut with anxiety but apart from that, her body felt as if she'd just had ten hours' sleep. By cautious degrees she lowered her hands from her eyes and flexed fingers that had been numb with cold a moment ago.

Freya stood gazing at her. *"Strength I can give you,"* she said calmly. *"And guidance. Little more, but of that a full measure."*

"I thank you," stammered Fraine, overwhelmed. "Can you help me reach Midgard?"

"Yes."

Fraine swallowed. "Take me there, please."

"Wait," said Caraid hoarsely—so she could still speak with that purpled mouth. "I cannot set foot in Midgard now. I can remain in the 'tweenlands only by Freya's grace and in her presence. If she goes to Midgard without me, I am lost to you, and I have yet some part to play."

"*She is right. We will not abandon you, Fraine, but if you wish to call upon us, you must be in the 'tweenlands or in trance. Therefore you should ask all your questions before you leave us."*

"Why is Owein trying to destroy the bridge?"

"He believes it is the only way to stop Loki from killing Matilda."

"Can he destroy it?"

"That I cannot See," said Caraid. "But I know that you must try to stop him."

"We will aid you all we can."

The goddess's promise should have heartened Fraine. Instead, before that shining presence she had never felt so small. "What must I do?" she asked as steadily as she could.

A compassionate look from Caraid. "First you must find Owein."

Fraine squared her shoulders. "I'll begin at Limecliff." Then she remembered something. "He said an exorcism would be performed at the estate. Can you still send me there?"

Caraid glanced at Freya, who smiled a little, more to herself than to Fraine. In the goddess's eyes was the certainty of nightfall, the persistence of the tides. Her face blurred, then grew young and wistful. Both cats retreated three measured paces and stood gazing at her. Soon her hair was crowned with budding vines that, after a moment, brought forth green leaves whose veins glowed with a rich tracery of light.

Fraine caught her breath, but Freya had not done changing. The greenery about her face, which had grown brown and sturdy, blazed with a medley of red and orange and yellow. Of a sudden the entire garland of fire-tinted leaves shriveled, and the goddess's skin grew white and lined, her eyes stark with shadows, her face gleaming pale and chill. Icicles shone ghostlike in her hair. In her glance was a vast and inexorable wisdom, far more age than Moira or even Tallah, and so much mystery that Fraine fell to her knees. Caraid was already kneeling.

As from a great distance, the goddess regarded them. Then she raised her arms, palms upward. Light poured from her face, swirled about her body. When it dimmed, the golden hue had returned to her newly flawless skin. Her yellow hair streamed unbound and uncovered to her knees, and her face was radiant.

She smiled down at Fraine. *"Entry to Midgard is barred to Caraid as she is now, but exorcism cannot keep Me from it,"* she said gently. *"It affects the Elves more than it does My various faces. Their Fate is more linked to Midgard, to the flesh of her soil and the bones of her rocks—and the beliefs of her children. Nor will exorcism keep you out, Fraine, if I choose to send you there."* Still smiling. *"I am older than that rite, and older than the Elves. While Midgard lives, however withered, so do I."*

CHAPTER TWENTY-NINE: SCHEMES

Midgard

In the heart of the oldest patch of woods he could find, Owein had climbed atop a fallen oak and now sat, cross-legged and heavily shielded, amid the vines scrambling over the corpse of the great trunk. It was cool and dim here, and he could see a fair distance among the widely spaced trees, all so large and their canopies of branches so extensive that they had choked out lesser growth that didn't thrive on dense shade. Apart from a scolding squirrel trying to shoo him away from her nest, the wood was relatively quiet.

Quiet, not mute, with all the tiny noises that accompany the ongoing life of such deep green enclaves. Soft air barely fingering the topmost leaves, sun slanting down through the branches. Small chewing presences above and below: moles, wood mice, grubs. Deer, drowsing in their hollows till sunset. A fox turned in its burrow, resettled itself nose to tail and dozed off again. Owein gazed at his open palm, which held his half of the Gebo Rune, the Rune of Partnership that he and Fraine bore between them, then tucked it back into his jerkin. He had no such partnership with Matilda, but how could he let her die?

He'd launched his assault on the bridge from Midgard and the 'tweenlands both, and he was close to exhaustion. How could he have destroyed what he and Fraine had worked so hard to create?

Not that he'd destroyed all of it. Much of the link between the Beltane and midsummer points had crumbled, along with most of the tie that stretched from the winter solstice to Imbolc, but the rest of what connective structure he and Fraine had built among the points still remained. The eight points themselves had trembled and swayed beneath his attack, and once or twice shot out eerie jagged sparks of light, but their scaffolding held.

He'd tried everything he could think of to topple it. Bolts of iron-essence. Energy siphoned off from his shield. Runic incantations, projections of the Runes' shapes. He'd even shrieked the Ørlög at the top of his lungs, aiming the words like so many flung stones. A mistake: if anything, the points seemed to grow stronger. Then a current of energy that he could partially sense but not see, some vast mysterious flux, began flowing among them. A ripple of it sent a slight shock through him, for with it had come images, mostly of Fraine.

Fraine, recoiling with each blow that Owein aimed at the bridge. The sight of her doubled over and clutching at her sides gave him another jolt, centered on his sternum, though it immediately spread from there through the length of his spine. That was when he'd stopped his attack and retreated to the woods. Was he making a terrible mistake? He wanted time. He wanted a choice. And as far as he could see, he had none.

That Fraine had reached Midgard unscathed must be wholly Freya's doing. Fraine traveled the rest of the way in Freya's arms, wrapped in the goddess's falcon-skin cloak that let its wearer fly between the worlds. From its feathers Fraine stared in wonder at the fiery latticework through which they were passing, with Caraid and the cats at Freya's sides. With each burning hexagon left by the ritual of exorcism, Fraine felt a flash of heat and heard garbled chanting. What most struck her, however, was the fear trapped in those convoluted honeycombs of energy, like a nest built by lunatic wasps. Fear of the unknown. Mistrust of anything not defined or measurable with specific words or deeds. Fear of the dark, the night, the Moon. Terror of the depths of the forest and the restless Sea. Fear of ecstasy and trance, of women, of the Earth itself.

Freya had left her in the 'tweenlands, but so close to Limecliff that all Fraine had to do was gather herself and, holding her breath, leap across the border between the worlds. There was a moment of jarring disorientation, as if both her mind and her body had scraped across chipped slate. Then, with her knees curled to her chest, she landed on the soft grass of the willow grove. She tucked her head, laced her hands protectively behind her neck and felt feathers there. Freya had left the falcon-skin cloak wrapped about her.

Awed at such a loan, Fraine slowly got to her feet. The cloak moved with her, smoothly, clinging a bit, as if it were made more from silk than from feathers. When she lifted her hand to stroke them, they made no sound beneath her fingers.

For a few seconds she stood irresolute. The cape allowed its wearer to travel between the worlds. Should she wear it here? Perhaps it was intended to help her travel back to Elfland. She took it off and studied it thoughtfully. Earth-toned falcon feathers, a hood, a long sweep of fabric from neck to knees. At a distance the colors would help her blend into the trees, but anyone close enough to tell what she wore would be taken aback. The Saxons dressed in wool or rough cloth, sometimes hides or pelts. Linen was rare, reserved for the wealthy. Even fine wool was rare.

Frowning, she glanced about the grove but saw nowhere to leave the garment. A chill crept down her spine at the thought, and she knew she should take the cloak with her. But she had nothing in which to carry it, and she was still dressed in the Saxon garb she'd worn to visit Matilda. She'd be too warm, but she'd have to don the feathered cape beneath her tinker's dirty cloak.

What if she rolled Freya's cape and tied it like a rope about her waist? To her surprise, it slipped and slid beneath her hands until it had coiled itself into a roll the width of perhaps three of her fingers. She stared at it as if challenging it to unravel. Nothing happened. She put it down and stepped back a pace. Again, nothing. If it would roll lengthwise so neatly, could she fold it into a packet that she could tuck into the front of her belted gown?

She could indeed. Marveling at the feathery bundle about the size of her hand, she slipped it into her dress.

Owein wasn't in the grove. Although she sensed his presence from every direction at once, she didn't know precisely where he was. But she had a plan. Since Daniel and the Bishop had persuaded Alfred to allow an exorcism at Limecliff, they might be pawns in Loki's game of human counters. The Bishop was powerful, at least in that Alfred paid heed to him. It was Daniel who might be the weakest of Loki's dupes and Owein's enemies, so if Fraine couldn't find Owein, she'd find the hermit instead.

"*Owein!*" Fraine called in mind-speech. Keeping her shield up, she hurried through the late-fallen summer twilight towards Cheddar gorge. Now that the Sun had finally set, a faint nip, a suggestion of dampness, began to seep into the otherwise soft air. The sky was a canopy of watered silk stained a deepening tint of lavender, jeweled with stars all intent upon their glittering tracks. At any other time Fraine would have stopped and tilted her face up to watch them, or found a dry patch of ground where she could lie on her back to drink in the night and breathe that caressing air. But not now.

"*Owein!*" Her shield might afford little protection when she was announcing her presence by calling him. If Loki could strike Matilda with an ageing sickness, perhaps he could overhear mind-speech. Fraine didn't know the extent of his powers. They might be changing as he grew stronger in Midgard, with its exorcisms that were slowly blocking the Elves' passage here.

After considerable thought, Owein decided not to enter trance and the 'tweenlands from the willow grove, but to use the estate's most seldom occupied sleeping lean-to instead. It was far from the great hall, and he'd be sheltered withindoors should he stay in trance an inordinate length of time, which might prove necessary given the condition of the bridge. The eight points still stood, and he'd torn down fewer than half of the links among them that he and Fraine had contrived to build. Destroying any more, he suspected, would require a greater and more sustained effort than he'd yet been able to manage.

What should he do? Somehow he must succeed in getting Matilda restored to herself again; he couldn't let her die like Caraid. He wanted to see Matilda so badly that it was a physical ache akin to hunger or cold. But every time his steps turned towards the great hall, the pit of his stomach knotted, his heart clenched and thudded beneath his ribs, and the soles of his feet burned icy-hot. No images of Matilda came to him, nor any flash of knowledge about what might await him there. Only his body's warning, and he'd best respect it. Aubrey had taught the twins that the Sight worked as reliably through one's physical self as in more easily interpreted ways. Perhaps more reliably, if one only heeded the body's messages.

Heed them Owein did. Hard as it was to avoid the great hall, if he met with some tragedy there, then the bridge would remain standing and Matilda would die. But if he could destroy the rest of his handiwork, then Loki would spare her.

Or so Loki said. But Owein dared not let his thoughts wander any great distance down that particular road, lest his nerve fail him.

Owein had meant to send only his entranced and gathered attention to the 'tweenlands, and indeed it had started that way...

In the darkened lean-to he lay on the straw, closed his eyes, slowed his breathing. Commanded his muscles to relax, starting with his toes and working his way up to his jaw, his tongue, his eyelids. Pictured the Lammas point, the brightest one and the easiest to remember.

An iridescent pinwheel with radiating spokes like a starfish formed of pulsing energy, and at its core a light like the August Sun. Blinding and disorienting if one looked directly at it. The trick was to avert one's vision from that molten center, observe the pinwheel's long glittering arms and never stare at any one spot for too long.

Owein stretched his concentrated awareness towards the Lammas point till he had it well-focused in his mind's eye. He extended a tendril of energy and felt its strength as it left his shield, as he might have felt, in his arms and shoulders, the vibration and follow-through of an arrow he had shot.

It was working. He had a link, a powerful one. Encouraged, he slowed his breathing again and sank more deeply into trance. His narrowed attention was nearly there: he should be able to manipulate the bridge's energies in the 'tweenlands, yet leave his body in Midgard.

Then a dazzling flash temporarily blinded his inner vision, and a jolt ran through his body as if someone had passed a burning torch down the length of it, searing him.

With a gasp and a strangled protest he heaved himself upright. Something was very wrong. He'd have to make a whole new beginning. No, he wouldn't; the link to the bridge was still there, stronger than before. But it should have been broken. It shouldn't be stronger unless he was—

In the 'tweenlands. Straw dropped away from underneath him; the air was spinning. Owein flailed at it; it was heavy, like water, as if he were swimming. When he opened his eyes, terror stabbed at his chest and robbed him of breath. He should be falling. He was floating instead.

Directly before him blazed the core of the Lammas point. At this distance it was almost unbearably brilliant yet not uniformly white. Not white at all, but a mixture of every shade of yellow: flame and saffron and citrine and gold. It didn't give off nearly so much heat as one might expect. Strangest of all, it varied in size: one moment towering over his thrashing limbs and the next shrinking to the dimensions of a bonfire. The fluctuations were regular enough that the point almost seemed to be breathing.

Almost but not quite. No sooner had Owein realized that he'd misjudged when the point would next reach its largest extent than he was upon it, and then he was falling in earnest. He tucked his chin and shielded his head just in time, right before he thumped down onto a solid yet very slightly yielding surface.

Its color was that familiar reddish-brown that must come from the iron-essence that he and Fraine had used to form it. His nose stung a little from the smell of it. He was sprawled on one of the rays from the Lammas point.

Having landed more or less on his left side, for a few moments he huddled there and caught his breath. Then he stretched his legs, flexed his arms. Nothing was broken, but his left hip would be bruised. The surface where he lay didn't seem to be moving.

Rubbing his hip, Owein sat up gingerly and eyed the core of the pinwheel. Now its size wasn't changing at all. He had helped build this thing, but he didn't understand it.

Nor did he understand how he'd come here. He'd entered trance in one of Limecliff's sleeping lean-tos. He'd built a mental link, a strong one, to the Lammas point. But down that link he'd made no effort to throw any more than his awareness and energy, not his body. His physical self had never traveled to the 'tweenlands alone. For it to have made the passage here, to the best of his knowledge he would have needed to intend that it did, to focus his will and use all his energy to propel his flesh and bones here in their wrapping of skin.

No such intent had been his and no such propulsion, yet here he was in both body and mind. The will and the impetus must have come from someone else, someone powerful enough to override his own intent.

In a word, he'd been pushed.

The muscles between his shoulderblades tensed. He scanned all he could see of the Lammas point and the void in which it was suspended. A moment ago he'd fancied that the pinwheel and its rays had started, very slowly, to revolve. Now he was sure of it: the point was rotating. He was alone, but he knew who had pushed him just as unmistakably as if Loki stood before him.

If he destroyed the Lammas point, what would support his weight here in the 'tweenlands? Would he go falling endlessly through this void, never finding his bearings? Or would he land on something hard with so much impact that it killed him?

He shivered as he studied the molten pinwheel before him. At its center the colors rippled and billowed like a variegated curtain shaken by unseen hands. Loki had sent him to this place. Loki, who wanted the bridge destroyed. Wouldn't Owein survive the razing of the Lammas point, since he was needed to destroy the others?

He glanced down at the ray where he stood. It glittered beneath his feet, subtly and with a dull reddish shimmer as if so many iron filings were trapped within its substance. If he attacked the core, would the rays hold? Could he cling to this one?

He crouched down and touched its surface. Rough and grainy. From this proximity he smelled iron again. When he examined the palms of his hands, nothing but the iron scent had clung to them.

Iron in the bridge, iron in his mortal blood. Iron that the Elves couldn't bear. If he'd built this thing, could he not tear it down?

As Tomas had taught him, he aimed his intent at the pinwheel, and from his compressed shield hurled the greatest bolt of iron-essence he could summon. Like a shooting star it flashed into the Lammas point, which flared even brighter for a moment as the pinwheel vibrated ever so slightly—but its substance held.

Owein considered the core; it was perhaps thirty paces from him. Prepared to leap backwards at any second, treading as lightly as he could, he moved closer. Nothing happened. No sensation of heat, no increase in the slight sensation of rotation by the point as a whole. No change in the infinitesimally yielding texture of the ray beneath his feet.

At ten paces away he slowed, began to inch forward. Five paces now. Three. He stopped and stood motionless, thinking. The pinwheel blazed heedlessly on. If only he were a bit above it, rather than level with it. Frowning, he glanced down at the ray beneath him. It gleamed faintly, like a bolt of raw silk the color of cinnabar.

He knew how to pull as well as push. The better to concentrate, he shut his eyes, then extended a fishhook of energy from his shield.

When he opened his eyes, he was looking down at the pinwheel rather than straight at it. He'd lifted the ray where he was standing perhaps three arm's lengths higher than before. It was enough.

He wasn't sure why he removed his clothing, except that he wanted fewer barriers between himself and the core of the Lammas point. No one had taught him how to launch an attack from every square inch of his skin, but he'd turned aside a few such assaults from Moira during his training. If he could withstand that sort of attack, it stood to reason that he could initiate one. A fair amount of what magic he'd learned involved reversing something one already knew how to do or had witnessed done, as he and Fraine had built the bridge by reversing a move that Tomas had taught them. A move that had used iron-essence to crumble the stones in the courtyards of Elfland, and to strike Deverell down.

Perhaps such a gambit would work better coming straight from Owein's pores, with less fabric to muffle whatever energy he exuded. And perhaps it would work better at close range.

Naked, he leaped silently into the heart of the pinwheel.

Fraine had not found Owein. Not a trace, not a whisper, not a footstep. She hadn't yet gone to the great hall, but she didn't harbor much hope that Owein would be there. Her sense of him was growing dimmer, like a noise receding in the distance or a feeble breeze moving away. Her sense of him was still diffuse as well, not one-pointed or traceable to a specific direction, all of which made her suspect he had left Midgard with its clearcut and predictable boundaries of time and space. Wherever he was, such parameters were far more hazy. Elfland, perhaps, or the 'tweenlands. Or a worse place, and harder to find.

Daniel, however, she had located, and with him the Bishop. Now Fraine stood on a narrow ledge below the entrance to the hermit's cave. Her back flat against a rough limestone wall and its scrubby outcroppings of rock-loving plants, she strained her ears—more acute than those of a full-blooded mortal—to catch every nuance of the lagging conversation above her head. So far they'd said only that Matilda was no better despite the exorcism, and Alfred more worried than before.

"What could the King do?" asked Daniel at last.

"Several things." The Bishop's tone was rather cool. "Send another search party after the boy, for one."

"You don't believe Linley knows where he is?"

A sound, a faint one, that might have been a snort. "Not he. Or he'd not look so worried."

"As well to send one quickly, if it's to be done at all," said the hermit. "He's not been gone but a day and a half. Unless he's stolen a horse, that's not long enough to get far."

"Long enough to reach the Saefren." The Bishop's voice was grim. "From there he could have bought passage home. He'd have no fear of the Norse."

The pause that followed contained, Fraine suspected, an exchange of glances.

"Why go back up the North Way if he's trying stake Tomas Rhymer's claim here?" muttered Daniel. "Unless he'd got wind of the exorcism and was fleeing it."

"Or unless he fled afterward."

Another silence.

"Do you *want* him found?"

"If he were in our custody, a charge could be brought against him," said the Bishop carefully.

"But if Linley were to find him..."

A creaking noise from above, as if Werferth had shifted his position on a bench or a chair.

"Ah," said the hermit.

Footsteps, barely audible on the cave's beaten earth floor. A thud, then a faint crackle. Someone had heaved another log on the fire.

"Alfred's not called for another search," Daniel said thoughtfully.

"Not yet."

"If Linley were harboring the lad..."

"It would have to be that, or something like. Alfred holds Linley too dear. They were boys together, and Simon with them." Then, measuring the words, "I fear he may have taken a misstep, our Simon."

"Influence."

"Influences." A lowered voice, fraught with meaning. "More than one."

Outside on the ledge, Fraine edged directly beneath the cave mouth, moving with an Elfin sureness of foot that dislodged no stone. Her fingertips were splayed out on the limestone wall, and from its friable surface she knocked a small pebble loose. It went tumbling into the gorge. She held her breath, listening. Since she could only just hear the impact below, she doubted that the Bishop and Daniel could.

"Has Linley taken that misstep along with his brother?"

"That's not for me to say," murmured Werferth after a few seconds had passed, with a hint of both sadness and patience in his voice. "Not in Simon's case either."

Fraine stiffened. She sensed what might follow, provided Daniel wasn't too thick to see it.

"As his superior, you could hardly—"

"Precisely."

"Your role is more to guide and to hope for change, rather than..." Was Daniel studying Werferth's face, guessing how far he might venture? "Rather than accuse."

"You see it as my lord Alfred would, I believe." Werferth's voice was calm.

A pause, so long a one that Fraine wanted to fidget.

"If," began the hermit, clearing his throat. "If the proper witnesses could be found and all went in accordance with—" A cough. "With what we know for the truth, you and I, might Alfred see the need for a double monastery?"

"He might. I could not say for certain."

"Yet your word carries some weight with him. I have much to lose in this affair, my lord," Daniel pointed out. "I'd feel bolder if I felt I had as much to gain."

A rustling of cloth as if someone had stood, or someone else knelt.

"You would gain the satisfaction of sparing a few souls from peril." The Bishop's tone was firm.

An intake of breath. "A monastery could spare still more."

Another silence.

"We shall see," Werferth said softly. "Many's the step to be taken, and all of them with care."

Fraine eased herself away from the wall and began soft-footing it down the ledge. If she'd understood rightly, Daniel was offering to bring a formal accusation of *maleficium* against Owein, and to implicate Linley and Simon for harboring him. The Bishop preferred not to make the charge himself against a priest of his diocese, while Alfred, who loved both brothers and needed Tomas's second Sight, would accuse neither them nor Owein. In return for lodging the complaint, Daniel wanted assurance that the Bishop would help provide witnesses to support it—and see that Daniel was given the charter to Limecliff, once Rose and Linley had been turned out of doors.

Fraine should warn them, though they doubtless knew that such an accusation might be forthcoming. But first she must find Owein. From the sweat on her palms and the cold sick feeling at the pit of her stomach, he was in more danger than before.

CHAPTER THIRTY: INJURIES

Elfland

Afraid that Tomas would dive into that whirling vortex of patterned air after their daughter, Moira flung her arms about his waist. Slowly and horribly, Fraine was disappearing: first her left leg and shoulder, rippling as they blurred from view, then the midline of her body. Tomas reached for her.

"Stay with me!" Moira shouted above the wind shrieking through Jared's quarters out of nowhere. They both ducked as the dark tunnel of air changed direction and bore down upon them. Tomas's empty glass danced and skittered off the table to land in splintered shards; three chairs tipped and fell backwards. Pulling Moira to the floor, Tomas flung himself over her and shielded her face. She yelled that he was the one more likely to be wounded by whatever was happening, but her voice was lost in a great deafening rumble like a landslide. As the vortex roared over their heads, she caught a glimpse of Fraine's right hand vanishing into the center of the cone—which was suddenly no longer there. The rumbling sound was the last thing to leave, fading with a long drawn-out clatter as if into immeasurable distances.

"Are you hurt?" asked Tomas next to Moira's ear. Still holding her, he rolled onto his side and she rolled with him.

"No. And you?"

He shook his head, his eyes wide and unfocused, as if using his Sight. "Fraine's in the 'tweenlands," he muttered. "Trying to enter Midgard." Wincing, he dug his finger-ends into his temples. "It's not come clear to me."

Moira started to get to her feet, but the room was behaving strangely: the fenodyree's tray was skating towards the edge of the table, while unfastened shutters banged against the outside wall. Small thumps and crashes could be heard in the pantry, and a muffled thud in the bath. From the corner of Jared's sitting room came a ripple of sound from Tomas's harp. She sank back on her haunches as he reached up and stopped the tray from sliding into their laps.

"It's an earthquake," said Tomas, one hand on her elbow and his eyes on his harp.

"In *Faerie?*" Earthquakes belonged to Midgard. The ground never moved here; here, all was stable. Rhys used to say that Elfland was the still point round which the other worlds turned. And so it had been, but no longer. The pivot world was Midgard now.

Tomas was studying her face. "You don't have earthquakes here," he said slowly. "Do you?"

More thumps in the hallway, an indignant shriek from a fenodyree, then small running feet, several pairs of them. Jared's table had stopped moving, but its final position wasn't quite level.

"We do not." Moira stood. "This is something worse."

On what was left of the greensward, Moira drew a troubled breath and gazed down a corridor of ravaged turf in the direction of the hawthorn circle and the well. Jagged trunks of what had been towering trees, snapped off a few ells above the ground as if they were no more than kindling, dotted the landscape like splintered teeth. Behind them more of the hall had crumbled, and a cloud of dust hung in the air above the scattered stones. Where the earth was bare it was grey and tumbled, a yellowing brown where slivers of grass still clung. The green was empty unless one counted the ravens a few ells away—and the Elf lying like a toppled statue near the hawthorns.

All Moira could see of the Elf's body was two motionless bare feet. Their owner was either unconscious, in the first stages of living apart or both. She began picking her way across the ruined lawn, but she'd not taken three steps when Tomas grasped her shoulder. He was so pale that she could see the pulse at his throat and a hint of the faint cobalt lacework of veins near the corners of his eyes, which were dark with shock.

"How long..." he began. His voice was huskier than usual. He swept an arm around to indicate the extent of the green. "When did this happen?"

He kept thinking in terms of mortal time, didn't always remember that events flowed differently here. "The worst of it began after you left for the shore," she said neutrally.

His brows drew together, but his gaze held steady on hers.

"The uprooted trees and the heaving of the earth, that's more recent. So is the collapse of more of the palace. I'd say that's what happened just now." She started towards the fallen Elf again. "Someone may be hurt," she said, pointing. "I don't know what's happened." She was shivering but there was no help for it; she'd raced out of their rooms without her cloak. "Except that we've drifted even further from Midgard."

She stopped because Tomas was standing where she'd left him, with one arm flung across his forehead and the other out to one side as if groping for balance. His eyes were rolling up to the tops of their sockets. By the time she reached him, his eyelids were closed.

"The bridge," he muttered. What little color he had left was gone now. "Someone's trying to tear it down it. Someone's succeeded in destroying almost half of what the twins built."

Moira knew better than to touch him. The Sight could not be rushed, and they needed whatever tidings it might bring. "May the Powers have mercy," she said at last, painfully aware of the Elf near the well. "Can you tell where the twins are?"

There was an agonizing pause before Tomas said despairingly, "No."

She inhaled. "Or who's attacking the bridge?"

He shook his head, then squeezed his eyes more tightly shut, as if the gesture could focus his Sight. He was coming out of trance, then. In trance, he'd never have attempted to force it.

"Loki." She turned towards the hawthorns. "Trying to cut us off. Or the Christians. Perhaps that last exorcism."

Tomas rubbed the back of his neck. "Could one ritual—"

"I don't know!" She headed for the unconscious Elf. "We must tend to whoever that is."

In two strides he caught up with her, blinking, a bit unsteady on his feet.

"The Nazarenes and Loki," Moira said bitterly. "Perhaps they've joined forces. They both want us to wither."

They drew level with the foot that protruded from the edge of the wood. An unshod foot, with thick leathery pads on its sole and a fine dusting of brown furlike hair. The foot was attached to a long unclothed shin, rather spare but beautifully formed, and covered with a thicker layer of fur.

"It's an Elf from the Inner Reaches. A group of them came to the twins' oath-taking." Tomas sounded more intrigued than surprised as he knelt down in the leaf mold. "This is the one who said the golden lady called them."

Moira squatted on her heels for a closer look. The Elf was unconscious, his lips parted and his breath shallow. Blood matted the thick dark hair at his right temple, but the wound didn't appear deep. Not far from him lay a weighty and dense-grained poplar branch that must have grazed his head when it fell from the tree above. The Elf's padded fingers were curled at his sides, his clawlike nails slightly extruded. Moira set the flat of her hand on his chest. His heartbeat was fast but steady.

Tomas took off his cape and spread it over the Elf. "Isn't his name Lir?" A sidelong glance at Moira. "I believe Jared knew him. Shall we take him to Jared?"

Jared would certainly do all he could to locate Lir's companions and have him tended by whatever healers could still be found. "An excellent idea. He'd never let a kinsman want for anything."

"A kinsman?"

Moira nodded. "A distant one."

Tomas was looking Lir over from head to toe. "He puts me in mind of a great cat, the way Aubrey's own shape still looks like a horse to me. The whole lot of them does, and sometimes Jared does too. Cats are sacred to Freya. She could be the golden lady." When Moira said nothing, he shot her a keen look. "Well? Are they shapeshifters?"

"Some of them were," Moira said carefully—Tomas hated to

shapeshift. "A very long time ago. Jared isn't. He believed that his branch of the family was the last to leave the Inner Reaches, until Lir and his followers appeared at the oath-taking." She eyed Tomas. "That doesn't startle you."

He shrugged. "Among my people are a very few who ride the wolf's pelt, or the bear's."

Berserkers, who wore the bear's shirt. Moira nodded.

"Though it's said that their animals more often ride them." Tomas studied the pads of Lir's feet. "We ought to move him. There could be another earthquake, or whatever it was."

"You know what it was."

That brought the grey eyes up to her. "So do you," he said quietly. "The attack on the bridge. It's driven us further from Midgard, and it's destroying our soil."

Our soil. Tomas had just said 'us' and 'our.' Relief prickled behind Moira's eyes. She inhaled deeply. He was close enough that she breathed in the smell of him: sweat and muskiness and something like hay, and something else like walnuts just past the point of ripeness. The smell of mortality: it made her chest ache with a sharp heavy pain like a hot stone laid upon it. They'd both been sufficiently angry that their quarrel could be slow in mending—and she would lose him so soon. For all she knew they had just lost their children. She said only, "Perhaps you could pick him up, and we'll take him to Jared."

"Very well." There was remorse in his glance about the devastated clearing. Then he surprised her; he reached out a tentative hand and touched her hair. "I hope you'll forgive me. I was grieving, but I shouldn't have deserted you."

Gentleness in his eyes. She couldn't lose herself in it yet, not with Lir lying at their feet, even if she'd not also read a caution in Tomas that mirrored her own. Still fragile, both of them. Yet it was a beginning. "Thank you," she murmured. "And I hope you'll forgive me for—making you feel as if you're of no account, only what you can do." It was probably too soon to apologize for the rest of it, how she'd flung Rhys's name at him, if indeed she should mention that at all. "Even if you'd stayed, Tomas, I don't know if we could have prevented this attack on the bridge."

His expression was dubious.

"I'll make them rebuild it, Loki or the Nazarenes," she said through clenched teeth. "There will be no half measures."

With many a pause while she supported Lir's head or readjusted his weight, Tomas gathered up the unconscious Elf.

"There will be no compromise," she told Tomas. "With either faction."

CHAPTER THIRTY-ONE: ANOTHER ENCOUNTER

The 'tweenlands

When Owein leaped into the heart of the Lammas point, he had no clear idea what might happen. Since he intended to destroy the point, to hurl at it every last bit of iron-essence that he could extract from his halfbreed's body, he supposed that the point would somehow fight back. Attack him in turn, burn him or at least make some attempt on his shield. Instead, after a breathless moment or two during which he floated, turning heels over head with suspenseful slowness in dazzlingly bright air, there was a snapping sensation at the top of his head and another at the base of his spine. Then he landed on his rump, smack in the middle of the spiral arm from which he'd just launched himself. He clambered to his feet, shook himself head to toe like Linley's hounds after a swim, and glared at the Lammas point. It glowed unchanged above and before him.

Owein gathered himself and sprang into it again, with the same result as before. And again: the outcome was no different. Half a dozen jumps later he was out of breath and out of ideas. Fuming, he put his trousers on, sat cross-legged on the reddish gleaming flecks of the spiral arm and tried to think.

Perhaps he'd picked the wrong point to destroy, yet he doubted that any of the others would be easier to topple. Should he try somewhere between two of them? While he was still in Midgard, he'd razed some of the connections among the points, but now he couldn't see them; he could see only the Lammas pinwheel suspended in a featureless haze. Why? The 'tweenlands were far from empty. During his previous trips here, he'd seen the shimmering debris left by exorcisms and heard Tomas's stories of Hecate and her crossroads. The Powers only knew who else frequented this place, but just now it seemed empty but for Owein.

"Giving up?" drawled a light tenor voice behind him. "When your task's not done?"

Reinforcing his shield, Owein scrambled to his feet as fast as he could. Arms folded, standing hipshot, the ginger-haired man—Loki—was smiling at him, although the hardness of his expression made it more of a sneer. Ill will radiated from him along with the faintest whiff of sulphur. "I'm not certain you've made your best attempt," he said sadly, as if Owein had somehow betrayed his trust. When Owein made the mistake of meeting his eyes, it cost him an effort to look away from the eerie amber light that flickered in their depths.

Too much power in those eyes. Too much rage, bizarrely mingled with callousness, and too little self-control. Something in the godling's loose-jointed stance and the curl of his lip and his long twitching hands all said that he was completely unpredictable. Owein's throat went dry; his heartbeat was a breathless rat-a-tat in his ears. The muscles of his legs tensed. *Run away,* his body was screaming. *Run. He isn't even sane.*

There was nowhere to go. Fighting a wave of dizziness, he said, "I've tried."

Loki folded his arms. "You've razed some of the bridge, so you should be capable of destroying the rest. Why haven't you?"

"I can't." Owein's palms were slick with sweat, but his throat tightened with anger that he knew he should hide along with his fear.

"If that's true, it's a pity. Pity about your little Saxon maid, too."

Owein drew a breath that felt hot in his lungs. His hands wanted to clench; he hooked his thumbs in the waistband of his trousers. His bare chest and feet made him feel still more vulnerable, but when he looked about for his shoes and jerkin he couldn't spot them. He had no way to attack Loki, nothing that would threaten him. Nothing that Owein could do would bother Loki in the slightest, except leaving the rest of the bridge intact. And he had no idea how to destroy it.

But Loki didn't know that. And Loki was killing Matilda.

"You'd do well to leave her alone," Owein said as imperturbably as he could, the way he thought Moira would have said it.

Loki raised his sparse auburn eyebrows.

"If she dies, the bridge will never come down," said Owein, bluffing.

The sudden murderous rage that flared in Loki's eyes made Owein's heart take a panicky stab at his ribcage. Loki's lip curled; could he tell that Owein was frightened? The realization that he'd been trying to avoid came back full force: he had made a mistake and a very serious one in agreeing to any bargain with this creature. What had he been thinking; where had his wits been? Now it was too late to break the agreement without being humiliated before he was killed. Owein's hands turned to ice; for a moment his breath stopped in his chest.

If he showed any fear, Loki might kill him where he stood, and he just might still find a way out of it. He had to stay alive. Owein lifted his chin. "For that matter, the bridge stands till you've healed her."

Loki darted forward, one fist raised, the other hand pointing at Owein. It happened so fast he had no time to duck and no time to think. A long yellow tongue of flame shot from Loki's fingertip towards the left side of Owein's face; by reflex Owein shied violently away to the right—and collided with a hard-driven fist, half on his right cheekbone and half on his temple, with his own momentum doubling the impact.

For an instant the pain ground everything to a halt: his eyesight, his breathing, his thoughts. Then his knees sagged and he crumpled into a mindless heap at Loki's feet.

CHAPTER THIRTY-TWO: OFFERS FROM THE SAXONS

Midgard

Halfway between Limecliff and the caves, taking a short cut through the forest, Fraine moved among the trees as quietly as she could. She'd not found Owein anywhere, so she'd set off to ask Rose and Linley when they'd last seen him, and to warn them about the hermit.

Her sense of Owein was still diffuse rather than painful, as if he'd called off his attack on the bridge for the moment. Pale golden light sifted down through the branches, setting the leaves aglow and changing a few of them into all but translucent green veils. Beneath her feet lay a carpet of variegated brown, gray and green: pine needles, moss, and last year's fallen leaves, sprinkled with dead twigs and branches large and small, all crumbling slowly into the soil. The air was quiet and soft and slightly moist, but not completely still.

Without warning there came a swift hard blow to the back of her knees. She stumbled, breaking her fall only by grabbing the low-hanging branch of an oak sapling. Heat flashed before her face, but she saw nothing burning, nor any source for the impact that glanced off her right temple. But she most certainly smelled something. Sulphur.

Then her sense of Owein completely disappeared.

Fraine straightened up and let go of the branch, feeling queasy and more than a little confused. What had happened? The sulphur must mean that Loki was involved.

"Owein. Where are you?" she whispered aloud and then in mind-speech. No answer, and no awareness of him, however remote, came back to her.

She started walking again, as fast as she could without making so much racket that any Saxons in the wood might hear her before she saw them. Never before had she lost her sense of Owein's presence, however faintly, somewhere in or between the nine worlds. Without that awareness she felt as naked as if all her garments had been stripped from her. And raw, as though some of her skin was gone too. She was shivering. Should she go back to the 'tweenlands and ask Freya for help? But what if Owein were still in Midgard?

Linley had a bit of the Sight. Maybe he could help Fraine locate her brother. Tomas said that Linley's Sight ran mostly to an understanding of people—and to astrology. Perhaps the twins' horoscopes could reveal something useful.

At the edge of the clearing about Limecliff's great hall, Fraine stopped amid the last concealing clump of trees. Smoke from both hearthfires rose above the roof, though the midsummer day was mild by Saxon standards. It was about the hour for the evening meal. Wasn't that thickset redheaded woman the cook Hroswitha, emerging from the kitchen with a covered tray? Walking carefully, concentrating on the platter she held, she was followed by a kitchenmaid who carried a second tray. Probably Alfred and Werferth were not within, or there would have been more food and more ceremony. Perhaps a man-at-arms by the door, and someone running to fetch a bottle from the store of wine that Owein said Alfred always brought, or a small cask of ale from the pantry. And Hroswitha might have looked tense as well as sad. Fraine waited till both cook and kitchenmaid had gone away empty-handed before she slipped up to the door and tapped upon it.

Almost immediately she heard Linley's voice, strained and low. "Who goes there?"

"Fraine. May I—"

The door was already swinging open, and Linley's hand reaching through it. "Get inside, girl, and welcome! Has anyone seen you?"

"No one," she said, blinking at the murk withindoors. Her nose itched at the smell of iron, and the everpresent smoke made her cough. Both hearthfires were blazing. Above one a kettle boiled, infusing the air with the scent of herbs. She accepted a seat at the table across from Rose.

Hands on his hips, shirt open at the neck and sleeves rolled above his elbows, Linley stood gazing down at Fraine. His dark eyes were sorrowful, his face taut, and he and Rose both smelled of grief and fatigue: mud, cypress and something faintly resinous, like old pine sap. Rose's oval face had lost much of its high healthy coloring and was smudged with hearthsmoke. Her features were drawn, her eyes hollow, and a few tendrils of straight brown hair had escaped from beneath her kerchief.

Simon was sitting at the edge of the open bedcloset with one hand on Matilda's forehead. He gave Fraine a tired smile; he was bloodlessly pale and his shoulders were slumped. Next to him sat Susannah, looking as if she'd lost a night's sleep, and in her arms was Matilda, wrapped in blankets, her face nearly as grey as her hair, her eyes closed. Unconscious.

Fraine had come prepared to ask a barrage of questions as fast as she could get them answered, but the sorrow in the room stopped her. Very quietly, she said, "Matilda's worse."

Rose nodded. Her eyes filled; she turned her head aside. Linley dropped onto the bench and put an arm around her. To Fraine he said, "We had wondered...is it anything akin to the iron-sick?"

Fraine shook her head. "And Matilda has no—" She caught the flickering of Linley's eyes in Simon's direction. "No Elf blood." Linley must realize it wasn't anything that Simon hadn't already known or been told in one way or another. "This is Loki's doing."

From the Saxons' grim expressions, they'd accepted as much.

"Can you help us?" asked Rose.

"I wish I could." A bead of sweat rolled down Fraine's forehead, another down her neck, and her back felt sticky. Sighing, she took off her outer cloak. Linley eyed the roll of feathers about her waist but said nothing. "Part of the bridge is damaged," said Fraine. They'd no need to know it was at Owein's hand, and loyalty to him kept her silent in that regard. "I must find Owein. Do you know where he is?"

"No," said Linley, studying her eyes. "You're troubled for him, aren't you?"

She nodded. "When did you last see him?"

"Two days ago," Rose told her. Then, after a minute hesitation, "The exorcism was yesterday."

Fraine glanced at the door. "Where are Werferth and Daniel?"

"Praying in the chapel. With Alfred." A whiff of tar came from Rose. "We should warn you," she said. "Werferth's eager to question the tinker woman who was seen with Owein under the chestnut tree near the path to the caves, and even more eager to question Owein. Daniel overheard the two of you talking."

"That's partly why I've come. To warn you they'll accuse Owein of *maleficium* if they can, and implicate you as well."

"You're worried over more than what Werferth might do," said Linley. He lowered his voice as Simon, moving stiffly, came to join them. "Is Owein also in danger from Loki?"

Fraine nodded.

"He's not been taken ill like Matilda?" asked Rose, paling.

"I doubt it. I think I would know if he were." The Saxons had probably heard the slight catch in her voice. She didn't know, not for certain. None of her sense of Owein had returned. She found herself twining her hands together beneath the table.

When Simon put a hand on her shoulder, she was startled at the heat in his palm. From it a small steadying current began to flow, traveling towards her heart, soothing her. The priest was regarding her gravely, with kindness in his melancholy brown eyes—and a fatigued depression that smelled like sour pears and black water from the bottom of a rain barrel.

She touched his small sturdy hand. "Rest," she said firmly. "You needn't help me, though I thank you. Give a thought to restoring yourself instead."

For an instant Simon looked taken aback. Then, with a hint of a smile, he sat down rather heavily on the bench beside her.

Had Linley just winked? "You must give us your secret," he told Fraine. "Simon never pays us any heed."

"She has all her mother's presence," said Rose.

"Her father has not a little of his own," said Linley in a cheerful voice, but Fraine caught the mingled undernotes of tact and worry, like bitter apples. "How fares our Tomas these days?"

"Well, I think." She should have told Linley about him before now. "I just saw him. He knew of the exorcism."

Relief welled into Linley's eyes, but the tension didn't leave his bearing. "What did he tell you?"

Noticing Rose's minute glance at Simon, Fraine looked at him too.

"You needn't hold your tongue in my presence, Fraine," said the priest. "Nothing you could say would make an enemy of me, nor will Werferth or Alfred hear a word of it."

Linley sat back a little on the bench, his eyes widening. Then, slowly and tentatively, he began to smile. An affectionate glance, querying and answering and sometimes apologetic, held between the brothers before Simon told Linley, "There are powers greater than the law. Of Church or King."

Linley reached across the table to touch his hand, and the gaze between them deepened.

As if responding to something his brother had just said, Simon added softly, "And not all vows are spoken."

For an instant Linley appeared a trifle abashed. Then he grinned and Simon grinned back, and Rose's face brightened as she watched them.

The warmth in all their eyes made Fraine miss Owein so much that her throat closed. Looking down at her plate, she fingered the folds of her Saxon gown, still dirty from her role as the tinker woman. Because of their little game, Owein was in deeper jeopardy from the Bishop. Though not so much as he was from Loki.

"Linley?" she began when she could speak again. Immediately she had everyone's full attention. "You have Owein's horoscope, do you not?"

"And yours with it."

"Could they help you locate him, or tell you how he's faring?"

"I don't know. But by all means, let's have a look at them." He headed for the ladder to the loft.

"Another look, mind you," murmured Rose, smiling sidelong at Fraine.

"I didn't intend to put him to work again, if he's already studied them—"

Simon touched her elbow. "Never fret; he loves fussing with charts." Overhead, the lid of one of the storage chests thumped against the wall. "And you're a fresh audience. Rose can calculate a nativity perfectly well herself."

"Do you ever ask Linley for advice?" ventured Fraine. "I mean, of this nature?"

Simon met her gaze. "I have done," he said quietly. "And I always hear him out if he begins."

"But I thought you didn't..." She ignored the increasingly expressionless look Rose was giving her. "You're not like Werferth or Daniel."

Simon shook his head. "Not in that way, no."

"Not at all, as far as I can see. How many Christians are like you?"

"I hope that most of them are a good deal better," he said, his face grave.

"Damnation!" muttered Linley, still in the loft. Another two lids thumped open.

Fraine smiled. Rose caught her eye and, to Fraine's surprise, started to giggle, then laughed outright. So did Fraine. Simon put his face in his hand; he was grinning.

"Going to share the joke, are you?" Linley called down to them softly.

"Later." Rose blew him a kiss.

"Astrology is rooted in the earth. It studies her seasons and the heavens' effect upon her," Simon told Fraine. "All were made by the divine, so I can't quite credit that their study is wrong."

"But Werferth would," Fraine said steadily.

Simon's shrug and opaque glance could mean several things: that he wouldn't speak for the Bishop, wouldn't contradict him aloud, had no idea what Werferth thought, or agreed with Fraine. She rather thought it was the latter. To her surprise, Simon didn't smell wary and neither did Rose: no scent of wormwood came from them. They must trust her. She felt warmed by the thought.

A leather envelope tucked under his arm, Linley was descending the ladder. Simon got up to let him sit next to Fraine, and he spread the charts out before her and weighted their curling ends flat with a mug and the milk pitcher.

"Hard to believe you were born only six years ago," he told her.

It was Fraine's turn to shrug. The twins' charts were scribbled over with strange symbols, all curves and circles and hard angled lines, and more than one hand had made notes on the parchment.

"I expect it's hard for her to believe, too," said Rose.

Linley was frowning at the charts. "During those six years, you and Owein were in Elfland at least as much as you were here."

Rose darted a glance at Simon. Was that a flicker of surprise in her face to find him calmly listening?

"So we have a riddle, my friend," Linley was telling Fraine. "Astrology relates to the earth and those who walk upon it. I've no idea if your horoscope affects you as it would if you'd been living here those six years."

"If it does, what could it tell you about Owein?"

Linley drew a flat round metal object, a pile of interlocking plates, from its case. He moved one plate, then another, turned them over and studied their backs. Next he set the twins' horoscopes to one side and, referring to the metal plates and the handwritten notes, started drawing yet another chart with a nub of charcoal. Fraine looked at Rose, who smiled reassuringly.

"Blessed little," muttered Linley after an intent scrutiny of his handiwork. "Owein's attention is on exploring his roots. So is yours, Fraine; you've virtually the same chart. He needs to make a sustained effort of will. Not quite three years ago, he..." When Linley rubbed the side of his nose and unwittingly smeared it with charcoal, Rose hid a smile. Still poring over the parchment, he cast a glance up at Fraine. "I just can't say how it applies to the pair of you, when you weren't living under these skies." Two small vertical lines she'd not seen before had appeared between his eyebrows. "I'd hoped this other chart I've just drawn might help us determine Owein's whereabouts."

"But it doesn't," she said, reading his expression.

"I'm afraid not," said Linley in the gentlest of tones. "The Moon rules him here." Tapping on the new chart. "To begin with, it's void of—"

"You needn't explain," she said, all at once feeling exhausted. "I believe you."

Without another word, Linley swept all the parchment aside and hugged her.

"Thank you for looking at them," she said, her voice muffled by the cloth of his jerkin. "When Matilda's so ill." Blinking back tears, she let go of him and smoothed the feathers of Freya's cloak.

Simon was kneeling by Matilda now, holding one of her limp hands in both of his. Susannah had slumped against the back of her chair and closed her eyes. When Linley shot the priest a questioning glance, Simon nodded.

"'Tilda's still with us," said Rose, sounding awed. "I'll go sit with her; Mother and Simon both need rest."

Yet after a brief intent conversation with Susannah, who folded her lips and crossed her arms and stared unwaveringly at her daughter, it was Rose and the priest who meekly came to join Fraine and Linley.

"I've a question for you," said Simon, sliding onto the bench across from Fraine. "Your mother once told me that if ever I had need of her, I could call upon her." He took a breath, let it out again harshly. "Matilda has need of whatever aid I can find for her. Could Moira offer us any?"

"I don't know," Fraine said slowly.

"Have you healers in Elfland?" Simon asked. Gently; he wasn't pressing her. Good will, with a scent like hot fresh bread, wafted from him.

"Many of them. The last I heard, they were much occupied with a horrible case of the iron-sick. Tomas—"

Linley turned a shade paler, no mean feat beneath that midsummer-olive skin.

"It's not Tomas who's ailing," she told him. Never mind the rest; she shouldn't have begun and it would be hard to explain. None of the Saxons knew Deverell.

"Matilda's sickness was brought on by enchantment of a kind," said Simon, very low. "From Loki."

Fraine nodded.

"The Elves know more of magic than we do," continued Simon.

Linley was gazing at him with an expression midway between shock and delight, as if Simon had unexpectedly returned from a very long journey.

The priest ran his hands through his short dark hair. "So their healers might know better than I how to combat a magically induced illness."

"But Simon, you yourself are a healer," said Fraine. "You have the gift."

"I don't deny I've been granted it." The priest's tired face, round as the Moon, grew more sad, and the lines about his mouth deepened. "But others have a greater store of that gift, among your mother's people and mine alike." He waited a beat. "Would it be possible for Moira to bring one of your healers here?"

Linley and Rose were both gaping.

"You could ask." Fraine hunted for words. "It would be difficult. We're all in a shambles; the earth itself is heaving and buckling. We've drifted so far from Midgard—" She almost said how hard it had been for her to travel here, but then he might have asked how she'd won through. Increasingly open though Simon might be, and as much as Fraine found herself trusting Tomas's friends, she didn't care to reveal Freya's aid to her just yet.

Simon steepled his fingers on the tabletop. In Moira's palace that uneven wooden surface would have been sanded to a glasslike sheen, but here all was built for immediate service, rough and workmanlike, and planed only till the danger of splinters was gone. "What if..." he began. Stopped, took a sip of water, looked straight into Fraine's eyes. "If the passage here is too hard for an Elf, what if I went to Faerie instead?"

"You?" Fraine was astonished.

Simon nodded. "Could you take me?" he asked in a rush. "And once I'd met with your healers, could you bring me back straightaway, not years later?"

"I don't know."

Linley stirred. "What if Alfred were to send for you, Simon? Or if Werferth did?" he asked. Concerned: he wasn't arguing. "And should you leave 'Tilda for so long?"

The priest clasped his hands behind his head. "I would." Fatigue crept into his voice. "If it gave me the slightest chance of healing her, I would go to Elfland this moment." He looked at Fraine.

"I can't promise I could take you there," she said haltingly. "Let alone return you here safely before any time had passed. Nor whether you'd learn anything useful."

"I should go in your place," Linley put in, pale and round-eyed, squaring his shoulders. "'Tilda could slip away from us in no time without you here, Simon. I could talk to Moira's healers for you and remember all they said."

Simon opened his mouth, but Rose spoke first. "If one of us ventures into Elfland, it should be I," she said thinly. She reached across the table for Linley's hand and brushed her other hand across her mouth, as if fingering an old wound. "You're needed on the estate." Her voice was almost steady. "What if Daniel were to take advantage of your absence and fabricate a claim upon Limecliff? But he and Werferth would never notice I was gone, and even if they did, I'm of no account to them."

Linley raised her fingers to his lips. "And the Elf who struck you when Moira was here? What if you fell afoul of him?"

Who had hit Rose? Fraine was confused. Not about the Saxons' mutual respect: that could not have been more clear. No one was bickering; no one was issuing ultimatums. Nor about their courage: they were all terrified, yet every one of them had volunteered to go to Elfland if it could possibly help Matilda. What confused Fraine was that Simon was one of the Christians with whom Moira refused all compromise. Simon had the most to lose by such a journey, and it was Simon who had first offered to go.

If Fraine had any of her mother's presence, now was the time to use it, along with some tact. She sat straight and easily on the bench, kept her hands quiet in her lap, and asked, "Would you care to hear my opinion?"

Nods all around.

"None of you should try to go. Even if I could take you there and back again promptly, and I'm not at all sure that I could, there's no guarantee it would help Matilda in the slightest. And it could do all of you great harm."

Linley appeared relieved, if a bit wistful, while Rose looked as if she'd just escaped death by drowning. Simon closed his eyes for an instant before assuming a calm expression, but grief and a rebellious desperation floated from him, smelling of cypress, scorched barley and smoke, and overpowering whatever scents came from the others.

Fraine laid a tentative hand on his arm. "It would haunt me forever if I lost you there or in the 'tweenlands."

The brown eyes looked into hers for a moment. "That I understand." He appeared to conduct a brief argument with himself. "It would haunt me to bury Matilda," he said flatly, and glanced at Linley. "If we do, it will be in Limecliff's soil. We're not returning her to her mother."

"Alfred agreed, then," said Rose.

"So he did. There's been no time to tell you." Simon got to his feet, turned towards the bedcloset.

"Wait!" Fraine made a grab for his arm.

Hope flared in his eyes. "You'll take me to Elfland?"

"No, no, no. Root and branch, you're as stubborn as Tomas," she said. "I remembered something!"

From Linley came a faint choking sound, a match for the mirth in his eyes. Simon glared at him.

Fraine was fumbling in her pouch for Freya's earth. When her fingertips found the compacted lump, a tingling warmth shot from it clear to her heart. If she'd had any doubts, that sensation removed them.

"Here," she said, pressing the lump into Simon's hand. "It isn't Limecliff's soil, but it just might help you keep Matilda above ground. Use it however you see fit, healer." With more bravado than she felt, she added, "I'm off to find Owein. When I do, we'll see to the rest." *If* she found Owein, and if Loki could be stopped. But the Saxons needed hope as much as they needed whatever Freya's earth might be able to do.

Simon stared at the rich loamy soil in his palm, extended it away from his torso, narrowed his eyes and stood utterly still. His face withdrew a little. He was using his Sight on Freya's earth. After half a moment, appearing reassured but mystified, he glanced at Fraine and asked, "Where did you get this?"

Linley appeared curious and expectant, but Rose had guessed what Fraine would say, and was glad of it. Fraine could tell from the glow in the Saxon woman's eyes and the scent of honey about her. She gave Rose a small triumphant look, as one gives a comrade. With her hand on the doorlatch, Fraine said, "From the Goddess and a friend."

CHAPTER THIRTY-THREE: A SMALL SOAPSTONE BOWL

The 'tweenlands

Owein lay on his belly, head turned to one side, his left cheekbone flat against something smooth and slightly yielding. The pressure of the contact hurt the left side of his face. The other side, where Loki had first hit him, was even more painful. He ached all over, but worst of all were his right cheekbone and temple and his puffy right eye.

Had someone spoken? He didn't want to listen, wanted to sink back into unconsciousness where the pain wouldn't follow him.

"Get up."

Loki's voice. Bruised ribs protested as Owein caught his breath. He wasn't certain he could stand, but staying prone was dangerous, because Loki could—

Kick him, hard, right at the hipbone. Owein gasped as a river of stars burst into whitewater in his head. He rolled away from the next kick too late; a booted foot caught him almost in the groin. He brought his knees to his chest, wrapped his arms around them, tucked his head and kept rolling. Staggered to his feet. Bent forward a bit from the waist, hands on his thighs, breathing as deeply as he could. At least one of his ribs must be broken.

At his feet was the familiar reddish mottled substance that connected the eight points of the bridge. Not three ells to his left, the red stuff ended in a jagged tear and then there was nothingness, just opaque grey haze. If he'd rolled too far, would he have fallen? And where would he have landed?

He blinked up at the glowing point before him. Not the Lammas pinwheel. Other than the rays that connected them, the points were all different. Like the narrow end of a giant ellipse, this one's streams of particulate energy curved above his head in rich chalky shades of viridian and cobalt and crimson, beaded with silvery light like a spiderweb at dawn.

Now he remembered: it was the summer solstice point. His last chance, Loki had said, but Owein had no more succeeded at razing it than any of the others. One by one, Loki had forced him to attack them all. He put up his shield, but it was feeble. He wasn't sure how much longer he could stand.

"You've some fight left, I see. Maybe you'll tear down this point for me after all."

Owein turned his head and saw Loki a few ells away, sitting where the red substance was torn apart, at the very edge where that gaping grey void began. Dangling his lower legs into it as casually as Linley might have perched on the fence of a sheep pen. Even swinging his feet a bit. Loki's feet and calves and knees were all still visible; they hadn't disappeared into the emptiness.

"Oh, *I'm* quite safe here," said Loki, grinning. "I wouldn't want you to have any false hopes. So disheartening."

"Tear it down yourself," muttered Owein, then tried not to wince. His lip might be bleeding again. "I want the rest of my clothes," he said, keeping his voice as steady as he could."

"You left them at the Lammas point. All but your trousers. Don't you remember?" asked Loki solicitously. "That's one thing you can't lay at my door." Eyeing him again, and the half smile had returned, the speculative one.

"I think you could find them," said Owein. "It might be worth your while."

Loki giggled. "Still trying to bargain? You're such a slow learner."

Owein forced a deep and painful breath into his lungs and unclenched his fists. He hadn't succeeded in hitting Loki. Twice he had lost his head and, incoherent with rage, launched himself at the godling instead of the bridge—and got his rib broken. Since then he'd focused on staying alive. And on not showing that he was frightened, that he knew he'd made a mistake.

Nimbly, Loki rose and came to Owein, stopping directly before him. That loose-jointed shambling walk, that demented smile... The worst of it was how much Loki was enjoying himself.

Owein stood his ground. If he backed away, Loki would follow. Loki would grab Owein's arm and shove his face up against Owein's, and the glittering amber eyes would bore into him and make his stomach churn and his head spin even more than it already was. He knew why he hadn't curled into a shuddering ball, let Loki batter him to death and have done with it. His reasons were personal. At first he'd been obsessed with saving Matilda, then guilty over how he'd let that obsession blind him to the improbability of Loki's keeping any bargain—blind him to such a degree that he'd betrayed Fraine and the bridge. Now sheer hatred motivated him: if he gave up, Loki would humiliate him. Loki would win.

"Care to have another go at the point?"

"No."

The hazel eyes blazed, then assumed an inward stare of concentration. Owein braced himself; he was going to be struck again.

Instead, the upper left quadrant of Loki's skull silently rolled back like a drawbridge of bone or the secret door of a cave. Where the encased brains of an Elf or a mortal would have been, Owein saw a miniature replica of the midsummer point blazing away within that partially opened skull.

What he saw wasn't real, he reminded himself, feeling his knees weaken and his gorge rise. Loki was a shape-changer. A quarter section of his head might appear to have been sliced away like an apple paring—perfectly, seamlessly, bloodlessly—and transformed into a model of the midsummer point, but it was an illusion. Only an illusion, however nightmarish.

"Hit me," said Loki, fixing Owein with his remaining eye. "I give you leave. I'll not stop you and I won't strike back." A truncated cackle. "Hit the little point before you hit the real one. What do you say?"

Owein choked on a dry heave.

"Squeamish? Let's try something else." The image blurred like a shaken veil. Then, instead of the midsummer point, one quarter of Loki's face and skull held a bird's nest. A raven's nest, crammed with far more fledglings than a real nest would contain, all hopping up and down and flapping their stubby wings, shrieking, their mouths gaping open as if demanding their mother's return. To their right could be seen half of Loki's forehead and his ginger hair and one visible eye, while underneath the nest were the remainder of Loki's cheek and nose and the sarcastic twist of his mouth.

He was smirking at Owein. "Maybe two of them are Thought and Memory! Care to see them eat? Mama bird spits their food into their beaks. Much less fun than you must have had sucking Moira's teats with that pretty mouth of yours. How big were you when Tomas made you stop? *She'd* have let you keep on and on—"

Before he knew what he intended, Owein was driving his fist as hard as he could, not at the phantom bird's nest but straight at Loki's remaining eye. To that flesh-and-blood blow he added another: all the iron-essence he could muster. Chuckling, Loki sidestepped him with dizzying speed. Before Owein realized that his target had moved, he was careening headfirst into the midsummer point with his fists flailing and murder in his heart.

He heard a triumphant shout from behind him. There were a few free-floating seconds of confusion, of warmth and whirling lights and shifting energetic structures. Then Loki let out a howl of pure frustration, for the midsummer point had just ejected Owein again.

He landed hard at Loki's feet. His bruised ribs gave a throb of protest, but the point didn't seem harmed and neither did he. Haltingly, Owein pulled himself upright, then stood, wary of a kick in the face.

Loki was frowning, abstractedly, not in anger. As if Owein were a riddle he hadn't quite solved. The godling's head looked normal again, the skull sealed shut now, the ginger hair unruffled.

Feeling desperate and overwhelmed, Owein backed away a few paces. "I can do no more. Now will you believe me?" He couldn't slow his breathing, and a scream was threatening to rise in his throat. "Destroy the rest of the bridge yourself if you can."

Loki shook his head as though dismissing a fly, and transferred his absent stare to the midsummer point.

"Send me back to Midgard and let Matilda live," Owein said dully, then dropped into a crouch and waited. His ribs ached. His face hurt. All at once he felt half starved and thirsty to boot. He wanted his shirt, too, but at least he wasn't cold. The midsummer point shimmered untouched above his head. Around and immediately beneath him, the grey of the 'tweenlands and the soft-packed glittering crimson surface where he squatted remained precisely the same. And all the while Loki stood immobile, his ginger hair so vivid that it seemed a living aureole about his frozen white face.

"What did you just say about the bridge?" he finally asked, in the same tone he might have used to inquire about the time. He didn't look at Owein.

His chest tightening with apprehension, Owein scrambled to his feet.

"What was it? Give me every word."

"'Destroy the rest of the bridge yourself if you can.'"

"Ha!" Loki's pale face was sharp with malevolence. "I couldn't and neither could you. Not by yourself." The hazel eyes were narrowed and alight, still puzzling something out, yet with growing certainty. "Two of you built it; two must tear it down." He folded his arms. "We need your sister, my friend. Where is she?"

"I have no idea." Owein tried not to hold his breath as Loki studied him.

"So you don't," said the godling at last. "You look too relieved on her account, and too afraid for your own skin. Rest easy, I won't hit you again. But I'll see to it that you stay put while I find her."

Before Owein could move, Loki darted up to him and breathed in his ear. No, more than that: Loki had just said something. A single word that Owein couldn't quite make out. Perhaps he'd not heard it properly because Loki's voice was so soft, and besides, he'd not paid much attention because his eyes had mysteriously started to close and all he wanted to do was—

"Sleep," whispered Loki a second time, smiling down at the unconscious young halfbreed.

First Loki searched the rest of the bridge, in the hope of catching Fraine trying to repair the connections between the points that her brother had managed to destroy. No one was there but a few sylphs, who skittered away at the sight of Loki, and one thick-necked and stubby-fingered salamander gazing in worshipful stupefaction at the Imbolc point's nexus of light. When Loki appeared, it threw itself onto its face and babbled something about how it might serve his Radiance.

"You mightn't," said Loki peevishly. "Unless you've seen a halfbreed girl about? Blonde, looks more like an Elf than a mortal."

Alas, the salamander was mortified to have seen no such person. Somewhat out of temper, Loki left the bridge and set off through the 'tweenlands.

He began with Hecate's crossroads but found no sign of Fraine there. Hecate would very seldom speak to him, and this visit was no exception. She wouldn't even appear. When he asked if She had seen Fraine, all three of Her statue's faces, maiden, mother and crone, gazed at him forbiddingly and remained silent.

He kept exploring. Let Her be hateful; he didn't need Her. He didn't need anyone. The nine worlds were drifting inconveniently far apart, but he was more powerful than an Elf or a mortal Mage, and he could do enough reconnoitering to eliminate some possibilities. Fraine wasn't in Niflheim with Loki's daughter Hel. Nor was she in what was left of Asgard, where he had posted a salamander or two, so she must still be alive. She wasn't in Jötunheim, land of the giants. Loki's kin there assured him as much and in this matter, at least, they'd little reason to deceive him.

He doubted that the girl was in the 'tweenlands. Most of his salamanders had fanned out there to look for her, and when he returned, all the reports were negative. He should search a bit longer himself, though he was rapidly growing weary of the prospect. Not that it was particularly difficult for him to move about here. The weird thorny blocks erected by the Christian rite of exorcism like so many nightmare hedges, glowing and alive, had never caused him much more than minor annoyance. So far he'd run across very few that were aimed specifically at him, Loki, the Norse fire deity. Most of them were meant to bar Elves and various beings whom the Christians took for demons. They seemed to have a particular horror of salamanders, though almost no idea what any of the Elementals were.

As Loki grew into Lucifer's role, the rite of exorcism might begin to affect him. Still, he doubted that it would prove very troublesome even then, since it would be aimed at his assumed identity and not at him. But exorcisms would go a long way toward keeping the Elves where he wanted them—out of Midgard—so he was all for encouraging the ritual. Odd, how the Elves seemed more susceptible to it. Perhaps because they were fond of oaths, or because they couldn't lie. And beliefs held nearly as much power for the Elves as their true names did.

Idiots, the whole weasel-faced lot of them. Loki didn't care a fig for oaths or truths or calling things by their names, and lying was among his foremost talents. Therefore he was more versatile and powerful than the entire Elfin race. And soon would wield still greater power, once he'd found Fraine and destroyed the Elves' route to his new fiefdom. Where in blazes was the girl?

Scowling, Loki made his way back to Hecate's crossroads, more to annoy the goddess than because he thought he'd learn anything useful there. She wasn't visible, but that didn't mean She wasn't watching him from somewhere close by. In a parody of a supplicant's posture, Loki threw himself down on his belly before Her statue, propped his chin in his hands and considered his situation.

He'd found nothing in the 'tweenlands but a few suspiciously blurred places, as though someone were shielding something. Yet the 'tweenlands, older than the nine worlds that had sprung from them, had always been riddled with bizarre and fragmented little pockets of energy.

Owein was completely ignorant of his sister's whereabouts. Loki could read faces, particularly mortal ones, and young Owein's was an unusually open book. His mother must have spent hardly any time with him; else he'd have learned more subtlety.

Annoying little wretch. The only hindrance to killing him was that, as Loki had just been clever enough to guess, both twins were necessary to destroy the bridge. And both to build it. Suppose they were reunited before Loki found Fraine? Or suppose someone happened upon the sleeping Owein and murdered him? The boy was both a fledgling Mage and the King of Elfland, or soon would be, and his rivals would be plentiful.

Loki frowned at the bare marble toes of Hecate's statue and the small soapstone bowl that someone had placed between Her feet. Some sort of offering, no doubt. He lifted the lid; the bowl was empty.

He should have left Owein shielded or hidden or posted a salamander nearby, but he'd been in a tearing hurry to find Fraine, and even he couldn't always think of everything. Still, now that he'd turned his mind to it, was there a way to render Owein both safe and harmless before resuming the search for Fraine?

There might very well be. Loki had heard tales of mortal Magicians, powerful and ambitious, who'd sent their own souls out of their bodies to be encased in glass or a gemstone or some such whatnot, which was then well-concealed. With the soul elsewhere, the body couldn't be killed. A daring move: it made such Mages seem invincible, and struck terror in their enemies. A risky move, too, for it left the Magician, and anyone so rash as to love him or her, utterly at the mercy of whoever found that hidden and vulnerable soul. If the glass were broken or the pearl smashed, the soulless body would perish.

Well content with himself, Loki began humming a little tune. Another luminous strategy: he would force Owein's soul out of his body before he, Loki, found Fraine, and thereby bend both twins to his will. Of Fraine's love for her brother there was no doubt whatsoever.

Owein opened his eyes. His mouth was parched, his joints stiff, his head full of fog. He was lying on his side near one of the points of the bridge. And he wasn't alone. He rolled over to discover Loki squatting nearby and staring at him speculatively.

He yanked himself upright. Though he moved as fast as he could, he felt as if he were slogging through quicksand, and he had to use his hands to push himself to a sitting position. Why had he been asleep? Had Loki been watching him the whole time?

His first instinct was to experiment with his shield. To his relieved surprise, energy coursed out of his solar plexus, flowed in a warm reassuring layer over his body and sealed itself into place precisely as it always had. The rest must have done him some good. Heartened, he sent another pulse from his midsection and felt his shield grow stronger, just as it should have done.

He still had no sense of Fraine's whereabouts. Come to think of it, he'd not felt his link to her since Loki had pushed him into the 'tweenlands, but he'd been too intent on surviving his encounter with Loki to spare much thought for that loss of awareness. He felt it now, though, and acutely, as if he were breathing with only one lung. It was disorienting. He wouldn't wish Fraine here with him and Loki, but he'd never missed her so much in all his short life.

"Bother," said Loki, his brow furrowed. "I waited too long."

"Waited? For what?"

"Oh, nothing." Loki reached into his jerkin and pulled out a small soapstone bowl. It was beige, flecked with brown and peach and red, highly polished, shallow, and not quite the width of Loki's palm. He put the bowl between himself and Owein, removed its lid and set it beside the bowl.

A tremor snaked up Owein's spine and tingled down his limbs. Not gooseflesh: a warning. "What is that?" he asked. It was dangerous, whatever it was, and he reinforced his shield a second time.

"A bowl," said Loki blandly. Squatting easily on his heels, elbows propped on his knees and chin in his hands, he was watching Owein. "Someone left it by Hecate's statue. She wasn't using it, so I brought it back with me."

"Why?"

Loki smiled. "It's for you." His relaxed bearing didn't change in the slightest, but his face did; suddenly it was drenched in sweat. It hardened and twisted, and his eyes flared like boiling topaz. Jabbing one long narrow finger as if it were a skewer, he pointed first at Owein and then at the soapstone. "*Enter...that...bowl,*" he intoned. Not in his usual voice, an amiable and affected tenor, but in something between a low guttural growl and a hiss that crackled like fired kindling.

Owein smelled smoke. A wave of heat struck him, and a second and a third, all washing over him as if he stood at a volcano's mouth. He jumped to his feet and looked wildly about for the flames. He saw none, yet the soles of his bare feet were so hot they felt all but ablaze. His throat was dry; his eyes were streaming. At any second his hair would catch fire, and every inch of his skin was pink and running with sweat and must be blistering—

An invisible mallet struck him full in the chest. He staggered and fell to his knees, wincing as they touched that sizzling ground, but the pain was nothing compared to the blows at his solar plexus. Loki was trying to shatter his shield.

That was the greatest danger; perhaps the heat was only meant to distract him. He concentrated on reinforcing his shield as that phantom sledgehammer struck him again and again. Groaning, he huddled over his knees and wrapped his arms about the back of his head, but the next blow came straight to his chest just as easily as if he were standing and Loki were drubbing him with an axe handle.

"Enter that bowl."

The pounding redoubled, rocked Owein upward, away from his knees, and he clutched at them.

Enter the bowl? How? Another assault left him gasping. It was impossible. A mortal child, even an infant, wouldn't fit. And Loki seemed to be trying to hammer his way into Owein's ribcage, not push him into the—

Thunk. Another cracked rib? Was he bleeding?

"Damned Elfin shields," muttered Loki.

Was he forcing Owein to go live apart? But Owein wasn't an Elf; he was mortal, and at this rate he'd die before Loki finished whatever he'd started. Die without seeing Fraine again, without warning her about Loki.

Thunk. Loki was cursing.

Kneeling with his chest and face on his thighs and his hands locked behind his head, Owein sent out a silent howl in mind-speech: *Fraine! Stay away!* Was he dying? *Loki's forcing me to live apart!*

Not the next blow, but the one after, set him screaming out loud.

CHAPTER THIRTY-FOUR:
A MEETING AT HECATE'S CROSSROADS

Midgard

Headed for the willow grove, Fraine loped through her father's silent ivy-covered trees. She'd just left the nearby town of Axbridge, after having satisfied herself that Owein wasn't there, and she wanted to make one last sweep of the estate before searching the 'tweenlands.

Twilight was starting to creep close, the shadows lengthening, the hushed summer air increasingly tinged with mauve. Moisture was carried on that air, and along with it the promise of rain on the morrow. Fraine kept her footfalls soft upon the rich and slightly damp humus, crumbling oak leaves and pine needles. Since she followed no path but was taking the shortest route to her destination, she turned and meandered and leaped over moss-eaten boulders and more than one small noisy rill. Rabbits scattered at her approach. Once she disturbed a sleeping bat but kept moving, stopping only to drink from a stream that ran towards the grove.

At last she saw the willows, the westernmost sweep of their branches lit to an arc of pale green falling stars by the last rays of the Sun. From this distance the grove looked empty. Nonetheless she approached it silently, keeping within the cover of the neighboring trees as long as possible.

Owein wasn't in the grove. Frustrated, she sank onto the thick soft grass beneath the willows, stretched out on her back and frowned at the fingernail Moon peering over the treetops to the east. When she ran her hand through the plush carpet of green where she lay, her fingers came away moist but smelled of sun and air.

She knew what stars would rise next. She knew where the Sun would sink beneath the western skyline and where, later that evening, the stars of the Plough would be visible—Tomas called it Odin's Wain. She could have pointed directly at Limecliff's great hall, the stable, the kitchen, the mews. And the gorge and the caves, or Axbridge town. But where Owein was she had no idea. If that thin curving wafer of Moon knew, it hadn't told Linley and it wasn't telling her.

Something was wrong. What else could account for her loss of any sense of Owein's whereabouts, and the blows she'd felt just before it disappeared? She'd no proof that Owein had left Midgard, but neither had she any proof he'd remained. He could be anywhere in the nine worlds.

Sighing, she got to her feet and began untying the roll of feathers about her waist. She'd go to the 'tweenlands and ask for whatever help the goddess could give.

Fraine drew the cape about her shoulders, the hood over her head, and closed her eyes. She knew how to project a tendril of her energy from her shield to the 'tweenlands; she'd done so to build the bridge. But then she'd known where to find Owein, and where to aim. She waited, letting her shield build, letting a current of energy flow from her solar plexus and tingle through her arms and down to her fingertips, through her legs and down to her toes. It felt rather as if her limbs were asleep, but the sensation had more to do with being energized than numbed or slowed. Some of the current flowed a few inches above her skin as well as on and beneath it. She planted her feet more firmly, kept her back straight, flexed her fingers. She'd thought the cape would be heavy, but instead it felt oddly light.

At last she felt strong enough to begin. She issued a narrow ribbon of energy from her shield—it felt a bit like removing a splinter, but without any pain. Next she pictured Caraid and Freya, and reached towards their image in her mind.

And found darkness. Found nothing.

Fraine stumbled forward. She was falling. Just as she opened her mouth to scream, warm air enfolded her. The world turned black, then disappeared.

"Welcome, my daughter," said a vast echoing voice that she knew.

Fraine's feet thumped down onto something solid. Flinging her arms out to keep her balance, she took one tottering step sideways and opened her eyes. She was in the 'tweenlands; she knew its topography by now, and the immense enveloping stillness of its air. Just here it was grey, grey air and soil almost as far as the eye could see, but for Freya who stood before her, radiant and smiling. Fraine bowed her head.

At the goddess's side was Caraid, her blue eyes dull, and more sunken in the puffy discolored flesh of her face than when Fraine last saw her. The scent of decay that clung to her was worse. Leaning against Freya, as if without that support she would collapse, she was smiling feebly nonetheless.

Then Fraine noticed the statue: a woman with three faces. On each marble forehead the mortal Moon was carved, waxing, full and on the wane. Fraine could see only the Mother's face from where she stood, but she knew about the others, the Maiden and the Crone. Moira had told her of the goddess who rules all turning points. And yes, three lanes stretched away from Hecate's statue, and one of Her faces overlooked each road.

Awed, Fraine said, "I have heard of this crossroads. How is it that I'm here?"

"My cape. And My will. When you sought me, I added Mine to yours." Freya's smile softened. *"And Hecate is kin to me, after a fashion."*

"You've come about your brother." Caraid's whisper was guttural, almost liquid. "Loki's trying to force his soul from his body. If you won't help him tear down the bridge, Loki will kill him."

Fraine's blood roared in her ears. Deafened, as if she were under water, she stared at Caraid, then at Freya, who nodded. Fraine let out a long exhalation, and only then realized she'd been holding her breath. Her throat was burning and her chest felt hollow and her heart was thudding. All reactions that she recognized as fear, yet only her body felt afraid. She herself was cold and determined and acutely alert. "Can he do that? Force a mortal soul from its body?"

"It lies within his power, given enough time. Owein's shield is more than Loki expected, but he's tiring. You must send him strength."

"I must go to him," said Fraine. Her legs were trembling; her shoulders felt stiff.

"If Loki seizes you too, the bridge is lost. Better to strengthen Owein from a distance. We will aid you all we can."

Anxiety gleamed in Caraid's filmy eyes. "The sooner the better, Fraine."

"Show me how."

"I will shield the three of us, and loan you what power I can spare from that task. Owein is in the 'tweenlands; go into trance and find him. Both Caraid and I may be of assistance there." With a compassionate glance, Freya added, *"But to strengthen him, you must trust Caraid's guidance. I do not fully understand the mortal body, for I have never had one."*

"How much longer I can help you, I do not know," said Caraid. "I am here by Freya's grace, and the Ørlög limits her as it does you and me."

Fraine took off Freya's cloak, stretched out on her back and draped the feathered garment over the length of her body. Laboriously and with Freya's help, Caraid lowered herself to a sitting position nearby, while Fraine fought a wave of queasiness at the proximity of that decaying flesh and its accompanying stench.

Caraid was looking at her. "I must touch you, to see what you will see in trance. Your pardon, I know that I—"

"I thank you for your help," said Fraine, ashamed of the bile in her throat and hoping her revulsion hadn't shown. She reached for Caraid's swollen hand with its blackened fingernails. It felt cold to the bone, faintly slick and moist, as if the slightest pressure of Fraine's fingers could leave indentations in that clammy flesh. Her gorge rose again. With her other hand, she clasped her half of Gebo, the Rune of Partnership. Was Owein still wearing his?

"You may begin." Freya's expression grew calm and intent. Fraine wouldn't have thought it possible for the goddess's skin to glow any more than it had during the transformations of Her face, yet now it was radiating both heat and light. A glittering luminescence welled from Her face and hair and hands, enveloping Her body and pouring down over Fraine and Caraid. The same warmth that had surrounded Fraine on her passage here

reached her now, flowing on a river of shining energy like dust motes set aflame. With the warmth came a reassurance that eased all of Fraine's muscles almost like a physical touch.

Feeling safer than she ever had, and guilty that she should be so protected when Owein was most in danger, she closed her eyes and began the descent, swifter than usual, into trance.

Floating. Disembodied. No breath, no weight, no gravity. Only a consciousness, an immaterial eye that could see in all directions at once and change its focus as Fraine willed. She was dimly aware of her body lying tranced at Freya's perfect feet, and completely unable to feel Caraid's hand in hers, although if she turned her attention that way she could see the two of them, along with the barest hint of the long shining cord that connected her to her body.

But they were irrelevant, she and Caraid, their physical forms. What mattered was that she could see Owein now, and that she was drawing closer to him.

Stripped to the waist, huddled over his bent knees, he was hiding his face and shielding the back of his neck with both hands. His breath came in long heaving gasps. Fraine could sense his fatigue, not in her own abandoned body but because she could gently and stealthily touch her awareness to his, as lightly as if she were melting a snowflake with only the heat of her breath. She could feel how Owein's muscles ached, how his thoughts were slowed and his heart thumped against his ribcage like an imprisoned moth.

The ground where he knelt was packed and glittering with a red-gold hue that she recognized: the iron-riddled substance of the lanes that connected the points of the bridge. Above Owein blazed the midsummer point, a rainbow of lapis and cornflower, citrine and saffron and emerald. Next to him stood Loki, scowling abstractedly.

Fraine withdrew a little. Could Loki see her?

"Not while I shield you," said Freya in mind-speech. *"He can neither see nor sense you, even when your awareness touches Owein. Do not reveal your presence. Loki should think that Owein's resistance is entirely his own. If Owein senses you, tell him not to give you away."*

With the toe of one impeccably cut boot, Loki prodded Owein. "The problem," he said fretfully, "is how to force your soul from your body but leave it alive." Another nudge at Owein's ribs. "You've got your mother's shield, I must say. Why not drop it and spare yourself more pain? I'll win regardless."

No answer. At the pit of his stomach and across his shoulderblades, Fraine could feel the anger in her twin, hot and sullen and controlled, could feel how the skin of his face and neck grew warmer and his belly tightened. But he didn't stir, and she knew he was saving his energy for Loki's next attack.

"You look like a turtle," muttered Loki. "An albino turtle out of its shell." He shut his eyes, extended his hands. A sizzling current, slower than lightning but twice as hot, leapt from them and struck Owein's naked back in a hollow between two vertebrae. Fraine was miserable; she could sense the heat and the pressure bearing down on Owein's spine, and how he clenched his teeth to stifle a groan.

"Now!" said Caraid in Fraine's mind.

Fraine sent Owein a pulse of energy, aiming precisely where Loki had.

"Not there. Where his shield emerges from his body."

The living arc of energy that Fraine had sent carried so much force that it took a moment to retract. Like a boomerang, she thought, and fought an irrational urge to duck as the tendril came arrowing back to her. She couldn't have ducked; her body lay tranced at Freya's feet. It took another moment to begin her second attempt to send Owein strength, and all the while he was panting and his mind was full of pain and stubbornness and rising panic.

"Stay calm. I can shield whatever you send."

With all the intent she could muster, Fraine aimed at Owein's solar plexus—she couldn't see it, but she could sense it—and hurled another pulse of energy at him.

"Not so much," warned Caraid. "You'll startle him. It should feel like his own strength."

Owein gasped as the current merged with his shield. Fraine felt him inhaling deeply, exhaling, felt his confusion. She didn't want to reach for his thoughts; he might not conceal his reaction. Besides, she could sense his emotions all too easily. Primary among them was relief. He seemed to be accepting this new strength, wherever it came from. Likely he was too tired to question it.

Loki, however, was another matter. He was turning about in a circle, his face sharp with suspicion, studying the midsummer point and what remained of its rays. He took a measured step forward, folded his arms and gave Owein a menacing stare.

"Let go!" urged Caraid. "You needn't stay connected to Owein's shield now that your energy's part of it. Turn your attention aside, but don't—"

Pain, everywhere, from the skin down through the flesh and piercing Fraine's bones like so many hot needles. She couldn't breathe. But that shouldn't matter; she wasn't in her body. She was in trance, in the 'tweenlands, floating near Owein.

Then she was sitting stark upright, clawing at her throat and gasping for air. An appalling smell filled her nostrils.

Beside her Caraid let out a little moan. "Don't return to your body," she finished feebly. "But you just did. Be easy; you've come to no harm."

Fraine could scarcely breathe and Owein, whom she could sense almost as vividly as before, was still in danger; Loki was eyeing him, wondering why he'd grown more resilient, and she had to go to him but she couldn't enter trance if she couldn't catch her breath—

"Be still," said Freya, leaning down. The luminous golden face, the mild ancient knowing eyes, were very close. Then a warm hand was laid firmly across Fraine's forehead and another against the back of her neck. *"Hush. You are safe. You can breathe."*

Fraine gulped down a bushel of air, let it out again. The soothing hands were removed from her skin, leaving a comfortable tingling wherever they had touched. But when she looked at Caraid, tears started in her eyes. The Seer's face was dark and bloated, almost unrecognizable, and her skin had begun to slough away.

"My time grows short," she whispered.

Swallowing hard, Fraine said, "I'll enter trance again."

"Go with confidence, and listen to Caraid. You have already helped Owein."

Fraine reached for the feather cloak she'd tossed aside in her panic, pulled it over her legs and torso and lay supine. She closed her eyes; she steadied her mind, even when the moist clammy weight of Caraid's hand fell on her bare arm.

CHAPTER THIRTY-FIVE: THREATS AND ULTIMATUMS

Elfland

The cataclysm that had driven Moira and Tomas out of doors and destroyed more of the palace had left piles of rubble in every corridor. Either Tomas or Moira could have opened a path with magic, but doing so would have betrayed their whereabouts to anyone in search of them. Clambering over the debris, slowly and carefully so as not to hurt Lir, had been their best option for avoiding detection.

The best, albeit the slowest. Making their way to Jared's rooms had taken a great deal of time. Shields up, they picked their way through the gutted palace, every sense on alert, with the ravens flying ahead to ascertain that the path was clear. A few times the birds suggested detours that had taken longer still. Hunger pangs gnawed at Tomas's stomach, and his eyes kept closing. If he were in Midgard, he would have guessed they'd put nearly two days into the journey, but in Elfland there was no telling how long it had been. Lir's color was better and his breathing stronger and more regular, but he remained unconscious.

Jared's door, when they finally reached it, was heavier and plainer than most that Tomas had seen here. Although the ubiquitous torch holders flanked it on either side, there was no carving on the lintel, no mat before the sill and no nameplates. A pale wooden knocker, carved into a face as androgynous as Nissyen's, was the door's only ornament. Moira lifted the door knocker and let it fall. No answer.

Lir's head drooped against Tomas's shoulder. The Elf's body was a limp weight in his arms; he'd be glad when he could put the fellow down. How much longer would Moira stand there frowning? Tomas caught her sidelong glance at Nissyen, and the seraphic green-eyed smile that the sylph gave her in return. Nissyen had joined them on their way to Jared's quarters. After inquiring where they'd found Lir, the Elemental had been uncharacteristically quiet, its expression bland and innocent, all of which meant it was thinking furiously.

Looking relieved at the sight of Tomas, Aubrey came panting up to greet them, then asked, ears swiveling forward, "Have you found the twins?"

Tomas hated to disappoint him by admitting they hadn't. Moira tapped on Jared's door a second time. Again, no reply. Even the ravens, perched on the empty torch brackets, were silent.

"Someone's within," murmured Nissyen.

Moira looked pointedly at the sylph: had anyone asked it a question? With a half-amused twist of its mouth, Nissyen retreated a few steps. They could all hear soft hurried footfalls within Jared's rooms now.

"Coming!" said a low voice. The door opened wide, revealing, framed like a portrait on the threshold, a pale and slender Elf with a long whimsical face. All he wore was a pair of red silk trousers with a loose and flowing cut. A mare's nest of hair hung half in his face. He pushed a dark curl out of his eyes, which were a clear brilliant shade of blue even though half-fogged with sleep, and gave his visitors a smile. It was Aidan.

Stepping aside with a bow, he said, "Enter and welcome." And to Tomas, formally but with warmth in his glance, "Well met, my lord."

They filed in, Moira and Aubrey and Nissyen, followed by the ravens, with Tomas and his burden last.

"Put him on the sofa." Aidan was eyeing Lir thoughtfully. "You'll want Jared; I'll tell him you've come." He hurried down a hallway that opened from the center of the main room's left-hand wall and, without knocking, slipped through the only door in the corridor that stood slightly ajar.

As gently as he could, Tomas set Lir down on a long couch with a low curving back and arms, all covered with pale blue, rather worn upholstery in what had once been a foliate pattern. He looked about for a cushion for Lir's head, but Aubrey was already handing him a cylindrical tattered one, and a narrow bolster which the two of them slipped beneath the Elf's knees. At their touch, Lir mumbled something but didn't open his eyes.

"He's coming round," said Moira, relieved. She dropped to her knees by the sofa and studied Lir's face. "Is there a blanket—"

Aubrey had already whipped a dusty sheet from a chair in the next room, all of whose furniture was shrouded in white. These quarters must not have been used for some time before Jared's tenancy. The pooka draped the cloth over Lir but made no attempt to tuck it in, and shook his head when Nissyen suggested a second coverlet. "I don't want him feeling restrained when he wakens," said Aubrey.

"That's probably wise," said Jared from behind them. When Moira stood, he went straight to her, though he gave Tomas a brief grave look and a murmured "m'lord." He was belting his trousers as he spoke; his hair was mussed, and he was barefoot and shirtless. Tomas tried not to stare: Jared was nearly as muscular as Lir, though he was neither so tall nor so broad of shoulder. Moreover, the hair on the captain's chest bore some resemblance to the fur-like pelt that covered Lir's back and torso and what could be seen of his shins.

Jared knelt beside the unconscious Elf. Down the hallway, Aidan closed the door that the captain had just come through, disappeared behind another door hard by the main room, and emerged carrying a platter of fruit, bread and cheese.

Moira was explaining where they'd found Lir. "Tomas suggested we bring him here."

Jared's dark gypsy's face softened a trifle. "I thank you," he told Tomas.

"That was well done." He was frowning as he studied Lir, but his expression was more perplexed and wondering than displeased, and so full of concentration that Tomas and Moira exchanged a speculative glance.

Aidan set the tray on a table by the sofa and moved quietly to Jared's side. Without taking his eyes from Lir, Jared said, "You were right; he's still with us."

"And has a part to play," murmured Aidan. Slowly and tentatively, he stretched a hand towards Lir's forehead.

"That might startle him." Jared clasped Aidan's wrist. "Best to let him waken on his own." A barely perceptible pause. "Apprise the Regents of our situation, would you please?"

The Seer rested his hand on Jared's shoulder for an instant before joining Moira and Tomas. "We've suspected that Evan's faction has attempted to surround your quarters for some time. But his Elves were well-shielded and we hadn't any proof, while they had enough support that imprisoning their ring-leaders might have made heros of them."

Moira didn't appear surprised. The briefing must be for Tomas's benefit.

"It's well that last tremor came when it did," said Aidan. "Two corridors collapsed not far from your suite, and Evan's Guards hidden there were in too much pain and shock to maintain their shields. They're in custody now." His face was grim. "We'd our own Guards concealed nearer your rooms. Not a one of them was hurt. Luck was with us."

"Only in that regard," said Jared. "There was so much confusion that I'd not swear your quarters are still secure, my lady. Someone could have slipped in while our Guards were pursuing theirs."

When Lir let out a long plaintive sigh, Aidan took a flask of water from the tray and handed it to Jared, who set it on the floor by the sofa. "This one," said Jared, nodding at Lir, "was patrolling the wood and the green for any activity from Evan's folk. And looking for Fraine—"

"How?" interrupted Nissyen.

They all turned to the sylph who, its fingers twitching, was gripping the back of the pale blue couch. Nissyen's expression was both intent and elated, as though Lir were a long-sought puzzle piece that the sylph hadn't decided quite how to use.

Jared glanced at Tomas, who nodded: the question could be answered. Yet from the veiled and calculating gleam in the sylph's greenish-blue eyes, the sylph might already know the answer and be playing games to elicit more information, or to see if Jared would conceal what he knew.

"They are trackers, they who come from the Inner Reaches," said the captain. "From birth. They have their own methods." His voice was neutral, his face wary.

Nissyen gave Jared a knowing look, clasped its bony hands behind its back and started to pace.

At that moment several things happened at once. Tomas smelled sulphur, overwhelmingly, and reinforced his shield. The ravens disappeared, but he sensed that they were still present. Aidan hunched over and clutched at his temples; Jared leapt to his feet. Its eyes slitted, the sylph turned to gaze at the door to the hallway and the rest of the palace. Aubrey made a grab for the water flask that Jared had set by the sofa, then flung himself between the white-lipped Moira and the door. They were all staring at it now, because a faint wisp of smoke was seeping in beneath the sill.

Lightly, almost playfully, someone knocked.

Tomas took a step forward. Aubrey threw him a frazzled look, then grabbed Jared's heaviest two armchairs and shoved them towards the door.

"No. Let him enter," Moira said quietly. When she clasped Tomas's arm, her finger were trembling. "Let him speak."

Aubrey cast a protesting glance over his shoulder. The pooka's ears were flat against his skull, and the whites of his eyes showed.

"She's right," said Tomas softly. He knew who their visitor was. "We cannot stop him." They'd had no warning, but that was another matter. "He'll do more damage if we try to prevent him."

He started for the door, but Jared shook his head. Only the knotting of the muscles along his spine betrayed the captain's tension. As calmly as if he expected the fenodyree with their supper, he pushed the armchairs aside and opened the door.

A slightly built, ginger-haired young man stood on the threshold. He was dressed in Saxon garments: trousers, soft-soled leather boots, a hip-length tunic. His thumbs were hooked in his belt, the rest of his hands hidden from view, his stance wide-legged and his head held high. Humming a tune under his breath, Loki made Jared an ironic bow, darted an assessing glance at the rest of the company, then fixed Tomas with a hot liquid stare.

"State your business here," said Jared, moving to block the doorway.

Loki ignored him. "My errand's with you, Mage," he said softly to Tomas.

"I'm listening."

"May I come in?"

Dangerous to provoke him by forbidding it. "Enter."

A wide and supple smile. "But your friend's in my path."

The captain stepped back but not fast enough: Loki's left hand made a deft motion. Iron-smell in the room: bitter, sour, stinging the nostrils. Light flashed from metal. Coughing, Aidan started towards Jared who, despite his watering eyes and puckered mouth, twisted nimbly away from Loki's knife, leapt backward and went into a crouch.

Aubrey was bent double, hacking. Jared was panting, but there was no blood on him that Tomas could see. Wheezing, his horrified gaze fastened on the knife, Aidan stopped a few paces from the captain's side. Moira stood very straight, her back and neck stiff, tears streaming down her face. Only Nissyen and the ravens, all perched on Jared's table, showed no trace of the iron-sick. Apart from them, Tomas was the least incapacitated; he had a prickly throat and his eyes stung, but he felt no nausea. Not yet. Fear coiled around the base of his spine.

He crossed the space between Loki and himself until less than an arm's length separated them. "Put the knife away if you wish to speak with me." He could spare it only one glance that made use of his Sight. The entire weapon was pulsing with an oily brownish-red energy, and its blade was carved with Runes that glowed like a forge and seemed to shift position on the metal. Then for the barest instant he glimpsed, floating above the knife, a man's face. A long pale face beneath a cap of boiled leather, mouth open in a soundless scream, a jagged oozing cut across his throat.

Shaken, Tomas blinked the face away. No ordinary weapon: it had been infused with spells that he didn't want to See, and some of them were even darker than the one he'd just detected. Blood magic. Little wonder Aidan looked so appalled.

Loki gazed at him, smiling, satisfaction plain in his face. "You finished the lesson I started," he said airily. "You've learned to control the iron-sick. Gratifying to have so apt a pupil."

"Put the blade away."

"Why?" Cauldrons now, those hazel eyes. "You've one of your own. Shielded, but you do."

Tomas nodded, unsettled by how quickly and completely Loki's expression could change. He hated to meet that smoldering gaze and his throat was drier and more painful by the second, but at least he didn't feel addled, as he often had in Loki's presence. Perhaps the iron-sick helped keep his mind sharp. Certainly it made him more aware of his body.

"I am outnumbered here," said Loki, assuming an injured tone. "As I was when we last met."

"You're far from defenseless. Put it away or—"

Or give it to me, he was about to add. But the sudden blaze of triumph in Loki's eyes would have stopped him, even before Nissyen began shrieking in mind-speech: *No, do not ask for it! Never touch it! It will turn on any hand but his.*

"Or destroy it," said Tomas. "Or begone."

"I'd throw it if it would strike flesh and not prating air," muttered Loki, not looking at Nissyen, not quite, but with an ominous curl of his lip. "If you give me your word I shan't be attacked, I will sheath the knife. Then and only then." A slow mirthless grin. "And you have true speech, friend

Thief. So I'll have the promise from you, not your Lord of the Air."

"I am not his Lord of the Air. I am not bound to this Mage," said Nissyen. It spoke patiently, as if to a small child. And with a hint of exasperated condescension, as if that child were both dim-witted and something of a pest. Tomas shot Nissyen a glance midway between warning and astonishment. Because the presence of a fire godling would excite any air Elemental, he'd expected to see the glitter in Nissyen's eyes and its tangled brown hair standing up in wisps, as though the sylph's substance could barely be contained within its illusory shape. But he'd not anticipated the casual way that Nissyen was sprawled beside the ravens on the table, propped on its elbows with its legs stretched straight out before it and its ankles crossed. As if Loki were nothing to worry about, and Nissyen were bored.

Don't underestimate him. And don't provoke him.

The angrier he is, the easier he is for me to read. I have observed that treating him dismissively or indifferently makes him angry.

Not a comforting reply. Nissyen had judged Loki's maniacal self-centeredness perfectly, but did the sylph realize how dangerous a game it was playing?

Loki was giving it an expressionless stare."I'll accept your word only," he said curtly, turning to Tomas.

"You shall have it once you shield that knife."

Slowly, his gaze never wavering, Loki folded his arms.

"I want its presence blotted out. No iron-sick and no blood magic."

The narrow lips tightened. "You have been learning, haven't you? Very well." He sheathed the knife, passed the flat of his hand over its hilt.

Tomas's throat gradually stopped prickling. He darted a glance at the others: Aidan could breathe again, and Moira's eyes were no longer watering, though her face was an alabaster carving. Ears flat against his skull, grey hide a-quiver, Aubrey straightened up. So did Jared.

"Well?" asked Loki, eyebrows aloft.

"You may enter," Tomas said neutrally and stepped aside. Another chill shot along his spine.

Lips pursed, moving with sure, light-footed steps, Loki crossed the threshold.

When the godling had come to a halt three paces away, Tomas asked, "Why have you come?"

"I'll tell you. If I'm blunt, pray excuse me; I'd just as soon not waste your time or mine." Oiled smoothness in Loki's voice. Like a spear, like the knife he had sheathed, the amber eyes were trained on Tomas alone. "First, if you want your son Owein alive, you will yield to me. In every particular."

As if Tomas were falling, his stomach lost its center of gravity, then tried to climb to his throat. The room grew still as new-fallen snow. Beside him, Moira drew herself to her full height, a small, tense, almost imperceptible movement. Aware of the red that flared in Aubrey's eyes, of Jared's poised immobility, Tomas studied Loki's face. "Where is Owein?"

"Do you think I would tell you?" Loki was enjoying himself: it showed in the smug set of that thin-lipped and mobile mouth, in the malevolent gleam at the back of his eyes. "All you need know is that I can easily kill him." His voice hardened. "I want him and Fraine to destroy the bridge, and for that I'll need the pair of them. Where is Fraine?"

"I have no idea."

Without taking his gaze from Tomas, Loki jerked his chin in Nissyen's direction. "Does the Lord of the Air?"

"I do not," said Nissyen a split second later, as if it hadn't been following the conversation. "We none of us do. Those with the Sight tell me they are too close to the matter to See clearly."

No one had said any such thing to Nissyen in Tomas's hearing, though it was certainly true. Loki looked at Moira. "Do you know where your daughter is, madame?"

"No," she said, very low. Her face might have been a death mask.

No and no and no, said the others. Loki flicked an enigmatic glance at Lir, who now appeared deep in ordinary slumber rather than unconscious. "Like as not your friend is equally ignorant." A glittering stare at Tomas, who maintained his outward calm. When Loki took a step closer, Aubrey's ears swiveled forward, then lay even flatter than before, and his upper lip curled back from his protruding yellow teeth. Moira gave him a tiny shake of her head.

"You'd best find her," said Loki, ignoring the pooka. The look he gave Tomas contained so much concentrated venom that it was almost a physical force. To Tomas's Sight, the air between them had gone as simmering and yellow and deadly as Loki's eyes, and carried a peculiar pressure, a gathering heaviness like the atmosphere before a storm. The pressure grew, constricting Tomas's chest. From the corner of his eye he could see that Aidan appeared pale and nauseated and was gripping the back of a chair. Moira's face had taken on her roots-of-a-mountain look: solid and immovable and infinitely old, with a hard flinty core. A mountain that had stood for thousands of years and would stand for thousands more. An Elfin expression, not remotely human and with no softness in it.

Tomas would not retreat before Loki. As unobtrusively as he could, he took a breath, a deep one, but so labored against that building pressure that it pained his ribs as if they were cracked. Although fear had chilled and stiffened his hands to the point of numbness, sweat started on his brow.

"I want that bridge down and your lot gone from Midgard forever. Find your daughter for me, or Owein dies."

Tomas said quietly, "What if she were found after he's dead? If you kill him, you'll leave the bridge standing."

"What there is of it. If either twin dies, it won't be finished." A wolf's grin. "But that won't suffice. I want it all the way down. Find your daughter for me, Mage." In a flash of motion, Loki raised both hands overhead. Flames shot from his fingertips, spiraled down around his body—and were gone and Loki with them, leaving only the smell of sulphur where he had been.

CHAPTER THIRTY-SIX: STRATEGIES

Tomas was still staring at the empty space where Loki had just been standing when he heard a hoarse indignant caw, and Thought landed squarely on his right shoulder. A second flapping of wings made him turn his head to see Memory settling on the arm of the couch just above Lir's head.

"Owein," whispered Moira, coming to Tomas. "Root and branch." He caught her to him, aware of the pale silent Elves, their faces either bleak or stunned, all watching the two of them. Aware of how intensely private Moira was, of their recent quarrel, of how his gesture might sit ill with her. Her body was tense, but although she didn't lean into his hold, neither did she make any move to pull away.

Across the room, a loud startled voice let out something between a grunt and a wail. Lir was sitting up, his long arms flailing, pushing the sheet aside. Memory hopped from the Elf's chest to the back of the sofa, feathers dark and glossy against that expanse of powder blue. Lir started to cough.

Jared muttered something unintelligible, then said to Tomas, "Your bird roused him. Landed on his chest and took his hair in its beak and pulled. By the gods *pulled.*" He held Lir's arm and said a rushed phrase in a language throatier and harsher than Elvish. Chest heaving, Lir stared at the captain with round startled eyes.

It was Nissyen's reaction that made Tomas reluctantly let go of Moira. The sylph's assumed indolence gone, bolt upright on the table, its lips moving soundlessly and its eyes full of feverish light, it was staring at Lir. Like a child with a new toy, thought Tomas; what was it thinking? Unnerved, he headed for the table before the sylph could leap from it and cut a caper or something worse. Nissyen didn't stir.

Do nothing to startle Lir, Tomas advised.

No need! Memory was brilliant.

Eerie yellow bird-gaze trained upon Lir and Jared, Memory was perched calmly on the back of the couch. The two Elves were deep in conversation now, that same thick liquid lilting language pouring from them both. A ridge of the coarse dark hair along Lir's spine was bristling.

Jared turned to Tomas. "He has bruises but says he'll mend quickly. Some of it was shock from the branch striking him when he was exhausted." His expression was grave. "He can find Fraine nowhere in Elfland, he tells me."

Lir nodded. "Long I searched for her." His voice was low and faintly sing-song, with vibrato undernotes that Tomas found pleasant and an accent that he couldn't place.

"Beyond your borders, she must be," said Lir, including Moira in his glance. "Else I could have found her." Suddenly his eyes and nostrils flared; his pupils narrowed to slits. Ignoring Jared's offered arm, he jumped to his feet and faced the main room's open door and the corridor that led to the rest of the palace.

Catching a familiar stench, Tomas turned just in time to see the first slight, brown-skinned winged Elf sail through the doorway, precisely level with the watchful face of the door knocker. Two of her kin followed, then another eight or ten. They all had snarled black hair, disproportionately long arms and legs, pine-green whiteless eyes and not a stitch of clothing. Parcae, a troop of thirteen, and just as rank as before. Nonetheless he would always welcome the sight of them; they'd kept Moira from dying in childbirth.

Women and men formed this troop. It was the first time that Tomas had seen a male Parca. They weren't much taller than the women, though broader of chest and wingspan and heavier of bone. He shot a glance at Moira, who was wearing one of her more neutral expressions. Still, he thought she hadn't expected the Parcae. Neither had Jared and Aidan, who exchanged a puzzled glance. Both Nissyen and Lir were studying the newcomers intently, while the ravens looked much as they always did. Aubrey, to Tomas's surprise, appeared almost resigned.

The foremost Parca was gazing expectantly up at Tomas, who still couldn't tell them apart from one another. "Tallah?" he ventured. He'd guessed well, for she beamed and nodded. As if at a signal, moving in unison, the other twelve Parcae chose that moment to sit cross-legged on the rug. They seemed ill at ease. After a few seconds he realized why: they'd left their wings half unfurled, as though prepared to take off again at any moment.

Pointing at Lir and the ravens, Tallah chirped a few words. Moira shook her head and pronounced three syllables.

Tallah frowned, chittered something else. That was when, to Tomas's eyes, the air in the room shifted, thickened, filled with oscillating specks that slowly began to swirl. An episode of his Sight, and a powerful one. The images that could follow might well be so strong that they'd temporarily blot out the room for him. Light-headed, he took a step or two towards the couch and reached as casually as he could for its back. Without interrupting her conversation with Tallah, Moira shot him an acute glance; she knew what was happening.

What do you See? asked Nissyen in mind-speech.

Nothing yet.

Nor did he, but the specks before his eyes had stretched themselves into small dots and ellipses and were all streaming in the same direction now. Streaming towards Lir who was still seated on the sofa, his face alight with curiosity, dividing his attention between Jared and Tallah. Lir's skin began to emit a coppery glow that Tomas felt sure was visible to no one else, and his gaze was equally luminous.

Tomas had just time to wonder why the images hadn't yet arrived, when what came in their stead was an overwhelming certainty. He knew what must happen next, what he should say and, in detail, what he must persuade the others to do—but not what the end would be. The final result was as clouded as if the third Norn, Skuld, blocked his Sight.

He moved to the center of the room, where he could watch the Elves and Nissyen and the ravens all at once. He felt balanced and agile and not light-headed at all; that had passed when the knowledge came. Instead he'd rarely been more calm.

After tilting her head to one side and surveying him thoughtfully, Tallah furled her wings and followed him. The rest of the Parcae remained seated on the rug, while the other Elves all stayed where they were: Aidan and Jared on the sofa with Lir; and Aubrey with Moira close to one of the armchairs near the door. Only Nissyen and Thought moved, the sylph to lean on the back of the couch next to Memory, and Thought to join the two of them. Lir spared the ravens and the Elemental an uneasy glance, then returned his attention to Tomas.

"Fraine is the key," began Tomas. "Lir, I ask you to accept a task. Not merely at my behest, but for all of us."

Lir rose. "What task is that?" Behind his back, Aidan gave Jared an intent look and the slightest of nods; perhaps Aidan's own Sight had spoken.

"Find Fraine. In Midgard or the 'tweenlands."

Lir was motionless. Shadows began to gather in the round lustrous eyes fixed unblinkingly upon Tomas, while the copper tint kept radiating from the tall Elf's face and hands and the muscles on his torso.

"I believe your golden lady knows where Fraine is. She might lend you aid."

Silence, taut and weighted. Then, slowly, "You have Seen the Lady, my lord?"

"No visions. Knowledge. That is also the Sight."

Lir's eyes narrowed. He looked at Aidan and Jared, who nodded, then at Moira. Her chin held high, she regarded Lir steadily. A scant second later he dropped his gaze and turned back to Tomas. "I will hunt for your daughter. Where should I begin?"

"Midgard. Before the way is closed to you."

"How shall I go there?"

Tomas pointed at Tallah. "She'll guide you."

Moira said a few words to Tallah. Glancing from Tomas to Lir, the Parca twitched her wings once and nodded. Mutters rose from her kin. Lir was studying them, with some strain about his eyes that revealed the effort it cost him to keep his expression as composed as it was.

"Tallah and no more than two other Parcae, if she wishes it," said Tomas. "Aidan, will you track their progress for us as far as you're able?"

Aidan murmured an assent. Lir flashed Tomas what might have been a grateful look; so did Jared.

Moira was translating again. A few of the Parcae scowled, one or two leaned forward eagerly, and the others developed a sudden fascination with the carpet. None of them said anything till Tallah made a brief speech, which earned her three protests, one gusty sigh of relief and a muffled hiss. Something—the hiss, Tomas supposed—provoked a shower of rebuke from the others. In a trice all the Parcae had jumped to their feet and were quarrelling.

There were no sides or factions to the squabble, at least none that Tomas could see. It looked completely random and sounded like a flock of rioting starlings; the volume was deafening. Wings were unfurled and batted, claw-tips brandished. Once someone reached for the pouch of stones that hung from her chest but was shouted down by the others. Finally, abandoning Tomas and her dignity, Tallah waded into their midst.

Nissyen, eyes alight, bounded to the edge of the dispute to listen. The sylph had made progress learning the Parcae's language; soon it spoke to them in their own tongue. From the way Moira's eyes widened and her brows lifted, the words were intelligible, but the Parcae ignored them. Catching Moira's reaction, the sylph's expression changed from mild consternation to intrigued reassessment so quickly that for an instant Tomas wanted to grin. One of the Parcae women was jumping up and down and caterwauling now. Tomas glanced aside only to look straight at the pooka, who was trying so hard not to laugh that his long bony face was twitching. Their eyes met; Aubrey's lips trembled, and a tiny high-pitched whistling sound escaped him.

Tallah chose that moment to bellow something at the top of her lungs. With shocked looks, as if they'd been slapped, the Parcae fell silent. After giving her kin a prolonged scathing look, during which all but one of them sat down, Tallah folded her wings, looked at Moira and uttered a few formal phrases. To Nissyen she paid no attention at all, though the sylph had clearly followed the gist of the argument and its resolution as least as well as Moira had.

"Tallah and Gavin will accompany Lir," said Moira, as unruffled as if she were ordering supper. The Parca standing beside Tallah made Lir a small bow.

"My thanks," said Lir, missing a beat.

Just then a small gleeful choking noise came from the pooka and he bolted for the kitchen, where they could hear him thunderously opening and shutting a series of cupboard doors, as if to muffle other sounds. With his eyes downcast and the hint of a quiver about the corners of his mouth, he returned with a pitcher, mugs, and a damp cloth which he handed to Lir.

Tomas said quietly, "Owein must also be found. But Fraine first. Fraine is the key."

As Lir began swabbing the blood from his temple, Jared's gaze flickered towards the ravens.

"We have need of Thought and Memory here," Tomas continued smoothly. "They can tell us the whereabouts of Evan's Guards, and the state of the palace and the rest of Elfland." And where Lir had gone, should Aidan lose track of him—but that Tomas didn't say. Nor did he mention that he'd part from the ravens only if Lir's errand failed, and as a last resort. Odin had sent the birds through the nine worlds daily, but Odin was a god, not a mortal Mage at a disadvantage among the Elves.

He turned to Lir. "Warn Fraine of Loki and bring her to me. She'll know where Owein is." Next came the part where Tomas's certainty faltered and with it his hopes, but that he would hide if he could. Slowly, meeting each pair of eyes, he looked at the assembled Elves and the sylph. "Together, we'll find a way to free him." He also wanted the ravens with him for any advice they could give about Owein's predicament. Besides, who among Tomas's allies could better predict how Loki might behave?

Aubrey cleared his throat.

"Speak," said Tomas courteously.

"Loki wants nothing more than for Fraine to be found. Won't he be prying and sneaking about? Won't he follow Lir back to us?"

"We won't be here," said Tomas. "Not in these rooms."

"Where, then?"

He drew breath, met Moira's eyes. "In the Parcae-wood," she said quietly—they'd had the same idea. "It would be more difficult for Loki to trespass unnoticed there than anywhere else in Faerie, and for Evan's spies, too."

But would the Parcae be willing to play host? Her face serene, Moira said something to Tallah and got an enthusiastic nod. A lump of tension in Tomas's throat began to dissolve. He looked at Jared, who was stifling a frown. "You're wishing your Guards could communicate with the Parcae."

"That I am," said Jared unemotionally.

"A pair of your sentries can mind-link with a pair of theirs." This part Tomas had also Seen, and in detail. "Tell the rest to bring Runestones and charcoal, and post themselves with the Parcae along the border of the wood, two by two. Have them stand where they can scratch out pictures in the dirt or draw on stone with charcoal. At the end of each watch, they should erase anything they've written." He turned to Aubrey. "Find all the water-Elves you can trust, and send two to every pair of Guard and Parca.

Lir, your kin will move one by one among all the sentries. Nissyen—"

"Two of our sylphs will join each patrol, and more sylphs travel among them," said Nissyen, its eyes gleaming. *The border of the Parcae-wood shifts, my Mage, all the more so when heavily guarded. Someone should track its changes and inform your sentries where to follow the border.*

Can you do so?

I would be honored.

"Nissyen will coordinate the sentries' movements," said Tomas. Jared's face closed. "Because," Tomas continued, "Nissyen can easily follow the shifts in the border of the Parcae-wood, and send sylphs to tell each patrol where to go next."

Jared still looked as though he were trying not to protest. As if to reason with him, Nissyen began to speak, but stopped when Tomas caught its eye. Moira was explaining something to the Parcae. A few of them shot Nissyen a glance of approval, but Tallah was studying Jared's expression. Suddenly she grabbed another Parca by the wrist, marched over to the captain, held out her kinswoman's small hairy hand and chittered insistently. Jared's jaw tightened, but he took the Parca's hand in his and closed his eyes.

"She's suggesting," said Jared with a pucker about his mouth, "that I remain with Nissyen to order the defense. In the heart of the Parcae-wood, in the great platform in the—" He released the little Elf's hand and turned to Tomas. "It looks like a great ugly birds' nest at the top of an oak, my lord, and they want you and Moira and Aidan up there, too. Whether it can hold all of us and Fraine and Lir as well—"

"It can," said Moira curtly. "I've been there." She came to Tomas's side and gestured for silence. "Save for the Guards, we Elves seldom join together for a common purpose," she began. "It has been more our wont to act in twos and threes, with few words and less trust exchanged." Her face was serious. "Why we adopted that practice is easy to see, for who cannot lie may avoid speech and inconvenient questions. Lately I have thought that in doing so, we run too great a risk of working against one another unwittingly." A glance at Tomas. "I believe that this ordering of a defense is well-advised, however new to us." She had the Elves' full attention; only the Parcae looked puzzled. "Are there any further suggestions?"

Jared cleared his throat. "I would not have anyone left in trance. We may need to act swiftly."

"Agreed," Moira told him.

"If we see Loki," asked the pooka, a crease between his brows, "do we grant him passage?"

"Send him to me," said Tomas. "He'd cause too much harm if you try to stop him, not that you could."

Aubrey's face looked pinched. "What if he wants speech with one of us?"

"Listen and report. Don't negotiate."

"Over the twins?"

"Over anything." Moira's eyes were flinty. "It's well that's been asked, and that all here have heard the answer. Loki may propose every manner of bargain, but I'll have none of them. What he wants is our exile from Midgard, completely and irrevocably. That would mean its destruction and ours." She raked her hands through her hair. "The Christians are in the ascendancy there since Asgard fell, and they want what Loki wants: our expulsion from Midgard. I will not haggle with him, and I will bargain with neither of them."

This may not be well-advised— began Nissyen.

Later, said Tomas peremptorily, watching Moira.

Her hands were clenched at her sides. "We will find Owein and finish the bridge. Is that clear?"

One by one, the Elves nodded, though none of them looked any more confident of the outcome than Tomas felt.

CHAPTER THIRTY-SEVEN: MIDDLE GROUND

The 'tweenlands

When pain and fatigue at last pushed Owein over the border of consciousness, Loki scooped up a small soapstone box from the ground near Owein's limp hand, summoned six groveling and incandescent salamanders to guard him, and left, scowling. Fraine knew neither why nor where Loki had gone. Would he return? Had she failed to protect Owein? He was unconscious, but still in his body. For how long? If she'd been in any form but this incorporeal awareness, she would have taken Owein and fled, even if it meant dragging him.

"Can you bring him to me, Lady?" she asked Freya. "I cannot touch him as I am now."

"Support and counsel. Shielding and transport between the worlds. No more can I offer."

"Why not?" Fraine asked as respectfully as she could. She was desperate.

"The Ørlög limits us all," said Caraid patiently.

"Better to remain as you are and tell Owein we are giving aid. Do not reveal yourself to the salamanders."

Fraine's consciousness was nowhere near her body; she was suspended in the air above Owein's head. Still, she felt a heaviness, a constriction, and the cord linking her to her body gave a twitch from the region closest to her chest. Owein was there, directly below her, and Loki was gone. There might be no better opportunity to fetch him away. "How do you know the Ørlög prevents us?"

There was a pause before Caraid said haltingly, "The dead know many things, and I was a Seer. I can See more of the Norns' weaving now, and who is bound and loosed by it."

Could she see Skuld, who'd recited the Ørlög at the twins' name-fastening? Rebellion rose in Fraine, arguments, protests. It was neither a goddess nor a dead Seer nor a Norn who lay crumpled at the salamanders' glowing cloven feet. It was Owein.

"Speak to him," Freya's voice was gentle, more than a bit sad, and infinitely compassionate. *"He wakens enough to hear you."*

Fraine aimed a current of attention and warning at her brother. More diffuse and warmer than a tendril extended from her shield, it felt a little like fanning the air in his direction, and made the skin of her forehead tingle. "Owein," she thought at him. "Don't let on that you've heard me. I'm sending you strength, and we are aided by Freya." She feared that any mention of Caraid might upset or startle him enough that his reaction would show.

He made Fraine no answer. He was curled on his side, knees drawn towards his chest, his half of the Gebo Rune lying on its cord near his chin. His breathing was ragged. Perhaps he wasn't sufficiently conscious to register her words. She built a mental picture of the other half of the Gebo Rune, the half she wore which completed his, and projected it at him as strongly as she could.

Owein's fingers flexed. Fraine waited. His hand crept feebly towards the half-Rune at his throat, stopped, moved again.

"Don't let your guards see you're awake," Fraine told him, still concentrating on the Rune's image. "Loki left six salamanders with you."

Owein lay motionless. Then she heard him, feebly, in her mind. "Fraine. Where are you?"

"Tranced. My body's with Freya in the 'tweenlands. We're sending you strength."

"Knew you'd come."

His mind-voice was thready and faint, but the trust in it rang out so powerfully that for a moment Fraine couldn't speak. *She* had known no such thing.

"Loki?" asked Owein.

"Gone. He could reappear any moment."

"So he could." Freya's voice was so soft that for an instant Fraine wasn't sure she had heard it. She was certain that Owein had not. *"He is in Elfland. He told Tomas to send you to him, Fraine, so that you and Owein could topple the bridge, or Owein would be killed."*

Fraine decided not to relay that threat to her brother, though it was likely he already knew of it.

"Caraid says she must speak to you before Loki returns."

"Rest," Fraine told her twin. "Gather strength."

"'Tilda?" he asked.

"She lives."

A wave of relief, then remorse. "Bridge...all down but the points. Forgive me. He was killing her—"

"Hush," said Fraine gently. "The points stand, and Matilda lives." Putting conviction she didn't feel into her mind-voice. "We'll find a way through this. Now rest."

Abruptly, Fraine was back in her body, her stomach heaving at the scent of her companion. Caraid's entire body was swollen. Patches of the Seer's skin, green and yellow and purple, were sloughing off, and the rest of it was approaching a state that wasn't entirely solid. Caraid lay on her back at Freya's feet. Stooping over the Seer, the goddess looked her full in the face, sorrowfully, tenderly, and stroked what was left of her hair with a gleaming hand. "My time grows short," Caraid said thickly.

"Remember the Ørlög."

"How can that help? Fraine was shaking. She wanted to go back into trance, back to Owein, away from what passed for a second death long overdue.

"Say it," Caraid mumbled. "The Ørlög."

Fraine looked despairingly at Freya, who gave her a nod and such an understanding glance that she felt shamed. She recited:

In the midst of darkness, light;
In the midst of death, life;
In the midst of chaos, order.

In the midst of order, chaos;
In the midst of life, death;
In the midst of light, darkness.

Thus has it ever been,
Thus is it now, and
Thus shall it always be.

"Think," said the Seer with an effort. "The Ørlög. The earth."

Freya's earth, that Fraine had given to Simon? Or the earth of all Midgard? Or of Elfland for that matter, where she wished she and Owein were now, wished it so hard and so bitterly that tears burned behind her eyes. She might never see Elfland again. She might be stranded in the 'tweenlands. She could die here and so could Owein. Without the bridge, according to the prophecy that had predicted the twins' birth, Midgard and Elfland would eventually die as well. Without the bridge the green of Midgard would fade, the earth wither, the streams run dry and poison fill the air. Mortals would have to hide from the Sun, the glory and anchor of Midgard, and perhaps even from the Moon that sailed its starred and orderly skies.

"I have to get Owein away from him," blurted Fraine. She'd no time to puzzle over the Ørlög. "Whatever I must offer. Whatever I must do." Would Loki take her instead? But if he killed either twin, the bridge would never be completely destroyed.

"Yes," said Caraid all but inaudibly. "Offer him."

Offer him what? Tomas and Moira wanted no compromise with either Loki or the Christians. No bargains, no concessions, partial or otherwise. Fraine touched the half-Rune at her throat, then pressed her fingertips to her temples and tried to concentrate.

What did Loki want? Total rulership of a Midgard utterly severed from Elfland. Chaos.

What did the Elves want? Loki expelled or powerless in a Midgard fully linked to Elfland. Order, of a kind.

In the midst of order, chaos. In the midst of chaos, order. Fraine put her head in her hands to block out the half-light of the 'tweenlands. She needed darkness to think clearly.

At long last it came to her, sitting hunched over with her eyes squeezed shut, sitting in the self-imposed darkness of her closed eyelids. *In the midst of darkness, light. In the midst of light, darkness.* Just as she needed darkness to think clearly, to attain clarity, the Ørlög meant that neither darkness nor light could hold undisputed sway in any of the nine worlds. It spoke of the vast and all-encompassing *balance* between light and darkness—and of the equally tortuous dance between life and death, between order and chaos.

Neither Loki nor her parents could have it all one way or the other. Moira might refuse to compromise, yet compromise was her only hope. Balance. The intricate and enigmatic whole described by the Ørlög, where nothing was either wholly evil or wholly good.

It was too great a truth for Fraine to compass. Her head ached. She laid her hand against Caraid's hair and met the Seer's dimming blue eyes. "My thanks," whispered Fraine. "You have shown me." *In the midst of death, life.* She blinked back tears. Caraid wanted to keep Tomas's children alive so much that she'd endured imprisonment in a rotting body long after she should have been at peace with Freya, or with another of the goddess's faces, one that ruled love. "Now I know why Freya helped you."

Power struck Fraine like heat, like the Sun, radiating from Freya, pulsing like a current of balmy air. Fraine glanced up, expecting to see the goddess's head bent towards her and Caraid. Instead the autumnal deity whom Fraine had once seen overshadowing Freya, a tall and powerfully built woman in late middle years, was reaching for the Seer. Her eyes were Freya's eyes: hazel, gleaming, and so full of warmth that Fraine felt buoyed and comforted.

She sank onto her heels and reverently watched Caraid being gathered into the bare brown arms. A sweep of greying ruddy hair, twined with leaves of yellow and gold, trailed over the goddess's strong hands and brushed Caraid's face. Where it touched the Seer, her skin began to smooth, the mottled hues and the swelling to ebb away. Slowly a new tint, very pale but nonetheless more human than corpse-like, crept across Caraid's face, her neck, her limbs. The Seer's eyes filled with tears of their own, of release rather than grief—and of leave-taking.

"Don't go," stammered Fraine.

"You have the falcon cape, my daughter." The goddess got to Her feet, holding Caraid. "*The healers in Wessex have my earth. And your next task*

is known to you."

But it wasn't, not entirely. Fraine only guessed, and now they were leaving her to act alone. She stood; she was trembling.

The goddess's hair was turning silver. *"Fraine,"* She said quietly, though Her voice was as full and resonant as before. *"Stranger, your mother named you. Stranger to all worlds, yet you see them clearly."* She held Fraine's gaze. *"Remember the Ørlög: a partial victory may not be wholly a loss. And remember Me."*

"I love you both." Fraine had not planned to say those words, had said them to only a very few. She was glad that she'd uttered them now. She fell to her knees. "Stay," she pleaded. "Or take me with you and help Owein from wherever you're bound."

"*Not yet*," said the goddess. *"Your road does not end here."*

Then, smiling, one hand raised in benediction, She and Caraid slowly faded from view. When they were completely gone, the statue of Hecate had disappeared along with them.

With Freya's departure, Fraine lost her sense of Owein again. Her first task was finding Loki, who knew Owein's whereabouts. She could go into trance again, but might she be too vulnerable with no one to watch over her body? She would try to use her Sight while fully alert.

After a prolonged effort she gave up, frowning. She couldn't find Loki. Did that mean he was with Owein, that he'd returned from Elfland? She knew where Elfland was, much as she could sense the direction of the Sun in Midgard: down a narrow glittering track that rolled away from where the statue had been. Elfland wasn't in sight, although Tomas told her that he could see part of it from Hecate's crossroads when he first came to them. When she turned her attention that way, she could sense that Elfland's location wasn't stable. There were small shifts in its position, always away from her and the other eight worlds.

She knew where Niflheim was too, down another track, a wide and easy and inviting one. No path led to Midgard from the crossroads, but she could have pointed straight to it, at a forty-five degree angle above and to the right of where she sat. She couldn't see any of the points of the bridge, though she sensed where all of them lay.

She'd never understood how the 'tweenlands were structured. Chambered like a wasps' nest, perhaps. And not fixed in position: they seemed to move about in space rather as the Parcae-wood did in Faerie. Perhaps the 'tweenlands moved about in time as well, and Loki was still in Elfland. Or perhaps he'd returned and was with Owein again now.

With that thought an icicle took form in Fraine's chest. She put on Freya's falcon cape, crossed her arms and gripped her elbows. But the cold that she felt wasn't physical, and she grew no warmer. There must be a way to find Loki before he began pounding at Owein again.

She had resources: she could call on Freya and be sent strength as promised, although she suspected the goddess would not reappear. Another advantage was Loki's ignorance: he didn't know that Fraine was in the 'tweenlands, nor her part in strengthening Owein's resistance. Beyond needing her to destroy the bridge, Loki probably considered her irrelevant. He might underestimate her. And he'd not kill her any more than he'd kill Owein; both twins were needed to raze the bridge.

If Loki couldn't force Owein from his body, then likely as not he couldn't force her either. Still, he'd attack her if he could, try to restrain her, perhaps use one twin to bribe the other, as he was using Owein to pressure Tomas to find her. Fraine had to provoke Loki's curiosity, make him eager to talk with her before he tried any sort of attempt upon her person. Or she had to make herself seem a difficult target, not one to be attacked before taking her measure.

She rubbed her hands together, frowned at them. What or who might give Loki pause? She'd not yet learned to shapeshift, so she couldn't appear as Moira or Hecate or Freya. She huddled into the falcon cloak and pulled up the hood. It might not warm her but it was comforting, and it reminded her of Freya.

The cloak. The cloak itself was a resource.

Fraine stared at the feathers draping her legs. Loki would recognize it; he'd borrowed it at least once, according to Tomas. Never would he mistake Fraine for Freya, but he'd know that with the cloak she had the goddess's protection. And while Freya wielded less power and Loki more than they'd once had, he might not dismiss Her out of hand. At the very least he'd have a few questions for Fraine about Her.

Fraine stood and closed her eyes. From her reinforced shield she sent a current of energy and swept it about her in a great circle. It seemed silver-blue to her inner vision, fading to grey in the distance, while the effort of extending its circumference made beads of sweat start on her brow.

She might be mad, but she was looking for Loki. She, Fraine, the halfbreed mortal. Feeling her unpracticed youth, tenuous maturity and uncertain strength, most of all feeling naked bereft of her twin, she had nevertheless begun. She might have the support of a goddess and the full weight of the Ørlög behind her, but she'd never been more afraid.

Her nerves were alive, her heart thudding, her palms damp. Breathe, she reminded herself. Everything that she sensed in that long searching sweep felt different now, sharper, more charged with menace. With her first deep inhalation came a mental image of the nine worlds with the 'tweenlands both enfolding and penetrating them, as if the worlds were substance and the 'tweenlands no more than air. At first the image was small, as if seen from a great distance, then slowly began creeping closer.

With her stomach in knots, she made herself imagine Loki as Owein had described him: a frail-looking young man, bonelessly supple, with ginger hair and malevolent smoldering hazel eyes. Loki. Where was he?

She'd begun seeing the points of the bridge now, interspersed among the nine worlds, sending out fading streamers of colored light where they'd once been partially connected. Where among them might Loki be?

She was no longer cold. Her heart was racing, her throat parched. She must keep her wits about her. She drew herself to her full height and lifted her chin. Slowing her respiration, she touched the Rune at her throat and thought, briefly, of Owein. She should focus on Loki and Loki alone.

At last she saw, in profile, a morbidly white face crowned with a reddish shock of hair, narrow at the temples, pointed at the chin, with sharp features and a thin compressed mouth. A weasel's face, nervy and suspicious and cunning. When the head turned, Fraine caught her breath at the sight of those flawed-amber eyes, sullen and flaring and shallow-lidded, with pupils of slightly different sizes. Loki knew someone was looking for him.

For an instant she cowered away, tried to block out the vision. Then she steeled herself. Where was he? If she knew, she would go there.

No sooner had the thought formed in her mind than her feet left the packed surface where she stood. She was hovering; she was flying, and she'd intended nothing of the sort. It must be the cape's doing. Air rushed past her face, fanning the falcon feathers, billowing the cloak out behind her. She clutched at it, gasping. She wasn't horizontal, but she was leaning forward as if into a hard wind, and all the while the nine worlds in the image were looming closer and larger. Then one of them—Jötunheim, the giant's realm?—was towering over her in a whirl of color and was gone. One of the bridge's eight points sailed past her head, then another, and through it all she saw Loki's face, his head tilted to one side, his expression alert.

Then she could see his whole body. She was approaching him more rapidly than she'd ever traveled. From the glittering and hard-packed surface beneath his feet, he was in the 'tweenlands. He took a few steps forward, stopped, peered overhead, glanced behind him, then turned back, slowly and thoughtfully, to face Fraine's oncoming trajectory, lips pursed and hands on his hips. Would she stop when she reached him?

To Loki and no farther, she thought, glancing down at the cape. Stop there. I would speak with him.

He had seen her. His eyes widened, narrowed, then went bland and innocent. The hardness, the tension melted from his body. His shoulders stooped as if in defeat; his hands hung loose and purposeless at his sides. The sizzling eyes were dull now, half veiled by drooping eyelids.

So fast was his transformation from incendiary schemer to this wreck and shambles of a man that Fraine was left shaken and doubly suspicious. Before she knew it she'd floated neatly to earth three paces before him, where she stood for a moment, reinforcing her shield and hoping her heartbeat would return to normal. When it didn't, she let the cape's hood fall back, revealing her face.

Loki blinked like a halfwit, but she thought she saw the barest flash of recognition at the back of his eyes. "Hullo," he said after a moment. "Who might you be?"

"You know who I am," she said. Calmly, even a trifle carelessly, or so she hoped. He had no scent, which would make reading him far more difficult. "And I know you, Loki."

He smiled, then made her a dancer's bow. When he straightened up, a chill threaded its way down Fraine's spine. He stood squarely now, shoulders down and back, hands open and relaxed. There was nothing but friendly curiosity in his face. The demented shimmer in his eyes was gone; they looked as human as Linley's honest gaze. "I'm delighted we've met at last," said Loki, all warmth. "A most dramatic entrance, I might add. Tell me, where did you find that cape?"

"That you also know."

Another smile. Conceding a point. "Is Freya well?"

"I believe so."

The barest flicker of ill will in the hazel eyes, yet it was enough to close a fist around Fraine's ribs, and her palms felt slick.

"Still bedding her twin brother, is she?" asked Loki in precisely the same tone as before.

"I wouldn't know," said Fraine, tensing.

"Oh, I think you could tell me quite a lot about twins." The voice was low and insinuating now. For a long moment he studied her face. "You have one yourself. Might you know where he is?"

"Wherever you left him," she said. "That's why I've come."

"Is it, now?" One corner of Loki's mouth lifted slightly, and an anticipatory gleam crept into his eyes. "Go on, my dear. Don't let me stop you."

He was toying with her. He thought he had her precisely where he wanted her, and that she and Owein were doomed. For a moment Fraine heard nothing but the beat of her blood in her ears. Her heart gave a twisted and painful thud, then another. She felt her breath growing fast and shallow, strove to deepen it. Something was wrong with the ground, too. It was tilting.

"Feeling light-headed?" asked Loki sweetly. "One does travel fast in that cape. I well remember." He dropped nimbly to a sitting position. "Now that you've come all this way, have a seat and tell me about it."

Awkwardly, fighting nausea and a touch of dizziness, Fraine joined him. Loki was watching her, smiling to himself. She felt galled by a hint of smugness in his expression, as if he'd already won a round. When he made a show of glancing aside, as if allowing her time to recover, she had just enough presence of mind to use her Sight on him. She dared call on it only for an instant, but long enough to spot the current of roiling energy that flowed from him, a small and furiously whirling funnel like a lunatic tornado. It seemed to be caroming off her shield for the most part, yet the glimpse of it increased her confusion.

The suffocating sensation in her chest was her own fear, but the confusion came from Loki's attempt to unsettle her. Some part of that attempt was affecting her, shield or not. He was more powerful than a mortal, more powerful than an Elf: he was nearly a god. Tomas had once said it was difficult to think clearly in Loki's presence. She should have remembered that.

She dug her fingernails into her palms as hard as she could. The pain seemed to clear her mind a bit, the pain or the anger. But she should feign bewilderment as long as she could.

"You've come about Owein?" Loki prompted. Then, when she said nothing, "What of him?"

"Let him go," she blurted after a few seconds, as if she had trouble speaking.

Sadly, the hazel eyes incandescent, Loki shook his head. "No, my dear, that I shan't do. But I'd gladly take you to him. You have only to ask."

She was so tempted that she sank her nails even deeper into her palms, and felt the skin stinging. "Not yet," she whispered.

The ginger eyebrows quirked upwards. "Why not?" Then, in the softest of voices, "You want to see him. Don't you?"

Fraine tried to give him a level stare, then shifted her gaze ever so slightly when she realized that looking him straight in the eyes might make her more dizzy.

"What has to happen first?" demanded Loki.

She blinked. She'd not seen that question coming.

"You must have some bargain in mind," he said expansively. "It's in your blood; you're more than half Elf. They haggle like dwarves, every last one of them." A thin giggle as he studied her. "Though it sits ill with them when I say so. They tell only the truth, your relations, but they've no end of trouble hearing it." He was grinning. "What do you want? And what will you give me for it?" He leaned forward. "That cape, for example?"

Fraine risked a glance at him, swift and direct. He was watching her, his hands on his knees and his face intent, but there was no tension in his expression. Only enjoyment and anticipation. And still more certainty, a satisfied gleam in his eyes, a slight twist to his smile.

Whereas she was hard pressed to breathe, and whenever the thought of Owein tugged at her, it was all she could do to shove it aside. She dared not let it distract her or she might start weeping, might agree to any terms Loki offered. And it was she who should be offering terms, and have the last word. For inspiration she thought of Moira. At first she intended to school her face to neutrality and put ice in her voice. Just in time she remembered that it was more to her advantage if Loki underestimated her.

"You have Owein," she said shakily. It was easy to shudder. "It's more a matter of what you want."

"I?" A hand laid on his chest, a pause of theatrical length. "I want you and your brother to destroy the bridge. Completely."

"Why is that?" Her head down, her voice breaking. She'd overdone it; Loki patted her knee in mock reassurance, and she recoiled from the burning touch.

"Because I would become the only Power in Midgard," he said with elaborate patience. "If its link to Elfland is severed, the Elves and their magic will no longer go there."

"But they don't worship you there. Asgard's fallen, and mortals hardly know of you outside of the North."

His face hardened. "That will change. The Christians are on the rise."

When she dared another glance at him, he was staring off to his right, where she saw nothing but the trackless-grey landscape that formed most of the 'tweenlands.

"They have only one god, weak enough to get himself executed. He has an enemy named Lucifer. A fallen angel, a bright shining being. He rules their Niflheim. They even call it Hell." A chuckle. "Named after my daughter. She'll be gratified. Though their Hell is fiery, not cold." His grin was hot with scorn. "I fit the part, don't you think? In most ways. And the others hardly matter. Not to me." An odd, contracted pause, during which he watched her beneath his eyelids. "But that I would be the only Power in Midgard if the Elves are exiled from it—that matters to me. A great deal."

A hand, white and spindly and unbelievably strong, grabbed Fraine's chin, wrenched her head up and forced her to meet his gaze. It was scalding. Another wave of dizziness washed over her, and close on its heels a hard dry terror that made her squeeze her eyes shut and clench her fists.

"We can bargain as long as you like. I've nothing to lose. And now, my very dear, what do *you* want?"

"Can't speak," she managed to gasp. Her chin was still gripped in that burning hand, her head lifted, her neck strained to an unnatural angle.

"Your pardon," he snapped, releasing her.

She rubbed the base of her skull. Like some noxious cloud of smoke, the terror was still there, in her lungs, in her heart, in her throat. But not in her mind: another force was flowing into it, steadying her. She'd no energy to spare wondering, but she thought that the calm came from Freya.

"Are you sure," she heard herself saying, "that Christianity is on the rise in Midgard? Asgard may have fallen and Midgard be the pivot world now, but the Norse still worship the Aesir and the Vanir."

He merely looked at her. Contemptuously. Humoring her. Because, she suddenly realized, the longer he waited to break her and Owein to his will, the greater their humiliation would be and the more he'd enjoy it.

"The Celtic lands have their own gods," she said as steadily as she could. "Gods who were old before the Christian one was born. With enough belief in them that they've not dwindled any more than the Elves have."

He shrugged.

"Can you uproot beliefs that are already there? Might it not be easier to use them instead?"

Loki's eyes flared. "Use them? I'm to be the only Power in Midgard."

He might kill her in a fit of pique, and Owein after her. But it was time to call upon what she'd learned, what Caraid had shown her. "There is a higher Power than the Aesir and the Elves and the Celtic gods put together. There always will be," said Fraine as firmly and coolly as she could, drawing herself upright. "It is the Ørlög. And you are as subject to it as every other being in the nine worlds."

Loki stared at her for three seconds, then started to laugh. "You do that very well," he said. "Quite the priestess you are. Pray go on." He was sputtering. "I can't recall when I was last so amused."

"The Ørlög," said Fraine. Her voice cracked; she ignored it. "The Ørlög says that nothing is all one way or the other. 'In the midst of light, darkness. In the midst of darkness, light.' You cannot be the only Power in Midgard or anywhere. No one can."

He was chuckling, a resonant full-bellied laugh.

"Think," she said. "You can't eradicate the older gods and their worship, be they Odin or Dana or the Elves. Not entirely, and the harder you try the stronger they'll become. 'In the midst of order, chaos.'"

Now she had his attention. She could tell by the slight stiffening of his back and the momentary shifting of his eyes, though he was still smiling.

"How can you impose Christianity and rule as Lucifer without using the older gods? Not expelling them."

"Using them," Loki drawled. He assumed a bored expression. "How might I do that? Theoretically, mind you."

"The old faiths mark eight festivals in the mortal year," she said. "And the eight points of the bridge correspond to them."

"Yes?" he asked politely—and attacked Fraine's shield.

She'd not expected it. She should have. But that thought was lost before the onslaught at her barriers. It came from everywhere at once, pressing and hammering at the same time, and with it a torrent of ill will rolled over her like an avalanche. In a trice she was kneeling with her head between her knees, gasping, clutching the nape of her neck. *Freya,* she called desperately, silently. *Help me.*

No answer. The assault redoubled. Panting, without a particle of energy to spare to do so much as groan, Fraine kept her shield intact. She couldn't sense the aid that Freya was sending, but it must be there. Then she had no strength even for wondering. She could focus on nothing but her shield, holding it against that mountainous force bearing down upon it: her shield, her shield, her shield...

"—just like your brother," said Loki's disgusted voice from somewhere above her.

Fraine could hear again. The pounding had stopped.

"Speak to me. What were you saying?"

She didn't move. She wasn't sure that she could.

"Oh, get *up,*" said Loki, exasperated. "I might as well hear you out."

Cautiously, maintaining her shield, Fraine removed her hands from the base of her skull and lifted her head. Nothing happened. Slowly and carefully, she pressed her palms to the ground and began pushing herself upright.

"Shall I help you?" Sarcasm in his voice.

"No!" she gasped, sinking back on her heels. She fell to one side, righted herself.

One corner of his lower lip caught between his teeth, Loki was studying her. Reassessing her. The underestimation was over. Trembling, Fraine spared just enough energy from her shield to shift to a cross-legged position.

Loki sat down in front of her. "Finish," he said, pointing. "Present your case."

She eyed him, still catching her breath.

"Do you wish me to grow impatient?" he asked sweetly.

"The eight points of the bridge," she said in a rush, fear focusing her mind. "Return Owein to me unharmed, and we'll leave them standing and tear down the rest. Then the Elves will be able to enter Midgard only on the ancient feast days."

"I see no advantage in it," Loki said after a moment, his mouth hardening.

"If you try to bar the old faiths from Midgard completely, along with the Elves—" Fraine was braced for another attack, but none came. "They could undermine your rule sooner or later, for the Ørlög tells us that nothing's all one way or the other."

He was staring at her, arms folded, fuming.

"Those feast days mark the turning of Midgard's year, and mortals are attuned to them. Mortals feel them in their blood, like the seasons. So if the festivals become part of the Christian faith, it can grow all the stronger, and so can you." She had a hazy idea. "Especially at Samhain, perhaps, when the earth sleeps and the darkness rules."

Loki folded his arms.

Fraine heard herself say, "'In the midst of death, life.' The new builds on the old." She strove to hide her shock; it was as if someone else had spoken through her. Holding stone-still, she hoped her face was expressionless, and watched the glitter of a sly and expedient intelligence in Loki's eyes as he pondered.

"An intriguing premise," he said at last, then shot her a measuring look. "Elves could cross into Midgard on those eight days and no other? Likewise mortals into Elfland?"

She nodded.

"If I harm neither you nor Owein. That is your condition?"

"One of them."

"I might have known there were others." Loki's face darkened. "How can I know your word is good? And that you speak for the Elves?"

Fraine let out a breath. "How can I know that yours is?

He grinned, widely and condescendingly.

"When the cost would be death for Owein and me, which of the Elves would break such a truce? If we start rebuilding the rest of the bridge, nothing's to stop you from tracking us down."

"True," said Loki with a deprecating wave of his hand, as if dismissing a compliment, then rested his chin in his palm. "There's something you've not told me about this bargain. What are the Elves giving up?"

"Moira and Tomas want no compromise with you at all," said Fraine as calmly as she could. "Time and again they have said so." Here it came: the great bluff. "The prophecy says that a mortal Mage and his twin children can keep the worlds linked and Midgard green. If Owein and I don't complete the bridge, then Tomas can and will." She paused, letting her words register.

Loki stiffened almost imperceptibly. Then his face closed, his eyes turned secretive and brooding. He hated Tomas. That much was abundantly clear and Fraine knew the reason, that Tomas had bested him in the realm of the Sidhe. From the tension in Loki's posture and the way his hands were clenched in his lap, he wasn't eager to cross Tomas again, particularly not when he saw a far easier way to get almost all he wanted. She had always heard that Loki was lazy.

"Tomas can and will," she repeated, praying she was right. "Unless he knows you'll come after Owein and me if he does."

Loki gave her a sharp curious glance. "Tomas doesn't know you're here," he said slowly, as if tasting the words. As if it were a revelation, a welcome one. "And neither does Moira. Do they?"

Fraine shook her head.

"You've gone behind their backs. You've come on your own."

She nodded.

His face aglow, Loki regarded her. Approval of an act that might mortify Tomas was stamped on his every feature. More than approval: a sly and triumphant affection for Fraine herself. She felt sickened, as if something slimy had brushed against her.

"My very dear," said Loki, "I congratulate you. And Tomas. He's sired someone far beyond him."

Worse than sickened. Shamed.

"A moment longer and I could almost wish you were my daughter."

Shamed and soiled. The skin at the back of her neck tried to creep down between her shoulderblades. She closed her eyes briefly, maintaining her shield.

"Enough sentiment for the time being," Loki said briskly, sounding closer to a decision. Fraine's heart lurched. "Your other conditions?"

"That you let Matilda be healed."

"Allow me to be quite sure I understand your conditions," began Loki, studying her with a gleam in his eyes. "Your brother and Matilda live—" He was counting on his fingers. "You and Owein destroy all but the eight points of the bridge; there is no traffic between Elfland and Midgard except upon those eight feast days, and your parents abide by our agreement?"

She nodded.

"Done!" he said gleefully. "And Tomas has to stomach it." He spat into his left hand, grabbed hers and clasped it, and jumped to his feet while she clutched her scalded palm and gaped up at him. "Don't care to touch my hand? You might not have survived the mingling of our blood," he said, grinning, and blew her a kiss. Then he disappeared, wholly and instantaneously.

Fraine still didn't know where Owein was, nor if Loki would honor his end of the bargain. How could she keep hers if she couldn't find Owein? She wiped her left palm on her dress, then on the ground, but her hand kept tingling and its skin was pink and lightly blistered. Was Loki lying, and hot-footing it back to Owein at that moment? From the relief of one kind of dread, from the birth of a whole new score of worries and most of all from sheer exhaustion, Fraine stretched out full length, pillowed her head on the falcon cape, and let out a sob.

CHAPTER THIRTY-EIGHT: AN END TO THE DRIFTING

"Fraine."

A deep lilting voice close to her ear. She was dreaming. But her hand smarted, while at her shoulder there came a touch, warm but not burning, and curiously padded.

"Fraine? My lady?"

Another touch. And a smell, one she'd know anywhere, rank, earthy, leathery and unwashed. A Parca, a tired one.

Comforted at the thought of allies, Fraine blinked up into a pair of black slanting eyes in a worried masculine face. The face slowly smiled, revealing a double row of short white teeth. Not a Parca. Two teeth in the row above and two below were pointed and a bit longer than the others—he had fangs, albeit small ones. He was an Elf, with fawn-colored trousers, a pouch slung across his back, bare feet and a muscular chest covered with a wealth of dark hair. An Elf she knew: Lir, from the Inner Reaches.

When she said his name, she smelled the violets and rainwater of relief, mingled with the stench of the Parcae. Directly behind Lir stood two of the winged Elves, a man and a woman, shifting from foot to foot with impatience.

"Tallah," said Fraine. She didn't know the other one's name.

"Gavin," said Tallah, pointing to him.

"Can you sit, Fraine?" asked Lir. And, when she was upright, "Where is Owein?"

"I don't know," she said, choking back tears.

Lir gave her a compassionate look but said only, "We will find him. Come."

Before she could protest, she was being hoisted aloft in those long arms, and feeling pinpricks where his fingers gripped her. "Ouch!" she said indignantly.

Lir looked contrite. "Your pardon." The pinpricks disappeared.

"Put me down," she demanded. "I can walk."

"As you wish." He set her on her feet, stretched head to toe and ended with a gaping yawn. Fraine tried not to stare at his fangs. He looked at her assessingly, as if she were a new tool that might or might not serve. "We will go faster if I carry you on my back. You cannot run as I can."

She pointed at the falcon cape, still bundled on the ground where she'd used it as a pillow. "But I can fly."

Lir's eyes widened. "May I?" When Fraine nodded, Lir picked up the garment, sniffed it, and sneezed when a feather brushed his nose. He cuffed it away, licked his lips, then spread the cape out admiringly. After a moment he draped it about Fraine's shoulders, backed away a few paces and bowed his head. "You are in Her favor. The golden lady. She who loves my kin." His eyes were shining. "I see why She called us."

So Freya had a special affinity for Lir and his relations. Fraine nodded again; she could think of no other reply, and she was so fearful about Owein that tears threatened again.

She thought she'd concealed them, but Lir said gently, "Do not weep; She will give aid. Shall we go?" Nose twitching, mouth open the better to catch every scent, he waited while Fraine fastened her cape at the neck.

"Do you know why I've lost my sense of Owein's whereabouts?" Fraine asked Lir. "Before now, I always knew where he was, the way I can tell where Midgard is now." She pointed.

Lir regarded her intently. "Could you also smell him?"

"Yes. But not now."

"As you can smell me?"

"Yes." How did he know she could smell him? "Though your scent is different from his."

"Only a spell can block a scent." He was shaking his head. "A very bad spell, to block your nose and your—" He finished with a lilting word she didn't know.

"My what?"

He said the word again, then patted her shoulder when she looked at him with a furrowed brow. "That is how you can tell where Midgard and Elfland are. And how you can smell me. Shall we go now?"

She agreed. Lir loped along in great ground-eating strides; Fraine floated effortlessly in the falcon cape just behind him, and the two Parcae followed. So Lir and his kin had a sense of orientation. And he must have known she was near tears from her scent. Someone else with Elf blood shared those traits with her and Owein. She was a bit surprised at how much that discovery came as a relief.

At the moment Lir appeared to be using both senses. Periodically he would stop and sniff the air, then turn about in a circle with his eyes closed and his hands extended. Fraine eyed his padded fingers and the flash of white she saw now and again at their tips. He had claws. That accounted for the pinpricks when he'd lifted her. Sometimes he seemed as much a cat as an Elf. Weren't cats sacred to Freya? If Lir were a shapeshifter, a great cat must be his preferred form, the way Aubrey most often became a horse.

Aubrey, with his bony face and tufted mobile ears and hard clumsy hands and feet. And those great liquid eyes, abrim with mischief for everyone, but soft for her and Owein. Not long ago, Aubrey had given Fraine the poppyseed cake he'd hoarded after the Cooks had run out of the wherewithal to make them. He adored poppyseed cake, the only Elfin food he would eat—she'd never cared to ask about the rest of his diet. She fought a stupid urge to cry. Lir reached up unerringly and patted her hand, and she laid her fingers in his for an instant.

The terrain had changed. No longer the flat featureless stretch of grey that formed most of the 'tweenlands, it was a forbidding landscape of tumbled earth punctuated by small hills, truncated ridges and long narrow outcroppings of shattered rock, as if an ailing dragon had emptied the contents of its gizzard here and there. Lir stopped, whuffed the air, and adjusted his course. Suddenly Tallah shot upward a few ells, soared ahead of Lir and came arrowing back, chittering excitedly and gesturing to her right. Lir and Fraine immediately followed her. The long streamers of rock that studded their new path had some color now. No longer grey, they were reddish and glittering and—

They were part of the bridge, the substance that connected the eight points, shredded and broken but unmistakable. As soon as Fraine topped the next ridge, she spotted the summer solstice point blazing away. Not far from it, lying in a crumpled heap of long legs and arms, was Owein.

Fraine never knew how she crossed the last bit of distance between them, only that she was kneeling beside him. He had no scent; its absence made her throat close with fear. He was stripped to the waist, and barefoot. She'd never seen him so pale. The lavender-blue veins about his eyes looked dark in contrast, and there were smudges beneath his closed eyes. When she saw his chest move with his breathing, the tears she'd been fighting since Lir's arrival finally overflowed.

She touched her twin's forehead; it was cold. The moment her skin came into contact with his, she could smell him again, and a sob of relief escaped her. He smelled of ashes; that was exhaustion. Everyone she'd ever met had a completely individual scent to their slumber, and Owein's was the faint hint of thyme that came from him now. Which meant that he wasn't ill or tranced or rendered unconscious by Loki; he was merely and deeply asleep. She draped the falcon cloak over him and looked up at the solemn Lir and the grinning Parcae. "Thank you."

She'd whispered, but Owein gave a start and opened his eyes. For an instant he goggled at them all, then heaved himself upright and caught Fraine to him.

"Knew you'd come," he was saying next to her ear. She was weeping in earnest now. "Stop," he pleaded. "Or I'll start."

"We won't go far," said Lir's retreating voice somewhere above their heads.

Fraine scarcely registered it. "Are you hurt, Owein? Are you cold?"

"I've got some bruised ribs, and I'm famished." He was rocking back and forth, holding her. "But I'll not let go of you yet."

* *

"I can't believe what you've wrought," said Owein. "With or without help." He'd listened to her tale of Freya in rapt silence, with both softness and pity in his face when Fraine cautiously spoke of Caraid. "It's marvelous. So are you." He settled the falcon cape about his shoulders. "So we're to destroy everything but the eight points. They'll form the lone bridge between Elfland and Midgard, but on only eight days of the mortal year. And Loki will spare Matilda?" He swallowed another bite of Lir's provisions.

"That was our agreement." When she reached for the water bottle, Owein waved it aside and took her hands, a habitual gesture. So was the way he would study their palms, noting how all the lines were the same. But this time she winced at the pressure of his fingers, and he drew a sharp breath, peering at her left hand.

"You've been burnt," he said, his face darkening.

"Loki sealed the bargain."

She'd half feared he'd pull away at that, but he only blew a kiss to her scorched hand, squeezed the uninjured one and released them both. "When shall we keep our end of it?"

"Before we return to Elfland. Or Moira and Tomas will object."

"That they will," he said wryly. Moving as if his ribs pained him, he stood and offered her his arm. "Shall we begin?" A glance at the glittering crimson surface beneath their feet. "Not here; this was one of the connections. We should work right by the midsummer point. The border around it before the rays begin is the widest of any of the points."

Fraine was afraid that the bridge would be even harder to destroy than it had been to build and, from Owein's taut silence, so was he. She couldn't dismiss the impression that the midsummer point glowed brighter upon their approach, as if responding to the presence of both its architects at once. Now it loomed behind their backs as, standing on the wide apron between the point and the red-flecked rays that spiraled out from it, they faced the rays and the rest of the connective structure that linked what remained of the bridge.

Lir and the Parcae were watching some twenty paces to the left. "Whatever happens, stay as close to the point as you can," Owein reminded them.

With their shields at maximum strength, their minds focused and intent, the twins clasped hands. Fraine started at the current of energy that pulsed up her arm, and Owein let out a gasp. Their eyes met.

"Like touching a lightning bolt," said Owein with a glance at their entwined fingers.

The tingling had reached the center of Fraine's chest. "And we're not even in trance. Let's make fast work of this, if we can."

They raised their linked arms and aimed them at the nearest glittering ray. Heat built in Fraine's hand; she closed her eyes. Then a pulse of energy leaped from the twins' locked fingers with such force that both she and Owein were rocked back on their heels. His grip tightened on her hand.

Tallah squealed; had they lost the little Elf? In a panic Fraine opened her eyes. Tallah, unhurt, gave her a triumphant wave.

The connective tissue of the bridge was dissolving into the air of the 'tweenlands, all the crimson particles scattering and dispersing and leaving no trace, as if bloodstained sand could melt away like snowflakes. Something tugged at Fraine's center of gravity, dwindled, subsided. When she took an awkward sideways step to keep her balance, so did Owein.

"The rest," she began in an awed voice. "Around the other points—"

"It's vanishing too," said Owein. "I can feel it. Like the tide receding." They exchanged an incredulous glance. After a moment Owein started to smile.

Just then heat licked at Fraine's back. "I'll look behind us," she said, alarmed. "Slowly. Let's keep hold of one another."

She peered over her shoulder. With nerve-racking slowness, the midsummer point was both shrinking and revolving. Owein craned his neck to see, then stepped so close to her that their sides touched. When she looked at Lir, worry was stamped on his pointed Elfin features. The Parcae were turned a little away from her now, staring up at the diminishing point. What if it vanished entirely? Would they all be trapped in the 'tweenlands?

At last the point settled into a fixed position and began to lose opacity. Fraine drew a relieved breath, returned Owein's squeeze of her hand. Soon she could see through the point to the tumbled grey landscape beyond it.

Something else had happened too. At that instant Fraine felt it on every inch of her skin, as if she'd dived into a pool of warm water.

"Elfland," said Owein, exulting. "It stopped drifting!"

"So have the other worlds." Perhaps while the bridge had been in flux, so had they.

Lir was eyeing the twins. He'd been grim-faced when they announced their intention to destroy the interstitial substance of the bridge, but made no move to stop them. Now he looked relieved and more than a little surprised. On the other hand, neither Parca appeared in the least startled. They were far from overjoyed, yet a wistful acceptance gleamed in both pairs of ivy-green eyes, along with a growing respect.

Smiling, Fraine turned to Lir. "Will you and the Parcae please take Owein to Elfland with us? I think this cloak will transport only one."

CHAPTER THIRTY-NINE: ENDINGS AND BEGINNINGS

Birka, a week shy of midsummer

After feeding Helga the goat and finishing their own meal, Aud and Brubakken lazed before her low fire, she with her spindle, he repairing his fishing nets. Aud had left her door open to admit the high clear evening light that they both loved. She kept setting her work down to gaze through the door and breathe the gentlest of juniper-scented breezes. At last she laid her spindle entirely aside and tilted her chair till it stood on its two back legs. When she glanced at her old friend, he was intent on his work, his strong square-knuckled fingers deft among the knots. He was squatting easily near the doorway, heels flat on her floor of beaten earth, a tallow lamp on a low table close beside him to augment the late sun that poured like cider across the sill. A stroll by the lake under that luminous heart-lifting sky might be a fine thing. When he finished that net, she'd suggest that they head down to the water for a chat with Gillian the lake-Elf.

It happened suddenly and all at once. A change, as if the air had grown thinner and the earth more heavy, and all the stars had faltered and dimmed. The front legs of Aud's chair thumped down; she got to her feet. She could have sworn that the face of the unseen Moon contracted for an instant; the wind stilled in the treetops and the lake paused against its banks. The atmosphere was charged, as if with the reverberations of a sound too low for her hearing. From the pen below the house, Helga gave a questioning bleat.

Brubakken was already outside, peering up at the sky and fishing in his pouch for an astrolabe. Aud joined him and glanced overhead. No storm was brewing.

She met his dark eyes. "It's stopped." As they both knew. "The drifting."

Someone was pelting up the path from the lake. "Did you feel it too?"called Gillian.

"Yes," said Aud as the lake-Elf, barefooted and soaking wet, charged into the clearing. "The drifting is at an end."

"Not only that," said Gillian, pale and wide-eyed. Six wet fingers gripped Aud's arm. "I was coming to pay the two of you a visit." Not surprising; they often got that neighborly notion at the same time. "Now I can't go back. To the lake, yes, but not to my home there. Not to the part that's in Elfland. The way is closed." She couldn't stifle a shudder.

A week later, Aud and Gillian were seated on a blanket in Aud's yard, sorting herbs and cuttings, with Aud's cat luxuriating in the sun near them. Midsummer morning had dawned too fine to work withindoors, warm and clear, with an entrancingly blue sky. Aud might know the greenery better, but Gillian was more dexterous and worked more quickly. Not only was Aud glad of the assistance, she suspected it wasn't wise for the lake-Elf to be too much alone. Gillian, Brubakken and his water Elemental, Linnea, had all spent endless hours searching the lake for Gillian's immediate kin, but as far as they knew, only Gillian had been in Midgard when the change came. She didn't complain, but there was a fine-tuned nervousness to her movements and a strain to her face that were both new, and she fell into uncharacteristically long silences.

Since the drifting was over, why was the way to Elfland barred? Brubakken's astrolabe told them nothing. He'd offered to make a spirit journey to see what he could learn, and Gillian had gratefully accepted. He would go that very night. Midsummer's night, when the journey should be easier.

"Not that I'm certain I can do more than have a look at the 'tweenlands," he'd told the lake-Elf.

"You'd think they would try to tell us what's afoot," said Gillian now, abandoning an attempt to rearrange her torn skirts and letting one brown knee protrude from them.

"That who would?"

"Tomas. And Moira." She emptied a double handful of juniper berries into her lap. "If they were to send word, it would be easiest for Aubrey to reach me. At least it would have been. I suppose everything's changed now."

"We can't be certain of that. Or of anything."

Gillian gave a short, sharp nod and began culling out berries.

Aud let a few moments pass. "You do that very well. It's a great help to me."

Helga the goat came trotting up and shouldered in by the two of them. The cat opened an eye, closed it, turned her belly to the luminous sky. Gillian put her work down to scratch Helga between the ears, shoved a bundle of greenery out of reach of the curious nose, and rested her face against Helga's coat.

"Now and again I've thought I could use an assistant," Aud said casually.

"At Birka market?" Even muffled as Gillian's voice was by goat fur, it sounded dubious. "I've two fingers too many."

"In the winter, with gloves on? And you'd need not be long away from the lake. I was thinking of here, though. Helga and I would be glad of your company."

The goat leaned contentedly into Gillian's caress. "I'll visit as often as you care to have me," she said a bit gruffly.

"I thank you." Aud knew that Gillian would never willingly take up residence with her. Even if they'd both been mortal, they lived by entirely different rhythms, and Gillian was a plucky creature, not given to brooding or neediness. Still, to know she had a permanent welcome beneath Aud's roof might ease some heartache.

The flesh at the back of Aud's neck sent her a message then, almost as if someone had brushed a finger across her skin, but the sensation wasn't one of touch. It was as if someone stood behind Aud, silently watching her and Gillian, someone who'd arrived without making a sound. Whoever it was didn't seem hostile, but she harbored no liking for spies, nor for anyone who approached her in any but a straightforward manner. Gillian shot her a meaningful look and froze where she sat, her hand stopped in mid-motion on Helga's fur.

"Who goes there?" asked Aud calmly, getting to her feet and facing their visitor.

She saw no one. Astonished, she turned about in a circle and studied the clearing. It was empty, the junipers beyond it innocent of callers, the path to the lake untrodden. Other than the light breeze kissing the treetops, she and Gillian were alone with the goat and the cat, who was now sitting upright with her ears pricked forward. Whatever they sensed had nothing to do with Brubakken. He was no slyboots and he was asleep, to be rested for his spirit journey that evening.

Gillian was giving the clearing a narrow-eyed scrutiny. "First it felt like an Elf, then it didn't," she muttered. "My shield says it's someone who uses magic, but that tells us nothing we didn't already—"

"Aud! Hullo!"

Tomas's voice and Tomas's step, jogging up the trail from the lake and crashing through the underwood with uncharacteristically reckless haste. Gillian leaped to her feet, scattering berries all over the indignant cat.

Tomas was loping through the last row of junipers. He hoisted Aud from her feet, hugged her, kissed her, set her on her feet, then hugged her again so hard that the kerchief binding her hair was knocked askew. She got a brief glimpse of gleaming white teeth and a merrier expression than she'd ever seen on Tomas's face, just before he scooped Gillian up in his arms, twirled her about, put her down and rumpled her hair with both hands. Then Moira joined them, her smile wide and indulgent, her pallor gone, and Aud found that she was clutching Tomas's arm as if to keep him from disappearing. The lake-Elf dipped her knee in a curtsy, then astonished Aud by letting out a great sniff that immediately became an expedient cough. She turned her back to them all, her shoulders not quite steady.

"Are you—" began Tomas, eyeing Gillian as the ravens swooped into the clearing.

"I'm quite well, thank you." Gillian faced him, her eyes suspiciously shiny. "Quite well indeed." She cleared her throat. "I'm *that* glad to see you! Been trying to go home for days, I have. However did you manage the journey?"

Moira and Tomas exchanged glances. "It's midsummer," began Tomas. "The bridge from here to Elfland is passable on this day, and seven others."

"Ah," said Aud. Then she knew, of a sudden and from pure intuition, as any non-Sighted Mortal might have guessed. "Only those portions of the bridge still stand," she said slowly. "And only then."

Gillian made a running start for the lake, caught herself mid-stride and came back, her face a study in mingled impatience and embarrassment. "My lady. My lord," she said formally. "If you would be kind enough to excuse me so soon after your arrival, I've been anxious about my kin in the lake. I'll come back as soon as ever I can. Today, not at Lammas."

Moira was shaking her head. "Tomas and I are no longer even Regents of Elfland. Do as you please, Gillian, and give your family my greeting."

The lake-Elf's eyes widened. "The twins?"

"Crowned King and Queen," said Tomas.

Gillian was already sprinting for the water. "I'll return!" she called over her shoulder.

From long experience, Aud refused to waken Brubakken when he was resting in preparation for a spirit journey. So it was Tomas who'd gone to her old friend's steading and, after an astonishingly short time, returned with him. Moreover, Brubakken's wide flat Saami face was wreathed in smiles, without a trace of the laconic ill humor that he'd warned her for years was inevitable were he to be disturbed at such a time. An observation she'd take up with him later.

"So that's to be the way of it," said Brubakken now, considering a mug of Aud's best ale as they sat with Tomas, Moira and the lake-Elf on a blanket in Aud's yard. "Loki more or less in power here, and all too much trouble left between mortal men and women." He took a swallow. "The drifting's stopped, but we've only a partial bridge to Elfland, and the Elves are no more than a partial presence here."

He turned to Moira, who was watching him steadily and without expression. When he spoke again, it was directly to her, and his voice was gentle. "Whether that's enough to keep this world green, I expect you know no better than I. We risk that brown and arid Fate that Tallah's sister saw in her Dream."

From Tomas and Gillian, a somber glance of concurrence, but Moira's nod was almost imperceptible.

"Still, we've neither wholly won nor wholly lost," said Brubakken. "I expect you had no better choice, or you'd have taken it."

"The choice was none of mine," she said quietly. "It was Fraine's doing. She and Loki worked it all out between them."

Very slowly, Brubakken set his mug down. "Tell me about it," he said.

"We'd no choice but to accept what was already done," Moira concluded, twining her fingers in her crisp black hair. She flashed an enigmatic smile at Tomas. "Fraine had her reasons. Our Saxon friends don't fear the old ways or those who practice them, be they men or women. A better man than Simon you could hardly find, and he has no quarrel with us. And he a priest." She picked up a sprig of mint that Aud had missed sweeping from the blanket. "With such it is no loss to compromise, though their numbers are few. And with Loki..." She shrugged. "He'd have forced Fraine to help Owein destroy the entire bridge, and we'd have lost everything. We've borrowed some time with her bargain." A long-lidded glance at Tomas. "It falls to your kin to decide what to make of this world: green or dead, just or no. I don't know if they'll see the necessity of balance as well as Fraine does."

Necessity. Of the three Fates, whose names were Fate, Being and Necessity, it was Skuld who had come to the twins' name-fastening. Skuld, whose name meant Necessity.

"What of your world?" asked Aud.

Moira gave her a small smile. "We are anchored now. I have hopes that some of our damage is mendable."

Gillian was nodding.

"Our distance from Midgard, the pivot world, and whatever dwindling of our power is still to come—" Moira turned a hand over in her lap. "We'll accept them. We must."

A flash of black wings; the ravens had left their perch in a nearby tree and settled on Tomas's shoulders. Slowly, he got to his feet. "I'll return at Lammas," he said to Aud, including Brubakken and Gillian in his glance. "And bring Owein or Fraine to meet you, I hope. Both, if they can be spared from court." He turned to Moira. "We should leave soon; we promised Owein we'd meet him at Limecliff. But first, may we all take a stroll to the market?"

Somerset

When the swift insistent tapping came at the door, Linley looked up from the vigil they were keeping around Matilda. She lay unconscious, her face slack and nearly as grey as her hair, her protruding ribs hardly moving with her breath. A peculiar quality to Linley's expression, midway between awe and relief, told Rose that he'd just had some form of the Sight. Without a word he got to his feet.

A swirl of dark green cape, the light footfalls of soft leather boots. After a hushed and affectionate exchange of greetings with Linley, Owein swept into the hall with his hood thrown back, his pointed and exotic face full of eagerness, his pale hair combed to a fare-thee-well. He looked older than when Rose had last seen him. It wasn't so much that he was perhaps an inch taller, nor that his shoulders and the bones of his face had broadened ever so slightly. Rather, it was the increased confidence in his bearing. He came straight to Matilda's bedside and dropped gracefully to his knees to speak to Alfred, who was trying not to frown.

Owein looked at Rose and Simon. "How has she been faring? Any turn for the better?"

The priest shook his head. "Though she's no longer failing. There's been no change at all for several days."

Owein glanced at the small table by Matilda's bedside, where some of Fraine's earth lay in a small shallow dish. "What use have you made of that?"

"Compresses. With herbs and oils." Simon pointed. "On her chest."

"You did well," said Owein, smiling. He reached for the dish. "May I?" He was looking at Alfred now, steadily, directly.

The King was hollow-eyed; he'd slept less than any of them, and not even Simon could bully him into taking much nourishment. Blue eyes full of foreboding studied Owein. "What are you proposing? And why?"

"I can help her, your Grace. A way has been shown to me."

They all heard Simon's intake of breath. Alfred flicked a glance at him, then turned back to Owein. "Where have you been?"

"I've seen Tomas."

Alfred's jaw knotted as he glanced aside. The skin about his eyelids grew taut; his knuckles whitened on the open door of the bedcloset. His gaze wandered about the room as if seeking help from it, then settled on Matilda's empty face. "Explain your intentions to Simon," he said at last. "If he approves, you may proceed."

The words had hardly left the King's mouth before Simon told him, his voice low and clear, "Owein may do whatever he wishes, with my full support."

Because Rose was well-acquainted with her brother-in-law, she knew both what a risk he'd just taken, in his own mind, and what a vote of confidence he'd given Owein. Perhaps Owein knew as well; the slanting grey eyes warmed and softened as he looked at the priest.

"Very well," said Alfred half a beat later. Standing, he brushed straw from his trousers. "Do you wish us to leave you alone with her?"

Another vote of confidence, less readily given but given nonetheless. Rose and Linley exchanged a fleeting glance.

"Not at all," said Owein, smiling. "Unless you prefer to go." He set down the dish of earth. "We'll want her feet bare."

Only Susannah had the presence of mind to respond right away; she pulled the blankets from Matilda's feet and began removing her socks.

"And her hands," said Owein, picking one up and gently removing its fingerless glove. He glanced reassuringly at Alfred, whose face had turned ashen as he watched. "And her throat, heart and belly."

When Rose opened the front of Matilda's gown, Owein looked down at her withered body for a long moment. Rose saw pity in his expression. He bowed his head and held the small saucer of earth aloft for three heartbeats. Moving deliberately, his expression intent, he took two pinches of dirt and rubbed them into Matilda's palms.

Rose stole a glance at Simon, who was watching Owein. The priest's expression was interested and alert, but not surprised.

Next Owein smoothed another few particles of earth onto Matilda's forehead, throat, breastbone and navel. This time Simon's eyes widened a trifle. She did seem to be breathing more easily, at that.

Finally Owein held the bowl overhead a second time, ground another bit of earth into his palms, rubbed them over the soles of Matilda's feet and stood holding his hands flat against them. Head bowed, face a mask of concentration. For an instant his brow creased. "Pray, if you would, please," he said quietly.

From the way both Alfred's and Simon's lips were moving soundlessly, they already were, and Rose had been praying all day.

Slowly, Matilda's breathing deepened. Alfred divided his attention between her and Owein, his eyes strained and his expression torn. Rose thought she must feel nearly the same: both desperate to hope, and dreading that any reawakened hope would come to naught. Linley and Susannah, eyes gleaming, hands relaxed at their sides and lips parted, appeared all but jubilant, while Simon was studying Owein's face as if trying to memorize it.

After perhaps twenty minutes, Owein hadn't moved; he was looking only at Matilda. His manner was calm and his eyes steady, but could he maintain that one-pointed focus without any respite? As for Matilda, her face had attained the repose that comes with ordinary sleep, not the blank mask of unconsciousness it had worn for so long.

Finally Rose could bear Owein's immobility no longer, and Susannah was casting her a speculative glance that meant she was wondering the same. "Owein?" Rose asked tentatively, as if he were speaking and she had to interrupt.

"Mm?" He sounded as he always did, albeit preoccupied. Matilda let out a small sigh and turned her head, for all the world as if naturally asleep. When awe and delight in equal measures crept into Simon's expression, Alfred's shoulders sagged with relief.

"Is there aught we can do for you? Are you tired?" Rose asked.
A shake of the white-blond head.
"How long can you go without a rest?"
"As long as need be," he said, and flashed her a smile.

The miracle happened in increments.
When Matilda rolled onto her side and pillowed her head in one hand, a sleeper's normal movements, Owein smiled into Alfred's brimming eyes. Then he released Matilda's feet, came round the bedcloset, placed a long narrow palm on her forehead and took her fingers in his other hand.
"Keep her warm," he murmured, then gazed calmly down at Matilda as if no one else were in the room or the world.
Susannah tucked another blanket over Matilda as Alfred went to Simon and said something too low for Rose to hear. The King's eyes were alight, and his hand on Simon's arm not entirely steady.
Rose groped for Linley's hand. More and more color was suffusing Matilda's skin, her face very slowly filling out, her limbs appearing more rounded beneath the quilts. Alfred returned to kneel beside Owein and gaze at his niece's sleeping face.

Now and again Owein took a pinch of the earth Fraine had left. He would rub it into Matilda's palms, her temples, her scalp, and once, gently, over her lips. He kept one of her hands folded in his. Mostly, however, he did no more than study her face with a profound and wordless concentration that none of the awed Saxons dared break. No empty stare, Owein's gaze held so much warmth and intent that when it passed over Rose, on the one occasion when he asked for some water, she felt the look almost as a physical touch.
The miracle continued. Matilda's hair remained grey, yet gradually and steadily her color returned. Her breathing eased, she turned and murmured in her sleep like any healthy dreamer.
After a time, Rose noticed that the room itself felt singularly different to her: hushed and restful. She must have watched Owein for hours, but she no longer felt any fatigue, whereas when he arrived she'd been ready to drop. When she glanced at Linley, his face was relaxed for the first time in days, and he was breathing as deeply as if the air itself were rejuvenating. Rose had no Sight, but she guessed that Owein was weaving a spell so subtle and potent at once that it had them all in its hold.
On his knees beside Owein, Alfred was reverently watching Matilda, who was fathoms deep in easeful sleep.

At last Owein released Matilda's hand, stepped back a pace and said, "We'll let her waken on her own."

Perhaps half an hour later, Matilda opened her eyes to find her uncle, Simon, Linley, Rose, Susannah and Owein all gathered about her bed. Every last one of them was beaming, from Owein's faint, satisfied and weary smile to Alfred's overjoyed gratitude. She blinked up at their radiant faces, then gave Rose a puzzled stare. "Why are you here? Have I been ill?"

"That you have, my dear, but you're out of danger now. Thanks to Owein," said Alfred, pressing her fingers.

She glanced at Owein and promptly away again, then drew the blanket high beneath her chin. "I don't understand," she said haltingly, avoiding Owein's startled look.

"You don't need to," said Simon. "We'll clear out in a moment and let you rest. As soon as you've had some broth."

"Indeed yes," muttered Susannah, and started for the hearth.

"How do you feel?" asked Alfred.

"Confused." Matilda's lip began quivering; she steeled her jaw, turned her head away from Owein's gaze. "I don't remember... What day is it?"

"It's midsummer, and a very fine day," Owein told her. He reached out to smooth a tendril of her hair from her face. When she stiffened at the touch, Owein appeared taken aback, then hurt. His face went blank; he withdrew his hand. There was an awkward pause before, his expression pensive, he untied the pouch at his belt. "I've a present for you, 'Tilda. A pair of jesses, a hood and a line."

All were made of fine supple leather. When Owein laid them on the table by the bedcloset, Alfred glanced at them with approval.

"I thank you," Matilda said hesitantly. It seemed all she could to do meet Owein's eyes. "But I've no bird of my own."

"You soon will." Then, looking sheepish, he turned to Rose. "I forgot to tell you. Tomas and Moira are on their way here."

Alfred gave Owein his sunniest smile. "And a welcome sight they'll be. So will you, Owein, anywhere in my realm and under any circumstances." There were promises in his face, of safety and support and unswerving loyalty. No one mentioned the Bishop, but Rose was sure that everyone thought of him, and that they all breathed an inward sigh of relief.

Elfland

Aubrey, in horse shape, was swimming in great confident strokes in his favorite stream. It was the twins' favorite stream too, all the more so now that its waters were calm again, and they could enjoy it from the vantage point of the pooka's broad grey back. Fraine sat nearest his withers and Owein directly behind her, resting one hand easily on her waist.

"Was Matilda pleased with the white gyrfalcon Tomas brought her from

Birka?" the pooka asked lazily, breaking a long companionable silence.

"Yes," Owein told him, glancing aside. "She was delighted. It's seldom that women own falcons there, let alone train them. Alfred and Linley liked theirs, too."

"Is she well enough to fly hers?"

"Almost," said Owein, a trifle remote, gazing at the water. Fraine smelled cypress about him. "I expect she soon will be."

"Will you be going there at Lammas?" persisted Aubrey. Fraine gave him a slight kick in the ribs, and he flicked his ears at her in a way that meant: be easy; I know what I'm about.

She hoped so. She avoided mentioning Matilda to Owein at all, at least for the time being. That the girl had lost none of her new fear of him before he left Limecliff still troubled him.

"I could smell it," he had told Fraine. "Linley says she associates me with having fallen so ill. Alfred told her I healed her, but I'm not sure that helped. Perhaps she thinks that I was only mending what I'd broken, or that I could have done it more quickly."

"You couldn't have," Fraine had reminded him. "You didn't know how until the Sight told you, on our way back from the 'tweenlands with Lir."

She suspected that what Owein had first taken entirely for the Sight might also have been a communication from Freya and Caraid, one that had awakened the twins' own gift of healing. Owein agreed, but neither of them had mentioned Caraid to Tomas. One day they would tell him of the help she had given the twins by Freya's grace, and at what cost. That day had not yet come, even though Tomas and Moira appeared less strained since the coronation, when their work had dwindled to answering the twins' questions and providing counsel. Fraine preferred to sense a deeper rapprochement between her parents before she brought up anything that would remind them of Caraid's death.

Yet had the Seer's essence truly died? It had endured even bound by the nightmare shape of her corpse and, Fraine had no doubt, was continuing free of it elsewhere now.

The pooka had reached a narrower part of the stream, all overhanging banks and stooping vines, near the Parcae's territory. Tallah had proclaimed him permanently welcome there.

"I asked," said Aubrey patiently, "if you would go to Limecliff when next it's Lammas there?"

"I think not," said Owein, and Fraine could feel his moody gaze at her back. "I like our Saxon friends," he added, choosing his words. "But I'll never belong there. I'm a halfbreed."

Silence. Fraine refrained from touching his hand.

"I might do better to go to Birka instead. And spend some time with Aud and Brubakken, and be schooled by them. I expect Tomas is right about that." He reached forward and patted Fraine's knee. "What would you think if I stayed in Birka until the fall equinox? Would I be too long away from here?"

"It would be the fall equinox there. I don't know how long that is here—"

"Neither do I," Owein broke in, exasperated. "Neither of us knows any of that yet. Everything's new this first round of their year."

"Aud and Brubakken would train you well," put in Aubrey a little too quickly. Fraine was tempted to kick him again.

"Are they halfbreeds?"

"Not by blood," said the pooka. And, when the twins pressed him for an explanation of that mysterious remark, he would do no more than smile.

GLOSSARY

This glossary is meant only as the briefest of guides to unfamiliar words and concepts in the third novel of the Rhymer trilogy.

In the telling of Tomas's tale, a work of fiction, I have taken considerable novelistic license with Norse mythology. I apologize to any scholars or purists I may have offended. To set the record straight and for the sheer pleasure of exploring these rich stories, I encourage consulting such works as Kevin Crossley-Holland's *The Norse Myths,* Ralph Metzner's *The Well of Remembrance,* Freya Aswynn's *Leaves of Yggdrasil,* and Dag Rossman's *The Nine Worlds: A Dictionary of Norse Mythology.*

Aesir: one of the two types of Norse gods. Patriarchal and warlike, by the Viking Age the Aesir were thought to be higher in rank and power than the Vanir or fertility gods.

Alfred the Great: c. 848-899; king of the West Saxons or Wessex, from 871-c. 899.

All Soul's Night, or All Soul's Eve: November 6, also called Halloween, or Samhain. One of the eight festivals of the pagan year. See the description of these festivals near the beginning of this novel.

Ars Magica: the magic arts.

Asgard: Norse realm of the gods called the Aesir.

Baldur: the mildest and fairest Norse god, son of Odin and Frigg. His foretold death at Hödur's hand, prompted by Loki's treachery, signals the beginning of Ragnarök, the fall of the gods.

Beltane: also called May Eve or May Day. May 6, one of the eight festivals of the pagan year. See the description of these festivals near the beginning of this novel.

berserkers: piratical worshippers of Odin to whom the god sometimes granted violent and fearless trances.

Bifrost: the rainbow bridge connecting Asgard to other realms.

Birka: c. 800-1000 A.D., a lucrative Norse trading port on the island of Björkö, or Birch Island, in Lake Mälaren (Lake Malar) in what is now

Sweden. A fine historical museum is now located on the island.

bondman or woman: an indentured servant or slave.

Bretons: a Celtic people who lived in what is now Brittany, France.

cadge: a wooden box for carrying birds of prey.

Cornish: adjective describing inhabitants of Cornwall, a Celtic stronghold.

Éire: Ireland.

Elementals: spirits composed of only one Element: usually fire, earth, air or water.

ell: a unit of measurement, about two feet.

fenodyree: a small house-Elf, a brownie.

Fimbulvetr: three years of continuous harsh winter, unbroken by any summer, that will precede Ragnarök, the fall of the Norse gods.

Freya or Freyja: Norse Vanir goddess of love, beauty, fertility and sorcery. Cats are sacred to her. Gold is associated with her; some writers believe she may have dwindled from ancient matrifocal roots as a powerful solar goddess. Half the warriors slain in battle are hers, and half are Odin's. Medieval Icelandic writer Snorri Sturluson said words to the effect that "She alone of all the gods yet lives."

Freyr or Frey: Norse god of fertility and harvests, Freya's handsome twin brother, son of the sea god Njörd. Invoked for peace, prosperity and plenty. His sacred animal is the boar.

Frigg: Odin's wife, invoked at childbirth. Said to be perhaps the wisest of the Aesir. She knows the Fate of all men and women, but does not speak of it. Her symbol is the distaff.

Gentry: an Irish name for the Elves.

gnome: an earth Elemental, a spirit composed of only the earth element.

Hecate: Greek or Thracian goddess of triple aspect (Maiden, Mother, Crone) who rules crossroads, turning points, magic, night, the dark, and women's life cycles and mysteries.

Heimdall: Norse god who guards Bifrost, the rainbow bridge to Asgard, with his keen sight and hearing. At Ragnarök he and Loki, ancient enemies, will kill each other. Disguised as Rig, Heimdall fathered the three classes of Norse society: thrall, yeoman and noble.

Hel: daughter of Loki and a troll, the Norse goddess of the dead in freezing Niflheim. The dead not taken by Odin or Freya, and those who die of old age, belong to Hel.

Hödur: one of Odin's sons. Hödur is blind. Loki tricks him into killing Baldur with a sprig of mistletoe, and thereby begins Ragnarök. .

huldre-folk: literally, the Hidden People. A Norse term for troll-like or Elf-like beings, whose women are very beautiful from the front but hollow in the back; they often have a tail. The huldre-folk's women are said to lose their beauty if they marry a mortal, but to make fine wives nonetheless.

Imbolc or Candlemas: February 6, one of the eight festivals of the pagan year. See the description of these festivals near the beginning of this novel.

Jötunheim: Norse realm of the giants, traditional enemies of the Aesir.

Lake Malar: Lake Mälaren, a nearly land-locked lake in what is now Sweden.

Lammas: August 6, one of the eight festivals of the pagan year. See the description of these festivals near the beginning of this novel.

Lode Star: the Pole star.

Loki: a Norse demigod, son of two giants and Odin's foster brother. A trickster, he gets the Aesir into many a scrape, then out of them again by sheer cunning (and to save his own skin). Bisexual and a shapeshifter, his children include Fenrir the giant wolf, Jörmungand the world-serpent, the halfbreed troll goddess Hel, and Odin's eight-legged horse Sleipnir. Loki tricks Hödur into killing Baldur with a supposedly harmless sprig of mistletoe. His punishment is to be chained to three rocks, where a serpent drips venom on him. He breaks free only at Ragnarök.

Manx: adjective describing inhabitants of the Isle of Man, a Celtic isle colonized by the Norse.

Memory: one of Odin's two ravens, also called Munin, who fly through all nine worlds and tell Odin what they see.

mews: a lodging for captive birds of prey or, less commonly, a stable, or sometimes both.

Midgard: the Middle Realm, Norse realm of the mortals.

nativity: a horoscope or astrological birthchart.

Niflheim: misty realm of the dead who were neither Odin's, slain in battle, nor claimed by Freyja. Ruled by Loki's daughter, the halfbreed troll Hel.

Nornir, or Norns: the three Norse Fates, the sisters Urd, Verdandi and Skuld, whose names mean Fate, Being and Necessity. They rule, respectively, the past, the present and the future, and even the gods are subject to them. Lesser Norns visit a child at birth and decree its Fate.

Odin: the chief Norse god, of war, magic, poetry and the dead, favored by aristocrats, warriors, skalds and those who attempt to wield magic. A shapeshifter, he often travels among mortals as a vigorous old man, wearing a blue cloak and having only one eye. He gave the other eye to receive wisdom at the well of Mimir.

Odin's Wain: Norse name for the Big Dipper.

Ørlög: Every day, as the three Nornir who rule the Past, the Present and the Future, apply healing water from Urd's well to the roots of Yggdrasil, the world's axis tree, they chant the Ørlög. It is the universal law that both circumscribes and propels all events, is profoundly related to the interplay of past, present and future, and even the gods are subject to it. A complete analysis of the Ørlög is impossible in this limited space. See the article by Dag Rossman mentioned in the acknowledgments, and the references listed at the beginning of this glossary.

Picts: a Celtic people who lived in the northern British isles.

pooka: a shapeshifting Welsh water-Elf who often appears as a horse.

Ragnarök: the destruction of the Norse gods and their realms, Asgard and Vanaheim. After Ragnarök there will be a new heaven and a new earth, and the two mortals who survive will repopulate it. Hödur and Baldur are said to return there as well.

Rhenish: an adjective applied to people or objects from the country around the Rhine river.

Runes: both an alphabet and an oracle, each Rune standing for a letter and a specific divinatory meaning. See my novelist's interpretation of the Runes near the beginning of this novel.

Saefren: now the Severn river between England and Wales.

salamander: a fire Elemental, a spirit composed of only the fire element.

Saami: the nomadic Laplanders' name for themselves.

Samhain: see All Soul's Night.

Saxons: the ruling people of England after about the fifth or sixth century A.D. until the Norman conquest in 1066 A.D. A Germanic people, the Saxons invaded and conquered the indigenous Britons, of whom the legendary Arthur was the most famous sovereign.

scramasax: a knife used by the Saxons.

Sidhe: a name for the Irish Elves.

skald: a Norse bard, a poet.

Skuld: the third Norse Fate, who rules the Future, or Necessity.

Svea: Norse name for the people who gave their name to modern Sweden.

sylph: an air Elemental, a spirit composed of only the air element.

Thor: Norse god of thunder and unmatched strength, much admired by the common people. He drives a goat-drawn chariot and wields a hammer that helps him fight his greatest foe, the giants. He and the world serpent, Loki's child Jörmungand, will kill one another at Ragnarök.

Thought: one of Odin's ravens, also called Hugin.

thrall: a slave or largely indentured servant.

Tuatha de Danaan: an Irish name for the Elves.

Tyr: boldest of the Norse gods, invoked by warriors in battle. He sacrificed a hand to help chain the great wolf Fenrir, Loki's son, who will be loosed at Ragnarök.

undine: a water Elemental, a spirit composed of only the water element.

Uppland: part of what is now Sweden.

Uppsala: an Uppland town with a temple to the Norse gods, where their worship probably lasted into the late eleventh century.

Urd: the first of the Norse Fates, who rules Fate and the Past.

Valholl: Old Norse term for Valhalla, Odin's hall of warrior dead in Asgard.

Vanaheim: realm of the Norse nature and fertility gods called the Vanir.

Vanir: one of the two types of Norse gods, gods of fertility and nature. Some authorities believe the Vanir were the gods of a more peaceful, matrifocal society, who were overrun by patriarchal and warlike tribes who worshipped the Aesir.

Varangian Sea: Norse name for the Baltic Sea.

Verdandi: the second of the Norse Fates, who rules Being and the Present.

Vestfold: a kingdom in ninth-century southern Norway.

Waleis: what is now modern Wales.

Well of Mimir: The Well of Wisdom, at one of the roots of Yggdrasil, the World Tree. Guarded by the wise giant Mimir, who drank from its waters. When the Vanir cut off his head, Odin preserved it and consults it for wisdom.

Wessex: what is now southwest England, mostly Wiltshire, Somerset and Hampshire.

Yggdrasil: the world axis tree, a great ash tree that connects the nine worlds of Norse cosmology. Its three roots lie in Asgard by the Well of Urd, tended by Norns; in Jötunheim of the giants by Mimir's Well; and in Niflheim by Hvergelmir, the well of creation, which teems with dragons.